Recruits.
Drawn by P. G. Jeanniot.
IDYLL AND THE EPIC (LES MISÉRABLES, IV.).

LES MISÉRABLES.

By VICTOR HUGO.

PART FOURTH.

THE IDYLL AND THE EPIC.

———◆———

BOSTON:

LITTLE, BROWN, AND COMPANY.

1907.

TABLE OF CONTENTS.

———◆———

THE RUE PLUMET IDYLL AND THE RUE ST. DENIS EPIC.

———

𝔅𝔬𝔬𝔨 I.

SOME PAGES OF HISTORY.

𝔅𝔬𝔬𝔨 II.

ÉPONINE.

46514

𝔅𝔬𝔬𝔨 III.

THE HOUSE OF THE RUE PLUMET.

𝔅𝔬𝔬𝔨 IV.

SUCCOR FROM BELOW MAY BE SUCCOR FROM ON HIGH.

𝔅𝔬𝔬𝔨 V.

IN WHICH THE END DOES NOT RESEMBLE THE BEGINNING.

𝕭𝖔𝖔𝖐 VI.

LITTLE GAVROCHE.

𝕭𝖔𝖔𝖐 VII.

SLANG.

𝕭𝖔𝖔𝖐 VIII.

ENCHANTMENTS AND DESOLATIONS.

𝔅𝔬𝔬𝔨 IX.

WHERE ARE THEY GOING?

𝔅𝔬𝔬𝔨 X.

THE FIFTH OF JUNE, 1832.

𝔅𝔬𝔬𝔨 XI.

THE ATOM FRATERNIZES WITH THE HURRICANE.

𝔅𝔬𝔬𝔨 XII.

CORINTH.

𝔅𝔬𝔬𝔨 XIII.

MARIUS ENTERS THE SHADOW.

𝔅𝔬𝔬𝔨 XIV.

THE GRANDEUR OF DESPAIR.

Book XV.

THE RUE DE L'HOMME ARMÉ.

THE RUE PLUMET IDYLL

AND

THE RUE ST. DENIS EPIC.

BOOK I.

SOME PAGES OF HISTORY.

CHAPTER I.

WELL CUT OUT.

1831 and 1832, the two years immediately attached to the revolution of July, contain the most peculiar and striking moments of history; and these two years, amid those that precede and follow them, stand out like mountains. They possess the true revolutionary grandeur, and precipices may be traced in them. The social masses, the foundations of civilization, the solid group of superimposed and adherent interests, and the secular profiles of the ancient Gallic formations, appear and disappear every moment through the stormy clouds of systems, passions, and theories. These apparitions and disappearances were called resistance and movement, but at intervals truth, the daylight of the human soul, flashes through all.

This remarkable epoch is so circumscribed, and is beginning to become so remote from us, that we are able to seize its principal outlines. We will make the attempt. The Restoration was one of those intermediate phases which are so difficult to define, in which are fatigue, buzzing, murmurs, sleep, and tumult, and which, after all, are nought but the arrival of a great nation at a halting-place. These epochs are peculiar, and deceive the politician who tries to take advantage of them. At the outset the nation only demands repose; there is but one thirst, for peace, and only one ambition, to be small, — which is the translation of keeping quiet. "Great events, great accidents, great adventures, great men, — O Lord! we have had enough of these, and more than enough." Cæsar would be given for Prusias, and Napoleon for the Roi d'Yvetôt, who was "such a merry little king." Folk have been marching since daybreak and arrive at the evening of a long and rough journey; they made their first halt with Mirabeau, the second with Robespierre, and the third with Napoleon, and they are exhausted. Everybody insists on a bed.

Worn-out devotions, crying heroisms, gorged ambitions, and made fortunes, seek, claim, implore, and solicit, — what? A resting-place, and they have it. They take possession of peace, tranquillity, and leisure, and feel satisfied. Still, at the same time certain facts arise, demand recognition, and knock at doors on their side. These facts have emerged from revolutions and wars; they exist, they live, and have the right, — the right of installing themselves in society, which they do; and in the majority of instances facts are the quarter-masters that only prepare a billet for principles.

In such a case, this is what occurs to political philosophers : at the same time as wearied men claim rest, accomplished facts demand guarantees, for guarantees for facts are the same thing as repose for men. It is this that England asked of the Stuart after the Protector, and what France asked of the Bourbons after the Empire. These guarantees are a necessity of the times, and they must be granted. The Princes concede them, but in reality it is the force of things that gives them. This is a profound truth and worth knowing, which the Stuarts did not suspect in 1662, and of which the Bourbons did not even gain a glimpse in 1814.

The predestined family which returned to France when Napoleon collapsed had the fatal simplicity of believing that it gave, and that it could take back what it had once given ; that the Bourbon family possessed the right divine, and France possessed nothing, and that the political right conceded in the charter of Louis XVIII. was nothing else but a branch of the divine right, detached by the House of Bourbon and graciously permitted to the people up to the day when the king thought proper to clutch it again. Still, from the displeasure which the gift caused it, the Bourbon family ought to have felt that it did not emanate from it. It behaved in a grudging way to the 19th century, and looked with an ugly smile at every expansion of the nation. To employ a trivial, that is to say, a popular

and true phrase, it was crabbed, and the people noticed it.

The Government believed that it had strength
because the Empire had been removed before it, like
a stage scene ; but it did not perceive that it had been
produced in the same way, nor see that it was held
in the same hand which had removed Napoleon.
It believed that it had roots, because it was the past,
and was mistaken : it formed a portion of the past,
but the whole of the past was France ; and the roots
of French society were not in the Bourbons, but in
the nation. These obscure and tenacious roots did
not constitute the right of a family, but the history
of a people, and were everywhere, except under the
throne. The House of Bourbon had been for France
the illustrious and blood-stained knot of her history,
but was no longer the principal element of her destiny or the necessary basis of her policy. She could
do without the Bourbons as she had done for two-
and-twenty years : there was a solution of continuity,
but they did not suspect it. And how could they
suspect it, when they imagined that Louis XVII.
reigned at the 9th Thermidor, and that Louis XVIII.
was reigning at the day of Marengo ? Never, since
the origin of history, have princes been so blind in
the presence of history and that portion of the divine
authority which facts contain and promulgate. Never
had the nether claim, which is called the right of
kings, denied to such a condition the supreme right.
It was a capital error that led this family to lay their
hand again on the " granted " guarantees in 1814, or
on the concessions, as they entitled them. It is a

sad thing that what they called their concessions were our conquests, and what they called our encroachments were our rights. When the hour appeared to have arrived, the Restoration, supposing itself victorious over Bonaparte, and rooted in the country, that is to say, believing itself strong and profound, suddenly made up its mind, and risked its stake. One morning it rose in the face of France, and, raising its voice, contested the collective title, and the individual title, the sovereignty of the nation, and the liberty of the citizen. In other terms, it denied the nation what made it a nation, and the citizen what made him a citizen. This is the substratum of those famous decrees which are called the "Ordonnances" of July. The Restoration fell, and fell justly. Still, let us add, it was not absolutely hostile to all the forms of progress, and grand things were accomplished while it stood aloof. During the Restoration the nation had grown accustomed to calm discussion, which the Republic had been deficient in, and to grandeur in peace, which was not known under the Empire. France, strong and free, had been an encouraging example for the other nations of Europe. Under Robespierre the Revolution ruled; under Bonaparte, cannon; while in the reigns of Louis XVIII. and Charles X. the turn arrived for intellect to speak. The wind ceased, and the torch was re-illumined, while a pure mental light played round the serene crests. It was a magnificent, useful, and delightful spectacle; and for fifteen years those great principles, which are so old for the thinker, so new for the statesman, — equality before the law, liberty of conscience, freedom of the press and speech, and the accessibility of all fitting men to office, — could be seen at work in a reign of peace, and publicly. Things went on thus till 1830, and the Bourbons were an instrument of civilization which broke in the hands of Providence.

The fall of the Bourbons was full of grandeur, not on their side, but on that of the nation. They left the throne with gravity, but without authority; their descent into night was not one of those solemn disappearances which impart a sombre emotion to history, and it was neither the spectral calmness of Charles I. nor the eagle cry of Napoleon. They went away, that was all; they deposited the crown and did not retain the glory, and though they were dignified, they were not august, and they were to a certain extent false to the majesty of their misfortune. Charles X., having a round table cut square during the Cherbourg voyage, seemed more anxious about the imperilled etiquette than the crumbling monarchy. This diminution saddened the devoted men who were attached to the Bourbons personally, and the serious men who honored their race. The people behaved admirably, however, and the nation, attacked one morning by a species of royalist insurrection, felt themselves so strong that they displayed no anger. They defended themselves, restrained themselves, and restored things to their place; the government in the law, the Bourbons in exile, alas! and stopped there. They took the old King Charles X. off the daïs which had sheltered Louis XIV., and gently placed him on the ground, and they only

touched the royal persons cautiously and sorrowfully.
It was not one man, or a few men, but France,
united France, France victorious, and intoxicated by
its victory, which appeared to remember, and practised
in the eyes of the whole world, the serious remarks
of Guillaume du Vair after the day of the Barricades. " It is easy for those who have been accustomed to obtain the favors of the great, and leap
like a bird from branch to branch, from a low to a
flourishing fortune, to show themselves bold against
their prince in his misfortunes; but for my part the
fortune of my kings will be ever venerable to me,
and principally of those who are in affliction." The
Bourbons bore away with them respect, but not
regret; as we have said, their misfortune was
greater than themselves, and they faded away on
the horizon.

The revolution of July at once found friends and
enemies in the whole world ; the former rushed toward it enthusiastically and joyfully, while the latter
turned away, each according to its nature. The
princes of Europe, the owls of this dawn, at the
first moment closed their eyes, which were hurt and
stupefied, and only opened them again to menace, —
it is a terror easy to understand and a pardonable
anger. This strange revolution had scarcely required
a blow, and had not even done conquered royalty the
honor of treating it as an enemy and shedding its
blood. In the sight of despotic governments which
also have an interest in liberty calumniating itself,
the revolution of July had the fault of being formidable and remaining gentle, but no attempt was

made or prepared against it. The most dissatisfied and irritated persons saluted it; for whatever their selfishness or rancor may be, men feel a mysterious respect issue from events in which they feel the co-operation of some one who labors higher than man. The revolution of July is the triumph of right overthrowing fact, and is a thing full of splendor. Hence came the brilliancy of the revolution of 1830, and at the same time their mildness, for right that triumphs has no need to be violent. Right is justice and truth, and it is the property of right to remain eternally beautiful and pure. Fact, even the most necessary in appearance and best accepted by contemporaries, if it only exist as fact, and contain too little right, is no right at all, and is infallibly des-tined to become, with the duration of time, mis-shapen, foul, and perhaps even monstrous. If we wish to discover at one glance what a degree of ugliness fact can attain, when looked at through the distance of centuries, let us regard Machiavelli. He is not an evil genius, a demon, or a cowardly and servile writer : he is nothing but the fact, and not merely the Italian fact, but the European fact, the fact of the sixteenth century. He appears hideous, and is so in the presence of the moral idea of the 19th century. This struggle between right and fact has endured since the origin of societies. It is the task of wise men to terminate the duel, amalgamate the pure idea with human reality, and to make right penetrate fact and fact right pacifically.

CHAPTER II.

BADLY STITCHED.

But the task of wise men differs greatly from that of clever men, and the revolution of 1830 quickly stopped ; for when a revolution has run ashore, the clever men plunder the wreck. Clever men in our century have decreed themselves the title of states- men, so that the phrase has eventually become a bit of slang. For it must not be forgotten that where there is only cleverness, littleness necessarily exists, and to say "the clever" is much like saying the "mediocrities." In the same way the word "states- man" is often equivalent to saying "traitor." If we believe clever men, then revolutions like that of July are severed arteries, and a rapid ligature is required. Right, if too loudly proclaimed, threatens a general overthrow. Hence the right once secured, the gov- ernment must be strengthened. As soon as liberty is assured we must turn our attention to power. Here wise men, though they have not yet separated from clever men, begin to distrust them. Power, very good ! But, in the first place, what is power ; and secondly, whence does it come ? The clever men do not appear to hear the muttered objection and continue their ma- nœuvres. According to politicians who ingeniously place a mask of necessity upon profitable fiction, the first want of a people after a revolution, if that people form part of a monarchical continent, is to obtain a dynasty. In this way they say peace is secured after the revolution, that is to say, the neces- sary time for repairing the house and dressing the wounds. A dynasty hides the scaffolding and covers the hospital. Now, it is not always easy to obtain a dynasty, although the first man of genius or the first adventurer met with is sufficient to make a king. You have in the first case Bonaparte, and in the second Iturbide. But the first family come across is not sufficient to form a dynasty, for there is ne- cessarily a certain amount of antiquity required as a race, and the wrinkle of centuries cannot be improvised.

If we place ourselves at the standpoint of states- men, with all due reserves of course, what are the qualities of a king who issues from a revolution? He may be, and it is useful that he should be, revo- lutionary; that is to say, have played a personal part in the revolution, have become either compromised or renowned in it, and have wielded the axe or drawn the sword. What are the qualities of a dy- nasty? It must be national; that is to say, distantly revolutionary, not through acts done, but through ideas accepted. It must be composed of the past and be historical, and of the future and be sympa- thetic. All this explains why the first revolutions are satisfied with finding a man, Napoleon or Crom- well, while the second are determined on finding a family, like the House of Brunswick or the House of Orléans. Royal houses resemble those Indian fig-trees, each branch of which bends down, becomes rooted in the ground, and grows into a fig-tree. Each branch of the family may become a dynasty, on the sole condition that it bends down to the people. Such is the theory of clever men.

This, then, is the great art, — to give success the sound of a catastrophe, so that those who profit by it may also tremble at it ; to season every step taken with fear ; to increase the curve of the transition until progress is checked ; to spoil this daybreak, denounce and retrench the roughness of enthusiasm ; to cut angles and nails ; to pad the triumph, muffle the right, roll the giant people in flannel, and put it to bed at full speed ; to place this excess of health under medical treatment, and regard Hercules as a convalescent ; to dilute the event in expediency, and offer to minds thirsting for the ideal this weak nectar ; to take precautions against extreme success, and provide the revolution with a sunshade. 1830 practised this theory, which had already been applied to England by 1688. 1830 is a revolution arrested half-way, and a moiety of progress is almost right. Now, logic ignores this as absolutely as the sun ignores a rush-light. Who check revolutions half-way ? The bourgeoisie. Why ? Because the bourgeoisie represent satisfied self-interest. Yesterday appetite was felt, to-day fulness, and to-morrow satiety. The phenomenon of 1814, after Napoleon, was reproduced in 1830 after Charles X. Attempts have been made, though wrongly, to convert the bourgeoisie into a class, but they are merely the contented portion of

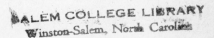

the population. The bourgeois is a man who has at last time to sit down, and a chair is not a caste. But through a desire to sit down too soon, the progress of the human race may be arrested, and this has frequently been the fault of the bourgeoisie; and people are not a class because they commit a fault, and selfishness is not one of the divisions of the social order. However, as. we must be just even towards selfishness, the condition for which that portion of the nation called the bourgeoisie yearned after the shock of 1830 was not inertness, which is complicated with indifference and sloth, and contains a little shame; nor was it sleep, which presupposes a momentary oblivion accessible to dreams, but it was a halt. This word contains a double, singular, and almost contradictory meaning, for it implies troops on the march, that is to say, movement, and a stoppage, that is to say, rest. A halt is the restoration of strength, it is repose armed and awake, it is the accomplished fact, posting its sentries and standing on guard. A halt presupposes a combat yesterday and a combat to-morrow, — it is the interlude between 1830 and 1848.

What we here call combat may also be called progress. Hence the bourgeoisie as well as the statesmen required a man who expressed the idea of a halt, an " although-because," a composite individuality signifying revolution and stability; in other words, strengthening the present by the evident compatibility of the past with the future. This man was found " ready-made," and his name was Louis Philippe d'Orléans. The 221 made Louis Philippe king, and Lafayette undertook the coronation. He named him " the best of Republics," and the Town Hall of Paris was substituted for the Cathedral of Rheims. This substitution of a half-throne for a complete throne was " the work of 1830." When the clever men had completed their task, the immense fault of their solution was apparent ; all this had been done beyond the pale of absolute right, which shouted, " I protest ! " and then, formidable thing, receded into the darkness.

CHAPTER III.

LOUIS PHILIPPE.

REVOLUTIONS have a terrible arm and a lucky hand; they hit hard and choose well. Even when incomplete, bastardized, and reduced to the state of a younger revolution, like that of 1830, they nearly always retain sufficient providential light not to fall badly, and their eclipse is never an abdication. Still, we must not boast too loudly, for revolutions themselves are mistaken, and grave errors have been witnessed ere now. Let us return to 1830, which was fortunate in its deviation. In the establishment which was called order after the revolution was cut short, the king was worth more than the Royalty. Louis Philippe was a rare man.

Son of a father to whom history will certainly grant extenuating circumstances, but as worthy of esteem as his father was of blame ; possessing all the private virtues and several of the public virtues ; careful of his health, his fortune, his person, and his business affairs ; knowing the value of a minute, but not always the value of a year ; sober, serious, peaceful, and patient ; a good man and a good prince ; sleeping with his wife, and having in his palace lackeys whose business it was to show the conjugal couch to the cits, — a regular ostentation which had grown useful after the old illegitimate displays of the elder branch ; acquainted with all the languages of Europe, and, what is rarer still, with all the languages of all the interests, and speaking them ; an admirable representative of the "middle classes," but surpassing them, and in every way greater ; possessing the excellent sense, while appreciating the blood from which he sprang, of claiming merit for his personal value, and very particular on the question of his race by declaring himself an Orléans and not a Bourbon ; a thorough first prince of the blood, so long as he had only been Most Serene Highness, but a frank bourgeois on the day when he became His Majesty ; diffuse in public, and concise in private life ; branded as a miser, but not proved to be one ; in reality, one of those saving men who are easily prodigal to satisfy their caprices or their duty ; well read and caring but little for literature ; a gentleman but not a cavalier ; simple, calm, and strong ; adored by his family and his household ; a seductive speaker, a statesman who had lost his illusions, cold-hearted, swayed by the immediate interest, governing from hand to mouth ; incapable of rancor and of gratitude ; pitilessly employing superiorities upon mediocrities, and clever in confounding by parliamentary majorities those mysterious unanimities which growl hoarsely beneath thrones ; expansive, at times imprudent in his expansiveness, but displaying marvellous skill in his imprudence ; fertile in expedients, faces, and masks ; terrifying France by Europe, and Europe by France ; loving

his country undeniably, but preferring his family ;
valuing domination more than authority, and authority more than dignity ; a temperament which has
this mournful feature about it, that by turning everything to success it admits of craft and does not
absolutely repudiate baseness, but at the same time
has this advantage, that it preserves politics from
violent shocks, the State from fractures, and society
from catastrophes ; minute, correct, vigilant, attentive,
sagacious, and indefatigable ; contradicting himself at
times, and belying himself ; bold against Austria at
Ancona, obstinate against England in Spain, bom-
barding Antwerp and paying Pritchard ; singing the
Marseillaise with conviction ; inaccessible to despondency, to fatigue, to a taste for the beautiful and ideal,
to rash generosity, to Utopias, chimeras, anger, vanity,
and fear ; possessing every form of personal bravery ;
a general at Valmy, a private at Jemmappes ; eight
times attacked by regicides, and always smiling ;
brave as a grenadier, and courageous as a thinker ;
merely anxious about the chances of a European convulsion, and unfitted for great political adventures ;
ever ready to risk his life, but not his work ; disguis-
ing his will in influence for the sake of being obeyed
as an intellect rather than as king ; gifted with observation and not with divination ; paying but slight
attention to minds, but a good judge of men, — that is
to say, requiring to see ere he could judge ; endowed
with prompt and penetrating sense, practical wisdom,
fluent tongue, and a prodigious memory, and incessantly drawing on that memory, his sole similitude
with Cæsar, Alexander, and Napoleon ; knowing

facts, details, dates, and proper names, but ignorant of the various passions and tendencies of the crowd, the internal aspirations and concealed agitation of minds, — in one word, of all that may be called the invisible currents of consciences ; accepted by the surface, but agreeing little with the lower strata of French society ; getting out of scrapes by skill ; governing too much and not reigning sufficiently ; his own Prime Minister ; excellent in the art of setting up the littleness of realities as an obstacle to the immensity of ideas ; mingling with a true creative faculty of civilization, order, and organization, I do not know what pettifogging temper and chicanery ; the founder of a family and at the same time its man-of-law ; having something of Charlemagne and something of an attorney in him ; but, on the whole, as a lofty and original figure, as a prince who managed to acquire power in spite of the anxiety of France, and influence in spite of the jealousy of Europe, — Louis Philippe would be ranked among the eminent men of his age, and among the most illustrious governors known in history, if he had loved glory a little, and had a feeling for what is grand to the same extent that he had a feeling for what is useful.

Louis Philippe had been handsome, and when aged, remained graceful : though not always admired by the nation he was always so by the mob, for he had the art of pleasing and the gift of charm. He was deficient in majesty, and neither wore a crown though king, nor displayed white hair though an old man. His manners belonged to the ancient

régime, and his habits to the new, — a mixture of
the noble and the citizen which suited 1830.   Louis
Philippe was transition on a throne, and retained the
old pronunciation and orthography, which he placed
at the service of modern opinions : he was fond of
Poland and Hungary, but he wrote " les Polonois,"
and pronounced, " les Hongrais."   He wore the uniform of the National Guard like Charles X., and
the ribbon of the Legion of Honor like Napoleon.
He went but rarely to Mass, not at all to the chase,
and never to the opera : he was incorruptible by
priests, whippers-in, and ballet girls, and this formed
part of his citizen popularity.   He had no Court,
and went out with an umbrella under his arm, and
this umbrella for a long time formed part of his
nimbus.   He was a bit of a mason, a bit of a gardener, and a bit of a surgeon: he bled a postilion
who had fallen from his horse, and no more thought
of going out without his lancet than Henry III.
would without his dagger.   The Royalists ridiculed
this absurd king, the first who shed blood in order
to cure.

A deduction must be made in the charges which
history brings against Louis Philippe, and they
formed three different columns, each of which gives
a different total, — one accusing royalty, the second
the reign, and the third the king. Democratic right
confiscated, progress made the second interest, the
protests of the streets violently repressed, the military execution of insurrections, revolt made to run
the gauntlet, the Rue Transnonain, the councils of
war, the absorption of the real country in the legal

country, and the government on joint account with three hundred thousand privileged persons — are the deeds of royalty : Belgium refused, Algeria too harshly conquered with more of barbarity than civilization, like India by the English, the breach of faith to Abd-el-Kader, Blaye, Deutz bought and Pritchard paid — are chargeable to the reign ; while the policy which cares more for the family than the nation belongs to the king. As we see, when the deductions have been made, the charge against the king is reduced ; but his great fault was that he was modest in the name of France. Whence comes this fault ?

Louis Philippe was a king who was too much a father, and this incubation of a family which is intended to produce a dynasty is frightened at everything, and does not like to be disturbed. Hence arises excessive timidity, which is offensive to a nation which has July 14th in its civil traditions and Austerlitz in its military annals. However, when we abstract public duties, which should ever be first fulfilled, the family deserved Louis Philippe's profound tenderness for it. This domestic group was admirable, and combined virtue with talent. One of the daughters of Louis Philippe, Marie d'Orléans, placed the name of her race among artists as Charles d'Orléans had done among the poets, and she created from her soul a statue which she called Joan of Arc. Two of Louis Philippe's sons drew from Metternich this demagogic praise : " They are young men whose like can be found nowhere, and such princes as were never seen before." Here is the truth, without ex-

tenuating or setting down aught in malice, about
Louis Philippe. It was his good fortune to be in
1830 the Prince Égalité, to bear within him the con-
tradiction between the Restoration and the Revolution, to possess that alarming revolutionary side
which becomes reassuring in the governor : and
there was never a more complete adaptation of the
man to the event, for one entered the other and the
incarnation took place. Louis Philippe is 1830 made
man, and he had also on his side that great designa-
tion to a throne, exile. He had been proscribed,
wandering, and poor, and had lived by his own
labor. In Switzerland, this heir to the richest
princely domains of France was obliged to sell a
horse, in order to eat ; at Reichenau, he had given
mathematical lessons while his sister Adelaide was
embroidering and sewing. These souvenirs blended
with a king rendered the bourgeoisie enthusiastic.
With his own hands he had demolished the last iron
cage at Mont St. Michel, erected by Louis XI. and
employed by Louis XV. He was the companion
of Dumouriez and the friend of Lafayette ; he had
belonged to the Jacobin Club, and Mirabeau had
tapped him on the shoulder, and Danton said to him,
" Young man." At the age of twenty-four in '93,
when M. de Chartres, he had witnessed from an obscure gallery in the Convention, the trial of Louis
XVI., so well named "that poor tyrant." The blind
clairvoyance of the revolution breaking royalty in
the king, and the king with royalty, while hardly
observing the man in the fierce crushing of the idea ;
the vast storm of the Convention Tribune ; Capet

not knowing what to answer; the frightful and stupefied vacillation of this royal head before the raging blast; the relative innocence of all mixed up in this catastrophe, of those who condemned as well as of him who was condemned, — he, Louis Philippe, had looked at these things and contemplated these vertigos; he had seen centuries appear at the bar of the Convention; he had seen behind Louis XVI., that unfortunate and responsible victim, the real culprit, monarchy, emerging from the darkness, and he retained in his soul a respectful terror of this immense justice of the people which is almost as impersonal as the justice of God. The traces which the revolution left upon him were prodigious, and his memory was a living imprint of these great years, minute by minute. One day, in the presence of a witness whose statements we cannot doubt, he corrected from memory the entire letter A in the list of the Constituent Assembly.

Louis Philippe was an open-air king; during his reign the press was free, debates were free, conscience and speech were free. The Laws of September had a clear track. Though he knew the corrosive power of light upon privileges, he left his throne exposed to the light, and history will give him credit for this honorable behavior. Louis Philippe, like all historic men who have quitted the stage, is at the present day being tried by the human conscience, but this trial has not yet gone through its first stage. The hour when history speaks with its venerable and free accent has not yet arrived for him; the moment has not yet come for the final judgment. Even the stern and illustrious historian, Louis Blanc, has recently toned down his first verdict. Louis Philippe was elected by the two hundred and twenty-one deputies in 1830, that is to say, by a semi-Parliament and a semi-revolution; and, in any case, we cannot judge him here philosophically, without making some reservations in the name of the absolute democratic principle. In the eyes of the absolute, everything is usurpation which is outside of these two rights, — first, the right of man and in the next place the right of the people; but what we are able to say at present is, that in whatever way we may regard him, Louis Philippe, taken by himself, and looked at from the stand-point of human goodness, will remain, to employ the old language of old history, one of the best princes that ever sat on a throne. What has he against him? This throne; take the king away from Louis Philippe and the man remains. This man is good, at times so good as to be admirable. Often in the midst of the gravest cares, after a day's struggle, after the whole diplomacy of the Continent, he returned to his apartments at night; and then, though exhausted by fatigue and want of sleep, what did he? He would take up a list of sentences and spend the night in revising a criminal trial, considering that it was something to hold his own against Europe, but even greater to tear a culprit from the hands of the executioner. He obstinately resisted his keeper of the seals, and disputed the scaffold inch by inch with his attorney-generals, those "chatterers of the law," as he called them. At times piles of sentences covered his table, and he examined them all, and felt an

agony at the thought of abandoning these wretched
condemned heads.   One day he said to the witness
whom we just now quoted, " I gained seven of them
last night."   During the earlier years of his reign the
penalty of death was, as it were, abolished, and the
re-erection of the scaffold was a violence done to
the king.   As the Grève disappeared with the elder
branch, a bourgeois Grève was established under the
name of the Barrière St. Jacques, for " practical men"
felt the necessity of a quasi-legitimate guillotine.
This was one of the victories of Casimir Perier, who
represented the narrow side of the bourgeoisie, over
Louis Philippe, who represented the liberal side.
The king annotated Beccaria with his own hand, and
after the Fieschi machine he exclaimed, " What a
pity that I was not wounded, for then I could have
shown mercy ! "   Another time, alluding to the resistance offered by his ministers, he wrote with refer-
ence to a political culprit, who is one of the most
illustrious men of the day, " His pardon is granted,
and all that I have to do now is to obtain it."   Louis
Philippe was as gentle as Louis IX., and as good as
Henri IV., and in our opinion, in history, where goodness is the rare pearl, to have been good is almost
better than to have been great.

As Louis Philippe has been sternly judged by some,
and perhaps harshly by others, it is very simple that
a man, himself a phantom at the present day, who
knew that king, should offer his testimony for him
in the presence of history ; this testimony, whatever
its value may be, is evidently, and before all, disinterested.   An epitaph written by a dead man is

sincere; one shadow may console another shadow, for sharing the same darkness gives the right to praise, and there is no fear that it will ever be said of two tombs in exile, — this man flattered the other.

CHAPTER IV.

CRACKS IN THE FOUNDATION.

At this moment, when the drama we are recounting is about to enter one of those tragic clouds which cover the beginning of the reign of Louis Philippe, it is quite necessary that this book should give an explanation about that king. Louis Philippe had entered upon the royal authority without violence or direct action on his part, through a revolutionary change of wind, which was evidently very distinct from the real object of the revolution, but in which he, the Duc d'Orléans, had no personal initiative. He was born a prince, and believed himself elected king; he had not given himself these functions, nor had he taken them; they were offered to him and he accepted, convinced — wrongly as we think, but still convinced — that the offer was in accordance with right, and the acceptance in harmony with duty. Hence came an honest possession, and we say in all conscience that, as Louis Philippe was honest in the possession, and democracy honest in its attack, the amount of terror disengaged from social struggles cannot be laid either on the king or the democracy. A collision of principles resembles a collision of elements; ocean defends the water and the hurricane the air ; the king defends royalty, democracy defends the people ; the relative, which is monarchy, resists the absolute, which is the republic ; society bleeds from this conflict, but what is its suffering to-day will be its salvation at a later date ; and in any case those who struggle must not be blamed, for one party must be mistaken. Right does not stand, like the Colossus of Rhodes, on two shores at once, with one foot in the republic, the other in royalty, but is indivisible, and entirely on one side ; those who are mistaken are honestly mistaken, and a blind man is no more a culprit than a Vendean is a brigand. We must, therefore, only impute these formidable collisions to the fatality of things, and, whatever these tempests may be, human irresponsibility is mixed up with them.

Let us finish our statement : The Government of 1830 had a hard life of it from the beginning, and born yesterday it was obliged to combat to-day. Scarce installed, it felt everywhere the vague movements of faction beneath the foundation of July, which had so recently been laid, and was still anything but solid. Resistance sprang up on the morrow, and might, perhaps, have been born on the day before, and from month to month the hostility increased, and instead of being dull became patent. The revolution of July, frowned upon by kings out of France, was diversely interpreted in France. God imparts to men His will visible in events, an obscure text written in a mysterious language. Men at once make themselves translations of it, — hasty, incorrect translations, full of errors, gaps, and misunderstandings. Very few minds comprehend the divine language; the more sagacious, the calmer, and the more profound decipher slowly, and when they arrive with their version, the work has been done long before ; there are already twenty translations offered for sale. From each translation springs a party, and from each misunderstanding a failure, and each party believes that it has the only true text, and each faction believes that it possesses the light. Often enough power itself is a faction, and there are in revolutions men who swim against the current; they are the old parties. As revolutions issue from the right to revolt, the old parties that cling to heirdom by grace of God fancy that they have a right to revolt against them; but this is an error, for in revolutions the rebel is not the people but the king. Revolution is precisely the contrary of revolt ; every revolution, being a normal accomplishment, contains its legitimacy within itself, which false revolutionists sometimes dishonor, but which endures even when sullied, and survives even when bleeding. Revolutions issue, not from an accident, but a necessity; for they are a return from the factitious to the real, and they take place because they must take place.

The old legitimist parties did not the less assail the revolution of 1830 with all the violence which springs from false reasoning. Errors are excellent projectiles, and they skilfully struck it at the spot where it was vulnerable, — the flaw in its cuirass, its want of logic, — and they attacked this revolution in its royalty. They cried to it, " Revolution, why this king ? " Factions are blind men who aim accurately. This cry the revolutionists also raised, but coming from them it was logical. What was blundering in the legitimists was clear-sightedness in the democrats; 1830 had made the people bankrupt, and indignant democracy reproached it with the deed. The establishment of July struggled between these attacks, made by the past and the future; it represented the minute contending on one side with monarchical ages, on the other with eternal right; and then, again, 1830, no longer a revolution, and becoming a monarchy, was obliged to take precedence of Europe, and it was a further difficulty to maintain peace, for a harmony desired against the grain is often more onerous than a war. From this sullen conflict, ever muzzled but ever grumbling, emerged armed peace, that ruinous expedient of civilization suspecting itself. The royalty of July reared in the team of European cabinets, although Metternich would have liked to put a kicking-strap upon it. Impelled by progress in France, it impelled in its turn the slowly-moving European monarchies, and while towed, it towed too.

At home, however, pauperism, beggary, wages, education, the penal code, prostitution, the fall of woman, wealth, misery, production, consumption, division, exchange, money, capital, the rights of capital, and the rights of labor, — all these questions were multiplied above society, and formed a crushing weight. Outside of political parties, properly so called, another movement became manifest, and a philosophic fermentation responded to the democratic fermentation, and chosen minds felt troubled like the crowd, — differently, but quite as much. Thinking men meditated, while the soil, that is to say, the people, traversed by revolutionary currents, trembled beneath them with vague epileptic shocks. These thinkers, some isolated, but others assembled in families and almost in communities, stirred up social questions peacefully but deeply; they were impassive miners, who quietly hollowed their galleries beneath volcanoes, scarce disturbed by the dull commotions and the fires of which they caught a glimpse. This tranquillity was not the least beautiful spectacle of this agitated epoch, and these men left to political parties the question of rights, to trouble themselves about the question of happiness. What they wished to extract from society was the welfare of man ; hence they elevated material questions, and questions about agriculture, trade, and commerce, almost to the dignity of a religion. In civilization, such as it has been constituted a little by God and a great deal by man, instincts are combined, aggregated, and amalgamated so as to form a real hard rock, by virtue of a law of dynamics which is carefully studied by social economists, those geologists of politics. These men, who grouped themselves under different appellations, but who may all be designated by the generic title of socialists, tried to pierce this rock and cause the living waters of human felicity to gush forth ; their labors embraced all questions, from that of the scaffold to that of war, and they added to the rights of man as proclaimed by the French revolutions, the rights of the woman and the child.

For various reasons we cannot thoroughly discuss

here, from the theoretical point of view, the questions raised by socialism, and we limit ourselves to an indication of them. All the questions which the socialists proposed — laying aside cosmogonic visions, reverie, and mysticism — may be carried back to two original problems, the first of which is, to produce wealth, and the second, to distribute it. The first problem contains the question of labor, the second the question of wages ; in the first, the point is the employment of strength, and in the second, the distribution of enjoyments. From a good employment of strength results public power, and from a good distribution of enjoyments individual happiness. By good distribution we mean, not equal, but equitable, distribution, for the first equality is equity. From these two things — combined public power abroad and individual happiness at home — results social prosperity ; that is to say, man happy, the citizen free, and the nation great.

England solves the first of these two problems, — she creates wealth admirably, but distributes it badly. This solution, which is completely on one side, fatally leads her to these two extremes, — monstrous opulence and monstrous misery ; all the enjoyments belong to the few, all the privations to the rest, that is to say, to the people, and privileges, exceptions, monopoly, and feudalism spring up from labor itself. It is a false and dangerous situation to base public power on private want, and to root the grandeur of the state in the sufferings of the individual ; it is a badly composed grandeur, in which all the material elements are combined, in which no moral element enters. Communism and the agrarian law fancy that they solve the second question, but they are mistaken. Their distribution kills production, and equal division destroys emulation and consequently labor. It is a distribution made by the butcher who slaughters what he divides. Hence it is impossible to be satisfied with these pretended solutions, for killing riches is not distributing them. The two problems must be solved together in order to be properly solved; the two solutions demand to be combined, and only form one. If you solve but the first of these problems you will be Venice, you will be England; you will have, like Venice, an artificial power, like England, a material power, and you will be the wicked rich man; you will perish by violence, as Venice died, or by bankruptcy, as England will fall; and the world will leave you to die and fall, because it allows everything to die and fall which is solely selfishness, and everything which does not represent a virtue or an idea to the human race. Of course it will be understood that by the words Venice and England we do not mean the peoples, but the social constructions; the oligarchies that weigh down the nations, but not the nations themselves. Nations ever have our respect and sympathy. Venice, as a people, will live again; England, as the aristocracy, will fall, but England the nation is immortal. This said, let us continue.

Solve the two problems, encourage the rich and protect the poor, suppress misery, put an end to the unjust exhaustion of the weak by the strong, bridle the iniquitous jealousy which the man still on the road feels for him who has reached the journey's end, adjust mathematically and paternally the wage to the labor, blend gratuitous and enforced education with the growth of childhood and render science the basis of manhood, develop intelligence while occupying the arms, be at once a powerful people and a family of happy men, democratize property, not by abolishing but by universalizing it, so that every citizen without exception may be a land-owner, — an easier task than it may be supposed, — in two words, know how to produce wealth and to distribute it, and you will possess at once material greatness and moral greatness, and be worthy to call yourself France. Such was what socialism, above and beyond a few mistaken sects, said; this is what it sought in facts and stirred up in minds: they were admirable efforts and sacred attempts !

These doctrines, theories, and resistances; the unexpected necessity for the statesman of settling with the philosophers; glimpses caught of confused evidences; a new policy to create, agreeing with the old world, while not disagreeing too greatly from the revolutionary ideal, a situation in which Lafayette must be used to defend Polignac, the intuition of progress apparent behind the riots, the chambers, and the street; the king's faith in the revolution; rivalries to be balanced around him, possibly some eventual resignation sprung from the vague acceptance of a definite and superior right; his wish to remain here, his race, his family affections, his sincere respect for the people, and his own honesty, — all these painfully affected Louis Philippe, and at times, though he was so strong and courageous, crushed him beneath the difficulty of being a king. He felt beneath his feet a formidable disintegration, which, however, was not a crumbling to dust, as France was more France than ever. Dark storm-clouds were collected on the horizon; a strange, gradually increasing shadow was extended over men, things, and ideas; it was a shadow that sprang from anger and systems. Everything that had been hastily suppressed stirred and fermented, and at times the conscience of the honest man held its breath, as there was such an uneasy feeling produced by this atmosphere, in which sophisms were mixed with truths. Minds trembled in the social anxiety, like leaves on the approach of a storm, and the electric tension was such that at some moments the first-comer, a stranger, would produce a flash, but then the twilight obscurity fell over the whole scene again. At intervals, deep and muttered rolling allowed an opinion to be formed of the amount of lightning which the cloud must contain.

Twenty months had scarce elapsed since the revolution of July, and the year 1832 opened with an imminent and menacing appearance. The distress of the people, workmen without bread; the Prince of Condé suddenly departed from the world; Brussels expelling the Nassaus, as Paris had done the Bourbons; Belgium offering itself to a French prince and given to an English prince; the Russian hatred of Nicholas; behind us two demons of the South, Ferdinand in Spain and Miguel in Portugal; the earth trembling in Italy; Metternich stretching out

his hand over Bologna; France confronting Austria
at Ancona; in the North the sinister sound of a hammer, enclosing Poland again in its coffin; throughout
Europe angry eyes watching France; England, a suspicious ally, prepared to push any one who staggered
and to throw herself on him who fell; the Peerage
taking refuge behind Beccaria to refuse four heads
to the law; the fleurs-de-lys erased from the king's
coaches; the cross dragged from Notre Dame; Lafayette enfeebled, Laffitte ruined; Benjamin Constant
dead in poverty; Casimir Perier dead in the exhaustion of power; a political and a social disease declaring themselves simultaneously in the two capitals
of the kingdom, — one the city of thought, the other
the city of toil; in Paris a civil war, in Lyons a servile war; and in both cities the same furnace-glow,
a volcanic purple on the brow of the people; the
South fanaticized, the West troubled, the Duchesse
de Berry in the Vendée; plots, conspiracies, insurrections, and cholera adding to the gloomy rumor of
ideas the gloomy tumult of events.

CHAPTER V.

FACTS FROM WHICH HISTORY IS DERIVED BUT WHICH HISTORY IGNORES.

TOWARD the end of April matters became aggravated, and the fermentation assumed the proportions of an ebullition. Since 1830 there had been small partial revolts, quickly suppressed, but breaking out again, which were the sign of a vast subjacent conflagration, and of something terrible smouldering. A glimpse could be caught of the lineaments of a possible revolution, though it was still indistinct and badly lighted. France was looking at Paris, and Paris at the Faubourg St. Antoine. The Faubourg St. Antoine, noiselessly heated, had begun to boil. The wine-shops in the Rue de Charonne were grave and stormy, though the conjunction of these two epithets applied to wine-shops appears singular. The Government was purely and simply put upon its trial on this, and men publicly discussed whether "they should fight or remain quiet." There were back-rooms in which workmen swore to go into the streets at the first cry of alarm, "and fight without counting their enemies." Once they had taken the pledge, a man seated in a corner of the wine-shop shouted in a sonorous voice, "You hear! You have sworn!" Sometimes they went up to a private room on the first floor, where scenes almost resembling masonic ceremonies took place, and the novice took oaths, " in order to render a service to himself as well as to the fathers of families," — such was the formula. In the tap-rooms, " subversive " pamphlets were read, and, as a secret report of the day says, " they spurned the Government." Remarks like the following could be heard : " I do not know the names of the chief, we shall not know the day till two hours before-hand." A workman said, " We are three hundred, let us each subscribe ten sous, and we shall have one hundred and fifty francs, with which to manufacture bullets and gunpowder." Another said, " I do not ask for six months, I do not ask for two. Within a fortnight we shall be face to face with the govern-ment, for it is possible to do so with twenty-five thousand men." Another said, " I do not go to bed at nights now, for I am making cartridges." From time to time well-dressed men came, feigning em-barrassment and having an air of command, and shook hands with the more important and then went away, never staying longer than ten minutes ; sig-nificant remarks were exchanged in whispers, " The plot is ripe, the thing is ready," — to borrow the re-mark of one of the audience, " this was buzzed by all present." The excitement was so great that one day a workman said openly in a wine-shop, " But we have no weapons," to which a comrade replied, " The soldiers have them," unconsciously parodying Bonaparte's proclamation to the army of Italy. " When they had any very great secret," a report adds, " they did not communicate it," though we do not understand what they could conceal after what they had said. The meetings were sometimes periodical; at certain ones there were never more than eight or ten members present, and they were always the same, but at others any one who liked went in, and the room was so crowded that they were obliged to stand; some went there through enthusiasm and passion, others "because it was the road to their work." In the same way as during the revolution, there were female patriots in these wine-shops, who kissed the new-comers.

Other expressive facts were collected: thus a man went into a wine-shop, drank, and went away, saying, "Wine-dealer, the revolution will pay what is due." Revolutionary agents were nominated at a wine-shop opposite the Rue de Charonne, and the ballot was made in caps. Workmen assembled at a fencing-master's who gave lessons in the Rue de Cotte. There was a trophy of arms, made of wooden sabres, canes, cudgels, and foils. One day the buttons were removed from the foils, and a workman said, "We are five-and-twenty, but they do not reckon upon me, as they consider me a machine." This man was at a later date Quénisset. Things that were premeditated gradually assumed a strange notoriety; a woman who was sweeping her door said to another woman, "They have been making cartridges for a long time past." In the open streets proclamations addressed to the National Guards of the departments were read aloud, and one of them was signed, "Burtot, wine-dealer."

One day a man with a large beard and an Italian

accent leaped on a bench at the door of a dram-shop
in the Marché Lenoir, and began reading a singular
document, which seemed to emanate from some occult power.   Groups assembled around him and applauded, and the passages which most excited the
mob were noted down at the time.   " Our doctrines
are impeded, our proclamations are torn down, our
bill-posters watched and thrown into prison. . . . The
collapse in cottons has brought over to us a good
many conservatives. . . . The future of the people
is being worked out in our obscure ranks. . . . These
are the terms laid down, action or reaction, revolution or counter-revolution, for in our age no one still
believes in inertia or immobility.   For the people, or
against the people, that is the question, and there is
no other. . . . On the day when we no longer please
you, break us, but till then aid us to progress."   All
this took place in broad daylight.   Other facts, of
even a more audacious nature, appeared suspicious to
the people, owing to their very audacity.   On April 4,
1832, a passer-by leaped on the bench at the corner
of the Rue Sainte Marguerite, and shouted, " I am
a Babouviste," but under Babœuf the people scented
Gisquet.   Among other things this man said :
" Down with property ! The opposition of the Left is
cowardly and treacherous : when they wish to be in
the right, they preach the revolution ; they are democratic that they may not be defeated, and royalist
so that they need not fight.   The republicans are
feathered beasts ; distrust the republicans, citizen-
workmen ! "   " Silence, citizen-spy ! " a workman
shouted, and this put an end to the speech.

Mysterious events occurred. At nightfall a workman met a "well-dressed" man near the canal, who
said to him, "Where art thou going, citizen?" "Sir,"
the workman answered, "I have not the honor of
knowing you" — "I know thee, though;" and the
man added, "Fear nothing, I am the agent of the
committee, and it is suspected that thou art not to
be trusted. But thou knowest that there is an eye
upon thee, if thou darest to reveal anything." Then
he shook the workman's hand and went away, saying,
"We shall meet again soon." The police, who were
listening, overheard singular dialogues, not only in
the wine-shops but in the streets. "Get yourself
ready soon," said a weaver to a cabinet-maker. "Why
so?" "There will be shots to fire." Two passers-
by in rags exchanged the following peculiar remarks,
which were big with an apparent Jacquerie: "Who
governs us?" "It is Monsieur Philippe." "No, the
bourgeoisie." It would be an error to suppose that
we attach a bad sense to the word "Jacquerie;" the
Jacques were the poor. Another time a man was
heard saying to his companion, "We have a famous
plan of attack." Of a private conversation between
four men seated in a ditch near the Barrière du
Trône only the following was picked up: "Everything possible will be done to prevent him walking
about Paris any longer." "Who is the *he?*" there
is a menacing obscurity about it. The "principal
chiefs," as they were called in the faubourg, kept
aloof, but were supposed to assemble to arrange matters at a wine-shop near the Point St. Eustache. A
man of the name of Aug, chief of the society for the

relief of tailors, was supposed to act as central inter-
mediary between the chiefs and the Faubourg St.
Antoine. Still, a considerable amount of obscurity
hangs over these chiefs, and no fact could weaken the
singular pride in the answer made at a later date, by
a prisoner brought before the Court of Peers.

" Who was your chief? "

" I did not know any, and I did not recognize any."

As yet they were but words, transparent but vague,
at times mere rumors and hearsays, but other signs
arrived ere long. A carpenter, engaged in the Rue
de Rueilly in nailing up a fence round a block of
ground on which a house was being built, found on
the ground a piece of a torn letter, on which the
following lines were still legible : " . . . . The Committee must take measures to prevent recruiting in
the sections for the different societies ; " and as a
postscript, " We have learned that there are guns at
No. 5, Rue du Faubourg, Poissonnière, to the number
of five or six thousand, at a gunmaker's in the yard.
The Section possesses no arms." What startled the
carpenter, and induced him to show the thing to his
neighbors, was that a few paces farther on he found
another paper, also torn, and even more significant,
of which we reproduce the shape, owing to the
historic interest of these strange documents.

Q	C	D	E	Apprenez cette liste par cœur. Après, vous la déchirerez : Les hommes ad-mis en feront autant lorsque vous leur aurez transmis des ordres. Salut et Fraternité. u og a^l fe L.

Persons at that time on the scent of this discovery did not learn till a later date the meaning of the four capitals, — *Quinturions, Centurions, Décurions,* and *Éclaireurs,* or the sense of the letters *u og a¹ fe,* which were a date, and indicated "this 15th April, 1832." Under each capital letter were written names followed by very characteristic remarks. Thus, " Q. Bannerel, 8 guns, 83 cartridges. A safe man. — C. Boubière, 1 pistol, 40 cartridges. — D. Rollet, 1 foil, 1 pistol, 1 lb. gunpowder. — E. Tessin, 1 sabre, 1 cartouche-box. Punctual. — Terreur, 8 guns. Brave," etc. Lastly, this carpenter found in the same enclosure a third paper, on which was written in pencil, but very legibly, this enigmatical list.

Unité. Blanchard : Arbre sec. 6.

Barra. Sixteen. Sall au Comte.

Kosciusko. Aubry the butcher ?

J. J. R.

Caius Graccus.

Right of revision. Dufond. Four.

Downfall of the Girondists. Derbac. Maubuée.

Washington. Pinson. 1 pist. 86 cart.

Marseillaise.

Sovereignty of the people. Michel. Quincampoix. Sabre.

Hoche.

Marceau. Plato. Arbre Sec.

Warsaw, Tilly, crier of the *Populaire.*

The honest citizen in whose hands this list remained learned its purport. It seems that the list was the complete nomenclature of the sections of the fourth arrondissement of the Society of the

Rights of Man, with the names and addresses of the chiefs of sections. At the present day, when these obscure facts have become historic, they may be published. We may add that the foundation of the Society of the Rights of Man seems to have been posterior to the date on which this paper was found, and so it was possibly only a sketch. After propositions and words and written information, material facts began to pierce through. In the Rue Popincourt, at the shop of a broker, seven pieces of paper, all folded alike, were found in a drawer; these papers contained twenty-six squares of the same gray paper, folded in the shape of cartridges, and a card on which was written: —

Saltpetre	12 oz.
Sulphur	2 "
Charcoal	2½ "
Water	2 "

The report of the seizure showed that there was a strong smell of gunpowder in the drawer.

A mason, returning home after his day's work, left a small parcel on the bench near the bridge of Austerlitz. It was carried to the guard-house and opened, and from it were taken two printed dialogues signed "Lahautière," a song called "Workmen, combine!" and a tin box full of cartridges. A workman drinking with his comrade bade him feel how hot he was; and the other noticed a pistol under his jacket. In a ditch on the boulevard between Père Lachaise and the Barrière du Trône, some children, playing at the most deserted spot, discovered under a heap of rubbish a bag containing a bullet mould, a mandrel for making cartridges, a pouch in which there were some grains of gunpowder, and an iron ladle on which were evident signs of melted lead. Some police agents suddenly entering at five A.M. the room of one Pardon, who was at a later date a sectionist belonging to the Barricade Merry section, found him sitting on his bed with cartridges in his hand, which he was in the act of making. At the hour when workmen are generally resting, two men were noticed to meet between the Picpus and Charenton barrières, in a lane running between two walls. One took a pistol from under his blouse, which he handed to the other; as he gave it him he noticed that the perspiration on his chest had dampened the gunpowder, he therefore filled the pan afresh, and the two men thereupon parted. A man of the name of Gallas, afterwards killed in the April affair in the Rue Beaubourg, used to boast that he had at home seven hundred cartridges and twenty-four gun flints. One day the Government received information that arms and two hundred thousand cartridges had just been distributed in the faubourg, and the next week thirty thousand more cartridges were given out. The remarkable thing was that the police could not seize any of them; but an intercepted letter stated: "The day is not far distant when eighty thousand patriots will be under arms in four hours."

All this fermentation was public, we might almost say calm, and the impending insurrection prepared its storm quietly in the face of the Government. No singularity was lacking in this crisis, which was still subterranean, but already perceptible. The citizens spoke peacefully to the workmen of what was preparing. They said, " How is the revolt going on ? " in the same tone as they could have said, " How is your wife ? "   A furniture broker in the Rue Moreau asked, " Well, when do you attack? " and another shop-keeper said, " They will attack soon, I know it. A month ago there were fifteen thousand of you, and now there are twenty-five thousand." He offered his gun, and a neighbor offered a pocket pistol which was marked for sale at seven francs. The revolutionary fever spread, and no point of Paris or of France escaped it. The artery throbbed everywhere, and the network of secret societies began spreading over the country like the membranes which spring up from certain inflammations, and are formed in the human body. From the Association of the Friends of the People, which was at the same time public and secret, sprang the Society of the Rights of Man, which dated one of its orders of the day, " Pluviose, year 40 of the republican era," which was destined even to survive the decrees of the Court of Assizes pronouncing its dissolution, and did not hesitate to give to its sections significant titles like the following : " Pikes. The Tocsin. The Alarm Gun. The Phrygian Cap. January 21. The Beggars. The Vagrants. March forward. Robespierre. The Level. Ça ira."

The Society of the Rights of Man engendered the Society of Action, composed of impatient men who detached themselves and hurried forward.   Other associations tried to recruit themselves in the great mother societies : and the sectionists complained of being tormented. Such were the " Gaulish Society " and the "Organizing Committee of the Municipalities ; " such the associations for the " Liberty of the Press," for " Individual Liberty," for the " Instruction of the People," and " Against Indirect Taxes." Next we have the Society of Equalitarian Workmen divided into three fractions, — the Equalitarians, the Communists, and the Reformers. Then, again, the Army of the Bastilles, a cohort possessing military organization, four men being commanded by a corporal, ten by a sergeant, twenty by a sub-lieutenant, and forty by a lieutenant ; there were never more than five men who knew each other. This is a creation where precaution is combined with audacity, and which seems to be stamped with the genius of Venice. The central committee which formed the head, had two arms, — the Society of Action and the Army of the Bastilles. A legitimist association, the " Knights of Fidelity," agitated among these republican affiliations, but was denounced and repudiated. The Parisian societies ramified through the principal cities. Lyons, Nantes, Lille, and Marseilles, had their Society of the Rights of Man, The Charbonnière, and the Free Men. Aix had a revolutionary society called the Cougourde. We have already mentioned that name.

At Paris the Faubourg Marceau buzzed no less than the Faubourg St. Antoine, and the schools were quite as excited as the faubourgs. A coffee-shop in the Rue Saint Hyacinthe, and the Estaminet des

Sept Billards in the Rue des Mathurins St. Jacques, served as the gathering-place for the students. The Society of the Friends of the A. B. C. affiliated with the Mutualists of Angers, and the Cougourde of Aix assembled, as we have seen, at the Café Musain. The same young men met, as we have also said, at a wine-shop and eating-house near the Rue Montdetour, called Corinthe. These meetings were secret, but others were as public as possible, and we may judge of their boldness by this fragment from an examination that was held in one of the ulterior trials. " Where was the meeting held ? " " In the Rue de la Paix." " At whose house ? " " In the street." " What sections were there ? " " Only one." " Which one ? " " The Manuel section." " Who was the chief ? " " Myself." " You are too young to have yourself formed this serious resolve of attacking the Government.   Whence came your instructions ? " " From the central committee." The army was un-dermined at the same time as the population, as was proved at a later date by the movements of Béford, Luneville, and Épinal. Hopes were built on the 52d, 5th, 8th, and 37th regiments, and on the 20th light infantry. In Burgundy and the southern towns the tree of liberty was planted, that is to say, a mast surmounted by a red cap.

Such was the situation.

This situation, as we said at the commencement, the Faubourg St. Antoine rendered keen and marked more than any other group of the population. This was the stitch in the side. This old faubourg, peopled like an ant-heap, laborious, courageous, and

passionate as a hive of bees, quivered in expectation and the desire of a commotion. All was agitation there, but labor was not suspended on that
account. Nothing could give an idea of these sharp
and sombre faces; there were in this faubourg
crushing distress hidden under the roofs of houses,
and also ardent and rare minds. It is especially
in the case of distress and intelligence that it is
dangerous for extremes to meet. The Faubourg St.
Antoine had other causes for excitement, as it received the counter-stroke of commercial crisis, bankruptcies, stoppages, and cessation of work, which
are inherent in all political convulsions. In revolutionary times misery is at once the cause and the
effect, and the blow which it deals falls upon itself again. This population, full of haughty virtue,
capable of the highest amount of latent caloric, ever
ready to take up arms, prompt to explode, irritated,
profound, and undermined, seemed to be only waiting
for the fall of a spark. Whenever certain sparks
float about the horizon, driven by the wind of events,
we cannot help thinking of the Faubourg St. Antoine
and the formidable chance which has placed at the
gates of Paris this powder-magazine of sufferings
and ideas.

The wine-shops of the Antoine suburb, which
have been more than once referred to in this sketch,
possess an historic notoriety. In times of trouble
people grow intoxicated in them more on words than
wine; and a species of prophetic spirit and an efflu-
vium of the future circulates there, swelling hearts
and ennobling minds. These wine-shops resemble

the taverns on the Mons Aventinus, built over the Sibyl's cave and communicating with the sacred blasts of the depths, — taverns in which the tables were almost tripods, and people drank what Ennius calls the Sibylline wine. The Faubourg St. Antoine is a reservoir of the people, in which the revolutionary earthquake makes fissures, through which the sovereignty of the people flows. This sovereignty can act badly, it deceives itself like other things, but even when led astray it remains grand. We may say of it, as of the blind Cyclops, "Ingens." In '93, according as the idea that floated was good or bad, or according as it was the day of fanaticism or enthusiasm, savage legions or heroic bands issued from this faubourg. Savage, — let us explain that word. What did these bristling men want, who, in the Genesis of the revolutionary chaos, rushed upon old overthrown Paris in rags, yelling and ferocious, with uplifted clubs and raised pikes ? They wanted the end of oppression, the end of tyranny, the end of the sword, work for the man, instruction for the child, social gentleness for the woman, liberty, equality, fraternity, bread for all, the idea for all, the Edenization of the world, and progress ; and this holy, good, and sweet thing called progress, they, driven to exasperation, claimed terribly with upraised weapons and curses. They were savages, we grant, but the savages of civilization. They proclaimed the right furiously, and wished to force the human race into Paradise, even were it through trembling and horror. They seemed barbarians, and were saviors ; they demanded light while wearing the mask of night. Opposite these men, — stern and frightful we admit, but stern and frightful for good, — there are other men, smiling, embroidered, gilded, be-ribboned, in silk stockings, with white feathers, yellow gloves, and kid shoes, who, leaning upon a velvet-covered table near a marble chimney-piece, gently insist on the maintenance and preservation of the past, of the middle ages, of divine right, of fanaticism, of ignorance, of slavery, of the punishment of death, and of war ; and who glorify in a low voice and with great politeness the sabre, the pyre, and the scaffold. For our part, were we compelled to make a choice between the barbarians of civilization and the civilized of barbarism, we would choose the barbarians. But, thanks be to Heaven, another choice is possible ; no fall down an abyss is required, either in front or behind, neither despotism nor terrorism. We wish for progress on a gentle incline, and God provides for this. Reducing inclines is the whole policy of God.

CHAPTER VI.

ENJOLRAS AND HIS LIEUTENANTS.

SHORTLY after this period, Enjolras made a sort of mysterious census, as if in the view of a possible event. All were assembled in council at the Café Musain. Enjolras spoke, mingling a few half-enigmatical but significant metaphors with his words :

" It behooves us to know where we are, and on whom we can count. If we want combatants we must make them ; and there is no harm in having weapons to strike with. Passers-by always run a greater chance of being gored when there are bulls in the road than when there are none. So, suppose we count the herd. How many are there of us ? This task must not be deferred till to-morrow, for revolutionists must always be in a hurry, as progress has no time to lose. Let us distrust the unexpected, and not allow ourselves to be taken unawares ; we have to go over all the seams which we have sewn, and see whether they hold , and the job must be done to-day. Courfeyrac, you will see the Polytechnic students, for this is their day for going out. Feuilly, you will see those of La Glacière, and Combeferre has promised to go to the Picpus. Bahorel will

visit the Estrapade.   Prouvaire, the masons are growing lukewarm, so you will obtain us news from the
lodge in the Rue de Grenelle St. Honoré.   Joly will
go to Dupuytren's clinical lecture, and feel the pulse
of the medical scholars, while Bossuet will stroll
round the courts and talk with the law students.
I take the Cougourde myself."

"That is all settled," said Courfeyrac.

"No.   There is another very important matter."

"What is it?" Combeferre asked.

"The Barrière du Maine."

Enjolras was absorbed in thought for a moment,
and then continued, —

"At the Barrière du Maine are stone-cutters and
painters, an enthusiastic body, but subject to chills.
I do not know what has been the matter with them
for some time past, but they are thinking of other
things.   They are dying out, and they spend their
time in playing at dominoes.   It is urgent to go
and talk to them rather seriously, and they meet at
Richefeu's, where they may be found between twelve
and one o'clock.   Those ashes must be blown up,
and I had intended to intrust the task to that absent
fellow Marius, who is all right, but no longer comes
here.   I need some one for the Barrière du Maine,
and have no one left."

"Why, I am here," said Grantaire.

"You?"

"I."

"You indoctrinate republicans? you warm up
chilled hearts in the name of principles?"

"Why not?"

" Can you possibly be fit for anything ? "

" Well, I have a vague ambition to be so."

" You believe in nothing."

" I believe in you."

" Grantaire, will you do a service ? "

" Any one ; clean your boots."

" Well, do not meddle in our affairs, sleep off your absinthe."

" You are an ungrateful fellow, Enjolras ! "

" You be the man capable of going to the Barrière du Maine ! "

" I am capable of going down the Rue des Grès, crossing St. Michael's Square, cutting through the Rue Monsieur le Prince, taking the Rue de Vaugirard, passing the Carmelites, turning into the Rue d'Assas, arriving at the Rue Cherche Midi, leaving behind me the Council of War, stepping across the Rue des Vieilles-Tuileries, following the main road, going through the gate and entering Richefeu's. I am capable of all that, and so are my shoes."

" Do you know the men at Richefeu's ? "

" Not much."

" What will you say to them ? "

" Talk to them about Robespierre, Danton, and principles."

" You ! "

" I. You really do not do me justice, for when I make up my mind to it I am terrible. I have read Prudhomme, I know the social contract, and have by heart my constitution of the year II. ' The liberty of the citizen ends where the liberty of another citizen begins.' Do you take me for a brute ? I have an old assignat in my draw, — The Rights of Man, the sovereignty of the people, sapristi! I am a bit of a Hébertist myself. I can discourse splendid things for six hours at a stretch, watch in hand."

" Be serious," said Enjolras.

" I am stern," Grantaire answered.

Enjolras reflected for a few seconds, and then seemed to have made up his mind.

" Grantaire," he said gravely, " I consent to try you. You shall go to the Barrière du Maine."

Grantaire lodged in a furnished room close to the Café Musain. He went away and returned five minutes after — he had been home to put on a waistcoat of the Robespierre cut.

" Red," he said on entering, and looked intently at Enjolras. ·

Then he energetically turned back on his chest the two scarlet points of the waistcoat, and, walking up to Enjolras, whispered in his ear, " Never fear!" He boldly cocked his hat, and went out. A quarter of an hour after, the back-room of the Café Musain was deserted, and all the Friends of the A. B. C. were going in various directions about their business. Enjolras, who had reserved the Cougourde for himself, was the last to leave. The Members of the Aix Cougourde who were in Paris assembled at that period on the plain of Issy, in one of the abandoned quarries so numerous on that side of Paris.

Enjolras, while walking toward the meeting-place, took a mental review of the situation. The gravity of the events was visible, for when the facts which

are the forerunners of latent social disease move
heavily, the slightest complication checks and im-
pedes their action. It is a phenomenon from which
collapse and regeneration issue. Enjolras caught a
glimpse of a luminous upheaving behind the dark
clouds of the future. Who knew whether the moment might not be at hand when the people would
seize their rights once again ? What a splendid
spectacle ! the revolution majestically taking possession of France once more, and saying to the world,
" To be continued to-morrow ! " Enjolras was satisfied,
for the furnace was aglow, and he had at that self-
same moment a gunpowder train of friends scattered
over Paris. He mentally compared Combeferre's
philosophic and penetrating eloquence, Feuilly's cos-
mopolitan enthusiasm, Courfeyrac's humor, Bahorel's
laugh, Jean Prouvaire's melancholy, Joly's learning,
and Bossuet's sarcasms, to a species of electrical
flash, which produced fire everywhere simultaneously. All were at work, and most certainly the
result would respond to the effort. That was good,
and it made him think of Grantaire. "Ah," he said
to himself, " the Barrière du Maine is hardly at
all out of my way, so suppose I go on to Richefeu's
and see what Grantaire is doing, and how far he
has got."

It was striking one by the Vaugirard church when
Enjolras reached Richefeu's. He pushed open the
door, went in, folded his arms, and looked about the
room, which was full of tables, men, and tobacco
smoke. A voice was audible in this fog, sharply
interrupted by another voice, — it was Grantaire

talking with some opponent of his. Grantaire was seated opposite another man, at a marble table covered with sawdust and studded with dominoes. He smote the marble with his fist, and this is what Enjolras heard : —

"Double six."

"A four."

"The pig ! I have n't any left."

"You are dead.   A two."

"A six."

"A three."

"An ace."

"My set."

"Four points."

"With difficulty."

"It is yours."

"I made an enormous mistake."

"You are getting on all right."

"Fifteen."

"Seven more."

"That makes me twenty-two [pensively].   Twenty-two ! "

"You did not expect the double six.   Had I played it at first it would have changed the whole game."

"Double two."

"An ace."

"An ace ! well, a five ! "

"I have n't one."

"You played first, I believe ? "

"Yes."

"A blank."

"What luck he has! Ah! you have luck; [a long reverie] a two."

"An ace."

"I've neither a five nor an ace. It is stupid for you."

"Domino!"

"Oh, the deuce!"

BOOK II.

ÉPONINE.

CHAPTER I.

THE LARK'S FIELD.

MARIUS witnessed the unexpected dénouement of the snare upon whose track he had placed Javert, but the Inspector had scarce left the house, taking his prisoners with him in three hackney coaches, ere Marius stepped out of the house in his turn. It was only nine in the evening, and Marius went to call on Courfeyrac, who was no longer the imperturbable inhabitant of the Pays Latin. He had gone to live in the Rue de la Verrière, "for political reasons;" and this district was one of those in which insurrectionists of the day were fond of installing themselves. Marius said to Courfeyrac, "I am going to sleep here," and Courfeyrac pulled off one of his two mattresses, laid it on the ground, and said, "There you are!" At seven o'clock the next morning Marius returned to No. 50–52, paid his quarter's rent, and what he owed to Mame Bougon, had his books, bed, table, chest-of-drawers, and two chairs, placed on a truck, and went away without leaving his address;

so that, when Javert returned in the morning to question Marius about the events of the previous evening, he only found Mame Bougon, who said to him, " Gone away." Mame Bougon was convinced that Marius was in some way an accomplice of the robbers arrested the previous evening. " Who would have thought it ! " she exclaimed to the porteresses of the quarter, " a young man whom you might have taken for a girl ! "

Marius had two reasons for moving so promptly, the first was that he now felt a horror of this house, in which he had seen so closely, and in all its most repulsive and ferocious development, a social ugliness more frightful still, perhaps, than the wicked rich man, — the wicked poor man. The second was that he did not wish to figure at the trial, — which would in all probability ensue, — and be obliged to give evidence against Thénardier. Javert believed that the young man, whose name he forgot, had been frightened and had run away, or else had not even returned home ; he made some efforts, however, to find him, which were unsuccessful. A month elapsed, then another. Marius was still living with Courfeyrac, and had learned from a young barrister, an habitual walker of the Salle des Pas Perdus, that Thénardier was in solitary confinement, and every Monday he left a five-franc piece for him at the wicket of La Force. Marius, having no money left, borrowed the five francs of Courfeyrac ; it was the first time in his life that he borrowed money. These periodical five francs were a double enigma for Courfeyrac who gave them, and for Thénardier who received them. "Where can they go to?" Courfeyrac thought. "Where can they come from?" Thénardier asked himself.

Marius, however, was heart-broken, for everything had disappeared again through a trap-door. He saw nothing ahead of him, and his life was once more plunged into the mystery in which he had been groping. He had seen again momentarily and very closely the girl whom he loved, the old man who appeared her father, — the strange beings who were his only interest and sole hope in this world,—and at the moment when he fancied that he should grasp them, a breath had carried off all these shadows. Not a spark of certainty and truth had flashed even from that most terrific collision, and no conjecture was possible. He no longer knew the name of which he had felt so certain, and it certainly was not Ursule, and the Lark was a nickname; and then, what must he think of the old man? Did he really hide himself from the police? The white-haired workman whom Marius had met in the vicinity of the Invalides reverted to his mind, and it now became probable that this workman and M. Leblanc were one and the same. He disguised himself then, and this man had his heroic side and his equivocal side. Why did he not call for help? why did he fly? was he, yes or no, the father of the girl? and, lastly, was he really the man whom Thénardier fancied he recognized? Thénardier might have been mistaken. These were all so many insoluble problems. All this, it is true, in no way lessened the angelic charm of the maiden of the Luxembourg. Poignant distress, — Marius had a passion in his heart, and night over his eyes. He was impelled, he was attracted, and he could not stir ; all had vanished, except love, and he had lost the sudden instincts and illuminations of even that love. Usually, this flame which burns us enlightens us a little, and casts some useful light without, but Marius no longer even heard the dumb counsel of passion. He never said to himself, Suppose I were to go there, or try this thing or the other? She whom he could no longer call Ursule was evidently somewhere, but nothing advised Marius in what direction he should seek her. All his life was now summed up in two words, — absolute uncertainty, in an impenetrable fog, — and though he still longed to see her, he no longer hoped it. As a climax, want returned, and he felt its icy breath close to him and behind him. In all these torments, and for a long time, he had discontinued his work, and nothing is more dangerous than discontinued work ; for it is a habit which a man loses, — a habit easy to give up, but difficult to re-acquire.

A certain amount of reverie is good, like a narcotic taken in discreet doses. It lulls to sleep the at times harsh fevers of the working brain, and produces in the mind a soft and fresh vapor which correct the too sharp outlines of pure thought, fills up gaps and spaces here and there, and rounds the angles of ideas. But excess of reverie submerges and drowns, and woe to the mental workman who allows himself to fall entirely from thinking into reverie ! He believes that he can easily rise again, and says that, after all, it is the same thing. Error !

Thought is the labor of the intellect, and reverie its voluptuousness; substituting reverie for thought is confounding poison with wholesome food. Marius, it will be remembered, began with that; passion arrived, and finished by hurling him into object-less and bottomless chimeras. In such a state a man only leaves his home to go and dream, and it is an indolent childishness, a tumultuous and stagnant gulf, and in proportion as work diminishes, necessities increase. This is a law; man in a dreamy state is naturally lavish and easily moved, and the relaxed mind can no longer endure the contracted life. There is, in this mode of existence, good mingled with evil, for if the softening be mournful, the generosity is healthy and good. But the poor, generous, and noble-minded man who does not work is ruined; the resources dry up, and necessity arises. This is a fatal incline, on which the most honest and the strongest men are dragged down like the weakest and the most vicious, and which leads to one of two holes, — suicide or crime. Through going out to dream, a day arrives when a man goes out to throw himself into the water. Excess of dreaminess produces such men as Escousse and Libras. Marius went down this incline slowly, with his eyes fixed upon her whom he no longer saw. What we have just written seems strange, and yet it is true, — the recollection of an absent being is illumined in the gloom of the heart; the more it disappears the more radiant it appears, and the despairing and obscure soul sees this light on its horizon, the star of its inner night. She was Marius's entire thought, he dreamed of nothing else. He felt confusedly that his old coat was becoming an outrageous coat, and that his new coat was growing an old coat, that his boots were wearing out, that his hat was wearing out, that his shirts were wearing out, — that is to say, that his life was wearing out ; and he said to himself, Could I but see her again before I die !

One sole sweet idea was left him, and it was that she had loved him, that her glance had told him so ; and that she did not know his name but that she knew his soul, and that however mysterious the spot might be where she now was, she loved him still. Might she not be dreaming of him as he was dreaming of her? At times in those inexplicable hours which every loving heart knows, as he had only reason to be sad, and yet felt within him a certain quivering of joy, he said to himself, " Her thoughts are visiting me," and then added, " Perhaps my thoughts also go to her." This illusion, at which he shook his head a moment after, sometimes, however, contrived to cast rays which resembled hope into his soul at intervals. Now and then, especially at that evening hour which most saddens dreamers, he poured out upon virgin paper the pure, impersonal, and ideal reveries with which love filled his brain. He called this " writing to her." We must not suppose, however, that his reason was in disorder, quite the contrary. He had lost the faculty of working and going firmly toward a determined object, but he retained clear-sightedness and rectitude more fully than ever. Marius saw by a calm and real, though singular, light, all that was taking place before him, even the most indifferent men and facts, and spoke correctly of everything with a sort of honest weariness and candid disinterestedness. His judgment, almost detached from hope, soared far above him. In this state of mind nothing escaped him, nothing deceived him, and he discovered at each moment the bases of life, — humanity and destiny. Happy, even in agony, is the man to whom God has granted a soul worthy of love and misfortune! He who has not seen the things of this world and the heart of man in this double light has seen nothing of the truth and knows nothing.

The soul that loves and suffers is in a sublime state.

Days succeeded each other, and nothing new occurred; it really seemed to him that the gloomy space which he still had to traverse was becoming daily reduced. He fancied that he could already see distinctly the brink of the bottomless abyss.

"What!" he repeated to himself, "shall I not see her again before that takes place?"

After going up the Rue St. Jacques, leaving the barrière on one side, and following for some distance the old inner boulevard, you reach the Rue de la Santé, then the Glacière, and just before coming to the small stream of the Gobelins, you notice a sort of field, the only spot on the long and monotonous belt of Parisian boulevards, where Ruysdael would be tempted to sit down. I know not whence the picturesque aspect is obtained, for you merely see a green field crossed by ropes, on which rags hang to dry; an old house built in the time of Louis XIII., with its high-pitched roof quaintly pierced with garret-windows; broken-down grating; a little water between poplar trees; women's laughter and voices; on the horizon you see the Panthéon, the tree of the Sourds-Muets, the Val de Grâce, black, stunted, fantastic, amusing, and magnificent, and far in the background the stern square towers of Notre Dame. As the place is worth the trouble of visiting, no one goes there; scarce a cart or a wagon passes in a quarter of an hour. It once happened that Marius's solitary rambles led him to this field, and on that day there was a rarity on the boulevard, a passer-by. Marius, really struck by the almost savage grace of the field, asked him: "What is the name of this spot?"

The passer-by answered, "It is the Lark's field;" and added, "It was here that Ulbach killed the shepherdess of Ivry."

But, after the words "the Lark," Marius heard no more, for a word at times suffices to produce a congelation in a man's dreamy condition: the whole thought is condensed round an idea, and is no longer capable of any other perception. The Lark, that was the appellation which had taken the place of Ursule in the depths of Marius's melancholy. "Stay," he said, with that sort of unreasoning stupor peculiar to such mysterious asides, "this is her field, I shall learn here where she lives." This was absurd but irresistible, and he came daily to this Lark's field.

CHAPTER II.

CRIMES IN EMBRYO INCUBATED IN PRISONS.

Javert's triumph at the Maison Gorbeau had seemed complete, but was not so. In the first place, and that was his chief anxiety, Javert had not been able to make a prisoner of the prisoner; the assassinated man who escapes is more suspicious than the assassin, and it was probable that this personage, such a precious capture for the bandits, might be an equally good prize for the authorities. Next, Montparnasse slipped out of Javert's clutches, and he must wait for another opportunity to lay hands on that "cursed dandy." Montparnasse, in fact, having met Éponine on the boulevard, keeping watch, went off with her, preferring to play the Nemorino with the daughter rather than Schinderhannes with the father, and it was lucky for him that he did so, as he was now free. As for Éponine, Javert "nailed" her, but it was a poor consolation, and sent her to join Azelma at the Madelonnettes. Lastly, in the drive from No. 50–52 to La Force, one of the chief men arrested, Claquesous, had disappeared. No one knew how he did it, and the sergeants and agents did not at all understand it; he had turned into vapor, slipped through the handcuffs, and passed through a crack

in the coach ; but no one could say anything except
that on reaching the prison there was no Claquesous.
There was in this either enchantment or a police
trick. Had Claquesous melted away in the darkness
like a snow-flake in the water? Was there an un-
avowed connivance on the part of the agents ? Did
this man belong to the double enigma of disorder and
order ? Had this Sphynx its front paws in crimes,
and its hind paws in the police ? Javert did not
accept these combinations, and struggled against
such compromises ; but his squad contained other
inspectors besides himself, and though his subordi-
nates, perhaps more thoroughly initiated in the secrets
of the Préfecture, and Claquesous was such a villain
that he might be a very excellent agent. To be on
such intimate juggling relations with the night is
excellent for plunder and admirable for the police,
and there are double-edged rogues of the sort. However this might be, Claquesous was lost and could
not be found, and Javert seemed more irritated than
surprised. As for Marius, " that scrub of a lawyer
who was probably frightened," and whose name he
had forgotten, Javert did not trouble himself much
about him, and besides, a lawyer can always be
found. But, was he only a lawyer ?

The examination began, and the magistrate thought
it advisable not to put one of the members of the
Patron Minette band in solitary confinement, as it
was hoped he might chatter. This was Brujon, the
hairy man of the Rue du Petit Banquier ; he was
turned into the Charlemagne Court, and the eyes of
the spies were kept upon him. This name of Brujon

is one of the recollections of La Force. In the hideous yard called the Bâtiment Neuf,— which the governor named the Court of St. Bernard, and the robbers christened the Lion's Den, — and on the wall covered with scars and leprosy, that rose on the left to the height of the roof, and close to a rusty old iron gate which led to the old chapel of the ducal house of La Force, converted into a sleeping-ward for prisoners, there might have been seen, twelve years ago, a species of Bastille, clumsily engraved with a nail in the stone, and beneath it this signature, —

BRUJON, 1811.

The Brujon of 1811 was the father of the Brujon of 1832. The latter, of whom we could only catch a glimpse in the Gorbeau trap, was a very crafty and artful young fellow, with a downcast and plaintive air. It was in consequence of this air that the magistrate turned him loose, believing him more useful in the Charlemagne yard than in a secret cell. Robbers do not interrupt their labors because they are in the hands of justice, and do not trouble themselves about such a trifle. Being in prison for one crime does not prevent another being commenced. There are artists who have a picture in the Exhibition, but for all that work at a new one in their studio. Brujon seemed stupefied by prison; he might be seen standing for hours in the yard near the canteen man's stall, contemplating like an idiot the mean tariff of prices of the canteen which began with "garlic, fifty-two centimes," and ended with "cigar, five centimes." Or else he passed his time in trembling, shaking his teeth, declaring he had the fever, and inquiring whether one of the twenty-six beds in the Infirmary were vacant.

All at once, toward the second half of February, 1832, it was discovered that Brujon, the sleepy-looking man, had had three messages delivered, not in his own name, but in those of his comrades, by the prison porters. These messages had cost him fifty sous altogether, an exorbitant sum, which attracted the sergeant's attention. After making inquiries and consulting the tariff of messages hung up in the prisoners' visiting room, this authority found out that the fifty sous were thus divided, — one message to the Panthéon, ten sous ; one to Val de Grâce, fifteen sous ; and one to the Barrière de Grenelle, twenty-five sous, the latter being the dearest in the whole list. Now at these very places resided these very dangerous prowlers at the barrière, Kruideniers *alias* Bizarro, Glorious an ex-convict, and Stop-the-coach, and the attention of the police was directed to these through this incident. It was assumed that these men belonged to Patron Minette, of which band two chiefs, Babet and Gueulemer, were locked up. It was supposed that Brujon's messages, which were not delivered at the houses, but to persons waiting in the street, contained information about some meditated crime. The three ruffians were arrested, and the police believed they had scented some machination of Brujon's.

A week after these measures had been taken, a night watchman who was inspecting the ground-floor sleeping ward of the Bâtiment Neuf, was just placing his chestnut in the box (this was the method employed to make sure that the watchmen did their duty properly; every hour a chestnut must be dropped into all the boxes nailed on the doors of the sleeping wards), when he saw through the peep-hole Brujon sitting up in bed and writing something. The watchman went in, Brujon was placed in solitary confinement for a month, but what he had written could not be found. Hence the police were just as wise as before. One thing is certain, that on the next day a "postilion" was thrown from Charlemagne into the Lion's Den over the five-storied building that separated the two yards. Prisoners give the name of "postilion" to a ball of artistically moulded bread, which is sent to "Ireland," that is to say, thrown from one yard into another. This ball falls into the yard, the man who picks it up opens it and finds in it a note addressed to some prisoner in the yard. If it be a prisoner who finds the note he delivers it to the right address; if it be a guard, or one of those secretly-bought prisoners, called "sheep" in prisons, and "foxes" at the galleys, the note is carried to the wicket and delivered to the police. This time the postilion reached its address, although the man for whom it was intended was at the time in a separate cell. This person was no other than Babet, one of the four heads of Patron Minette. It contained a rolled-up paper, on which only two lines were written.

"Babet, there's a job to be done in the Rue Plumet, a gate opening on the garden."

It was what Brujon had written during the night. In spite of male and female searchers, Babet contrived to send the note from La Force to the Salpêtrière to a "lady friend" of his locked up there. She in her turn handed the note to a girl she knew, of the name of Magnon, whom the police were actively seeking, but had not yet arrested. This Magnon, of whose name the reader has already caught a glimpse, was closely connected with the Thénardiers, as we shall show presently, and by going to see Éponine was able to serve as a bridge between the Salpêtrière and the Madelonnettes. At this very period Éponine and Azelma were discharged for want of evidence, and when Éponine went out, Magnon, who was watching for her at the gate of the Madelonnettes, handed her the note from Brujon to Babet, with instructions to look into the affair. Éponine went to the Rue Plumet, recognized the grating and the garden, observed the house, watched for some days, and then carried to Magnon a biscuit, which the latter sent to Babet's mistress at the Salpêtrière. A biscuit, in the dark language of prisons, means, "Nothing to be done."

In less than a week from this, Babet and Brujon happened to meet, as one was going before the magistrate, the other returning. "Well," Brujon asked, "the Rue P. ?" "Biscuit," Babet answered. Thus the fœtus of crime engendered by Brujon at La Force became abortive; but this abortion had consequences, for all that, perfectly foreign to Brujon's plans, as will be seen. In fancying we are tying one thread we often tie another.

CHAPTER III.

MARIUS no longer called on any one, but at times he came across Father Mabœuf. While Marius was slowly descending the mournful steps which might be called the cellar stairs, and lead to places without light, on which you hear the footsteps of the prosperous above your head, M. Mabœuf was also descending. The Flora of Cauteretz did not sell at all now, and the indigo experiments had not been successful in the little garden of Austerlitz, which was badly situated. M. Mabœuf could only cultivate in it a few rare plants which are fond of moisture and shade. For all that, though, he was not discouraged ; he had obtained a strip of ground at the Jardin des Plantes in a good situation, for making " at his own charge " experiments on indigo. To do this he pledged the plates of his *Flora,* and he reduced his breakfast to two eggs, of which he left one for his old servant, whose wages he had not paid for fifteen months past. And very frequently his breakfast was his sole meal. He no longer laughed with his childish laugh, he had grown morose, and declined to receive visitors, and Marius did well not to call on him. At times, at the hour when M.

Mabœuf proceeded to the Jardin des Plantes, the old man and the young man passed each other on the Boulevard de l'Hôpital ; they did not speak, and merely shook their heads sorrowfully. It is a sad thing that there comes a moment when misery un-knots friendships. There were two friends : there are two passers-by !

Royol the publisher was dead, and now M. Mabœuf knew nothing but his books, his garden, and his indigo ; these were the three shapes which happiness, pleasure, and hope had assumed for him. They were sufficient to live for, and he would say to him-self : " When I have made my blue-balls, I shall be rich ; I will redeem my plates from the Mont de Piété, bring my *Flora* into fashion again with char-latanism, the big drum, and advertisements in the papers, and buy, I know where, a copy of Pierre de Medine's "Art of Navigation," with woodcuts, edition 1539." In the mean while, he toiled all day at his indigo patch, and at night went home to water his garden and read his books. M. Mabœuf at this period was close on eighty years of age.

One evening he had a strange apparition. He had returned home while it was still daylight, and found that Mother Plutarch, whose health was not so good as it might be, had gone to bed. He dined upon a bone on which a little meat remained and a lump of bread which he had found on the kitchen table, and was seated on a stone post which acted as a bench in his garden. Near this bench there was, after the fashion of old kitchen-gardens, a sort of tall build-ing of planks in a very rickety condition, a hutch on

the ground-floor, and a store-room on the first floor.
There were no rabbits in the hutch, but there were
a few apples, the remnant of the winter stock, in
the store-room. M. Mabœuf was reading, with the
help of his spectacles, two books which interested
him greatly, and also, a thing more serious at his
age, preoccupied him. His natural timidity rendered him prone to accept superstitions. The first
of these books was the celebrated treatise of President Delancre, " On the Inconstancy of Spirits,"
and the other was the quarto work of Mutor de la
Rubaudière, " On the Devils of Vauvert and the
Goblins of la Bièvre." The latter book interested
him the more, because his garden had been in olden
times one of the places haunted by the goblins.
Twilight was beginning to whiten what is above and
blacken what is below. While reading, M. Mabœuf
looked over the book which he held in his hand at
his plants, and among others at a magnificent rhododendron which was one of his consolations. Four
days of wind and sun had passed without a drop of
rain, the stems were bending, the buds drooping, the
leaves falling, and they all required watering ; this
rhododendron especially looked in a very sad way.
M. Mabœuf was one of those men for whom plants
have souls ; he had been at work all day in his indigo
patch, and was worn out with fatigue, but for all
that he rose, laid his books on the bench, and walked
in a bent posture and with tottering steps, up to the
well. But when he seized the chain he had not sufficient strength to unhook it ; he then turned and
took a glance of agony at the sky, which was glit-

tering with stars. The evening had that serenity
which crushes human sorrow under a lugubrious and
eternal joy. The night promised to be as dry as the
day had been.

"Stars everywhere!" the old man thought, "not
the smallest cloud! not a drop of water!"

And his head, which had been raised a moment
before, fell again on his chest, then he looked once
more at the sky, murmuring, —

"A little dew! a little pity!"

He tried once again to unhook the well-chain, but
could not succeed; at this moment he heard a voice,
saying, —

"Father Mabœuf, shall I water the garden for you?"
At the same time a sound like that of a wild beast
breaking through was heard in the hedge, and he saw
a tall thin girl emerge, who stood before him, looking
at him boldly. She looked less like a human being
than some form engendered of the darkness. Before
Father Mabœuf, whom, as we said, a trifle terrified,
found time to answer a syllable, this creature, whose
movements had in the gloom a sort of strange sud-
denness, had unhooked the chain, let down and
drawn up the bucket, and filled the watering-pot;
and the old gentleman saw this apparition, which
was barefooted and wore a ragged skirt, running
along the flower-beds and distributing life around
her. The sound of the water pattering on the leaves
filled M. Mabœuf's soul with ravishment, and the
rhododendron now seemed to him to be happy. The
first bucket emptied, the girl drew a second, then a
third, and watered the whole garden. To see her

moving thus along the walks in which her outline appeared quite black, and waving on her long thin arms her ragged shawl, she bore a striking resemblance to a bat. When she had finished, Father Mabœuf went up to her with tears in his eyes, and laid his hand on her forehead.

" God will bless you," he said, " you are an angel, since you take care of flowers."

" No," she replied, " I am the Devil, but I don't care."

The old man continued, without waiting for or hearing the reply, —

" What a pity that I am so unhappy and so poor, and can do nothing for you ! "

" You can do something," she said.

" What is it ! "

" Tell me where M. Marius lives."

The old man did not understand.

" What Monsieur Marius ? "

He raised his glassy eyes and seemed seeking something which had vanished.

" A young man who used to come here."

" Ah, yes ! " he exclaimed, " I know whom you mean. Wait a minute ! Monsieur Marius, Baron Marius Pontmercy, pardieu ! lives, or rather he does not live — well, I do not know."

While speaking, he had stooped to straighten a rhododendron branch, and continued, —

" Ah yes, I remember now. He passes very frequently along the boulevard, and goes in the direction of the Lark's field in the Rue Croulebarbe. Look for him there, he will not be difficult to find."

When M. Mabœuf raised his head again, he was
alone, and the girl had disappeared.   He was decidedly a little frightened.

" Really," he thought, " if my garden were not
watered, I should fancy that it was a ghost."

An hour after, when he was in bed, this idea returned to him, and while falling asleep, he said to
himself confusedly at the disturbed moment when
thought gradually assumes the form of dream in order
to pass through sleep, like the fabulous bird which
metamorphoses itself into a fish to cross the sea,—

" Really now, this affair greatly resembles what La
Rubaudière records about the goblins.   Could it have
been a ghost ? "

CHAPTER IV.

MARIUS HAS AN APPARITION.

A FEW days after this visit of a ghost to Father Mabœuf, — it was on a Monday, the day of the five-franc piece which Marius borrowed of Courfeyrac for Thénardier, — Marius placed the coin in his pocket, and before carrying it to the prison, resolved to "take a little walk," hoping that on his return this would make him work. It was, however, eternally thus. As soon as he rose, he sat down before a book and paper to set about some translation, and his work at this time was the translation into French of a celebrated German quarrel, the controversy between Gans and Savigny. He took up Gans, he took up Savigny, read four pages, tried to write one but could not, saw a star between his paper and himself, and got up from his chair, saying, " I will go out, that will put me in the humor," and he proceeded to the Lark's field, where he saw the star more than ever, and Gans and Savigny less. He went home, tried to resume his task, and did not succeed; he could not join a single one of the threads broken in his brain, and so said to himself, " I will not go out to-morrow, for it prevents me from working." But he went out every day.

He lived in the Lark's field more than at Courfeyrac's lodging, and his right address was Boulevard de la Santé, at the seventh tree past the Rue Croulebarbe. On this morning he had left the seventh tree and was seated on the parapet of the bridge over the little stream. The merry sunbeams were flashing through the expanded and luminous leaves. He thought of " Her," and his reverie, becoming a reproach, fell back on himself; he thought bitterly of the indolence and mental paralysis which were gaining on him, and of the night which constantly grew denser before him, so that he could no longer even see the sun. Still, through this painful evolution of indistinct ideas which was not even a soliloquy, as action was so weak in him, and he had no longer the strength to try to feel sad ; through this melancholy absorption, we say, sensations from without reached him. He heard behind, below, and on both sides of him, the washerwomen of the Gobelins beating their linen, and above him the birds twittering and singing in the elms. On one side the sound of liberty, happy carelessness, and winged leisure, on the other the sound of labor. Two joyous sounds made him think deeply and almost reflect. All at once he heard amid his depressed esctasy a voice he knew, that said, —

" Ah, here he is ! "

He raised his eyes and recognized the unhappy girl who had come to him one morning, Éponine, the elder of Thénardier's daughters ; he now knew what her name was. Strange to say, she had grown poorer and more beautiful, two things which he had not thought possible. She had accomplished a double progress, toward light and toward distress. Her feet were bare and her clothes torn, as on the day when she so boldly entered his room, but the tatters were two months older, the holes larger, and the rags filthier. She had the same hoarse voice, the same forehead wrinkled and bronzed by exposure, the same free, absent, and wandering look, but she had, in addition, on her countenance, something startled and lamentable, which passing through prisons adds to misery. She had pieces of straw and hay in her hair, not that, like Ophelia, she had gone mad through contagion with Hamlet's lunacy, but because she had slept in some stable-loft.

And with all that she was beautiful. What a star thou art, O youth!

She had stopped in front of Marius with a little joy on her livid face, and something like a smile, and it was some minutes ere she could speak.

"I have found you!" she said at last. "Father Mabœuf was right, it was in this boulevard! How I have sought you, if you only knew! Do you know that I have been in quod for a fortnight? They let me go as there was no charge against me, and besides I had not attained years of discretion by two months. Oh, how I have looked for you the last six weeks! So you no longer live down there?"

"No," said Marius.

"Ah, I understand, on account of that thing; well, such disturbances are unpleasant, and you moved. Hilloh, why do you wear an old hat like that? A young man like you ought to be handsomely dressed. Do you know, Monsieur Marius, that M. Mabœuf calls you Baron Marius, — I forget what, but you are not a Baron, are you? Barons are old swells, who walk in front of the Luxembourg Palace, where there is the most sun, and read the *Quotidienne* for a sou. I went once with a letter for a Baron who was like that, and more than a hundred years of age. Tell me, where do you live now?"

Marius did not answer.

"Ah," she added, "you have a hole in your shirt-front, I must mend it for you."

Then she continued with an expression which gradually grew gloomier, —

"You do not seem pleased to see me?"

Marius held his tongue. She was also silent for a moment, and then exclaimed, —

"If I liked, I could compel you to look pleased."

"What do you mean?" Marius asked.

She bit her lip, and apparently hesitated, as if suffering from some internal struggle. At length she seemed to make up her mind.

"All the worse, but no matter, you look sad and I wish you to be pleased, only promise me, though, that you will laugh, for I want to see you laugh and hear you say, 'Ah! that is famous!' Poor Monsieur Marius! you know you promised you would give me all I wanted."

"Yes, but speak, can't you?"

She looked at Marius intently and said, "I have the address."

Marius turned pale, and all his blood flowed to his heart.

" What address ? "

" The address which you asked me for ; " and she added, as if with a great effort, " the address, — you surely understand ? "

" Yes," stammered Marius.

" The young lady's."

These words uttered, she heaved a deep sigh. Marius leaped from the parapet on which he was sitting, and wildly seized her hand.

" Oh, lead me to it !   Tell me !   Ask of me what you please !   Where is it ? "

" Come with me," she answered ; " I don't exactly know the street or the number, and it is quite on the other side of town ; but I know the house well, and will take you to it."

She withdrew her hand, and continued in a tone which would have made an observer's heart bleed, but did not at all affect the intoxicated and transported lover, —

" Oh, how pleased you are ! "

A cloud passed over Marius's forehead, and he clutched Éponine's arm.

" Swear one thing."

" Swear ? " she said.   " What do you mean by that ?   Indeed, you want me to swear ? "

And she burst into a laugh.

" Your father !   Promise me, Éponine, — swear to me that you will never tell your father that address."

She turned to him with an air of stupefaction. " Éponine ! how do you know that is my name ? "

" Promise me what I ask you."

But she did not seem to hear him.

" That is nice !   You called me Éponine ! "

Marius seized both her arms.

" Answer me in Heaven's name !   Pay attention to what I am saying, — swear to me that you will not tell your father the address which you know."

" My father ? " she remarked, "oh, yes, my father. He's all right in a secret cell.   Besides, what do I care for my father ? "

" But you have not promised ! " Marius exclaimed.

" Let me go ! " she said, as she burst into a laugh ; " how you are shaking me !   Yes, yes, I promise it ; I swear it !   How does it concern me ?   I will not tell my father the address.   There, does that suit you ; is that it ? "

" And no one else ? " said Marius.

" And no one else."

" Now," Marius continued, " lead me there."

" At once ? "

" Yes."

" Come on !   Oh, how glad he is ! " she said.

A few yards farther on she stopped.

" You are following me too closely, Monsieur Marius ; let me go on in front and do you follow me, as if you were not doing so.   A respectable young man like you must not be seen with such a woman as I am."

No language could render all that was contained in the word " woman," thus pronounced by this child.   She went a dozen paces and stopped again. Marius rejoined her, and she said to him aside without turning to him, —

" By the bye, you know that you promised me something ? "

Marius felt in his pocket; he had nothing in the world but the five-franc piece destined for Father Thénardier, but he laid the coin in Éponine's hand. She let it slip through her fingers on the ground, and looking at him frowningly said, —

" I do not want your money."

BOOK III.

THE HOUSE OF THE RUE PLUMET.

CHAPTER I.

THE MYSTERIOUS HOUSE.

About the middle of the last century a president of the Parliament of Paris who kept a mistress under the rose — for at that day the nobility displayed their mistresses and the bourgeois concealed theirs — had "une petite maison" built in the Faubourg St. Germain, in the deserted Rue Blomet, which is now called Rue Plumet, and not far from the spot which was formerly known as the "Combat des Animaux." This house consisted of a pavilion only one story in height, there were two sitting-rooms on the ground-floor, two bedrooms on the first, a kitchen below, a boudoir above, an attic beneath the roof, and the whole was surrounded by a large garden with railings looking out on the street. This was all that passers-by could see. But behind the pavilion was a narrow yard, with an outhouse containing two rooms, where a nurse and a child could be concealed if necessary. In the back of this outhouse was a secret door leading into a long, paved, winding passage, open to the sky, and bordered by two lofty walls. This passage, concealed with prodigious art, and, as it were, lost between the garden walls, whose every turn and winding it followed, led to another secret door, which opened about a quarter of a mile off almost in another quarter, at the solitary end of the Rue de Babylone. The president went in by this door, so that even those who might have watched him, and observed that he mysteriously went somewhere every day, could not have suspected that going to the Rue de Babylone was going to the Rue Blomet. By clever purchases of ground, the ingenious magistrate had been enabled to make this hidden road upon his own land, and consequently uncontrolled. At a later date he sold the land bordering the passage in small lots for gardens, and the owners of these gardens on either side believed that they had a parting-wall before them, and did not even suspect the existence of this long strip of pavement winding between two walls among their flower-beds and orchards. The birds alone saw this curiosity, and it is probable that the linnets and tomtits of the last century gossiped a good deal about the President.

The pavilion, built of stone, in the Mansard taste, and panelled and furnished in the Watteau style, rock-work outside, old-fashioned within, and begirt by a triple hedge of flowers, had something discreet, coquettish, and solemn about it, befitting the caprices of love and a magistrate. This house and this passage, which have now disappeared, still existed fifteen years ago. In 1793 a brazier bought the house for the purpose of demolishing it, but as he could not pay, the nation made him bankrupt, and thus it was the house that demolished the brazier. Since then the house had remained uninhabited, and fell slowly into ruins, like every residence to which the presence of man no longer communicates life. The old furniture was left in it, and the ten or twelve persons who pass along the Rue Plumet were informed that it was for sale or lease by a yellow and illegible placard which had been fastened to the garden gate since 1810. Toward the end of the Restoration the same passers-by might have noticed that the bill had disappeared, and even that the first-floor shutters were open. The house was really occupied, and there were short curtains at the windows, a sign that there was a lady in the house. In October, 1829, a middle-aged man presented himself and took the house as it stood, including of course the outhouse and the passage leading to the Rue de Babylone, and he had the two secret doors of this passage put in repair. The house was still furnished much as the president had left it, so the new tenant merely ordered a few necessary articles, had the paving of the yard put to rights, new stairs put in, and the windows mended, and eventually installed himself there with a young girl and an old woman, without any disturbance, and rather like a man slipping in than one entering his own house. The neighbors, however, did not chatter, for the simple reason that he had none.

The tenant was in reality Jean Valjean, and the

girl was Cosette. The domestic was a female of the
name of Toussaint, whom Jean Valjean had saved
from the hospital and wretchedness, and who was
old, rustic, and stammered, — three qualities which
determined Jean Valjean on taking her with him.
He hired the house in the name of M. Fauchelevent,
annuitant.   In all we have recently recorded, the
reader will have doubtless recognized Valjean even
sooner than Thénardier did. Why had he left the
convent of the Little Picpus, and what had occurred
there? Nothing had occurred. It will be borne in
mind that Jean Valjean was happy in the convent,
so happy that his conscience at last became disturbed
by it. He saw Cosette daily, he felt paternity spring-
ing up and being developed in him more and more;
he set his whole soul on the girl; he said to himself
that she was his, that no power on earth could rob
him of her, that it would be so indefinitely, that she
would certainly become a nun, as she was daily gently
urged to it, that henceforth the convent was the world
for him as for her, that he would grow old in it and
she grow up, that she would grow old and he die
there; and that, finally, no separation was possible.
While reflecting on this, he began falling into per-
plexities: he asked himself if all this happiness were
really his, if it were not composed of the happiness
of this child, which he confiscated and deprived her
of, and whether this were not a robbery? He said
to himself that this child had the right to know life
before renouncing it, that depriving her beforehand,
and without consulting her, of all joys under the
pretext of saving her from all trials, and profiting

by her ignorance and isolation to make an artificial vocation spring up in her, was denaturalizing a human creature and being false to God. And who knew whether Cosette, some day meditating on this, and feeling herself a reluctant nun, might not grow to hate him? It was a last thought, almost selfish and less heroic than the others, but it was insupportable to him. He resolved to leave the convent.

He resolved, and recognized with a breaking heart that he must do so. As for objections, there were none, for six years of residence between these walls, and of disappearance, had necessarily destroyed or dispersed the element of fear. He could return to human society at his ease, for he had grown old and all had changed. Who would recognize him now? And then, looking at the worst, there was only danger for himself, and he had not the right to condemn Cosette to a cloister, for the reason that he had been condemned to the galleys; besides, what is danger in the presence of duty? Lastly, nothing prevented him from being prudent and taking precautions; and as for Cosette's education, it was almost completed and terminated. Once the resolution was formed, he awaited the opportunity, which soon offered: old Fauchelevent died. Jean Valjean requested an audience of the reverend prioress, and told her that as he had inherited a small property by his brother's death, which would enable him to live without working, he was going to leave the convent, and take his daughter with him; but as it was not fair that Cosette, who was not going to profess, should have been educated gratuitously, he implored the reverend prioress to allow him to offer the community, for the five years which Cosette had passed among them, the sum of five thousand francs. It was thus that Jean Valjean quitted the Convent of the Perpetual Adoration.

On leaving it he carried with his own hands, and would not intrust to any porter, the small valise, of which he always had the key about him. This valise perplexed Cosette, owing to the aromatic smell which issued from it. Let us say at once that this trunk never quitted him again, he always had it in his bedroom, and it was the first and at times the only thing which he carried away in his removals. Cosette laughed, called this valise "the inseparable," and said, "I am jealous of it." Jean Valjean, however, felt a profound anxiety when he returned to the outer air. He discovered the house in the Rue Plumet, and hid himself in it, henceforth remaining in possession of the name of Ultime Fauchelevent. At the same time he hired two other lodgings in Paris, so that he might attract less attention than if he had always remained in the same quarter; that he might, if necessary, absent himself for a while if anything alarmed him; and, lastly, that he might not be taken unaware, as on the night when he so miraculously escaped from Javert. These two lodgings were of a very mean appearance, and in two quarters very distant from each other, one being in the Rue de l'Ouest, the other in the Rue de l'Homme-armé. He spent a few weeks now and then at one or the other of these lodgings, taking Cosette with him and leaving Toussaint behind. He was waited on by the porters, and represented himself as a person living in the country, who had a lodging in town. This lofty virtue had three domiciles in Paris in order to escape the police.

CHAPTER II.

PROPERLY speaking, however, Jean Valjean's house was at the Rue Plumet, and he had arranged his existence there in the following fashion : Cosette and the servant occupied the pavilion, she had the best bedroom, with the painted press, the boudoir with the gilt beading, the president's drawing-room with its hangings and vast easy chairs, and the garden. Jean Valjean placed in Cosette's room a bed with a canopy of old damask in three colors, and an old and handsome Persian carpet, purchased at Mother Gaucher's in the Rue Figuier St. Paul ; while, to correct the sternness of these old splendors, he added all the light gay furniture of girls, an étagère, book-shelves with gilt books, a desk and blotting-case, a work-table inlaid with mother-of-pearl, a silver dressing-case, and toilet articles of Japanese porcelain. Long damask curtains of three colors, like those on the bed, festooned the first-floor windows, while on the ground-floor they were of tapestry. All through the winter Cosette's small house was warmed from top to bottom, while Jean Valjean himself lived in the sort of porter's lodge at the end of the back yard, which was furnished with a mattress and com-

mon bedstead, a deal table, two straw-bottomed
chairs, an earthenware water-jug, a few books on a
plank, and his dear valise in a corner, but he never
had any fire. He dined with Cosette, and black
bread was put on the table for him ; and he had said
to Toussaint, when she came, "This young lady is
mistress of the house."   "And you, sir?"   Toussaint replied, quite stupefied.   "Oh! I am much
better than the master, — I am the father."

Cosette had been taught house-keeping in the convent, and checked the expenses, which were very
small.   Daily Jean Valjean took Cosette for a walk,
leading to the most sequestered path of the Luxembourg, and every Sunday they attended Mass at the
Church of St. Jacques du Haut-pas, because it was
a long distance off.   As it is a very poor district,
he gave away a considerable amount of alms, and
the wretched flocked around him in the church,
which produced the letter from Thénardier, "To the
Benevolent Gentleman of the Church of St. Jacques
du Haut-pas."   He was fond of taking Cosette to
visit the indigent and the sick, but no stranger ever
entered the house in the Rue Plumet.   Toussaint
bought the provision, and Jean Valjean himself
fetched the water from a fountain close by, on
the boulevard.   The wood and wine were kept in a
semi-subterranean building covered with rock-work,
near the door in the Rue de Babylone, which had
formerly served the president as a grotto, for in
the age of Follies and Petites Maisons, love was
not possible without a grotto.   In the door opening
on the Rue de Babylone there was a letter-box,

but, as the inhabitants of the house in the Rue
Plumet received no letters, this box, once on a time
the go-between in amourettes, and the confidant of
a love-sick lawyer, was now only of service to receive the tax-papers and the guard-notices.   For
M. Fauchelevent, annuitant, belonged to the National
Guard, and had been unable to escape the close
meshes of the census of 1831.   The municipal inquiries made at that period extended even to the
convent of the Little Picpus, whence Jean Valjean
emerged venerable in the eyes of the mayoralty, and
consequently worthy of mounting guard.   Three or
four times a year Jean Valjean donned his uniform
and went on duty, and did so readily enough, for it
was a disguise which enabled him to mix with everybody, while himself remaining solitary.   Jean Valjean had attained his sixtieth year, or the age of
legal exemption ; but he did not look more than
fifty ; besides, he had no wish to escape his sergeant-
major and cheat Count Lobau.   He had no civil
status, hid his name, his identity, his age, everything, and, as we just said, he was a willing National
Guard, — all his ambition was to resemble the first-
comer who pays taxes.   The ideal of this man was
internally an angel, externally a bourgeois.

Let us mention one fact, by the way.   When Jean
Valjean went out with Cosette he dressed himself
in the way we have seen, and looked like a retired
officer ; but when he went out alone, and he did so
usually at night, he was attired in a workman's jacket
and trousers, and a cap whose peak was pulled deep
over his eyes.   Was this precaution or humility ?

Both at once. Cosette was accustomed to the enigmatical side of her destiny, and hardly noticed her father's singularities ; as for Toussaint, she revered Jean Valjean, and considered everything he did right. One day her butcher, who got a glimpse of her master, said, " He 's a queer looking stick," and she replied, " He 's a — a — a — saint." All three never left the house except by the gate in the Rue de Babylone ; and unless they were noticed through the garden gate it would be difficult to guess that they lived in the Rue Plumet. This gate was always locked, and Jean Valjean left the garden untended that it might not be noticed. In this, perhaps, he deceived himself.

CHAPTER III.

FOLIIS AC FRONDIBUS.

THIS garden, left to itself for more than half a century, had become extraordinary and charming: passers-by forty years ago stopped in the street to gaze at it, without suspecting the secrets which it hid behind its fresh green screen. More than one dreamer at that day allowed his eyes and thoughts indiscreetly to penetrate the bars of the old locked, twisted, shaky gate, which hung from two mould-covered pillars and was surmounted by a pediment covered with undecipherable arabesques. There was a stone bank in a corner, there were one or two mouldering statues, and some trellis-work, unnailed by time, was rotting against the walls; there was no turf or walk left, but there was dog's-grass everywhere. The artificiality of gardening had departed, and nature had returned; weeds were abundant, and the festival of the gilly-flowers was splendid there. Nothing in this garden impeded the sacred efforts of things toward life, and growth was at home there and held high holiday. The trees had bent down to the briars, the briars had mounted toward the trees; the plants had clambered up, the branches had bent down. What crawls on the ground had gone to meet what expands in the air, and what floats in the wind stooped down to what drags along the moss; brambles, branches, leaves, fibres, tufts, twigs, tendrils, and thorns were mixed together, wedded and confounded; vegetation had celebrated and accomplished here, in a close and profound embrace, and beneath the satisfied eye of the Creator, the holy mystery of its fraternity, which is a symbol of human paternity. This garden was no longer a garden, but a colossal thicket; that is to say, something which is as impenetrable as a forest, as populous as a city, as rustling as a nest, as dark as a cathedral, as fragrant as a bouquet, as solitary as a tomb, and as lively as a crowd.

In spring this enormous thicket, at liberty within its four walls, played its part in the dull task of universal germination, and quivered in the rising sun almost like an animal that inhales the effluvia of cosmic love and feels the sap of April ascending and boiling in its veins, and shaking in the wind its prodigious green foliage, scattered over the damp ground, over the weather-beaten statues, over the crumbling steps of the pavilion, and even over the pavement of the deserted street, constellations of flowers, pearls of dew, fecundity, beauty, life, joy, and perfumes. At midday thousands of white butterflies took refuge in it, and it was a divine sight to watch this living snow of summer falling in flakes through the shadows. In the pleasant gloom of the foliage a multitude of soft voices gently addressed the soul, and what the twittering forgot to say, the buzzing completed. At night a dreamy vapor rose from the garden and enveloped it; a cere-cloth of mist, a celestial and calm melancholy, covered it; the intoxicating smell of the honeysuckle and the bindweed ascended from all sides like an exquisite and subtle poison; the last appeals of the woodpeckers and the goldfinches could be heard, ere they fell asleep under the branches, and the sacred intimacy between the bird and the trees was felt, for by day, wings gladden the leaves, and at night the leaves protect the wings. In winter, the thicket was black, dank, bristling, and shivering, and allowed a glimpse at the house to be taken. Instead of flowers among the stalks and dew upon the flowers, the long silvery trail of the snails could be seen on the cold thick bed of yellow leaves; but in any case, under any aspect, and at all seasons, spring, summer, autumn, and winter, this little enclosure exhaled melancholy contemplation, solitude, liberty, the absence of man and the presence of God, and the old rusty railings had an air of saying, "This garden is mine."

Although the pavement of Paris was all around, the classical and splendid mansions of the Rue de Varennes two yards off, the dome of the Invalides close by, and the Chamber of Deputies at no great distance, although the carriages from the Rues de Bourgogne and St. Dominique rolled along luxuriously in the vicinity, and yellow, brown, white, and red omnibuses crossed the adjoining square, — the Rue Plumet was a desert; and the death of the old proprietors, a revolution which had passed, the overthrow of old fortunes, absence, forgetfulness, and forty years of desertion and widowhood, had sufficed to bring back to this privileged spot ferns, torchweeds, hemlock, ragwort, tall grass, dock-leaves, lizards, beetles, and restless and rapid insects. A savage and stern grandeur had re-appeared between these four walls, and nature, who disconcerts all the paltry arrangements of man, and is as perfect in the ant as in the man, had displayed herself in a poor little Parisian garden with as much roughness and majesty as in a virgin forest of the New World. Nothing, in fact, is small, and any one who is affected by the profound penetrations of nature is aware of this fact. Although no absolute satisfaction is granted to philosophy, and though it can no more circumscribe the cause than limit the effect, the contemplator falls into unfathomable ecstasy when he watches all those decompositions of force which result in unity. Everything labors for everything; algebra is applied to the clouds, the irradiation of the planet benefits the rose, and no thinker would dare to say that the perfume of the hawthorn is useless to the constellations. Who can calculate the passage of a molecule? Who among us knows whether the creations of worlds are not determined by the fall of grains of sand? Who is acquainted with the reciprocal ebb and flow of the infinitely great and the infinitely little? A maggot is of importance, the little is great and the great little, all is in a state of equilibrium in nature. This is a terrific vision for the mind. There are prodigious relations between beings and things; and in this inexhaustible total, from the flea to the sun, nothing despises the other, for all have

need of each other. Light does not bear into the
sky terrestrial perfumes without knowing what to do
with them, and night distributes the planetary essence to the sleepy flowers. Every bird that flies
has round its foot the thread of infinity; germination
is equally displayed in the outburst of a meteor and
the peck of the swallow breaking the egg, and
it places the birth of a worm and the advent of
Socrates in the same parallel. Where the telescope
ends the microscope begins, and which of the two
has the grandest sight? you can choose. A patch
of green mould is a pleiad of flowers, and a nebula
is an ant-hill of stars. There is the same and even
a more extraordinary promiscuity of the things of
the intellect and the facts of the substance; elements
and principles are mingled, combined, wedded together, and multiply each other till they lead both
the moral and the material world into the same light.
In the vast cosmic exchanges universal life comes
and goes in unknown quantities, revolving everything
in the invisible mystery of effluvia, employing everything, losing not a single dream of a sleep, sowing an
animalcule here, crumbling away a star there, oscillating and winding, making of light a force, and of
thought an element, disseminated and invisible, and
dissolving everything save that geometrical point,
the *Ego ;* bringing back everything to the atom
soul, expanding everything in God; entangling all
activities from the highest to the lowest in the obscurity of a vertiginous mechanism; attaching the
flight of an insect to the movement of the earth,
and subordinating, perhaps, if only through the

identity of the law, the evolution of the comet in the firmament to the rotary movement of the Infusoria in the drop of water, — a machine made of soul ; an enormous gearing of which the prime mover is the gnat, and the last wheel is the Zodiac.

CHAPTER IV.

CHANGE OF GRATING.

IT seemed as if this garden, created in former times to conceal libertine mysteries, had been transformed and become fitting to shelter chaste mysteries. There were no longer any cradles, bowling-greens, covered walks, or grottos ; but there was a magnificent tangled obscurity which fell all around, and Paphos was changed into Eden. A penitent feeling had refreshed this retreat, and the coquettish garden, once on a time so compromised, had returned to virginity and modesty. A president assisted by a gardener, a good fellow who believed himself the successor of La-moignon, and another good fellow who fancied himself the successor of Lenôtre, had turned it about, clipped it, and prepared it for purposes of gallantry, but nature had seized it again, filled it with shadow, and prepared it for love. There was, too, in this solitude a heart which was quite ready, and love had only to show itself ; for there were here a temple composed of verdure, grass, moss, the sighs of birds, gentle shadows, waving branches, and a soul formed of gentleness, faith, candor, hope, aspirations, and illusions.

Cosette left the convent while still almost a child. She was but little more than fourteen, and at the "unpromising age," as we have said. With the

exception of her eyes, she seemed rather ugly than
pretty; still she had no ungraceful feature, but she
was awkward, thin, timid and bold at the same time,
in short, a grown-up little girl. Her education was
finished, that is to say, she had been taught religion,
and more especially devotion, also " history," that is
to say, the thing so called in a convent; geography,
grammar, the participles, the kings of France, and a
little music, drawing, etc.; but in other respects she
was ignorant of everything, which is at once a charm
and a peril. The mind of a young girl ought not to
be left in darkness, for at a later date, mirages too
sudden and vivid are produced in it as in a camera
obscura. She should be gently and discreetly enlightened, rather by the reflection of realities than
by their direct and harsh light; for this is a useful
and gracefully obscure semi-light which dissipates
childish fears and prevents falls. There is only the
maternal instinct,—that admirable intuition into which
the recollections of the virgin and the experience of
the wife enter, — that knows how or of what this semi-
light should be composed. Nothing can take the
place of this instinct, and in forming a girl's mind, all
the nuns in the world are not equal to one mother.
Cosette had had no mother, she had only had a great
many mothers : as for Jean Valjean, he had within
him every possible tenderness and every possible
anxiety ; but he was only an old man who knew
nothing at all. Now, in this work of education, in
this serious matter of preparing a woman for life,
what knowledge is needed to contend against the
other great ignorance which is called innocence !

Nothing prepares a girl for passions like the convent, for it directs her thoughts to the unknown. The heart is driven back on itself, and hence come visions, suppositions, conjectures, romances sketched, adventures longed for, fantastic constructions, and edifices built entirely on the inner darkness of the mind, — gloomy and secret dwellings in which the passions alone find a lodging so soon as passing through the convent gate allows it. The convent is a compression which must last the whole life, if it is to triumph over the human heart. On leaving the convent, Cosette could not have found anything sweeter or more dangerous than the house in the Rue Plumet. It was the commencement of solitude with the commencement of liberty, a closed garden, but a sharp, kind, rich, voluptuous, and odorous nature ; there were the same dreams as in the convent, but glimpses could be caught of young men, — it was a grating, but it looked on the street. Still, we repeat, when Cosette first came here, she was but a child. Jean Valjean gave over to her this uncultivated garden, and said to her, " Do what you like with it." This amused Cosette, she moved all the tufts and all the stones in search of " beasts ; " she played about while waiting till the time came to think, and she loved this garden for the sake of the insects which she found in the grass under her feet, while waiting till she should love it for the sake of the stars she could see through the branches above her head.

And then, too, she loved her father, that is to say, Jean Valjean, with all her soul, with a simple filial passion, which rendered the worthy man a desired

and delightful companion to her. Our readers will
remember that M. Madeleine was fond of reading,
and Jean Valjean continued in the same track ; he
had learned to speak well, and he possessed the
secret wealth and the eloquence of a humble, true,
and self-cultivated intellect. He had retained just
sufficient roughness to season his kindness, and he
had a rough mind and a soft heart. During their
tête-à-têtes in the Luxembourg garden he gave her
long explanations about all sorts of things, deriving
his information from what he had read, and also from
what he had suffered. While Cosette was listening
to him, her eyes vaguely wandered around. This
simple man was sufficient for Cosette's thoughts, in
the same way as the wild garden was for her eyes.
When she had chased the butterflies for a while she
would run up to him panting, and say, "Oh ! how
tired I am !" and he would kiss her forehead. Cosette
adored this good man, and she was ever at his heels,
for wherever Jean Valjean was, happiness was. As
he did not live either in the pavilion or the garden,
she was more attached to the paved back-yard than
to the flower-laden garden, and preferred the little
outhouse with the straw chairs to the large drawing-
room hung with tapestry, along which silk-covered
chairs were arranged. Jean Valjean at times said to
her with a smile of a man who is delighted to be
annoyed : "Come, go to your own rooms ! leave me
at peace for a little while."

She scolded him in that charming tender way
which is so graceful when addressed by a daughter
to a parent.

"Father, I feel very cold in your room ; why don't you have a carpet and a stove ? "

" My dear child, there are so many persons more deserving than myself who have not even a roof to cover them."

" Then, why is there fire in my room and every-thing that I want ? "

" Because you are a woman and a child."

" Nonsense ! then men must be cold and hungry ? "

" Some men."

" Very good ! I 'll come here so often that you will be obliged to have a fire."

Or else it was, —

" Father, why do you eat such wretched bread as that ? "

" Because I do, my daughter."

" Well, if you eat it I shall eat it too."

And so to prevent Cosette from eating black bread Jean Valjean ate white. Cosette remembered her childhood but confusedly, and she prayed night and morning for the mother whom she had never known. The Thénardiers were like two hideous beings seen in a dream, and she merely remembered that she had gone " one day at night " to fetch water in a wood, — she thought that it was a long distance from Paris. It seemed to her as if she had com-menced life in an abyss, and that Jean Valjean had drawn her out of it, and her childhood produced on her the effect of a time when she had had nought but centipedes, spiders, and snakes around her. When she thought at night before she fell asleep, as she had no very clear idea of being Jean Valjean's daughter,

she imagined that her mother's soul had passed into
this good man, and had come to dwell near her.
When he was sitting down she rested her cheek on
his white hair, and silently dropped a tear, while
saying to herself, " Perhaps this man is my mother ! "
Cosette, strange though it is to say, in her profound
ignorance as a girl educated in a convent, and as,
too, maternity is absolutely unintelligible to virginity,
eventually imagined that she had had as little of a
mother as was possible. This mother's name she
did not know, and whenever it happened that she
spoke to Jean Valjean on the subject he held his
tongue. If she repeated her question he answered
by a smile, and once, when she pressed him, the
smile terminated in a tear. This silence on his part
cast a night over Fantine. Was it through prudence ?
Was it through respect ? Or was it through a fear
of intrusting this name to the chances of another
memory besides his own ?

So long as Cosette was young Jean Valjean readily
talked to her about her mother ; but when she grew
up it was impossible for him to do so, — he felt as
if he dared not do it. Was it on account of Cosette
or of Fantine ? He felt a species of religious horror
at making this shadow enter Cosette's thoughts, and
rendering a dead woman a third person in their
society. The more sacred this shade was to him,
the more formidable was it. He thought of Fantine,
and felt himself overwhelmed by the silence. He
saw vaguely in the darkness something that resembled
a finger laid on a lip. Had all the modesty which
was in Fantine, and which during her life quitted

her with violence, returned after her death, to watch indignantly over the dead woman's peace, and sternly guard her in the tomb? Was Jean Valjean himself unconsciously oppressed by it? We who believe in death are not prepared to reject this mysterious explanation, and hence arose the impossibility of pronouncing, even to Cosette, the name of Fantine. One day Cosette said to him, —

"Father, I saw my mother last night in a dream. She had two large wings, and in life she must have been a sainted woman."

"Through martyrdom," Jean Valjean replied. Altogether, though, he was happy; when Cosette went out with him she leaned on his arm, proudly and happily, in the fulness of her heart. Jean Valjean felt his thoughts melt into delight at all these marks of a tenderness so exclusive and so satisfied with himself alone. The poor wretch, inundated with an angelic joy, trembled; he assured himself with transport that this would last his whole life; he said to himself that he had not really suffered enough to deserve such radiant happiness, and he thanked God in the depths of his soul for having allowed him — the wretched — to be thus loved by this innocent being.

CHAPTER V.

THE ROSE PERCEIVES THAT SHE IS AN IMPLEMENT OF WAR.

ONE day Cosette happened to look at herself in the glass, and said, " Good gracious ! " She fancied that she was almost pretty, and this threw her into a singular trouble. Up to this moment she had not thought of her face, and though she saw herself in the mirror she did not look at herself. And, then, she had often been told that she was ugly ; Jean Valjean alone would say gently, " Oh, no, oh, no ! " However this might be, Cosette had always believed herself ugly, and had grown up in this idea with the facile resignation of childhood. And now all at once her looking-glass said to her, as Jean Valjean had done, " Oh, no ! " She did not sleep that night. " Suppose I were pretty," she thought, "how droll it would be if I were pretty ! " and she remembered those of her companions whose beauty produced an effect in the convent, and said to herself, " What ! I might be like Mademoiselle So-and-so ! "

On the next day she looked at herself, but not accidentally, and doubted. " Where was my sense ? " she said ; " No, I am ugly." She had simply slept badly, her eyes were heavy and her cheeks pale.

She had not felt very joyous on the previous day when she fancied herself pretty ; but was sad at no longer believing it. She did not look at herself again, and for upwards of a fortnight tried to dress her hair with her back to the glass. In the evening, after dinner, she usually worked at her embroidery in the drawing-room, while Jean Valjean read by her side. Once she raised her eyes from her work, and was greatly surprised by the anxious way in which her father was gazing at her. Another time she was walking along the street, and fancied she heard some one behind her, whom she did not see, say, " A pretty woman, but badly dressed." " Nonsense," she thought, " it is not I, for I am well-dressed and ugly." At that time she wore her plush bonnet and merino dress. One day, at last, she was in the garden, and heard poor old Toussaint saying, " Master, do you notice how pretty our young lady is growing ? " Cosette did not hear her father's answer, for Toussaint's words produced a sort of commotion in her. She ran out of the garden up to her room, looked in the glass, which she had not done for three months, and uttered a cry, — she dazzled herself.

She was beautiful and pretty, and could not refrain from being of the same opinion as Toussaint and her glass. Her figure was formed, her skin had grown white, her hair was glossy, and an unknown splendor was kindled in her blue eyes. The consciousness of her beauty came to her fully in a minute, like the sudden dawn of day ; others, besides, noticed her, Toussaint said so ; it was evidently to her that the passer-by alluded, and doubt was no longer possible. She returned to the garden, believing herself a queen, hearing the birds sing, though it was winter, seeing the golden sky, the sun amid the trees, flowers on the shrubs; she was wild, distraught, and in a state of ineffable ravishment. On his side, Jean Valjean experienced a profound and inexplicable contraction of the heart; for some time past, in truth, he had contemplated with terror the beauty which daily appeared more radiant in Cosette's sweet face. It was a laughing dawn for all, but most mournful for him.

Cosette had been for a long time beautiful ere she perceived the fact, but, from the first day, this un-expected light which slowly rose and gradually enveloped the girl's entire person hurt Jean Valjean's sombre eyes. He felt that it was a change in a happy life, so happy that he did not dare stir in it, for fear of deranging it somewhere. This man, who had passed through every possible distress, who was still bleeding from the wounds dealt him by his destiny, who had been almost wicked, and had become almost a saint, who, after dragging the galley chain, was now dragging the invisible but weighty chain of indefinite infamy; this man whom the law had not liberated, and who might at any moment be recaptured and taken from the obscurity of virtue to the broad daylight of further opprobrium, — this man accepted everything, excused everything, pardoned everything, blessed everything, wished everything well, and only asked one thing of Providence, of men, of the laws, of society, of nature, of the world,

— that Cosette should love him, that Cosette might continue to love him; that God would not prevent the heart of this child turning to him and remaining with him! Loved by Cosette he felt cured, at rest, appeased, overwhelmed, rewarded, and crowned. With Cosette's love all was well, and he asked no more. Had any one said to him, "Would you like to be better off?" he would have answered, "No." Had God said to him, "Do you wish for heaven?" he would have answered, "I should lose by it." All that could affect this situation, even on the surface, appeared to him the beginning of something else. He had never known thoroughly what a woman's beauty was, but he understood instinctively that it was terrible. This beauty, which continually expanded more triumphantly and superbly by his side upon the ingenuous and formidable brow of the child, from the depths of his ugliness, old age, misery, reprobation, and despondency, terrified him, and he said to himself, "How beautiful she is! what will become of me?" Here lay the difference between his tenderness and that of a mother, — what he saw with agony a mother would have seen with joy.

The first symptoms speedily manifested themselves. From the day when Cosette said to herself, "I am decidedly good-looking," she paid attention to her toilet. She remembered the remark of the passer-by, — pretty, but badly dressed, — a blast of the oracle which passed by her and died out, after depositing in her heart one of those two germs which are destined at a later period to occupy a woman's entire life, — coquettishness. The other is love. With faith in her beauty, all her feminine soul was expanded within her; she had a horror of merinos, and felt ashamed of plush. Her father never refused her anything, and she knew at once the whole science of the hat, the dress, the mantle, the slipper, and the sleeve, of the fabric that suits, and the color that is becoming, — the science which makes the Parisian woman something so charming, profound, and dangerous. The expression "femme capiteuse" was invented for the Parisian. In less than a month little Cosette was in this Thebaïs of the Rue de Babylone, not only one of the prettiest women, which is something, but one of the best dressed in Paris, which is a great deal more. She would have liked to meet her "passer-by," to see what he would say, and teach him a lesson. The fact is, that she was in every respect ravishing, and could admirably distinguish a bonnet of Gérard's from one of Herbaut's. Jean Valjean regarded these ravages with anxiety, and while feeling that he could never do more than crawl or walk at the most, he could see Cosette's wings growing. However, by the simple inspection of Cosette's toilet, a woman would have seen that she had no mother. Certain small proprieties and social conventionalisms were not observed by Cosette; a mother, for instance, would have told her that an unmarried girl does not wear brocade.

The first day that Cosette went out in her dress and cloak of black brocade, and her white crape bonnet, she took Jean Valjean's arm, gay, radiant, blushing, proud, and striking. "Father," she said, "how do you think I look?" Jean Valjean replied,

in a voice which resembled the bitter voice of an
envious person, " Charming." During the walk
he was as usual, but when he returned home he
asked Cosette, —

" Will you not put on that dress and bonnet, you
know which, again ? "

This took place in Cosette's room ; she returned
to the wardrobe in which her boarding-school dress
was hanging.

" That disguise ? " she said, " how can you expect
it, father ? Oh, no, indeed, I shall never put on
those horrors again ; with that thing on my head I
look like a regular dowdy."

Jean Valjean heaved a deep sigh.

From that moment he noticed that Cosette, who
hitherto had wished to stay at home, saying, " Father,
I amuse myself much better here with you," now
constantly asked to go out. In truth, what good is
it for a girl to have a pretty face and a delicious
toilet if she does not show them ? He also noticed
that Cosette no longer had the same liking for the
back-yard, and at present preferred remaining in the
garden, where she walked, without displeasure, near
the railings. Jean Valjean never set foot in the
garden, but remained in the back-yard, like the dog.
Cosette, knowing herself to be beautiful, lost the
grace of being ignorant of the fact, an exquisite
grace, for beauty heightened by simplicity is ineffable,
and nothing is so adorable as a beauteous innocent
maiden who walks along unconsciously, holding in
her hand the key of a Paradise. But what she lost
in ingenuous grace she regained in a pensive and

serious charm.   Her whole person, impregnated with
the joys of youth, innocence, and beauty, exhaled a
splendid melancholy.   It was at this period that
Marius saw her again at the Luxembourg, after an
interval of six months.

CHAPTER VI.

THE BATTLE BEGINS.

COSETTE was in her shadow, as Marius was in his, all ready to be kindled. Destiny, with its mysterious and fatal patience, brought slowly together these two beings, all charged with, and pining in, the stormy electricity of passion, — these two souls which bore love as the clouds bore thunder, and were destined to come together and be blended in a glance like the clouds in a storm. The power of a glance has been so abused in love-romances that it has been discredited in the end, and a writer dares hardly assert nowadays that two beings fell in love because they looked at each other. And yet, that is the way, and the sole way, in which people fall in love ; the rest is merely the rest, and comes afterwards. Nothing is more real than the mighty shocks which two souls give each other by exchanging this spark. At the hour when Cosette unconsciously gave that glance which troubled Marius, Marius did not suspect that he too gave a glance which troubled Cosette. For a long time she had seen and examined him in the way girls see and examine, while looking elsewhere. Marius was still thinking Cosette ugly, when Cosette had already considered Marius handsome, but as the young man paid no

attention to her he was an object of indifference.
Still she could not refrain from saying to herself that
he had silky hair, fine eyes, regular teeth, an agreeable voice, when she heard him talking with his companions ; that he perhaps walked badly, but with a
grace of his own, that he did not appear at all silly,
that his whole person was noble, gentle, simple, and
proud ; and, lastly, that though he seemed poor, he
had the bearing of a gentleman.

On the day when their eyes met, and at length
suddenly said to each other the first obscure and
ineffable things which the eye stammers, Cosette
did not understand it at first. She returned pen-
sively to the house in the Rue de l'Ouest, where
Jean Valjean was spending six weeks, according to
his wont. When she awoke the next morning she
thought of the young stranger, so long indifferent
and cold, who now seemed to pay attention to her,
and this attention did not appear at all agreeable to
her ; on the contrary, she felt a little angry with the
handsome disdainful man. A warlike feeling was
aroused, and she felt a very childish joy at the
thought that she was at length about to be avenged ;
knowing herself to be lovely, she felt, though in an
indistinct way, that she had a weapon. Women
play with their beauty as lads do with their knife,
and cut themselves with it. Our readers will
remember Marius's hesitations, palpitations, and
terrors ; he remained on his bench, and did not
approach, and this vexed Cosette. One day she
said to Jean Valjean, "Father, suppose we take a
walk in that direction ? " Seeing that Marius did

not come to her, she went to him, for in such
cases, every woman resembles Mahomet. And then,
strange it is, the first symptom of true love in a
young man is timidity; in a girl it is boldness. This
will surprise, and yet nothing is more simple; the
two sexes have a tendency to approach, and each
assumes the qualities of the other. On this day
Cosette's glance drove Marius mad, while his glance
made Cosette tremble. Marius went away confiding,
and Cosette restless. Now they adored each other.
The first thing that Cosette experienced was a confused and deep sorrow; it seemed to her that her
soul had become black in one day, and she no longer
recognized herself. The whiteness of the soul of
maidens, which is composed of coldness and gayety,
resembles snow; it melts before love, which is its sun.

Cosette knew not what love was, and she had
never heard the word uttered in its earthly sense.
In the books of profane music which entered the
convent, *tambour* or *pandour* was substituted for
amour. This produced enigmas, which exercised
the imagination of the big girls, such as : " Ah! how
agreeable the drummer is ! " or, " Pity is not a pandour! " But Cosette left the convent at too early an
age to trouble herself much about the " drummer,"
and hence did not know what name to give to that
which now troubled her. But are we the less ill
through being ignorant of the name of our disease?
She loved with the more passion, because she loved
in ignorance; she did not know whether it was good
or bad, useful or dangerous, necessary or mortal,
eternal or transient, permitted or prohibited, — she

loved. She would have been greatly surprised had any one said to her, "You do not sleep? that is forbidden. You do not eat? that is very wrong. You have an oppression and beating of the heart? that cannot be tolerated. You blush and turn pale when a certain person dressed in black appears at the end of a certain green walk? why, that is abominable!" She would not have understood, and would have replied, "How can I be to blame in a matter in which I can do nothing, and of which I know nothing?"

It happened that the love which presented itself was the one most in harmony with the state of her soul; it was a sort of distant adoration, a dumb contemplation, the deification of an unknown man. It was the apparition of youth to youth, the dream of nights become a romance and remaining a dream, the wished-for phantom at length realized and incarnated, but as yet having no name, or wrong, or flaw, or claim, or defect; in a word, the distant lover who remained idealized, a chimera which assumed a shape. Any more palpable and nearer meeting would at this first stage have startled Cosette, who was still half plunged in the magnifying fog of the cloister. She had all the fears of children and all the fears of nuns blended together, and the essence of the convent, with which she had been impregnated for five years, was still slowly evaporating from her whole person, and making everything tremble around her. In this situation, it was not a lover she wanted, not even an admirer, but a vision, and she began adoring Marius as something charming, luminous, and impossible.

As extreme simplicity trenches on extreme coquetry, she smiled upon him most frankly. She daily awaited impatiently the hour for the walk ; she saw Marius, she felt indescribably happy, and sincerely believed that she was expressing her entire thoughts when she said to Jean Valjean, "What a delicious garden the Luxembourg is!" Marius and Cosette existed for one another in the night : they did not speak, they did not bow, they did not know each other, but they met ; and like the stars in the heavens, which are millions of leagues separate, they lived by looking at each other. It is thus that Cosette gradually became a woman, and was developed into a beautiful and loving woman, conscious of her beauty and ignorant of her love. She was a coquette into the bargain, through her innocence.

CHAPTER VII.

JEAN VALJEAN IS VERY SAD.

ALL situations have their instincts, and old and eternal mother Nature warned Jean Valjean darkly of the presence of Marius. Jean Valjean trembled in the depth of his mind ; he saw nothing, knew nothing, and yet regarded with obstinate attention the darkness in which he was, as if he felt on one side something being built up, on the other something crumbling away. Marius, who was also warned by the same mother Nature, did all in his power to conceal himself from the father, but for all that, Jean Valjean sometimes perceived him. Marius's manner was no longer wise ; he displayed clumsy prudence and awkward temerity. He no longer came quite close to them, as he had formerly done, he sat down at a distance, and remained in an ecstasy : he had a book, and pretended to read it ; why did he pretend ? Formerly he came in an old coat, and now he came every day in his new one. Jean Valjean was not quite sure whether he did not have his hair dressed ; he had a strange way of rolling his eyes, and wore gloves, — in short, Jean Valjean cordially detested the young man. Cosette did not allow anything to be guessed. Without knowing exactly what was the matter with her, she had a feeling that it was something which must be hidden. There was a parallelism which annoyed Jean Valjean between the taste for dress which had come to Cosette, and the habit of wearing new clothes displayed by this stranger. It was an accident, perhaps, — of course it was, — but a menacing accident.

He never opened his mouth to Cosette about this stranger. One day, however, he could not refrain, and said, with that vague despair which suddenly thrusts the probe into its own misfortune, " That young man looks like a pedant." Cosette, a year previously, when still a careless little girl, would have answered, " Oh, no, he is very good-looking." Ten years later, with the love of Marius in her heart, she would have replied, " An insufferable pedant, you are quite right." At the present moment of her life and heart, she restricted herself to saying, with supreme calmness, " That young man ! " as if she looked at him for the first time in her life. " How stupid I am," Jean Valjean thought, " she had not even noticed him, and now I have pointed him out to her." Oh, simplicity of old people ! oh, depth of children ! It is another law of these first years of suffering and care, of these sharp struggles of first love with first obstacles, that the maiden cannot be caught in any snare, while the young man falls into all. Jean Valjean had begun a secret war against Marius, which Marius, in the sublime stupidity of his passion and his age, did not guess. Jean Valjean laid all sorts of snares for him. He changed his hours, he changed his bench, he left his handkerchief, he went alone to the Luxembourg : and Marius went headlong into the trap, and to all these notes of interrogation which Jean Valjean planted in the road, ingenuously answered, " Yes." Cosette, however, remained immured in her apparent carelessness and imperturbable tranquillity, so that Jean Valjean arrived at this conclusion : "That humbug is madly in love with Cosette, but Cosette does not even know that he exists."

For all that, though, he had a painful tremor in his heart, for the minute when Cosette would love might arrive at any instant. Does not all this commence with indifference ? Only once did Cosette commit an error and startle him ; he arose from his bench to go home after three hours' sitting, and she said, "What, already ? " Jean Valjean did not give up his walks at the Luxembourg, as he did not wish to do anything singular, or arouse Cosette's attention ; but during the hours so sweet for the two lovers, while Cosette was sending her smile to the intoxicated Marius, who only perceived this, and now saw nothing more in the world than a radiant adored face, Jean Valjean fixed on Marius flashing and terrible eyes. He who had ended by no longer believing himself capable of a malevolent feeling, had moments when he felt, if Marius were present, as if he were growing savage and ferocious ; and those old depths of his soul which had formerly contained so much anger opened again against this young man. It seemed to him as if unknown craters were again being formed within him. What ! the fellow was there ! What did he come to do ? he came to sniff, examine, and attempt ; he came to say, Well, why not ? he came to prowl round his, Jean Valjean's, life, to prowl round his happiness, and carry it away from him. Jean Valjean added, " Yes, that is it ! What does he come to seek ? An adventure. What does he want ? A love-affair. A love-affair ? and I ! What ? I was first the most wretched of men, and then the most unhappy. I have spent sixty years on my knees, I have suffered all that a man can suffer, I have grown old without ever having been young. I have lived without family, parents, friends, children, or wife. I have left some of my blood on every stone, on every bramble, on every wall. I have been gentle, though men were harsh to me, and good though they were wicked. I have become an honest man again, in spite of everything ; I have repented of the evil I did, and pardoned the evil done to me, and at the moment when I am rewarded, when all is finished, when I touched my object, when I have what I wish, — and it is but fair as I have paid for it and earned it, — all this is to fade away, and I am to lose Cosette, my love, my joy, my soul, because it has pleased a long-legged ass to saunter about the Luxembourg garden ! "

Then his eyeballs were filled with a mournful and extraordinary brilliancy ; he was no longer a man looking at a man, no longer an enemy looking at an enemy, he was a dog watching a robber. Our readers know the rest. Marius continued to be foolish, and one day followed Cosette to the Rue de l'Ouest. Another day he spoke to the porter, and the porter spoke in his turn, and said to Jean Valjean, " Do you happen to know, sir, a curious young man, who has been making inquiries about you ? " The next day Jean Valjean gave Marius that look which Marius at length noticed, and a week later Jean Valjean went away. He made a vow that he would never again set foot in the Rue de l'Ouest or the Luxembourg, and returned to the Rue Plumet. Cosette did not complain, she said nothing, she asked no questions, she did not attempt to discover any motive, for she had reached that stage when a girl fears that her thoughts may be perused, or she may betray herself. Jean Valjean had no experience of these miseries, the only ones which are charming, and the only ones he did not know, and on this account he did not comprehend the grave significance of Cosette's silence. Still, he noticed that she became sad, and he became gloomy. Inexperience was contending on both sides. Once he made an essay, by asking Cosette, "Will you go to the Luxembourg?" A beam illuminated Cosette's pale face; "Yes," she said. They went there, but three months had elapsed, and Marius no longer went there, — there was no Marius present. The next day Jean Valjean again asked Cosette, "Will you go to the Luxembourg?" She answered sadly and gently, "No." Jean Valjean was hurt by the sadness, and heart-broken by the gentleness.

What was taking place in this young and already so impenetrable mind? What was going to be accomplished? What was happening to Cosette's soul? Sometimes, instead of going to bed, Jean Valjean would remain seated by his bedside with his head between his hands, and spent whole nights in asking himself, "What has Cosette on her mind?" and in thinking of the things of which she might be thinking.

Oh, at such moments what sad glances he turned toward the convent, that chaste summit, that abiding-place of angels, that inaccessible glacier of virtue! With what despairing ravishment did he contemplate that garden, full of ignored flowers and immured virgins, where all the perfumes and all the souls ascend direct to heaven! How he adored that Eden, now closed against him forever, and which he had voluntarily and madly left! How he lamented his self-denial and his madness in bringing Cosette back to the world! He was the poor hero of the sacrifice, seized and hurled down by his own devotion. How he said to himself, What have I done? However, nothing of this was visible to Cosette, — neither temper nor roughness, — it was ever the same serene kind face. Jean Valjean's manner was even more tender and paternal than before; and if anything could have shown that he was less joyous, it was his greater gentleness.

On her side, Cosette was pining; she suffered from Marius's absence, as she had revelled in his presence, singularly, and not exactly knowing why. When Jean Valjean ceased taking her for her usual walk, a feminine instinct had whispered to her heart that she must not appear to be attached to the Luxembourg, and that if she displayed indifference in the matter her father would take her back to it. But days, weeks, and months succeeded each other, for Jean Valjean had tacitly accepted Cosette's tacit consent. She regretted it, but it was too late, and on the day when they returned to the Luxembourg, Marius was no longer there. He had disappeared, then, it was all over. What could she do? Would she ever see him again? She felt a contraction of the heart which nothing dilated and which daily increased; she no longer knew whether it were summer or winter, sunshine or rain, whether the birds were singing, whether it was the dahlia or the daisy season, whether the Luxembourg was more charming than the Tuileries, whether the linen brought home by the washerwoman was too much or insufficiently starched, or if Toussaint had gone to market well or ill; and she remained crushed, absorbed, attentive to one thought alone, with a vague and fixed eye, like a person gazing through the darkness at the deep black spot where a phantom has just vanished. Still, she did not allow Jean Valjean to see anything but her pallor, and her face was ever gentle to him. This pallor, though, was more than sufficient to render Jean Valjean anxious, and at times he would ask her :

" What is the matter with you? "

And she answered, —

" Nothing."

After a silence, she would add, as if guessing that he was sad too, —

" And, father, is there anything the matter with you? "

" With me? Oh, nothing," he would reply.

These two beings who had loved each other so exclusively, and one of them with such a touching love, and had lived for a long time one through the other, were now suffering side by side, one on account of the other, without confessing it, without anger, and with a smile.

CHAPTER VIII.

THE CHAIN-GANG.

THE more unhappy of the two was Jean Valjean; for youth, even in its sorrow, has always a brilliancy of its own. At certain moments Jean Valjean suffered so intensely that he became childish, for it is the peculiarity of grief to bring out a man's childish side. He felt invincibly that Cosette was slipping from him; and he would have liked to struggle, hold her back, and excite her by some external and brilliant achievement. These ideas, childish, as we said, but at the same time senile, gave him through their very childishness a very fair notion of the influence of gold lace upon the imagination of girls. One day Count Coutard, Commandant of Paris, passed along the street on horseback, and in full-dress uniform. He envied this gilded man, and said to himself: What a happiness it would be to be able to put on that coat, which was an undeniable thing; that if Cosette saw him in it it would dazzle her, and when he passed before the Tuileries gates the sentinels would present arms to him, and that would be sufficient for Cosette, and prevent her looking at young men.

An unexpected shock was mingled with his sad

thoughts. In the isolated life they led, and since they had gone to reside in the Rue Plumet, they had one habit. They sometimes had the pleasure of going to see the sun rise, a species of sweet joy, which is agreeable to those who are entering life and those who are leaving it. To walk about at daybreak is equivalent, with the man who loves solitude, to walking about at night with the gayety of nature added. The streets are deserted and the birds sing. Cosette, herself a bird, generally woke at an early hour. These morning excursions were arranged on the previous evening ; he proposed and she accepted. This was arranged like a plot ; they went out before day, and it was a delight for Cosette, as these innocent eccentricities please youth. Jean Valjean had, as we know, a liking to go to but little frequented places, — to solitary nooks, and forgotten spots. There were at that time, in the vicinity of the gates of Paris, poor fields, almost forming part of the city, where sickly wheat grew in summer, and which in autumn, after the harvest was got in, did not look as if they had been reaped, but skinned. Jean Valjean had a predilection for these fields, and Cosette did not feel wearied there ; it was solitude for him and liberty for her. There she became a little girl again ; she ran about and almost played ; she took off her bonnet, laid it on Jean Valjean's knees, and plucked flowers. She watched the butterflies, but did not catch them ; for humanity and tenderness spring up with love, and the maiden who has in her heart a trembling and fragile ideal feels pity for the butterfly's wing. She twined poppies into wreaths, which she placed on her head, and when the sun poured its beams on them and rendered them almost purple, they formed a fiery crown for her fresh pink face.

Even after their life had grown saddened they kept up their habit of early walks. One October morning, then, tempted by the perfect serenity of the autumn of 1831, they went out, and found themselves just before daybreak near the Barrière du Maine. It was not quite morning yet, but it was dawn, a ravishing and wild minute. There were a few stars in the pale azure sky, the earth was all black, the heavens all white, a shiver ran along the grass, and all around displayed the mysterious influence of twilight. A lark, which seemed mingled with the stars, was singing at a prodigious height, and it seemed as if this hymn of littleness to infinitude calmed the immensity. In the east the dark mass of Val de Grâce stood out against the bright steel-blue horizon, and glittering Venus rose behind the dome and looked like a soul escaping from a gloomy edifice. All was peace and silence, there was no one in the highway; and a few workmen, going to their daily toil, could be indistinctly seen in the distance.

Jean Valjean was seated on some planks deposited at the gate of a timber-yard; his face was turned to the road, and his back to the light. He forgot all about the sunrise, for he had fallen into one of those profound reveries in which the mind is concentrated, which imprison even the glance and are equivalent to four walls. There are meditations which may be called wells, and when you are at the bottom it takes

some time to reach the ground again.   Jean Valjean
had descended into one of these reveries ; he was
thinking of Cosette, of the possible happiness if nothing came betwixt him and her, of that light with
which she filled his life, and which was the breath
of his soul.   He was almost happy in this reverie ;
and Cosette, standing by his side, was watching the
clouds turn pink.   All at once Cosette exclaimed,
" Father, there is something coming down there ! "
Jean Valjean raised his eyes ; Cosette was correct.
The road which leads to the old Barrière du Maine
is a prolongation of the Rue de Sèvres, and is intersected at right angles by the inner boulevard.   At
the spot where the roads cross, a sound difficult to
explain at such an hour could be heard, and a sort
of confused mass appeared.   Some shapeless thing
coming along the boulevard was turning into the
main road.   It grew larger, and seemed to be moving
in an orderly way ; although it shook and heaved,
it seemed to be a vehicle, but its load could not be
distinguished.   There were horses, wheels, shouts,
and the cracking of whips.   By degrees the lineaments became fixed, though drowned in darkness.
It was really a vehicle coming toward the barrière
near which Jean Valjean was seated ; a second
resembling it followed, then a third, then a fourth ;
seven carts debouched in turn, the heads of the
horses touching the back of the vehicles.   Figures
moved on these carts ; sparks could be seen in the
gloom, looking like bare sabres, and a clang could
be heard resembling chains being shaken.   All this
advanced, the voices became louder, and it was a

formidable thing, such as issues from the cavern of dreams.

On drawing nearer, this thing assumed a shape, and stood out behind the trees with the lividness of an apparition. The mass grew whiter, and the gradually dawning day threw a ghastly gleam over this mass, which was at once sepulchral and alive, — the heads of the shadows became the faces of corpses, and this is what it was. Seven vehicles were moving in file along the road, and the first six had a singular shape; they resembled brewers' drays, and consisted of long ladders laid upon two wheels, and forming a shaft at the front end. Each dray, or, to speak more correctly, each ladder, was drawn by a team of four horses, and strange clusters of men were dragged along upon these ladders. In the faint light these men could not be seen, so much as divined. Twenty-four on each ladder, twelve on either side, leaning against each other, had their faces turned to the passers-by, and their legs hanging down; and they had behind their back something which rang and was a chain, and something that glistened, which was a collar. Each man had his collar, but the chain was for all; so that these twenty-four men, if obliged to get down from the dray and walk, were seized by a species of inexorable unity, and were obliged to wind on the ground with the chain as backbone, very nearly like centipedes. At the front and back of each cart stood two men armed with guns, who stood with their feet on the end of the chain. The seventh vehicle, a vast fourgon with rack sides but no hood, had four wheels and six horses, and carried a resounding mass of coppers, boilers, chafing-dishes, and chains, among which were mingled a few bound men lying their full length, who seemed to be ill. This fourgon, which was quite open, was lined with broken-down hurdles, which seemed to have been used for old punishments.

These vehicles held the crown of the causeway; and on either side marched a double file of infamous-looking guards, wearing three-cornered hats, like the soldiers of the Directory, and dirty, torn, stained uniforms, half gray and blue, a coat of the Invalides and the trousers of the undertaker's men, red epaulettes and yellow belts, and were armed with short sabres, muskets, and sticks. These sbirri seemed compounded of the abjectness of the beggar and the authority of the hangman; and the one who appeared their leader held a postilion's whip in his hands. All these details grew more and more distinct in the advancing daylight; and at the head and rear of the train marched mounted gendarmes with drawn sabres. The train was so long that at the moment when the first vehicle reached the barrière the last had scarce turned out of the boulevard. A crowd, which came no one knew whence and formed in a second, as is so common in Paris, lined both sides of the road, and looked. In the side-lanes could be heard the shouts of people calling to each other, and the wooden shoes of the kitchen-gardeners running up to have a peep.

The men piled up on the drays allowed themselves to be jolted in silence, and were livid with the

morning chill. They all wore canvas trousers, and
their naked feet were thrust into wooden shoes;
but the rest of their attire was left to the fancy of
wretchedness. Their accoutrements were hideously
disaccordant, for nothing is more mournful than the
harlequin garb of rags. There were crushed hats,
oilskin caps, frightful woollen night-caps, and side
by side with the blouse, an out-at-elbow black coat.
Some wore women's bonnets, and others had baskets,
as head-gear; hairy chests were visible, and through
the rents of the clothes tattooing could be distinguished, — temples of love, burning hearts, and
cupids, — but ringworm and other unhealthy red
spots might also be noticed. Two or three had
passed a straw rope through the side rail of the
dray, which hung down like a stirrup and supported
their feet; while one of them held in his hand and
raised to his mouth something like a black stone,
which he seemed to be gnawing, — it was bread he
was eating. All the eyes were dry, and either dull
or luminous with a wicked light. The escort cursed,
but the chained men did not breathe a syllable;
from time to time the sound of a blow dealt with a
stick on shoulder-blades or heads could be heard.
Some of these men yawned; the rags were terrible;
their feet hung down, their shoulders oscillated, their
heads struck against each other, their irons rattled,
their eyeballs flashed ferociously, their fists clenched
or opened inertly like the hands of death, and in
the rear of the chain a band of children burst into a
laugh.

This file of vehicles, whatever their nature might

be, was lugubrious. It was plain that within an
hour a shower might fall, that it might be followed
by another, and then another, that the ragged clothing would be drenched; and that once wet through,
these men would not dry again, and once chilled,
would never grow warm any more; that their canvas
trousers would be glued to their bones by the rain,
that water would fill their wooden shoes, that lashes
could not prevent the chattering of teeth, that the
chain would continue to hold them by the neck, and
their feet would continue to hang; and it was impossible not to shudder on seeing these human creatures thus bound and passive beneath the cold
autumnal clouds, and surrendered to the rain, the
breezes, and all the furies of the atmosphere, like
trees and stones. The blows were not even spared
the sick who lay bound with ropes and motionless
in the seventh vehicle, and who seemed to have
been thrown down there like sacks filled with
wretchedness.

All at once the sun appeared, the immense beam
of the east flashed forth; and it seemed as if it set
fire to all these ferocious heads. Tongues became
untied, and a storm of furies, oaths, and songs ex-
ploded. The wide horizontal light cut the whole file
in two, illumining the heads and bodies, and leaving
the feet and wheels in obscurity. Thoughts appeared on faces, and it was a fearful thing to see
demons with their masks thrown away, and ferocious
souls laid bare. Some of the merrier ones had in
their mouths quills, through which they blew vermin
on the crowd, selecting women. The dawn caused

their lamentable faces to stand out in the darkness of the shadows. Not one of these beings but was misshapen through wretchedness; and it was so monstrous that it seemed to change the light of the sun into the gleam of a lightning flash. The first cartload had struck up, and were droning out at the top of their voices, with a haggard joviality, a pot-pourri of Desaugiers, at that time famous under the title of *La Vestale.* The trees shook mournfully, while in the side-walks bourgeois faces were listening with an idiotic beatitude to these comic songs chanted by spectres. In the chaos of this train were all kinds of wretchedness; there were there the facial angles of all animals, old men, youths, naked skulls, gray beards, cynical monstrosities, sulky resignation, savage grins, wild attitudes, youth, girlish heads with corkscrew curls on the temples, infantine, and for that reason horrible, faces, and then countenances of skeletons which only lacked death. On the first dray could be seen a negro, who had been a slave probably, and was enabled to compare the chains. The frightful leveller, shame, had passed over all these foreheads. At this stage of abasement the last transformations were undergone by all in the lowest depths; and ignorance, changed into dulness, was the equal of intellect changed into despair. No choice was possible among these men, who appeared to be the pick of the mud; and it was clear that the arranger of this unclean procession had not attempted to classify them. These beings had been bound and coupled pell-mell, probably in alphabetical disorder, and loaded haphazard on the vehicles. Still, horrors, when grouped, always end by disengaging a resultant. Every addition of wretched men produces a total; a common soul issued from each chain, and each dray-load had its physiognomy. By the side of the man who sang was one who yelled; a third begged; another could be seen gnashing his teeth; another threatened the passers-by; another blasphemed God, and the last was silent as the tomb. Dante would have fancied that he saw the seven circles of the Inferno in motion. It was the march of the damned to the torture, performed in a sinister way, not upon the formidable flashing car of the Apocalypse, but, more gloomy still, in the hangman's cart.

One of the keepers, who had a hook at the end of his stick, from time to time attempted to stir up this heap of human ordure. An old woman in the crowd pointed them to a little boy of five years of age, and said to him, "You scamp, that will teach you!" As the songs and blasphemy grew louder, the man who seemed the captain of the escort cracked his whip; and at this signal a blind, indiscriminate bastinado fell with the sound of hail upon the seven cart-loads. Many yelled and foamed at the lips, which redoubled the joy of the gamins who had come up like a cloud of flies settling upon wounds. Jean Valjean's eye had become frightful; it was no longer an eyeball, but that profound glass bulb which takes the place of the eye in some unfortunate men, which seems unconscious of reality, and in which the reflection of horrors and catastrophes flashes. He was not look-ing at a spectacle, but going through a vision; he had to rise, fly, escape, but could not move his foot. At times things which you see seize you and root you in the ground. He remained petrified and stupid, asking himself through a confused and inexpressible agony what was the meaning of this sepulchral persecution, and whence came this Pandemonium that pursued him. All at once he raised his hand to his forehead, — the usual gesture of those to whom memory suddenly returns; he remembered that this was substantially the road, that this détour was usual to avoid any meeting with royalty, — which was always possible on the Fontainebleau road, — and that five-and-thirty years before he had passed through that barrière. Cosette was not the less horrified, though in a different way; she did not understand, her breath failed her, and what she saw did not appear to her possible. At length she exclaimed, —

"Father! what is there in those vehicles?"

Jean Valjean answered, —

"Convicts."

"Where are they going?"

"To the galleys."

At this moment the bastinado, multiplied by a hundred hands, became tremendous; strokes of the flat of the sabre were mingled with it, and it resembled a tornado of whips and sticks. The galley-slaves bowed their heads; a hideous obedience was produced by the punishment, and all were silent, with the looks of chained wolves. Cosette, trembling in all her limbs, continued, —

"Father, are they still men?"

"Sometimes," the miserable man replied.

It was, in fact, the Chain, which, leaving Bicêtre

before daybreak, was taking the Mans road, to avoid
Fontainebleau, where the king then was. This
détour made the fearful journey last three or four
days longer ; but it surely may be prolonged to save
a royal personage the sight of a punishment ! Jean
Valjean went home crushed; for such encounters are
blows, and the recollections they leave behind resemble a concussion. While walking along the Rue
de Babylone, Jean Valjean did not notice that
Cosette asked him other questions about what they
had just seen ; perhaps he was himself too absorbed
in his despondency to notice her remarks and answer
them. At night, however, when Cosette left him to
go to bed, he heard her say in a low voice, and as
if speaking to herself: "I feel that if I were to meet
one of those men in the street, I should die only
from being so close to him."

Luckily, the next day after this tragic interlude,
there were festivals in Paris on account of some
official solemnity which I have forgotten, a review
at the Champ de Mars, a quintain on the Seine,
theatres in the Champs Élysées, fireworks at the
Étoile, and illuminations everywhere. Jean Valjean,
breaking through his habits, took Cosette to these
rejoicings in order to make her forget the scene of
the previous day, and efface, beneath the laughing
tumult of all Paris, the abominable thing which had
passed before her. The review, which seasoned the
fête, rendered uniforms very natural ; hence Jean
Valjean put on his National Guard coat, with the
vague inner feeling of a man who is seeking a refuge. However, the object of this jaunt seemed to

be attained; Cosette, who made it a law to please
her father, and to whom any festival was a novelty,
accepted the distraction with the easy and light
good-will of adolescents, and did not make too disdainful a pout at the porringer of joy which is called
a public holiday. Hence Jean Valjean might believe
that he had succeeded, and that no trace of the hideous vision remained. A few days after, one morning when the sun was shining, and both were on the
garden steps, — another infraction of the rules which
Jean Valjean seemed to have imposed on himself,
and that habit of remaining in her chamber which
sadness had caused Cosette to assume, — the girl,
wearing a combing jacket, was standing in that
morning négligé which adorably envelops maidens,
and looks like a cloud over a star; and with her head
in the light, her cheeks pink from a good night's rest,
and gazed at softly by the old man, she was plucking
the petals of a daisy. She did not know the delicious legend of, " I love you, a little, passionately,"
etc., — for who could have taught it to her? She
handled the flower instinctively and innocently, without suspecting that plucking a daisy to pieces is ques-
tioning a heart. If there were a fourth Grace called
Melancholy, she had the air of that Grace when
smiling. Jean Valjean was fascinated by the contemplation of these little fingers on this flower, forgetting everything in the radiance which surrounded
the child. A red-breast was twittering in a bush
hard by; and while clouds crossed the sky so gayly
that you might have said that they had just been
set at liberty, Cosette continued to pluck her flower

attentively.   She seemed to be thinking of something, but that something must be charming.   All at once she turned her head on her shoulder, with the delicate slowness of a swan, and said to Jean Valjean, " Tell me, father, what the galleys are."

BOOK IV.

SUCCOR FROM BELOW MAY BE SUCCOR FROM ON HIGH.

CHAPTER I.

AN EXTERNAL WOUND AND AN INTERNAL CURE.

THEIR life thus gradually became overcast ; only one amusement was left them which had formerly been a happiness, and that was to carry bread to those who were starving, and clothes to those who were cold. In these visits to the poor, in which Cosette frequently accompanied Jean Valjean, they found again some portion of their old expansiveness ; and at times, when the day had been good, when a good deal of distress had been relieved, and many children warmed and re-animated, Cosette displayed a little gayety at night. It was at this period that they paid the visit to Jondrette's den. The day after that visit, Jean Valjean appeared at an early hour in the pavilion, calm as usual, but with a large wound in his left arm, which was very inflamed and venomous, which resembled a burn, and which he accounted for in some way or other. This wound kept him at home with a fever for more than a month, for he would not see any medical man, and when Cosette pressed him, he said, "Call in the dog-doctor." Cosette dressed his wound morning and night with an air of such divine and angelic happiness at being useful to him, that Jean Valjean felt all his old joy return, his fears and anxieties dissipated ; and he gazed at Cosette, saying, " Oh, the excellent wound ! the good hurt ! "

Cosette, seeing her father ill, had deserted the pavilion, and regained her taste for the little out-house and the back court. She spent nearly the whole day by the side of Jean Valjean, and read to him any books he chose, which were generally travels. Jean Valjean was regenerated. His happiness returned with ineffable radiance ; the Luxembourg, the young unknown prowler, Cosette's coldness,—all these soul-clouds disappeared, and he found himself saying, " I imagined all that ; I am an old fool ! " His happiness was such that the frightful discovery of the Thénardiers made in Jondrette's den, which was so unexpected, had to some extent glided over him. He had succeeded in escaping, his trail was lost, and what did he care for the rest ? He only thought of it to pity those wretches. They were in prison, and henceforth incapable of mischief, he thought, but what a lamentable family in distress ! As for the hideous vision of the Barrière du Maine, Cosette had not spoken again about it. In the convent, Sister Sainte Mechtilde had taught Cosette music ; she had a voice such as a linnet would have if it possessed a soul ; and at times she sang sad songs in the wounded man's obscure room, which enlivened Jean

Valjean.   Spring arrived, and the garden was so delicious at that season of the year, that Jean Valjean
said to Cosette, " You never go out, and I wish you
to take a stroll."   " As you please, father," said
Cosette.   And to obey her father, she resumed her
walks in the garden, generally alone, for, as we have
mentioned, Jean Valjean, who was probably afraid of
being seen from the gate, hardly ever entered it.

Jean Valjean's wound had been a diversion ; when
Cosette saw that her father suffered less, and was
recovering and seemed happy, she felt a satisfaction
which she did not even notice, for it came so softly
and naturally.   Then, too, it was the month of
March ; the days were drawing out, winter was departing, and it always takes with it some portion of
our sorrow ; then came April, that daybreak of summer, fresh as every dawn, and gay like all childhoods,
and somewhat tearful at times like the new-born babe
it is.   Nature in that month has charming beams
which pass from the sky, the clouds, the trees, the
fields, and the flowers into the human heart.   Cosette was still too young for this April joy, which resembled her, not to penetrate her ; insensibly, and
without suspecting it, the dark cloud departed from
her mind.   In spring there is light in sad souls, as
there is at midday in cellars.   Cosette was no longer
so very sad ; it was so, but she did not attempt to
account for it.   In the morning, after breakfast,
when she succeeded in drawing her father into the
garden for a quarter of an hour, and walked him
up and down while supporting his bad arm, she
did not notice that she laughed every moment and

was happy.   Jean Valjean was delighted to see her become ruddy-cheeked and fresh once more.

"Oh, the famous wound!" he repeated to himself, in a low voice.

And he was grateful to the Thénardiers.   So soon as his wound was cured he recommenced his solitary night-rambles ; and it would be a mistake to suppose that a man can walk about alone in the uninhabited regions of Paris without meeting with some adventure.

CHAPTER II.

MOTHER PLUTARCH ACCOUNTS FOR A PHENOMENON.

ONE evening little Gavroche had eaten nothing;
he remembered that he had not dined either on the
previous day, and that was becoming ridiculous; so
he formed the resolution to try and sup. He went
prowling about at the deserted spots beyond the
Salpêtrière, for there are good windfalls there; where
there is nobody, something may be found. He thus
reached a suburb which seemed to him to be the
village of Austerlitz. In one of his previous strolls
he had noticed there an old garden frequented by an
old man and an old woman, and in this garden a
passable apple-tree. By the side of this tree was a
sort of badly closed fruit-loft, whence an apple might
be obtained. An apple is a supper, an apple is life;
and what ruined Adam might save Gavroche. The
garden skirted a solitary unpaved lane, bordered by
shrubs while waiting for houses, and a hedge separated it from the lane. Gavroche proceeded to the
garden. He found the lane again, he recognized the
apple-tree, and examined the hedge; a hedge is but
a stride. Day was declining; there was not a cat in
the lane, and the hour was good. Gavroche was
preparing to clamber over the hedge, when he stopped

short, — some people were talking in the garden. Gavroche looked through one of the interstices in the hedge. Two paces from him, at the foot of the hedge on the other side, at precisely the point where the hole he had intended to make would have opened, lay a stone which formed a species of bench ; and on this bench the old man of the garden was seated with the old woman standing in front of him. The old woman was grumbling, and Gavroche, who was not troubled with too much discretion, listened.

"Monsieur Mabœuf!" the old woman said.

"Mabœuf!" Gavroche thought, "that's a rum name."

The old man thus addressed did not stir, and the old woman repeated, —

"Monsieur Mabœuf!"

The old man, without taking his eyes off the ground, decided to answer, —

"Well, Mother Plutarch!"

"Mother Plutarch!" Gavroche thought, "that's another rum name."

Mother Plutarch continued, and the old gentleman was compelled to submit to the conversation.

"The landlord is not satisfied."

"Why so?"

"There are three quarters owing."

"In three months more we shall owe four."

"He says that he will turn you out."

"I will go."

"The green-grocer wants to be paid, or she will supply no more fagots. How shall we warm ourselves this winter if we have no wood?"

" There is the sun."

" The butcher has stopped our credit, and will not supply any more meat."

" That is lucky, for I cannot digest meat; it is heavy."

" But what shall we have for dinner? "

" Bread."

" The baker insists on receiving something on account ; no money, no bread, he says."

" Very good."

" What will you eat? "

" We have apples."

" But, really, sir, we cannot live in that way without money."

" I have none."

The old woman went away, and left the old gentleman alone. He began thinking, and Gavroche thought too ; it was almost night. The first result of Gavroche's reflection was, that instead of climbing over the hedge, he lay down under it. The branches parted a little at the bottom. " Hilloh," said Gavroche to himself, " it 's an alcove," and he crept into it. His back was almost against the octogenarian's bench, and he could hear him breathe. Then, in lieu of dining, Gavroche tried to sleep, but it was the sleep of a cat, with one eye open. While dozing, Gavroche watched. The whiteness of the twilight sky lit up the ground, and the lane formed a livid line between two rows of dark streets. All at once two figures appeared on this white stripe ; one was in front and the other a little distance behind.

" Here are two coves," Gavroche growled.

The first figure seemed to be some old bowed citizen, more than simply attired, who walked slowly, owing to his age, and was strolling about in the starlight. The second was straight, firm, and slim. He regulated his steps by those of the man in front; but suppleness and agility could be detected in his voluntary slowness. This figure had something ferocious and alarming about it, and the appearance of what was called a dandy in those days; the hat was of a good shape, and the coat was black, well cut, probably of fine cloth, and tight at the waist. He held his head up with a sort of robust grace; and under the hat a glimpse could be caught of a pale youthful profile in the twilight. This profile had a rose in its mouth, and was familiar to Gavroche, for it was Montparnasse; as for the other, there was nothing to be said save that he was a respectable old man. Gavroche at once began observing, for it was evident that one of these men had projects upon the other. Gavroche was well situated to see the finale; and the alcove had opportunely become a hiding-place. Montparnasse, hunting at such an hour in such a spot, — that was menacing. Gavroche felt his gamin entrails moved with pity for the old gentleman. What should he do, — interfere? One weakness helping another! Montparnasse would have laughed at it; for Gavroche did not conceal from himself that the old man first, and then the boy, would be only two mouthfuls for this formidable bandit of eighteen. While Gavroche was deliberating, the attack — a sudden and hideous attack — took place; it was the attack of a tiger on an onager, of a spider on a fly.

Montparnasse threw away the rose, leaped upon the old man, grappled him and clung to him; and Gavroche had difficulty in repressing a cry. A moment after, one of these men was beneath the other, crushed, gasping, and struggling with a knee of marble on his chest. But it was not exactly what Gavroche had anticipated; the man on the ground was Montparnasse, the one at the top the citizen. All this took place a few yards from Gavroche. The old man received the shock, and repaid it so terribly that in an instant the assailant and the assailed changed parts.

" That's a tough invalid," Gavroche thought. And he could not refrain from clapping his hands, but it was thrown away; it was not heard by the two combatants, who deafened one another, and mingled their breath in the struggle. At length there was a silence, and Montparnasse ceased writhing. Gavroche muttered this aside, " Is he dead ? " The worthy man had not uttered a word or given a cry ; he rose, and Gavroche heard him say to Montparnasse, " Get up."

Montparnasse did so, but the citizen still held him. Montparnasse had the humiliated and furious attitude of a wolf snapped at by a sheep. Gavroche looked and listened, making an effort to double his eyes with his ears ; he was enormously amused. He was rewarded for his conscientious anxiety, for he was able to catch the following dialogue, which borrowed from the darkness a sort of tragic accent. The gentleman questioned, and Montparnasse answered, —

" What is your age ? "

" Nineteen."

" You are strong and healthy, why do you not work ? "

" It is a bore."

" What is your trade ? "

" Idler."

" Speak seriously. Can anything be done for you ? What do you wish to be ? "

" A robber."

There was a silence, and the old gentleman seemed in profound thought; but he did not loose his hold of Montparnasse. Every now and then the young bandit, who was vigorous and active, gave starts like a wild beast caught in a snare; he shook himself, attempted a trip, wildly writhed his limbs, and tried to escape. The old gentleman did not appear to notice it, and held the ruffian's two arms in one hand with the sovereign indifference of absolute strength. The old man's reverie lasted some time; then, gazing fixedly at Montparnasse, he mildly raised his voice and addressed to him, in the darkness where they stood, a sort of solemn appeal, of which Gavroche did not lose a syllable.

" My boy, you are entering by sloth into the most laborious of existences. Ah! you declare yourself an idler, then prepare yourself for labor. Have you ever seen a formidable machine which is called a rolling-mill ? You must be on your guard against it; for it is a crafty and ferocious thing, and if it catch you by the skirt of the coat it drags you under it entirely. Such a machine is indolence. Stop

while there is yet time, and save yourself, otherwise
it is all over with you, and ere long you will be
among the cog-wheels.   Once caught, hope for nothing more.   You will be forced to fatigue yourself,
idler ; and no rest will be allowed you, for the iron
hand of implacable toil has seized you.   You refuse
to earn your livelihood, have a calling, and accomplish
a duty.   It bores you to be like the rest ; well, you
will be different.   Labor is the law, and whoever
repulses it as a bore must have it as a punishment.
You do not wish to be a laborer, and you will be
a slave.   Toil only lets you loose on one side to seize
you again on the other ; you do not wish to be its
friend, and you will be its negro.   Ah, you did not
care for the honest fatigue of men, and you are
about to know the sweat of the damned ; while
others sing you will groan.   You will see other men
working in the distance, and they will seem to you
to be resting.   The laborer, the reaper, the sailor,
the blacksmith, will appear to you in the light like
the blessed inmates of a paradise.   What a radiance
there is in the anvil !   What joy it is to guide the
plough, and tie up the sheaf !   What a holiday to fly
before the wind in a boat !   But you, idler, will
have to dig and drag, and roll and walk.   Pull at
your halter, for you are a beast of burden in the
service of hell !   So your desire is to do nothing ?
Well, you will not have a week, a day, an hour
without feeling crushed.   You will not be able to
lift anything without agony, and every passing minute
will make your muscles crack.   What is a feather for
others will be a rock for you, and the most simple

things will become steep. Life will become a monster around you, and coming, going, breathing, will
be so many terrible tasks for you. Your lungs will
produce in you the effect of a hundred-pound weight;
and going there sooner than here will be a problem
to solve. Any man who wishes to go out, merely
opens his door and finds himself in the street; but
if you wish to go out you must pierce through your
wall. What do honest men do to reach the street?
They go downstairs; but you will tear up your
sheets, make a cord of them fibre by fibre, then pass
through your window and hang by this thread over
an abyss. And it will take place at night, in the
storm, the rain, or the hurricane; and if the cord
be too short you will have but one way of descending, by falling — falling haphazard into the gulf, and
from any height, and on what? On some unknown
thing beneath. Or you will climb up a chimney
at the risk of burning yourself; or crawl through
a sewer at the risk of drowning. I will say nothing
of the holes which must be masked; of the stones
which you will have to remove and put back twenty
times a day, or of the plaster you must hide under
your mattress. A lock presents itself, and the citizen has in his pocket the key for it, made by the
locksmith; but you, if you wish to go out, are condemned to make a terrible masterpiece. You will
take a double sou and cut it asunder. With what
tools? You will invent them; that is your business. Then you will hollow out the interior of the
two parts, being careful not to injure the outside,
and form a thread all round the edge, so that the

two parts may fit closely like a box and its cover. When they are screwed together there will be nothing suspicious to the watchers, — for you will be watched. It will be a double sou, but for yourself a box. What will you place in this box ? A small piece of steel, a watch-spring in which you have made teeth, and which will be a saw. With this saw, about the length of a pin, you will be obliged to cut through the bolt of the lock, the padlock of your chain, the bar at your window, and the fetter on your leg. This masterpiece done, this prodigy accomplished, all the miracles of art, skill, cleverness, and patience executed, what will be your reward if you are detected ? A dungeon. Such is the future. What precipices are sloth and pleasure ! To do nothing is a melancholy resolution, are you aware of that ? To live in indolence on the social substance ; to be useless, that is to say, injurious, — this leads straight to the bottom of misery. Woe to the man who wishes to be a parasite, for he will be vermin ! Ah ! it does not please you to work. Ah ! you have only one thought, to drink well, eat well, and sleep well. You will drink water ; you will eat black bread ; you will sleep on a plank, with fetters riveted to your limbs, and feel their coldness at night in your flesh ! You will break these fetters and fly ; very good. You will drag yourself on your stomach into the shrubs and eat grass like the beasts of the field ; and you will be re-captured, and then you will pass years in a dungeon, chained to the wall, groping in the dark for your water-jug, biting at frightful black bread which dogs would refuse,

and eating beans which maggots have eaten before
you. You will be a wood-louse in a cellar. Ah,
ah! take pity on yourself, wretched boy, still so
young, who were at your nurse's breast not twenty
years ago, and have doubtless a mother still! I
implore you to listen to me. You want fine black
cloth, polished shoes, to scent your head with fragrant oil, to please bad women, and be a pretty fellow ;
you will have your hair close shaven, and wear a red
jacket and wooden shoes. You want a ring on your
finger ; and will wear a collar on your neck, and if
you look at a woman you will be beaten. And you
will go in there at twenty and come out at fifty years
of age. You will go in young, red-cheeked, healthy,
with your sparkling eyes and all your white teeth,
and your curly locks ; and you will come out again
broken, bent, wrinkled, toothless, horrible, and gray-
headed ! Ah, my poor boy, you are on the wrong
road, and indolence is a bad adviser ; for robbery is
the hardest of labors. Take my advice, and do not
undertake the laborious task of being an idler. To
become a rogue is inconvenient, and it is not nearly
so hard to be an honest man. Now go, and think
over what I have said to you. By the bye, what
did you want of me ? My purse ? Here it is."

And the old man, releasing Montparnasse, placed
his purse in his hand, which Montparnasse weighed
for a moment ; after which, with the same mechanical
precaution as if he had stolen it, Montparnasse let
it glide gently into the back-pocket of his coat. All
this said and done, the old gentleman turned his
back and quietly resumed his walk.

" Old humbug ! " Montparnasse muttered. Who was the old gentleman ? The reader has doubtless guessed. Montparnasse, in his stupefaction, watched him till he disappeared in the gloom, and this contemplation was fatal for him. While the old gentleman retired, Gavroche advanced. He had assured himself by a glance that Father Mabœuf was still seated on his bench, and was probably asleep ; then the gamin left the bushes, and began crawling in the shadow behind the motionless Montparnasse. He thus got up to the young bandit unnoticed, gently insinuated his hand into the back-pocket of the fine black cloth coat, seized the purse, withdrew his hand, and crawled back again into the shadow like a lizard. Montparnasse, who had no reason to be on his guard, and who was thinking for the first time in his life, perceived nothing ; and Gavroche, when he had returned to the spot where Father Mabœuf was sitting, threw the purse over the hedge and ran off at full speed. The purse fell on Father Mabœuf's foot and awoke him. He stooped down and picked up the purse, which he opened without comprehending anything. It was a purse, with two compartments ; in one was some change, in the other were six napoleons. M. Mabœuf, greatly startled, carried the thing to his housekeeper.

"It has fallen from heaven," said Mother Plutarch.

BOOK V.

IN WHICH THE END DOES NOT RESEMBLE THE BEGINNING.

CHAPTER I.

SOLITUDE AND THE BARRACKS COMBINED.

Cosette's sorrow, so poignant and so sharp four or five months previously, had without her knowledge attained the convalescent stage. Nature, spring, youth, love for her father, the gayety of the flowers and birds filtered gradually, day by day and drop by drop, something that almost resembled oblivion into her virginal and young soul. Was the fire entirely extinguished; or were layers of ashes merely formed? The fact is, that she hardly felt now the painful and burning point. One day she suddenly thought of Marius; "Why," she said, "I had almost forgotten him." This same week she noticed, while passing the garden gate, a very handsome officer in the Lancers, with a wasp-like waist, a delightful uniform, the cheeks of a girl, a sabre under his arm, waxed mustaches, and lacquered schapska. In other respects, he had light hair, blue eyes flush with his head, a round, vain, insolent, and pretty face; he was exactly the contrary of Marius. He had a cigar in his mouth, and Cosette supposed that he belonged to the regiment quartered in the barracks of the Rue de Babylone. The next day she saw him pass again, and remarked the hour. From this moment — was it an accident? — she saw him pass nearly every day. The officer's comrades perceived that there was in this badly kept garden, and behind this poor, old-fashioned railing, a very pretty creature who was nearly always there when the handsome lieutenant passed, who is no stranger to the reader, as his name was Théodule Gillenormand.

" Hilloh ! " they said to him, "there's a little girl making eyes at you, just look at her."

" Have I the time," the Lancer replied, " to look at all the girls who look at me ? "

It was at this identical time that Marius was slowly descending to the abyss, and said, " If I could only see her again before I die ! " If his wish had been realized, if he had at that moment seen Cosette looking at a Lancer, he would have been unable to utter a word, but expired of grief. Whose fault would it have been ? Nobody's. Marius possessed one of those temperaments which bury themselves in chagrin and abide in it : Cosette was one of those who plunge into it and again emerge. Cosette, however, was passing through that dangerous moment, — the fatal phase of feminine reverie left to itself, in which the heart of an isolated maiden resembles those vine tendrils which cling, according to chance, to the capital of a marble column or to the sign-post of an inn. It is a rapid

and decisive moment, critical for every orphan,
whether she be poor or rich ; for wealth does not
prevent a bad choice, and misalliances take place in
very high society.   But the true misalliance is that
of souls ; and in the same way as many an unknown
young man, without name, birth, or fortune, is a
marble capital supporting a temple of grand sen-
timents and grand ideas, so a man of the world,
satisfied and opulent, who has polished boots and
varnished words, if we look not at the exterior but
at the interior, — that is to say, what is reserved for
the wife, — is nought but a stupid log obscurely
haunted by violent, unclean, and drunken passions, —
the inn sign-post.

What was there in Cosette's soul ? Passion calmed
or lulled to sleep, love in a floating state ; something
which was limpid and brilliant, perturbed at a certain depth, and sombre lower still. The image of
the handsome officer was reflected on the surface,
but was there any reminiscence at the bottom,
quite at the bottom ? Perhaps so, but Cosette did
not know.

A singular incident occurred.

CHAPTER II.

IN the first fortnight of April Jean Valjean went on a journey; this, as we know, occurred from time to time at very lengthened intervals, and he remained away one or two days at the most. Where did he go? No one knew, not even Cosette; once only she had accompanied him in a hackney coach, upon the occasion of one of these absences, to the corner of a little lane which was called, "Impasse de la Plan-chette." He got out there, and the coach carried Cosette back to the Rue de Babylone. It was gen-erally when money ran short in the house that Jean Valjean took these trips. Jean Valjean, then, was absent; and he had said, "I shall be back in three days." At night Cosette was alone in the drawing-room, and in order to while away the time, she opened her piano and began singing to her own accompaniment the song of Euryanthe, "Hunters wandering in the wood," which is probably the finest thing we possess in the shape of music. When she had finished she remained passive. Suddenly she fancied she heard some one walking in the garden. It could not be her father, for he was away; and it could not be Touissant, as she was in bed, for it was

ten o'clock at night.   Cosette was near the drawing-
room shutters, which were closed, and put her ear
to them ; and it seemed to her that it was the footfall of a man who was walking very gently.   She
hurried up to her room on the first floor, opened a
Venetian frame in her shutter, and looked out into
the garden.   The moon was shining bright as day,
and there was nobody in it.   She opened her window ; the garden was perfectly calm, and all that
could be seen of the street was as deserted as usual.

Cosette thought that she was mistaken, and she
had supposed that she heard the noise.   It was an
hallucination produced by Weber's gloomy and won-
derful chorus, which opens before the mind bewil-
dering depths ; which trembles before the eye like a
dizzy forest in which we hear the cracking of the
dead branches under the restless feet of the hunters,
of whom we catch a glimpse in the obscurity.   She
thought no more of it.   Moreover, Cosette was not
naturally very timid : she had in her veins some of
the blood of the gypsy, and the adventurer who goes
about barefooted.   As we may remember, she was
rather a lark than a dove, and she had a stern and
brave temper.

The next evening, at nightfall, she was walking about
the garden.   In the midst of the confused thoughts
which occupied her mind, she fancied she could distinguish now and then a noise like that of the previous night, as if some one were walking in the gloom
under the trees not far from her ; but she said to herself that nothing so resembles the sound of a footfall on grass as the grating of two branches together,

and she took no heed of it, — besides, she saw nothing.   She left the "thicket," and had a small grass-plat to cross ere she reached the house.   The moon, which had just risen behind her, projected Cosette's shadow, as she left the clump of bushes, upon the grass in front of her, and she stopped in terror. By the side of her shadow the moon distinctly traced on the grass another singularly startling and terrible shadow, — a shadow with a hat on its head.   It was like the shadow of a man standing at the edge of the clump a few paces behind Cosette.   For a moment she was unable to speak or cry, or call out, or stir, or turn her head; but at last she collected all her courage and boldly turned round.   There was nobody; she looked on the ground and the shadow had disappeared.   She went back into the shrubs, bravely searched in every corner, went as far as the railings, and discovered nothing.   She felt really chilled.   Was it again an hallucination?   What! two days in succession?   One hallucination might pass, but two! The alarming point was, that the shadow was most certainly not a ghost, for ghosts never wear round hats.

The next day Jean Valjean returned, and Cosette told him what she fancied she had seen and heard. She expected to be reassured, and that her father would shrug his shoulders and say, "You are a little goose;" but Jean Valjean became anxious.

"Perhaps it is nothing," he said to her.   He left her with some excuse, and went into the garden, where she saw him examine the railings with considerable attention.   In the night she woke up.   This

time she was certain, and she distinctly heard some
one walking just under her windows. She walked
to her shutter and opened it. There was in the garden really a man holding a large stick in his hand.
At the moment when she was going to cry out, the
moon lit up the man's face, — it was her father. She
went to bed again saying, "He seems really very
anxious!" Jean Valjean passed that and the two
following nights in the garden, and Cosette saw him
throngh the hole in her shutter. On the third night
the moon was beginning to rise later, and it might
have been about one in the morning when she heard
a hearty burst of laughter, and her father's voice
calling her : —

"Cosette ! "

She leaped out of bed, put on her dressing-gown,
and opened her window ; her father was standing on
the grass-plat below.

"I have woke you up to reassure you," he said ;
"look at this, — here 's your shadow in the round
hat."

And he showed her on the grass a shadow which
the moon designed, and which really looked rather
like the spectre of a man wearing a round hat. It
was an outline produced by a zinc chimney-pot with
a cowl, which rose above an adjoining roof. Cosette
also began laughing, all her mournful suppositions
fell away, and the next morning at breakfast she
jested at the ill-omened garden, haunted by the
ghost of chimney-pots. Jean Valjean quite regained
his ease ; as for Cosette, she did not notice particularly whether the chimney-pot were really in the

direction of the shadow which she had seen or fancied she saw, and whether the moon were in the
same part of the heavens.   She did not cross-ques-
tion herself as to the singularity of a chimney-pot
which is afraid of being caught in the act, and re-
tires when its shadow is looked at ; for the shadow
did retire when Cosette turned round, and she fancied
herself quite certain of that fact.   Cosette became
quite reassured, for the demonstration seemed to her
perfect, and the thought left her brain that there
could have been any one walking about the garden
by night.   A few days after, however, a fresh incident occurred.

CHAPTER III.

ENRICHED WITH THE COMMENTS OF TOUSSAINT.

In the garden, near the railings looking out on the street, there was a stone bench, protected from the gaze of passers-by by a hedge, but it would have been an easy task to reach it by thrusting an arm through the railings and the hedge. One evening in this same month of April, Jean Valjean had gone out, and Cosette, after sunset, was seated on this bench. The wind was freshening in the trees, and Cosette was reflecting; an objectless sorrow was gradually gaining on her, the invincible sorrow which night produces, and which comes perhaps — for who knows ? — from the mystery of the tomb which is yawning at the moment. Possibly Fantine was in that shadow.

Cosette rose, and slowly went round the garden, walking on the dew-laden grass and saying to herself through the sort of melancholy somnambulism in which she was plunged : " I ought to have wooden shoes to walk in the garden at this hour; I shall catch cold." She returned to the bench; but at the moment when she was going to sit down, she noticed at the place she had left a rather large stone, which had evidently not been there a moment before.

Cosette looked at the stone, asking herself what it meant. All at once the idea that the stone had not reached the bench of itself, that some one had placed it there, and that an arm had been passed through the grating, occurred to her and frightened her. This time it was a real fear, for there was the stone. No doubt was possible. She did not touch it, but fled without daring to look behind her, sought refuge in the house, and at once shuttered, barred, and bolted the French window opening on the steps. Then she asked Toussaint, —

" Has my father come in ? "

" No, Miss."

(We have indicated once for all Toussaint's stammering, and we ask leave no longer to accentuate it, as we feel a musical notation of an infirmity to be repulsive.)

Jean Valjean, a thoughtful man, and stroller by night, often did not return till a late hour.

" Toussaint," Cosette continued, " be careful to put up the bars to the shutters looking on the garden, and to place the little iron things in the rings that close them."

" Oh, I am sure I will, Miss."

Toussaint did not fail, and Cosette was well aware of the fact, but she could not refrain from adding, —

" For it is so desolate here."

" Well, that's true," said Toussaint ; " we might be murdered before we had the time to say, Ouf ! and then, too, master does not sleep in the house. But don't be frightened, Miss. I fasten up the windows like Bastilles. Lone women ! I should think that is enough to make a body shudder. Only think! to see men coming into your bedroom and hear them say, ' Be quiet, you ! ' and then they begin to cut your throat. It is not so much the dying, for everybody dies, and we know that we must do so ; but it is the abomination of feeling those fellows touch you ; and then their knives are not sharp, perhaps ; oh, Lord ! "

" Hold your tongue," said Cosette, " and fasten up everything securely."

Cosette, terrified by the drama improvised by Toussaint, and perhaps too by the apparitions of the last week, which returned to her mind, did not even dare to say to her, " Just go and look at the stone laid on the bench ; " for fear of having to open the garden gate again, and the men might walk in. She had all the doors and windows carefully closed, made Toussaint examine the whole house from cellar to attic, locked herself in her bedroom, looked under the bed, and slept badly. The whole night through, she saw the stone as large as a mountain and full of caverns. At sunrise — the peculiarity of sunrise is to make us laugh at all our terrors of the night, and our laughter is always proportioned to the fear we have felt — at sunrise, Cosette, on waking, saw her terror like a nightmare, and said to herself : " What could I be thinking about ! It was like the steps which I fancied I heard last week in the garden at night ! It is like the shadow of the chimney-pot. Am I going to turn coward now ? " The sun, which poured through the crevices of her shutters and made the damask curtains one mass of purple, re-assured her so fully that all faded away in her mind, even to the stone.

"There was no more a stone on the bench than there was a man in a round hat in the garden. I dreamed of the stone like the rest."

She dressed herself, went down into the garden, and felt a cold perspiration all over her, — the stone was there. But this only lasted for a moment, for what is terror by night is curiosity by day.

"Nonsense!" she said, "I'll see."

She raised the stone, which was of some size, and there was something under it that resembled a letter; it was an envelope of white paper. Cosette seized it; there was no address on it, and it was not sealed up. Still, the envelope, though open, was not empty, for papers could be seen inside. Cosette no longer suffered from terror, nor was it curiosity; it was a commencement of anxiety. Cosette took out a small quire of paper, each page of which was numbered, and bore several lines written in a very nice and delicate hand, so Cosette thought. She looked for a name, but there was none; for a signature, but there was none either. For whom was the packet intended? Probably for herself, as a hand had laid it on the bench. From whom did it come? An irresistible fascination seized upon her; she tried to turn her eyes away from these pages, which trembled in her hand. She looked at the sky, the street, the acacias all bathed in light, the pigeons circling round an adjoining roof, and then her eye settled on the manuscript, and she said to herself that she must know what was inside it. This is what she read.

CHAPTER IV.

THE reduction of the Universe to a single being, the expansion of a single being as far as God, — such is love.

Love is the salutation of the angels to the stars.

How sad the soul is when it is sad through love! What a void is the absence of the being who of her own self fills the world! Oh, how true it is that the beloved being becomes God! We might understand how God might be jealous, had not the Father of all evidently made creation for the soul, and the soul for love.

The soul only needs to see a smile in a white crape bonnet in order to enter the palace of dreams.

God is behind everything, but everything conceals God. Things are black and creatures are opaque, but to love a being is to render her transparent.

Certain thoughts are prayers. There are moments when the soul is kneeling, no matter what the attitude of the body may be.

Separated lovers cheat absence by a thousand chimerical things, which, however, have their reality. They are prevented seeing each other, and they cannot write, but they find a number of mysterious ways to correspond. They send to each other the song of birds, the light of the sun, the sighs of the breeze, the rays of the stars, and the whole of creation ; and why should they not ? All the works of God are made to serve love. Love is sufficiently powerful to interest all nature in its messages.

Oh, Spring, thou art a letter which I write to her.

The future belongs even more to hearts than to minds. Loving is the only thing which can occupy and fill the immensity, for the infinite needs the inexhaustible.

Love is a portion of the soul itself, and is of the same nature as it. Like it, it is the divine spark ; like it, it is incorruptible, indivisible, and imperishable. It is a point of fire within us, which is immortal and infinite ; which nothing can limit, and nothing extinguish. We feel it burning even in the marrow of our bones, and see its flashing in the depths of the heavens.

Oh, love ! adoration ! voluptuousness of two minds which comprehend each other, of two hearts which are exchanged, of two glances that penetrate one another ! You will come to me, oh happiness, will you not ? Lovers' walks in the solitudes, blest and radiant days ! I have dreamed that from time to time hours were detached from the lives of the angels, and came down here to traverse the destinies of men.

God can add nothing to the happiness of those who love, except giving them endless duration. After a life of love, an eternity of love is in truth an augmentation; but it is impossible even for God to increase in its intensity the ineffable felicity which love gives to the soul in this world. God is the fulness of heaven, love is the fulness of man.

You gaze at a star for two motives, because it is luminous and because it is impenetrable. You have by your side a sweeter radiance and greater mystery, — woman.

All of us, whoever we may be, have our respirable beings. If they fail us, air fails us, and we stifle and die. Dying through want of love is frightful, for it is the asphyxia of the soul.

When love has blended and moulded two beings in an angelic and sacred union, they have found the secret of life; henceforth they are only the two terms of the same destiny, the two wings of one mind. Love and soar!

On the day when a woman who passes before you emits light as she walks, you are lost, for you love. You have from that moment but one thing to do; think of her so intently that she will be compelled to think of you.

That which love begins, God alone can finish.

True love is in despair, or enchanted by a lost glove or a found handkerchief, and it requires eternity for its devotion and its hopes. It is composed at once of the infinitely great and the infinitely little.

If you are a stone, be a magnet; if you are a plant, be sensitive; if you are a man, be love.

Nothing is sufficient for love. You have happiness and you wish for Paradise. You have Paradise, and you crave for heaven. Oh, ye who love each other, all this is in love, contrive to find it there. Love has, equally with heaven, contemplation, and more than heaven, voluptuousness.

Does she still go to the Luxembourg? No, sir. — Does she attend mass in that church? She does not go there any longer. — Does she still live in this house? She has removed. — Where has she gone to live? She did not leave her address.

What a gloomy thing it is not to know where to find one's soul.

Love has its childishness, and other passions have their littleness. Shame on the passions that make a man little! Honor to the one that makes him a child!

It is a strange thing, are you aware of it? I am in the night. There is a being who vanished and took heaven with her.

Oh! to lie side by side in the same tomb, hand in hand, and to gently caress a finger from time to time in the darkness, would suffice for my eternity.

You who suffer because you love, love more than ever. To die of love is to live through it.

Love, a gloomy starry transfiguration, is mingled with this punishment, and there is ecstasy in the agony.

Oh, joy of birds! they sing because they have the nest.

Love is the celestial breathing of the atmosphere of Paradise.

Profound hearts, wise minds, take life as God makes it; it is a long trial, an unintelligible preparation for the unknown destiny. This destiny, the true one, begins for man with the first step in the interior of the tomb. Then something appears to him, and he begins to distinguish the definite. The definite, reflect on that word. The living see the infinite, but the definite only shows itself to the dead. In the mean while, love and suffer, hope and contemplate. Woe, alas, to the man who has only loved bodies, shapes, and appearances! Death will strip him of all that. Try to love souls, and you will meet them again.

I have met in the street a very poor young man who was in love. His hat was old, his coat worn, the elbows in holes ; the water passed through his shoes, and the stars through his soul.

What a grand thing it is to be loved ! What a grander thing still to love ! The heart becomes heroic by the might of passion. Henceforth it is composed of nought but what is pure, and is only supported by what is elevated and great. An unworthy thought can no more germinate in it than a nettle on a glacier. The lofty and serene soul, inaccessible to emotions and vulgar passions, soaring above the clouds and shadows of the world, — follies, falsehoods, hatreds, vanities, and miseries,— dwells in the azure of the sky, and henceforth only feels the profound and subterranean heavings of destiny as the summit of the mountains feels earthquakes.

If there were nobody who loved, the sun would be extinguished.

CHAPTER V.

WHILE reading these lines Cosette gradually fell into a reverie, and at the moment when she raised her eyes from the last page the handsome officer passed triumphantly in front of the gate ; for it was his hour. Cosette found him hideous. She began gazing at the roll of paper again ; it was in an exquisite hand-writing, Cosette thought, all written by the same hand, but with different inks, some very black, others pale, as when ink is put in the stand, and consequently on different days. It was, therefore, a thought expanded on the paper, sigh by sigh, irregularly, without order, without choice, without purpose, accidentally. Cosette had never read anything like it ; this manuscript, in which she saw more light than obscurity, produced on her the effect of the door of a shrine left ajar. Each of these mysterious lines flashed in her eyes, and flooded her heart with a strange light. The education which she had received had always spoken to her of the soul, and not of love, much as if a person were to speak of the burning log and say nothing about the flame. This manuscript of fifteen pages suddenly and gently revealed to her the whole of love, sorrow, destiny, life, eternity, the beginning and the end. It was like a hand which opened and threw upon her a galaxy of beams. She felt in these lines an impassioned, ardent, generous, and honest nature, a sacred will, an immense grief and an immense hope, a contracted heart, and an expanded ecstasy. What was the manuscript? A letter. A letter without address, name, or signature, pressing and disinterested, an enigma composed of truths, a love-message fit to be borne by an angel and read by a virgin; a rendezvous appointed off the world, a sweet love-letter written by a phantom to a shadow. It was a tranquil and crushed absent man, who seemed ready to seek a refuge in death, and who sent to his absent love the secret of destiny, the key of life. It had been written with one foot in the grave and the hand in heaven, and these lines, which had fallen one by one on the paper, were what might be called drops of the soul.

And now, from whom could these pages come? Who could have written them? Cosette did not hesitate for a moment, — only from one man, from *him!* Daylight had returned to her mind and everything reappeared. She experienced an extraordinary joy and a profound agony. It was he! He who wrote to her; he had been there; his arm had been passed through the railings! While she was forgetting him he had found her again! But had she forgotten him? No, never! she was mad to have thought so for a moment; for she had ever loved, ever adored him. The fire was covered, and had smouldered for a while, but, as she now plainly saw, it had spread its ravages, and again burst into a flame which entirely kindled her. This letter was like a spark that had fallen from the other soul into hers; she felt the fire begin again, and she was penetrated by every word of the manuscript. "Oh, yes," she said to herself, "how well I recognize all this! I had read it all already in his eyes."

As she finished reading it for the third time, Lieutenant Théodule returned past the railings, and clanked his spurs on the pavement. Cosette was obliged to raise her eyes, and she found him insipid, silly, stupid, useless, fatuous, displeasing, impertinent, and very ugly. The officer thought himself bound to smile, and she turned away ashamed and indignant; she would have gladly thrown something at his head. She ran away, re-entered the house, and locked herself in her bedroom, to re-read the letter, learn it by heart, and dream. When she had read it thoroughly, she kissed it and hid it in her bosom. It was all over. Cosette had fallen back into the profound seraphic love; the Paradisaic abyss had opened again. The whole day through, Cosette was in a state of bewilderment; she hardly thought, and her ideas were confused in her brain; she could not succeed in forming any conjectures, and she hoped through a tremor, what? Vague things. She did not dare promise herself anything, and she would not refuse herself anything. A pallor passed over her face, and a quiver over her limbs; and she fancied at moments that it was all a chimera, and said to herself, "Is it real?" Then she felt the well-beloved paper under her dress, pressed it to her heart, felt the corners against her flesh, and if Jean Valjean had

seen her at that moment he would have shuddered
at the luminous and strange joy which overflowed
from her eyelids.   " Oh, yes," she thought, " it is certainly his ! This comes from him for me ! "   And she
said to herself that an intervention of the angels, a
celestial accident, had restored him to her.   Oh, transfiguration of love ! oh, dreams ! this celestial accident,
this intervention of angels, was the ball of bread cast
by one robber to another from the Charlemagne yard
to the Lions' den, over the buildings of La Force.

CHAPTER VI.

THE OLD PEOPLE ARE OPPORTUNELY OBLIGED TO GO OUT.

WHEN night came Jean Valjean went out, and Cosette dressed herself. She arranged her hair in the way that best became her, and put on a dress whose body, being cut a little too low, displayed the whole of the neck, and was therefore, as girls say, " rather indecent." It was not the least in the world indecent, but it was prettier than the former fashion. She dressed herself in this way without knowing why. Was she going out ? No. Did she expect a visitor ? No. She went down into the garden as it grew dark ; Toussaint was engaged in her kitchen, which looked out on the back-yard. Cosette began walking under the branches, removing them from time to time with her hand, as some were very low, and thus reached the bench. The stone was still there, and she sat down and laid her beautiful white hand on the stone, as if to caress and thank it. All at once she had that indescribable feeling which people experience even without seeing, when some one is standing behind them. She turned her head and rose, — it was he. He was bareheaded, and seemed pale and thin, and his black clothes could scarcely be distinguished. The twilight rendered his glorious forehead livid, and covered his eyes with darkness; and he had, beneath a veil of incomparable gentleness, something belonging to death and night. His face was lit up by the flush of departing day, and by the thoughts of an expiring soul. He seemed as if he were not yet a spectre, but was no longer a man. His hat was thrown among the shrubs a few paces from him. Cosette, though ready to faint, did not utter a cry; she slowly recoiled, as she felt herself attracted, but he did not stir. Through the ineffable sadness that enveloped him she felt the glance of the eyes which she could not see. Cosette, in recoiling, came to a tree, and leaned against it; had it not been for this tree she would have fallen. Then she heard his voice, that voice which she had really never heard before, scarce louder than the rustling of the foliage, as he murmured, —

"Pardon me for being here; my heart is swollen. I could not live as I was, and I have come. Have you read what I placed on that bench? Do you recognize me at all? Do not be frightened at me. Do you remember that day when you looked at me, now so long ago? It was in the Luxembourg garden near the Gladiator, and the days on which you passed before me were June 16 and July 2; it is nearly a year ago. I have not seen you again for a very long time. I inquired of the woman who lets out chairs, and she said that you no longer came there. You lived in the Rue de l'Ouest on the third-floor front of a new house. You see that I know. I followed you, what else could I do? And then you disappeared. I fancied that I saw you pass once as

I was reading the papers under the Odéon Arcade, and ran after you, but no, it was a person wearing a bonnet like yours. At night I come here — fear nothing, no one sees me. I come to gaze and be near your windows, and I walk very softly that you may not hear me, for you might be alarmed. The other evening I was behind you; you turned round, and I fled. Once I heard you sing; I was happy. Does it harm you that I should listen to you through the shutters while singing? No, it cannot harm you. You see, you are my angel, so let me come now and then. I believe that I am going to die. If you only knew how I adore you! Forgive me for speaking to you. I know not what I am saying, perhaps I offend you — do I offend you? — "

" Oh, my mother! " said she.

And she sank down as if she were dying. He seized her in his arms and pressed her to his heart, not knowing what he did. Though reeling himself, he supported her. He felt as if his head were full of smoke ; flashes passed between his eye-lashes. His ideas left him ; and it seemed to him as if he were accomplishing a religious act, and yet committing a profanation. However, he had not the least desire for this ravishing creature, whose form he felt against his bosom ; he was distractedly in love. She took his hand, and laid it on her heart ; he felt the paper there, and stammered, —

" You love me, then ? "

She answered in so low a voice that it was almost an inaudible breath, —

" Silence ! you know I do."

And she hid her blushing face in the bosom of the proud and intoxicated young man. He fell on to the bench, and she by his side. They no longer found words, and the stars were beginning to twinkle. How came it that their lips met? How comes it that the bird sings, the snow melts, the rose opens, May bursts into life, and the dawn grows white behind the black trees on the rustling tops of the hills? One kiss, and that was all. Both trembled and gazed at each other in the darkness with flashing eyes. They neither felt the fresh night nor the cold stone, nor the damp grass, nor the moist soil, — they looked at each other, and their hearts were full of thought. Their hands were clasped without their cognizance. She did not ask him, did not even think of it, how he had managed to enter the garden; for it seemed to her so simple that he should be there. From time to time Marius's knee touched Cosette's knee, and both quivered. At intervals Cosette stammered a word; her soul trembled on her lips like the dewdrop on a flower.

Gradually they conversed, and expansiveness succeeded the silence which is plenitude. The night was serene and splendid above their heads, and these two beings, pure as spirits, told each other everything, — their dreams, their intoxication, their ecstasy, their chimeras, their depressions, how they had adored and longed for each other at a distance, and their mutual despair when they ceased to meet. They confided to each other in an ideal intimacy, which nothing henceforth could increase, all their most hidden and mysterious thoughts. They told each other, with a candid faith in their illusions, all that love, youth, and the remnant of childhood which they still had, brought to their minds. Their two hearts were poured into each other; so that at the end of an hour the young man had the maiden's soul and the maiden his. They were mutually penetrated, enchanted, and dazzled. When they had finished, when they had told each other everything, she laid her head on his shoulder and asked him, —

"What is your name?"

"Marius," he said; "and yours?"

"Mine is Cosette."

BOOK VI.

LITTLE GAVROCHE.

CHAPTER I.

A MALICIOUS TRICK OF THE WIND.

SINCE 1823, while the public-house at Montfermeil was sinking and gradually being swallowed up, not in the abyss of a bankruptcy, but in the sewer of small debts, the Thénardiers had had two more children, both male. These made five, two daughters and three boys, and they were a good many. The mother had got rid of the latter while still babies by a singular piece of good luck. Got rid of, that is exactly the term, for in this woman there was only a fragment of nature; it is a phenomenon, however, of which there is more than one instance. Like the Maréchale de Lamothe-Houdancourt, the Thénardier was only a mother as far as her daughters, and her maternity ended there. Her hatred of the human race began with her boys; on the side of her sons her cruelty was perpendicular, and her heart had in this respect a dismal steepness. As we have seen, she detested the eldest, and execrated the two others. Why? Because she did. The most terrible of motives and most indisputable of answers is, Because. " I do not want a pack of squalling brats," this mother said.

Let us now explain how the Thénardiers managed to dispose of their last two children, and even make a profit of them. That Magnon, to whom we referred a few pages back, was the same who continued to get an annuity out of old Gillenormand for the two children she had. She lived on the Quai des Célestins, at the corner of that ancient Rue du Petit-Musc, which has done all it could to change its bad reputation into a good odor. Our readers will remember the great croup epidemic, which, thirty-five years ago, desolated the banks of the Seine in Paris, and of which science took advantage to make experiments on a grand scale as to the efficacy of inhaling alum, for which the external application of tincture of iodine has been so usefully substituted in our day. In this epidemic Magnon lost her two boys, still very young, on the same day, one in the morning, the other in the evening. It was a blow, for these children were precious to their mother, as they represented eighty francs a month. These eighty francs were very punctually paid by the receiver of M. Gillenormand's rents, a M. Barge, a retired bailiff who lived in the Rue de Sicile. When the children were dead the annuity was buried, and so Magnon sought an expedient. In the dark free-masonry of evil of which she formed part everything is known, secrets are kept, and people help each other. Magnon wanted two children, and Madame Thénardier had two of the same size and age ; it was a good arrangement for one, and an excellent investment for the other. The little Thénardiers became the little Magnons, and Magnon left the Quai des Célestins, and went to live in the Rue Cloche-Perce. In Paris the identity which attaches an individual to himself is broken by moving from one street to the others. The authorities, not being warned by anything, made no objections, and the substitution was effected in the simplest way in the world. Thénardier, however, demanded for this loan of children ten francs a month, which Magnon promised, and even paid. We need not say that M. Gillenormand continued to sacrifice himself, and went every six months to see the children. He did not notice the change. "Oh, sir," Magnon would say to him, "how like you they are, to be sure."

Thénardier, to whom avatars were an easy task, seized this opportunity to become Jondrette. His two daughters and Gavroche had scarcely had time to perceive that they had two little brothers; for in a certain stage of misery people are affected by a sort of spectral indifference, and regard human beings as ghosts. Your nearest relatives are often to you no more than vague forms of the shadow, hardly to be distinguished from the nebulous back-ground of life, and which easily become blended again with the invisible. On the evening of the day when Mother Thénardier handed over her two babes to Magnon, with the well-expressed will of renouncing them forever, she felt, or pretended to feel, a scruple, and said to her husband, "Why, that is deserting one's children!" But Thénardier, magisterial and phlegmatic, cauterized the scruple with this remark, "Jean Jacques Rousseau did better." From scruple the mother passed to anxiety: "But suppose the police were to trouble us? Tell me, Monsieur Thénardier, whether what we have done is permitted?" Thénardier replied: "Everything is permitted. Nobody will see through it out of the blue. Besides, no one has any interest in inquiring closely after children that have not a sou." Magnon was a sort of she-dandy in crime, and dressed handsomely. She shared her rooms, which were furnished in a conventional and miserable way, with a very clever Gallicized English thief. This Englishwoman, a naturalized Parisian, respectable through her powerful and rich connections, who was closely connected with medals of the library and the diamonds of Mademoiselle Mars, was at a later date celebrated in the annals of crime. She was called "Mamselle Miss." The two little ones who had fallen into Magnon's clutches had no cause to complain; recommended by the eighty francs, they were taken care of, like everything which brings in a profit. They were not badly clothed, not badly fed, treated almost like "little gentlemen," and better off with their false mother than the true one. Magnon acted the lady, and never talked slang in their presence. They spent several years there, and Thénardier augured well of it. One day he happened to say to Magnon as she handed him the monthly ten francs, "The 'father' must give them an education."

All at once these two poor little creatures, hitherto tolerably well protected, even by their evil destiny,

were suddenly hurled into life, and forced to begin
it.   An arrest of criminals *en masse*, like that in
the Jondrette garret, being necessarily complicated
with researches and ulterior incarcerations, is a ver-
itable disaster for that hideous and occult counter-
society which lives beneath public society ; and an
adventure of this nature produces all sorts of convulsions in this gloomy world.   The catastrophe of
the Thénardiers was the catastrophe of Magnon.
One day, a little while after Magnon had given
Éponine the note relating to the Rue Plumet, the
police made a sudden descent on the Rue Cloche-
Perce.   Magnon was arrested, as was Mamselle
Miss, and all the inhabitants of the house which
were suspected were caught in the haul.   The two
little boys were playing at the time in the back-yard,
and saw nothing of the raid ; but when they tried to
go in they found the door locked and the house
empty.   A cobbler whose stall was opposite called
to them and gave them a paper which "their mother"
had left for them.   On the paper was this address,
" M. Barge, receiver of rents, No. 8, Rue du Roi de
Sicile."   The cobbler said to them :   "You no longer
live here.   Go there, it is close by, the first street on
your left.   Ask your way with that paper."   The
boys set off, the elder leading the younger, and holding in his hand the paper which was to serve as their
guide.   It was cold, and his little numbed fingers
held the paper badly, and at the corner of a lane a
puff of wind tore it from him ; and as it was night the
boy could not find it again.   They began wandering
about the streets haphazard.

CHAPTER II.

SPRING in Paris is very frequently traversed by
sharp, violent breezes which, if they do not freeze,
chill. These breezes, which sadden the brightest
days, produce exactly the same effect as the blasts
of cold wind which enter a warm room through the
crevices of a badly closed door or window. It seems
as if the gloomy gate of winter has been left ajar,
and that the wind comes from there. In the spring
of 1832, the period when the first great epidemic of
this century broke out in Europe, these breezes were
sharper and more cutting than ever, and some door
even more icy than that of winter had been left
ajar. It was the door of the sepulchre, and the
breath of cholera could be felt in these breezes.
From a meteorological point of view these cold
winds had the peculiarity that they did not exclude
a powerful electric tension. Frequent storms, accompanied by thunder and lightning, broke out at
this period.

One evening, when these breezes were blowing
sharply, so sharply that January seemed to have
returned, and the citizens had put on their cloaks
again, little Gavroche, still shivering gayly under his

rags, was standing as if in ecstasy in front of a hair-
dresser's shop in the vicinity of the Orme-Saint
Gervais. He was adorned with a woman's woollen
shawl, picked up no one knew where, of which he
had made a muffler. Little Gavroche appeared to
be lost in admiration of a waxen image of a bride,
wearing a very low-necked dress, and a wreath of
orange-flowers in her hair, which revolved between
two lamps, and lavished its smiles on the passers-by ;
but in reality he was watching the shop to see
whether he could not " prig " a cake of soap, which
he would afterwards sell for a sou to a barber in
the suburbs. He frequently breakfasted on one of
these cakes, and he called this style of work, for
which he had a talent, "shaving the barbers." While
regarding the bride, and casting sheep's eyes on the
cake of soap, he growled between his teeth : " Tuesday ; this is not Tuesday. Is it Tuesday ? Perhaps
it is Tuesday ; yes, it is Tuesday." What this
soliloquy referred to was never known ; but if it
was to the last time he had dined, it was three days
ago, for the present day was a Friday. The barber,
in his shop warmed with a good stove, was shaving
a customer and taking every now and then a side-
glance at this enemy, — this shivering and impudent
gamin who had his two hands in his pockets, but
his mind evidently elsewhere.

While Gavroche was examining the bride, the
window, and the Windsor soap, two boys of unequal
height, very decently dressed, and younger than himself, one apparently seven, the other five years of
age, timidly turned the handle and entered the shop,

asking for something, charity possibly, in a plaintive murmur which was more like a sob than a prayer. They both spoke together, and their words were unintelligible, because sobs choked the voice of the younger boy, and cold made the teeth of the elder rattle. The barber turned with a furious face, and without laying down his razor drove the older boy into the street with his left hand, and the little one with his knee, and closed the door again, saying, —

"To come and chill people for nothing!"

The two lads set out again, crying. A cloud had come up in the mean while, and it began raining. Little Gavroche ran up to them, and accosted them thus, —

"What's the matter with you, brats?"

"We don't know where to sleep," the elder replied.

"Is that all?" said Gavroche; "that's a great thing. Is that anything to cry about, simpletons?" And assuming an accent of tender affection and gentle protection, which was visible through his somewhat pompous superiority, he said, —

"Come with me, kids."

"Yes, sir," said the elder boy.

And the two children followed him as they would have done an archbishop, and left off crying. Gavroche led them along the Rue St. Antoine, in the direction of the Bastille, and while going off took an indignant and retrospective glance at the barber's shop.

"That whiting has no heart," he growled; "he's an Englishman."

A girl, seeing the three walking in file, Gavroche at the head, burst into a loud laugh. This laugh was disrespectful to the party.

"Good day, Mamselle Omnibus," Gavroche said to her.

A moment after the hair-dresser returning to his mind, he added, —

"I made a mistake about the brute; he is not a whiting, but a snake. Barber, I'll go and fetch a locksmith, and order him to put a bell on your tail."

This barber had made him aggressive; as he stepped across a gutter, he addressed a bearded porteress, worthy to meet Faust on the Brocken, and who was holding her broom in her hand, —

"Madame," he said to her, "I see that you go out with your horse."

And after this he plashed the varnished boots of a passer-by.

"Scoundrel!" the gentleman said furiously. Gavroche raised his nose out of the shawl.

"Have you a complaint to make, sir?"

"Yes, of you," said the gentleman.

"The office is closed," Gavroche remarked. "I don't receive any more complaints to-day."

As he went along the street he noticed a girl of thirteen or fourteen, shivering in a gateway, in such short petticoats that she showed her knees. But the little girl was beginning to get too tall a girl for that. Growth plays you such tricks, and the petticoat becomes short the moment that nudity becomes indecent.

" Poor girl," said Gavroche, " she has n't even a pair of breeches. Here, collar this."

And taking off all the good wool which he had round his neck he threw it over the thin violet shoulders of the beggar-girl, when the muffler became once again a shawl. The little girl looked at him with an astonished air, and received the shawl in silence. At a certain stage of distress a poor man in his stupor no longer groans at evil, and gives no thanks for kindness. This done, —

"B-r-r!" said Gavroche, colder than Saint Martin, who, at any rate, retained one half his cloak. On hearing this " Brr," the shower, redoubling its passion, poured down; those wicked skies punish good actions.

" Hilloh ! " Gavroche shouted, " what 's the meaning of this ? It is raining again. Bon Dieu ! if this goes on, I shall withdraw my subscription."

And he set out again.

" No matter," he said as he took a glance at the beggar-girl crouching under her shawl, " she 's got a first-rate skin."

And, looking at the clouds, he cried, — " Sold you are ! "

The two children limped after him, and as they passed one of those thick close gratings which indicate a baker's, for bread, like gold, is placed behind a grating, Gavroche turned round.

" By the bye, brats, have you dined ? "

" We have had nothing to eat, sir, since early this morning," the elder answered.

" Then you have n't either father or mother ? " Gavroche continued magisterially.

" I beg your pardon, sir ; we have a pa and a ma, but we don't know where they are."

" Sometimes that is better than knowing," said Gavroche, who was a philosopher in his small way.

" We have been walking about for two hours," the lad continued, " and looked for things at the corners of the streets, but found nothing."

" I know," said Gavroche ; " the dogs eat everything."

He resumed after a pause, —

" And so we have lost our authors. We don't know what we have done with them. That is n't right, gamins. It is foolish to mislay grown-up people. Well, one must swig, for all that."

He did not ask them any more questions, for what could be more simple than to have no domicile ? The elder of the boys, who had almost entirely recovered the happy carelessness of childhood, made this remark : " It is funny all the same. Mamma said she would take us to look for blessed box, on Palm Sunday. Mamma is a lady who lives with Mamselle Miss."

" Tanflute ! " added Gavroche.

He stopped, and for some minutes searched all sorts of corners which he had in his rags : at length he raised his head with an air which only meant to represent satisfaction, but which was in reality triumphant, —

" Calm yourselves, kids ; here is supper for three."

And he drew a sou from one of his pockets ; without giving the lads time to feel amazed, he pushed

them both before him into the baker's shop, and laid
his sou on the counter, exclaiming, —

"Garçon, five centimes' worth of bread."

The baker, who was the master in person, took up
a loaf and a knife.

"In three pieces, garçon," remarked Gavroche,
and he added with dignity, —

"We are three."

And seeing that the baker, after examining the
three suppers, had taken a loaf of black bread, he
thrust his finger into his nose, with as imperious a
sniff as if he had the great Frederick's pinch of snuff
on his thumb, and cast in the baker's face this indignant remark, —

"Keksekça ? "

Those of our readers who might be tempted to see
in this remark of Gavroche's to the baker a Russian
or Polish word, or one of the savage cries which the
Ioways or the Botocudos hurl at each other across
the deserted streams, are warned that this is a word
which they (our readers) employ daily, and which
signifies, *qu'est ce que c'est que cela?* The baker
perfectly comprehended, and replied, —

"Why, it is bread, very good seconds bread."

"You mean black bread," Gavroche remarked, with
a calm and cold disdain.   "White bread, my lad; I
stand treat."

The baker could not refrain from smiling, and
while cutting some white bread gazed at them in a
compassionate way which offended Gavroche.

"Well, baker's man," he said, "what is there about
us that you measure us in that way? "

When the bread was cut, the baker put the sou in the till, and Gavroche said to the two boys, —

" Grub away."

The boys looked at him in surprise, and Gavroche burst into a laugh.

" Oh, yes, that's true, they don't understand yet, they are so little."

And he continued, " Eat."

At the same time he gave each of them a lump of bread. Thinking that the elder, who appeared to him more worthy of his conversation, merited some special encouragement, and ought to have any hesitation about satisfying his hunger removed, he added, as he gave him the larger lump, —

" Shove that into your gun."

There was one piece smaller than the two others, and he took that for himself. The poor boys, Gavroche included, were starving; while tearing the bread with their teeth, they blocked up the baker's shop, who, now that he was paid, looked at them angrily.

" Let us return to the street," said Gavroche.

They started again in the direction of the Bastille; and from time to time as they passed lighted shops, the younger boy stopped to see what o'clock it was by a leaden watch hung round his neck by a string.

" Well, he is a great fool," said Gavroche.

Then he thoughtfully growled between his teeth, " No matter, if I had kids of my own I would take more care of them than that."

As they were finishing their bread, they reached the corner of that gloomy Rue de Ballet at the end of which the low and hostile wicket of La Force is visible.

"Hilloh, is that you, Gavroche?" some one said.

"Hilloh, is that you, Montparnasse?" said Gavroche.

It was a man who accosted Gavroche, no other than Montparnasse disguised with blue spectacles, but Gavroche was able to recognize him.

"My eye!" Gavroche went on, "you have a skin of the color of a linseed poultice and blue spectacles like a doctor. That's your style, on the word of an old man!"

"Silence," said Montparnasse, "not so loud;" and he quickly dragged Gavroche out of the light of the shops. The two little boys followed mechanically, holding each other by the hand. When they were under the black arch of a gateway, protected from eyes and rain, Montparnasse remarked, —

"Do you know where I am going?"

"To the abbey of Go-up-with-regret" (the scaffold), said Gavroche.

"Joker!"

And Montparnasse added, —

"I am going to meet Babet."

"Ah!" said Gavroche, "her name is Babet, is it?"

Montparnasse lowered his voice, —

"It is not a she, but a he."

"I thought he was buckled up."

"He has unfastened the buckle," Montparnasse replied.

And he hurriedly told the boy that on that very morning Babet, while being removed to the Conciergerie, escaped by turning to the left instead of the right in the " police-office passage."

Gavroche admired his skill.

" What a dentist ! " said he.

Montparnasse added a few details about Babet's escape, and ended with, " Oh, that is not all."

Gavroche, while talking, had seized a cane which Montparnasse held in his hand; he mechanically pulled at the upper part, and a dagger blade became visible.

" Ah ! " he said as he quickly thrust it back, " you have brought your gendarme with you disguised as a civilian."

Montparnasse winked.

" The deuce ! " Gavroche continued, "are you going to have a fight with some one ? "

" There 's no knowing," Montparnasse answered carelessly; " it 's always as well to have a pin about you."

Gavroche pressed him.

" What are you going to do to-night ? "

Montparnasse again became serious, and said, mincing his words, —

" Some things."

And he suddenly changed the conversation.

" By the bye — "

" What ? "

" Something that happened the other day. Just fancy. I meet a bourgeois, and he makes me a present of a sermon, and a purse. I put it in my pocket, a moment later I feel for it, and there was nothing there."

" Only the sermon," said Gavroche.

" But where are you going now ? "   Montparnasse continued.

Gavroche pointed to his two protégés, and said, —

" I am going to put these two children to bed."

" Where ? "

" At my house."

" Have you a lodging ? "

" Yes."

" Where ? "

" Inside the elephant," said Gavroche.

Montparnasse, though naturally not easy to astonish, could not refrain from the exclamation, —

" Inside the elephant ? "

" Well, yes, kekçaa ? "

This is another word belonging to the language which nobody reads and everybody speaks ; kekçaa signifies, *qu'est-ce-que cela a ?*   The gamin's profound remark brought Montparnasse back to calmness and good sense : he seemed to entertain a better opinion of Gavroche's lodgings.

" Ah, yes," he said, " the ' elephant.'   Are you comfortable there ? "

" Very," Gavroche replied.   " Most comfortable. There are no draughts as there are under the bridges."

" How do you get in ?   Is there a hole ? "

" Of course there is, but you have no need to mention it ; it 's between the front legs, and the police-spies don't know it."

" And you climb in ?   yes, I understand."

" A turn of the hand, cric crac, it 's done ; and there 's no one to be seen."

After a pause Gavroche added, —

" I shall have a ladder for these young ones."

Montparnasse burst into a laugh.

" Where the devil did you pick up those kids ? "

" A barber made me a present of them."

In the mean while Montparnasse had become pensive.

" You recognized me very easily," he said.

He took from his pocket two small objects, which were quills wrapped in cotton, and thrust one into each nostril ; they made him quite a different nose.

" That changes you," said Gavroche ; " you are not so ugly now, and you ought to keep them in for good."

Montparnasse was a handsome fellow, but Gavroche was fond of a joke.

" Without any humbug," Montparnasse asked ; " what do you think of me now ? "

It was also a different sound of voice : in a second Montparnasse had become unrecognizable.

" Oh ! play Porrichinelle for us ! " Gavroche exclaimed.

The two lads, who had heard nothing up to this moment, engaged as they were themselves in thrusting their fingers up their noses, drew nearer on hearing this name, and gazed at Montparnasse with a beginning of joy and admiration. Unhappily Montparnasse was in no humor for jesting ; he laid his hand on Gavroche's shoulder, and said, with a stress on each word, —

" Listen to what I tell you, boy ; if I were on the spot, with my dog, my knife, and my wife, and you were to offer me ten double sous I would not refuse to work, but we are not at Mardi Gras." [1]

This strange sentence produced a singular effect on the gamin; he turned around sharply, looked with his little bright eyes all around, and noticed a few yards off a policeman with his back turned to them. Gavroche let an " all-right " slip from him, which he at once repressed, and shook Montparnasse's hand.

"Well, good-night," he said; " I am off to my elephant with my brats. Should you happen to want me any night you'll find me there. I lodge in the *entresol*, and there's no porter; ask for Monsieur Gavroche."

" All right," said Montparnasse.

And they parted, Montparnasse going toward the Grève, and Gavroche toward the Bastille. The youngest boy, dragged on by his brother, whom Gavroche dragged along in his turn, looked round several times to watch " Porrichinelle " go away.

The enigmatical sentence by which Montparnasse informed Gavroche of the presence of the policeman contained no other talisman but the sound *dig* repeated five or six times under various forms. This syllable, not pronounced separately, but artistically mingled with the words of a sentence, means, " Take care, we cannot speak freely." There was also in Montparnasse's remark a literary beauty which escaped Gavroche's notice, that is, *mon dogue, ma*

---

[1] Écoute ce que je te dis, garçon, si j'étais sur la place, avec mon dogue, ma dague, et ma digue, et si vous me prodiguiez dix gros sous, je ne refuserais pas d'y goupiner, mais nous ne sommes pas le Mardi Gras.

dague, et ma digue, — a phrase of the Temple slang
greatly in use among the merry-andrews and queues
rouges of the great age in which Molière wrote and
Callot designed.

Twenty years back there might have been seen in
the southeastern corner of the square of the Bastille
near the canal dock, dug in the old moat of the
citadel-prison, a quaint monument, which has already
been effaced from the memory of Parisians, and
which should have left some trace, as it was an idea
of the "Member of the Institute, Commander-in-
Chief of the army of Egypt." We say monument,
though it was only a plaster cast; but this cast itself,
a prodigious sketch, the grand corpse of a Napoleonic
idea which two or three successive puffs of wind
carried away each time farther from us, had become
historic, and assumed something definitive, which
formed a contrast with its temporary appearance.
It was an elephant, forty feet high, constructed of
carpentry and masonry, bearing on its back a castle
which resembled a house, once painted green by
some plasterer, and now painted black by the heavens, the rain, and time. In this deserted and uncovered corner of the square the wide forehead of
the colossus, its trunk, its tusks, its castle, its enormous back, and its four feet like columns, produced
at night upon the starlit sky a surprising and terrible
outline. No one knew what it meant, and it seemed
a sort of symbol of the popular strength. It was
gloomy, enigmatical, and immense; it looked like a
powerful phantom visible and erect by the side of
the invisible spectre of the Bastille. Few strangers

visited this edifice, and no passer-by looked at it. It was falling in ruins, and each season plaster becoming detached from its flanks, made horrible wounds upon it. The "Édiles," as they were called in the fashionable slang, had forgotten it since 1814. It stood there in its corner, gloomy, sickly, crumbling away, surrounded by rotting palings, which were sullied every moment by drunken drivers. There were yawning cracks in its stomach, a lath issued from its tail, and tall grass grew between its legs; and as the level of the square had risen during the last thirty years through that slow and continuous movement which insensibly elevates the soil of great cities, it was in a hollow, and it seemed as if the earth were giving way beneath it. It was unclean, despised, repulsive, and superb; ugly in the eyes of cits, but melancholy in the eyes of the thinker. It had something about it of the ordure which is swept away, and something of the majesty which is decapitated.

As we said, at night its appearance changed; for night is the real medium of everything which is shadow. So soon as twilight set in the old elephant was transfigured; and it assumed a placid and re-doubtable appearance in the formidable serenity of the darkness. As it belonged to the past it belonged to night, and this obscurity suited its grandeur. This monument, rude, broad, heavy, rough, austere, and almost shapeless, but most assuredly majestic, and imprinted with a species of magnificent and savage gravity, has disappeared to allow the sort of gigantic stove adorned with its pipe to reign in peace, which was substituted for the frowning fortalice with its nine towers much in the same way as the bourgeoisie are substituted for feudalism. It is very simple that a stove should be the symbol of an epoch in which a copper contains the power. This period will pass away; it is already passing away. People are beginning to understand that if there may be strength in a boiler there can only be power in a brain; in other words, that what leads and carries away the world is not locomotives, but ideas. Attach locomotives to ideas, and then it is all right; but do not take the horse for the rider.

However this may be, to return to the Bastille square, the architect of the elephant managed to produce something grand with plaster, while the architect of the stove-pipe has succeeded in making something little out of bronze. This stove-pipe, which was christened a sonorous name and called the Column of July, this spoiled monument of an abortive revolution, was still wrapped up, in 1832, in an immense sheet of carpentry-work, — which we regret for our part, — and a vast enclosure of planks, which completed the isolation of the elephant. It was to this corner of this square, which was scarce lighted by the reflection of a distant oil-lamp, that the gamin led the two urchins.

(Allow us to interrupt our narrative here, and remind our readers that we are recording the simple truth ; and that twenty years ago a boy, who was caught sleeping in the inside of the elephant of the Bastille, was brought before the police on the charge of vagabondage and breaking a public monument.)

On coming near the colossus, Gavroche understood the effect which the infinitely great may produce on the infinitely little, and said, —

"Don't be frightened, brats."

Then he went through a hole in the palings into the ground round the elephant, and helped the children to pass through the breach. The lads, a little frightened, followed Gavroche without a word, and confided in this little Providence in rags who had given them bread and promised them a bed. A ladder, employed by workmen at the column by day, was lying along the palings; Gavroche raised it with singular vigor, and placed it against one of the elephant's fore legs. At the point where the ladder ended, a sort of black hole could be distinguished in the belly of the colossus. Gavroche pointed out the ladder and the hole to his guests, and said, "Go up, and go in." The two little boys looked at each other in terror.

"You are frightened, kids!" Gavroche exclaimed, and added, "you shall see."

He clung round the elephant's wrinkled foot, and in a twinkling, without deigning to employ the ladder, he reached the hole. He went in like a lizard gliding into a crevice, and a moment after the boys saw his head vaguely appear, like a white livid form, on the edge of the hole, which was full of darkness.

"Well," he cried, "come up, my blessed babes. You will see how snug it is. Come up, you," he said to the elder. "I will hold your hand."

The little boys nudged each other, for the gamin at once frightened and reassured them; and then it

was raining very hard. The elder boy ventured, and
the younger, on seeing his brother ascending and
himself left alone between the feet of this great
beast, felt greatly inclined to cry, but did not dare.
The elder climbed up the rungs of the ladder in
a very tottering way, and as he did so Gavroche
encouraged him by exclamations of a fencing-master
to his pupils, or of a muleteer to his mules.

" Don't be frightened ! That is it — keep on moving ; set your foot there ; now, your hand here —
bravo ! "

And when he was within reach he quickly and
powerfully seized him by the arm, and drew him
to him.

" Swallowed ! " he said.

The boy had passed through the crevice.

" Now," said Gavroche, " wait for me. Pray sit
down, sir."

And leaving the hole in the same way as he had
entered it, he slid down the elephant's leg with the
agility of a monkey, fell on his feet in the grass,
seized the youngest boy round the waist and planted
him on the middle of the ladder ; then he began
ascending behind him, shouting to the elder boy, —

" I 'll push him and you 'll pull him."

In a second the little fellow was pushed up,
dragged, pulled, and drawn through the hole before
he knew where he was ; and Gavroche, entering after
him, kicked away the ladder, which fell in the grass,
and clapped his hands as he shouted, " There we
are ! Long live General Lafayette ! " This explosion
over, he added, " Brats, you are in my house."

Gavroche was, in fact, at home. Oh, unexpected utility of the useless! Oh, charity of great things! Oh, goodness of the giants! This huge monument, which had contained a thought of the Emperor, had become the lodging of a gamin. The brat had been accepted and sheltered by the colossus. The cits in their Sunday clothes who passed by the elephant of the Bastille were prone to say, as they measured it with a contemptuous look from the eyes flush with their head, Of what service is that? It served to save from cold, from frost, from damp and rain; to protect from the winter wind; to preserve from sleeping in the mud, which entails fever, and from sleeping in the snow, which causes death, a little fatherless and motherless boy without bread, clothes, or shelter. It served to shelter the innocent boy whom society repulsed. It served to diminish the public wrong. It was a lair opened to him against whom all doors were closed. It seemed as if the old wretched mastodon, attacked by vermin and oblivion, covered with warts, mould, and ulcers, tottering, crumbling, abandoned, and condemned, — a species of colossal mendicant asking in vain the alms of a benevolent glance in the midst of the highway, — had taken pity on this other beggar, the poor pygmy who walked about without shoes on his feet, without a ceiling over his head, blowing his fingers, dressed in rags, and supporting life on what was thrown away. This is of what use the elephant of the Bastille was; and this idea of Napoleon, disdained by men, had been taken up again by God. What had only been illustrious had become august. The Em-

peror would have needed, in order to realize what
he meditated, porphyry, bronze, iron, gold, and marble ; but for God the old collection of planks, beams,
and plaster was sufficient.   The Emperor had had a
dream of genius.   In this Titanic elephant, armed,
prodigious, raising its trunk, and spouting all around
glad and living waters, he wished to incarnate the
people ; and God had made a greater thing of it,
for He lodged a child in it.

The hole by which Gavroche entered was a breach
scarce visible from the outside, as it was concealed,
as we said, under the elephant's belly, and so narrow
that only cats and boys could pass through it.

" Let us begin," said Gavroche, " by telling the
porter that we are not at home."

And plunging into the darkness with certainty
like a man who knows every corner of the room,
he took a plank and stopped up the hole.   Gavroche
plunged again into the darkness ; the children heard
the fizzing of a match dipped into the bottle of
phosphorus, — for lucifer matches did not yet exist,
and the Fumade fire-producer represented progress
at that day.   A sudden light made them wink.
Gavroche had lit one of those bits of string dipped
in pitch which are called " cellar rats ; " and this
thing, which smoked more than it illumined, rendered the inside of the elephant indistinctly visible.
Gavroche's two guests looked around them, and had
much such a feeling as any one would have if shut
up in the Heidelberg tun, or, better still, what Jonas
must have experienced in the biblical belly of the
whale.   An entire gigantic skeleton was visible to

them and enveloped them ; above their heads a long
brown beam, from which sprang at regular distances
massive cross-bars, represented the spine with the
ribs ; stalactites of plaster hung down like viscera,
and vast spider webs formed from one side to the
other dusty diaphragms.   Here and there in corners
could be seen large black spots which seemed alive,
and changed places rapidly with a quick and startled
movement.   The pieces which had fallen from the
elephant's back on its belly had filled up the con-
cavity, so that it was possible to walk on it as on
a flooring.   The youngest lad nudged his brother
and said, —

" It is black."

This remark made Gavroche cry out, for the petrified air of the two lads rendered a check necessary.

" What 's that you give me ? " he shouted ; " do
you gab ?   You have dislikes, eh !   I suppose you
want the Tuileries ?   Are you brutes ?   Tell me, but
I warn you that I do not belong to the regiment of
spoonies.   Well, to hear you talk one would think
that your father was a prince of the blood."

A little roughness is good in terror, for it reas-
sures ; the two children drew nearer to Gavroche,
who, affected paternally by this confidence, passed
from sternness to gentleness, and addressing the
younger lad, —

" Blockhead," he said, toning down the insult
with a caressing inflection of the voice, " it is outside that it 's black.   Outside it rains, and here it
does not rain ; outside it is cold, and here there is
not a breath of wind ; outside there is a heap of

people, and here there's nobody ; outside there's not even the moon, and here there's a candle, the deuce take it all !"

The two lads began looking round the apartment with less terror, but Gavroche did not allow them any leisure for contemplation.

"Quick," he said.

And he thrust them toward what we are very happy to call the end of the room, where his bed was. Gavroche's bed was perfect, that is to say, there was a mattress, a coverlet, and an alcove with curtains. The mattress was a straw mat, and the coverlet was a rather wide wrapper of coarse gray wool, very warm, and nearly new. This is what the alcove was, — three long props were driven securely into the plaster soil, that is to say, the elephant's belly, two in front and one behind, and were fastened by a cord at the top, so as to form a hollow pyramid. These props supported a grating of brass wire, simply laid upon them, but artistically fastened with iron wire, so that it entirely surrounded the three poles. A row of large stones fastened the lattice-work down to the ground, so that nothing could pass ; and this lattice was merely a piece of the brass-work put up in aviaries in menageries. Gavroche's bed was under the wire-work as in a cage, and the whole resembled an Esquimaux's tent. Gavroche moved a few of the stones that held down the lattice-work in front, and shouted to the lads, —

"Now then, on all fours."

He made his guests enter the cage cautiously,

then went in after them, brought the stones together again, and hermetically closed the opening. They lay down all three on the mat, and though they were all so short, not one of them could stand upright in the alcove. Gavroche still held the "cellar rat" in his hand.

"Now," he said, "to roost; I am going to suppress the chandelier."

"What is that, sir?" the elder of the lads asked Gavroche, pointing to the brass grating.

"That," said Gavroche, gravely, "is on account of the rats. Go to roost!"

Still he thought himself obliged to add a few words of instruction for these young creatures, and continued, —

"It comes from the Jardin des Plantes, and is employed to guard ferocious animals. There is a whole store-house full; you have only to climb over a wall, crawl through a window, and pass under a door, and you can have as much as you like."

While speaking he wrapped up the little boy in the blanket, who murmured, —

"Oh, that is nice, it's so warm!"

Gavroche took a glance of satisfaction at the coverlet.

"That also comes from the Jardin des Plantes," he said, "I took it from the monkeys."

And pointing out to the elder one the straw mat on which he was lying, which was very thick and admirably made, he added, —

"That belonged to the giraffe."

After a pause he continued, —

" The beasts had all those things, and I took them from them; they were not at all angry, for I told them that I wanted them for the elephant."

There was another interval of silence, after which he continued, " You climb over walls and snap your fingers at the Government."

The two lads gazed with a timid and stupefied respect at this intrepid and inventive being, a vagabond like them, isolated like them, weak like them, who had something admirable and omnipotent about him, who appeared to them supernatural, and whose face was composed of all the grimaces of an old mountebank, mingled with the simplest and most charming smile.

" Then, sir," the elder lad said timidly, " you are not afraid of the policemen ? "

Gavroche limited himself to answering, —

"Brat ! we don't say ' policemen,' we say ' slops.'"

The younger had his eyes wide open, but said nothing ; as he was at the edge of the mat, the elder being in the centre, Gavroche tucked in the coverlet around him as a mother would have done, and raised the mat under his head with old rags, so as to make him a pillow. Then he turned to the elder boy, —

" Well ! it is jolly here, eh ? "

" Oh, yes ! " the lad answered, as he looked at Gavroche with the expression of a saved angel.

The two poor little fellows, who were wet through, began to grow warm again.

" By the bye," Gavroche went on, " why were you blubbering ? "

And pointing to the younger boy he said to his brother, —

"A baby like that, I don't say no ; but for a tall chap like you to cry is idiotic, you look like a calf."

"Well, sir," the lad said, " we had n't any lodging to go to."

"Brat," Gavroche remarked, " we don't say 'lodging,' but ' crib.' "

"And then we felt afraid of being all alone like that in the night."

"We don't say ' night,' but ' sorgue.' "

"Thank you, sir," said the boy.

"Listen to me," Gavroche went on. " You must never blubber for anything. I 'll take care of you, and you 'll see what fun we shall have. In summer we 'll go to the Glacière with Navet, a pal of mine ; we 'll bathe in the dock, and run about naked on the timber floats in front of the bridge of Austerlitz, for that makes the washerwomen rage. They yell, they kick, and, Lord ! if you only knew how ridiculous they are ! We 'll go and see the skeleton man; he 's alive at the Champs Élysées, and the cove is as thin as blazes. And then I will take you to the play, and let you see Frederick Lemaître ; I get tickets, for I know some actors, and even performed myself once in a piece. We were a lot of boys who ran about under a canvas, and that made the sea. I will get you an engagement at my theatre. We will go and see the savages, but they ain't real savages, they wear pink fleshing which forms creases, and you can see repairs made at their elbows with white thread. After that

we will go to the Opera, and enter with the claquers.
The claque at the Opera is very well selected, though
I would n't care to be seen with the claque on the
boulevard. At the Opera, just fancy, they 're people
who pay their twenty sous, but they are asses, and
we call them dish-clouts. And then we will go and
see a man guillotined, and I 'll point out the executioner to you, Monsieur Sanson ; he lives in the Rue
de Marais, and he 's got a letter-box at his door.
Ah ! we shall amuse ourselves famously."

At this moment a drop of pitch fell on Gavroche's
hand, and recalled him to the realities of life.

"The devil," he said, " the match is wearing out.
Pay attention ! I can't afford more than a sou a
month for lighting, and when people go to bed they
are expected to sleep. We have n't the time to read
M. Paul de Kock's romances. Besides, the light
might pass through the crevices of the gate, and
the slops might see it."

"And then," timidly observed the elder lad, who
alone dared to speak to Gavroche and answer him,
"a spark might fall on the straw, and we must be
careful not to set the house on fire."

"You must n't say 'set the house on fire,'"
Gavroche remarked, " but ' blaze the crib.' "

The storm grew more furious, and through the
thunder-peals the rain could be heard pattering on
the back of the colossus.

"The rain 's sold ! " said Gavroche. " I like to
hear the contents of the water-bottle running down
the legs of the house. Winter 's an ass ; it loses its
time, it loses its trouble ; it can't drown us, and so

that is the reason why the old water-carrier is so growling with us."

This allusion to the thunder, whose consequences Gavroche, in his quality as a nineteenth-century philosopher, accepted, was followed by a lengthened flash, so dazzling that a portion of it passed through the hole in the elephant's belly. Almost at the same moment the thunder roared, and very furiously. The two little boys uttered a cry, and rose so quickly that the brass grating was almost thrown down; but Gavroche turned toward them his bold face, and profited by the thunder-clap to burst into a laugh.

"Be calm, children, and do not upset the edifice. That's fine thunder of the right sort, and it is n't like that humbugging lightning. It's almost as fine as at the 'Ambigu.'"

This said, he restored order in the grating, softly pushed the two lads on to the bed, pressed their knees to make them lie full length, and cried, —

"Since le Bon Dieu is lighting his candle, I can put out mine. Children, my young humans, we must sleep, for it's very bad not to sleep. It makes you stink in the throat, as people say in fashionable society. Wrap yourselves well up in the blanket, for I am going to put the light out; are you all right?"

"Yes," said the elder boy, "I'm all right, and feel as if I had a feather pillow under my head."

"You must n't say 'head,'" Gavroche cried, "but 'nut.'"

The two lads crept close together; Gavroche made them all right on the mat, and pulled the blanket up to their ears; then he repeated for the third time in the hieratic language, " Roost."

And he blew out the rope's end. The light was scarce extinguished ere a singular trembling began to shake the trellis-work under which the three children were lying. It was a multitude of dull rubbings which produced a metallic sound, as if claws and teeth were assailing the copper wire, and this was accompanied by all sorts of little shrill cries. The little boy of five years of age, hearing this noise above his head, and chilled with terror, nudged his elder brother, but he was " roosting " already, as Gavroche had ordered him; then the little one, unable to hold out any longer for fright, dared to address Gavroche, but in a very low voice and holding his breath.

" Sir ? "

" Hilloh ! " said Gavroche, who had just closed his eyes.

" What is that ? "

" It 's the rats," Gavroche answered.

And he laid his head again on the mat. The rats, which were really by thousands in the elephant's carcass, and were the live black spots to which we have alluded, had been held in check by the flame of the link so long as it was alight; but as soon as this cavern, which was, so to speak, their city, had been restored to night, sniffing what that famous storyteller, Perrault, calls " fresh meat," they rushed in bands to Gavroche's tent, climbed to the top, and were biting the meshes, as if trying to enter this novel sort of trap. In the mean while the little one did not sleep.

"Sir?" he began again.

"Well?" Gavroche asked.

"What are rats?"

"They're mice."

This explanation slightly reassured the child, for he had seen white mice in his life, and had not been afraid of them; still, he raised his voice again.

"Sir?"

"Well?" Gavroche repeated.

"Why don't you keep a cat?"

"I had one," Gavroche answered; "I brought it here, but they ate it for me."

This second explanation undid the work of the first, and the child began trembling once more; the dialogue between him and Gavroche was resumed for the fourth time.

"Sir?"

"Well?"

"What was eaten?"

"The cat."

"What ate the cat?"

"The rats."

"The mice?"

"Yes, the rats."

The child, terrified by these mice which ate the cats, continued, —

"Would those mice eat us?"

"Oh, Lord, yes!" Gavroche said.

The child's terror was at its height, but Gavroche added, —

"Don't be frightened, they can't get in.   And

then, I am here. Stay; take my hand, hold your tongue, and sleep."

Gavroche at the same time took the boy's hand across his brother, and the child pressed the hand against his body and felt reassured; for courage and strength have mysterious communications. Silence had set in again around them, the sound of voices had startled and driven away the rats; and when they returned a few minutes later and furiously attacked, the three boys, plunged in sleep, heard nothing more. The night hours passed away; darkness covered the immense Bastille Square. A winter wind, which was mingled with the rain, blew in gusts. The patrols examined doors, enclosures, and dark corners, and, while searching for nocturnal vagabonds, passed silently before the elephant; the monster, erect and motionless, with its eyes open in the darkness, seemed to be dreaming, as if satisfied at its good deed, and sheltered from the sky and from man the three poor sleeping children. In order to understand what is going to follow, it must be remembered that at this period the main-guard of the Bastille was situated at the other end of the square, and that what took place near the elephant could neither be prevented nor heard by the sentry. Toward the end of the hour which immediately precedes daybreak, a man came running out of the Rue St. Antoine, crossed the square, went round the great enclosure of the Column of July, and slipped through the palings under the elephant's belly. If any light had fallen on this man, it might have been guessed from his thoroughly drenched state that he had passed the night in the rain. On getting under the elephant he uttered a peculiar cry, which belongs to no human language, and which a parrot alone could reproduce. He repeated twice this cry, of which the following orthography scarce supplies any idea, " Kirikikiou ! " At the second cry a clear, gay, and young voice answered from the elephant's belly, " Yes ! " Almost immediately the plank that closed the hole was removed, and left a passage for a lad, who slid down the elephant's leg and fell at the man's feet. It was Gavroche, and the man was Montparnasse. As for the cry of " Kirikikiou," it was doubtless what the lad meant to say by, " You will ask for Monsieur Gavroche." On hearing it, he jumped up with a start, crept out of his alcove by moving the grating a little, and then carefully closing it again, after which he opened the trap and went down. The man and the child silently recognized each other in the night, and Montparnasse confined himself to saying, —

" We want you, come and give us a lift."

The gamin asked for no other explanation.

" Here I am," he said.

And the pair proceeded toward the Rue St. Antoine, whence Montparnasse had come, winding rapidly through the long file of market-carts which were coming into town at the time. The gardeners, lying on their wagons among their salads and vegetables, half asleep, and rolled up to the eyes in their greatcoats, owing to the beating rain, did not even look at these strange passers-by.

CHAPTER III.

INCIDENTS OF AN ESCAPE.

THIS is what occurred on this same night at La Force. An escape had been concerted between Babet, Brujon, Gueulemer, and Thénardier, although Thénardier was in secret confinement. Babet had managed the affair on his own account during the day, as we heard from Montparnasse's narrative to Gavroche, and Montparnasse was to help them outside. Brujon, while spending a month in a punishment room, had time, first, to make a rope, and, secondly, to ripen a plan. Formerly, these severe places, in which prison discipline leaves the prisoner to himself, were composed of four stone walls, a stone ceiling, a brick pavement, a camp-bed, a grated skylight, and a gate lined with iron, and were called dungeons ; but the dungeon was considered too horrible, so now it is composed of an iron gate, a grated skylight, a camp-bed, a brick pavement, a stone ceiling, four stone walls, and it is called a "punishment room." A little daylight is visible about midday. The inconvenience of these rooms, which, as we see, are not dungeons, is to leave beings to think who ought to be set to work. Brujon therefore reflected, and he left the punishment room with a cord. As

he was considered very dangerous in the Charlemagne yard, he was placed in the Bâtiment Neuf,
and the first thing he found there was Gueulemer,
the second a nail, — Gueulemer, that is to say, crime;
and a nail, that is to say, liberty.

Brujon, of whom it is time to form a complete idea,
was, with the appearance of a delicate complexion
and a deeply premeditated languor, a polished, intelligent robber, who possessed a caressing look and an
atrocious smile. His look was the result of his will,
and his smile the result of his nature. His first
studies in his art were directed to roofs; and he had
given a great impulse to the trade of lead-stealers,
who strip roofs and carry away gutters by the process
called *au gras double*. What finally rendered the
moment favorable for an attempted escape was that
workmen were at this very moment engaged in re-
laying and re-tipping a part of the prison slates. The
St. Bernard was not absolutely isolated from the
Charlemagne and St. Louis yards, for there were on
the roof scaffolding and ladders, — in other words,
bridges and staircases, on the side of deliverance.
The Bâtiment Neuf, which was the most cracked
and decrepit affair possible to imagine, was the weak
point of the prison. Saltpetre had so gnawed the
walls that it had been found necessary to prop up
and shore the ceilings of the dormitories; because
stones became detached and fell on the prisoners'
beds. In spite of this antiquity, the error was committed of confining in there the most dangerous prisoners, and placing in it the " heavy cases," as is said in
the prison jargon. The Bâtiment Neuf contained four

sleeping-wards, one above the other, and a garret-floor called "Le Bel Air." A large chimney-flue, probably belonging to some old kitchen of the Ducs de la Force, started from the ground-floor, passed through the four stories, cut in two the sleeping-wards, in which it figured as a sort of flattened pillar, and issued through a hole in the roof. Gueulemer and Brujon were in the same ward, and had been placed through precaution on the ground-floor. Accident willed it that the head of their beds rested against the chimney-flue. Thénardier was exactly above their heads in the garret called Bel Air.

The passer-by who stops in the Rue Culture Sainte Catherine, after passing the fire-brigade station, and in front of the bath-house gateway, sees a court-yard full of flowers and shrubs in boxes, at the end of which is a small white rotunda with two wings, enlivened by green shutters, — the bucolic dream of Jean Jacques. Not ten years ago there rose above this rotunda a black, enormous, frightful, naked wall, which was the outer wall of La Force. This wall behind this rotunda was like a glimpse of Milton caught behind Berquin. High though it was, this wall was surmounted by an even blacker roof, which could be seen beyond, — it was the roof of the Bâtiment Neuf.

Four dormer-windows protected by bars could be seen in it, and they were the windows of Bel Air; and a chimney passed through the roof, which was the chimney of the sleeping-wards. Bel Air, the attic-floor of the Bâtiment Neuf, was a species of large hall, closed with triple gratings and iron-lined doors, starred with enormous nails. When you entered by the north end, you had on your left the four dormers, and on your right facing these, four square and spacious cages, separated by narrow passages, built up to breast-height of masonry, and the rest to the roof of iron bars. Thénardier had been confined in solitary punishment since the night of February 3. It was never discovered how, or by what connivance, he succeeded in procuring and concealing a bottle of that prepared wine, invented, so it is said, by Desrues, in which a narcotic is mixed, and which the band of the Endormeurs rendered celebrated. There are in many prisons treacherous turnkeys, half jailers, half robbers, who assist in escapes, sell to the police a faithless domesticity, and " make the handle of the salad-basket dance."

On this very night, then, when little Gavroche picked up the two straying children, Brujon and Gueulemer, who knew that Babet, who had escaped that same morning, was waiting for them in the street with Montparnasse, gently rose, and began breaking open with a nail which Brujon had found the stove-pipe against which their beds were. The rubbish fell on Brujon's bed, so that it was not heard ; and the gusts of wind mingled with the thunder shook the doors on their hinges, and produced a frightful and hideous row in the prison. Those prisoners who awoke pretended to fall asleep again, and left Brujon and Gueulemer to do as they pleased ; and Brujon was skilful, and Gueulemer was vigorous. Before any sound had reached the watchman sleeping in the grated cell which looked into the ward, the wall was broken through, the chimney escaladed,

the iron trellis-work which closed the upper opening
of the flue forced, and the two formidable bandits
were on the roof. The rain and the wind were tremendous, and the roof was slippery.

"What a fine sorgue [night] for a bolt!" said
Brujon.

An abyss of six feet in width and eighty feet deep
separated them from the surrounding wall, and at
the bottom of this abyss they could see a sentry's
musket gleaming in the darkness. They fastened to
the ends of the chimney-bars which they had just
broken the rope which Brujon had woven in the cell,
threw the other end over the outer wall, crossed the
abyss at a bound, clung to the coping of the wall, be-
straddled it, glided in turn along the rope to a little
roof which joins the bath-house, pulled their rope
to them, jumped into the yard of the bath-house,
pushed open the porter's casement, close to which
hung his cord, pulled the cord, opened the gate, and
found themselves in the street. Not three quarters
of an hour had elapsed since they were standing on
the bed, nail in hand, and with their plan in their
heads; a few minutes after, they had rejoined Babet
and Montparnasse, who were prowling in the neighborhood. On drawing the cord to them they broke it,
and a piece had remained fastened to the chimney on
the roof, but they had met with no other accident beyond almost entirely skinning their fingers. On this
night Thénardier was warned, though it was impossible to discover how, and did not go to sleep. At
about one in the morning, when the night was very
black, he saw two shadows passing, in the rain and

gusts, the window opposite his cage. One stopped just long enough to give a look; it was Brujon. Thénardier saw him, and understood, — that was enough for him. Thénardier, reported to be a burglar, and detained on the charge of attempting to obtain money at night by violence, was kept under constant watch; and a sentry, relieved every two hours, walked in front of his cage with a loaded musket. Bel Air was lighted by a sky-light, and the prisoner had on his feet a pair of fetters weighing fifty pounds. Every day at four in the afternoon, a turnkey, escorted by two mastiffs, — such things still happened at that day, — entered his cage, placed near his bed a black loaf of two pounds' weight, a water-jug, and a bowl of very weak broth in which a few beans floated, inspected his fetters, and tapped the bars. This man with his dogs returned twice during the night.

Thénardier had obtained permission to keep a sort of iron pin which he used to nail his bread to the wall, in order, as he said, " to preserve it from the rats." As Thénardier was under a constant watch, this pin did not seem dangerous ; still it was remembered at a later day that a turnkey said, " It would have been better only to leave him a wooden skewer." At two in the morning the sentry, who was an old soldier, was changed, and a recruit substituted for him. A few minutes after, the man with the dogs paid his visit, and went away without having noticed anything, except the youthful and peasant look of the " tourlourou." Two hours after, when they came to relieve this conscript, they found

him asleep, and lying like a log by the side of
Thénardier's cage. As for the prisoner, he was no
longer there ; his severed fetters lay on the ground,
and there was a hole in the ceiling of his cage, and
another above it in the roof. A plank of his bed
had been torn out and carried off; for it could not be
found. In the cell was also found the half empty
bottle, containing the rest of the drugged wine with
which the young soldier had been sent to sleep. The
soldier's bayonet had disappeared. At the moment
when all this was discovered, Thénardier was supposed to be out of reach ; the truth was, that he
was no longer in the Bâtiment Neuf, but was still in
great danger. Thénardier, on reaching the roof of the
Bâtiment Neuf, found the remainder of Brujon's rope
hanging from the chimney-bars ; but as the broken
cord was much too short, he was unable to cross the
outer wall as Brujon and Gueulemer had done.

When you turn out of the Rue des Ballets into
the Rue du Roi de Sicile, you notice almost directly
on your right a dirty hollow. In the last century a
house stood here, of which only the back wall exists,
a perfect ruin of a wall which rises to the height of
a third story between the adjacent buildings. This
ruin can be recognized by two large square windows,
still visible. The centre one, the one nearest the
right-hand gable, is barred by a worm-eaten joist
adjusted in the supporting rafter; and through these
windows could be seen, formerly, a lofty lugubrious
wall, which was a portion of the outer wall of La
Force. The gap which the demolished house has
left in the street is half filled up with a palisade of

rotten planks, supported by five stone pillars, and inside is a small hut built against the still standing ruin. The boarding has a door in it which a few years ago was merely closed with a latch. It was the top of this ruin which Thénardier had attained a little after three in the morning. How did he get there? This was never explained or understood. The lightning-flashes must at once have impeded and helped him. Did he employ the ladders and scaffolding of the slaters to pass from roof to roof, over the buildings of the Charlemagne yard, those of the St. Louis yard, the outer, and thence reach the ruined wall in the Rue du Roi de Sicile? But there were in this passage breaks of continuity, which seemed to render it impossible. Had he laid the plank from his bed as a bridge from the roof of Bel Air to the outer wall, and crawled on his stomach along the coping, all round the prison till he reached the ruin? But the outer wall of La Force was very irregular; it rose and sank; it was low at the fire-brigade station, and rose again at the bath-house; it was intersected by buildings, and had everywhere drops and right angles; and then, too, the sentries must have seen the fugitive's dark outline, — and thus the road taken by Thénardier remains almost inexplicable. Had he, illumined by that frightful thirst for liberty which changes precipices into ditches, iron bars into reeds, a cripple into an athlete, a gouty patient into a bird, stupidity into instinct, instinct into intellect, and intellect into genius, invented and improvised a third mode of escape? No one ever knew.

It is not always possible to explain the marvels of an escape ; the man who breaks prison is, we repeat, inspired. There is something of a star, of the lightning, in the mysterious light of the flight. The effort made for deliverance is no less surprising than the soaring toward the sublime, and people say of an escaped robber, " How did he manage to scale that roof ? " in the same way as they say of Corneille, " Where did he find his *qu'il mourût* ? " However this may be, Thénardier, dripping with perspiration, wet through with rain, with his clothes in rags, his hands skinned, his elbows bleeding, and his knees lacerated, reached the ruin-wall, lay down full length on it, and then his strength failed him. A perpendicular wall as high as a three-storied house separated him from the street, and the rope he had was too short. He waited there, pale, exhausted, despairing, though just now so hopeful, still covered by night, but saying to himself that day would soon come ; horrified at the thought that he should shortly hear it strike four from the neighboring clock of St. Paul, the hour when the sentry would be changed, and be found asleep under the hole in the roof. He regarded with stupor the wet black pavement, in the light of the lamps, and at such a terrible depth, — that desired and terrific pavement which was death and which was liberty. He asked himself whether his three accomplices had succeeded in escaping, whether they were waiting for him, and if they would come to his help ? He listened : excepting a patrol, no one had passed through the street since he had been lying there. Nearly all the market carts from Montreuil,

Charonne, Vincennes, and Bercy came into town by
the Rue St. Antoine.

Four o'clock struck, and Thénardier trembled. A
few minutes after, the startled and confused noise
which follows the discovery of an escape broke out
in the prison. The sound of doors being opened and
shut, the creaking of gates on their hinges, the
tumult at the guard-room, and the clang of musket
butts on the pavement of the yards, reached his ears.
Lights flashed past the grated windows of the sleeping wards ; a torch ran along the roof of the Bâtiment Neuf, and the firemen were called out. Three
caps, which the torch lit up in the rain, came
and went along the roofs, and at the same time
Thénardier saw, in the direction of the Bastille, a
livid gleam mournfully whitening the sky. He was
on the top of a wall ten inches wide, lying in the
pitiless rain, with a gulf on his right hand and on
his left, unable to stir, suffering from the dizziness
of a possible fall and the horror of a certain arrest,
and his mind, like the clapper of a bell, went from
one of these ideas to the other : " Dead if I fall ;
caught if I remain." In this state of agony he suddenly saw in the still perfectly dark street a man,
who glided along the walls and came from the Rue
Pavée, stop in the gap over which Thénardier was,
as it were, suspended. This man was joined by a
second, who walked with similar caution, then by
a third, and then by a fourth. When these men
were together, one of them raised the latch of the
paling gate, and all four entered the enclosure where
the hut is, and stood exactly under Thénardier.

These men had evidently selected this place to consult in, in order not to be seen by passers-by, or the sentry guarding the wicket of La Force a few paces distant. We must say, too, that the rain kept this sentry confined to his box. Thénardier, unable to distinguish their faces, listened to their remarks with the desperate attention of a wretch who feels himself lost. He felt something like hope pass before his eyes, when he heard these men talking slang. The first said, in a low voice, but distinctly, something which we had better translate : —

"Let us be off. What are we doing here?"

The second replied, —

"It is raining hard enough to put out the fire of hell. And then the police will pass soon ; besides, there is a sentry on. We shall get ourselves arrested here."

Two words employed, *icigo* and *icicaille*, which both mean "here," and which belong, the first to the flash language of the barrières, and the second to that of the Temple, were rays of light for Thénardier. By the *icigo* he recognized Brujon, who was a prowler at the barrières, and by *icicaille* Babet, who, among all his other trades, had been a second-hand clothes-dealer at the Temple. The antique slang of the great century is only talked now at the Temple, and Babet was the only man who spoke it in its purity. Had it not been for the *icicaille*, Thénardier could not have recognized him, for he had completely altered his voice. In the mean while the third man had interfered.

"There is nothing to hurry us, so let us wait a

little. What is there to tell us that he does not want us ? "

Through this, which was only French, Thénardier recognized Montparnasse, whose pride it was to understand all the slang dialects and not speak one of them. As for the fourth man, he held his tongue, but his wide shoulders denounced him, and Thénardier did not hesitate, — it was Gueulemer. Brujon replied almost impetuously, but still in a low voice : —

" What is that you are saying ? The innkeeper has not been able to bolt. He does n't understand the dodge. A man must be a clever hand to tear up his shirt and cut his sheets in slips to make a rope ; to make holes in doors ; manufacture false papers ; make false keys ; file his fetters through ; hang his rope out of the window ; hide and disguise himself. The old man cannot have done this, for he does not know how to work."

Babet added, still in the correct classic slang which Poiailler and Cartouche spoke, and which is to the new, bold, and colored slang which Brujon employed what the language of Racine is to that of André Chénier, —

" Your friend the innkeeper must have been taken in the attempt. One ought to be wide awake. He is a flat. He must have been bamboozled by a detective, perhaps even by a prison spy, who played the simpleton. Listen, Montparnasse ; do you hear those shouts in the prison ? You saw all those candles ; he is caught again, and will get off with twenty years. I am not frightened. I am no coward, as is well known ; but the only thing to be done now is to bolt, or we shall be trapped. Do not feel offended ; but come with us, and let us drink a bottle of old wine together."

" Friends must not be left in a difficulty," Montparnasse growled.

" I tell you he is caught again," Brujon resumed, " and at this moment the landlord is not worth a farthing. We can do nothing for him, so let us be off. I feel at every moment as if a policeman were holding me in his hand."

Montparnasse resisted but feebly ; the truth is, that these four men, with the fidelity which bandits have of never deserting each other, had prowled the whole night around La Force, in spite of the peril they incurred, in the hope of seeing Thénardier appear on the top of some wall. But the night, which became really too favorable, for the rain rendered all the streets deserted, the cold which attacked them, their dripping clothes, their worn-out shoes, the alarming noises which had broken out in the prison, the hours which had elapsed, the patrols they had met, the hope which departed, and the fear that returned, — all this urged them to retreat. Montparnasse himself, who was perhaps Thénardier's son-in-law in a certain sense, yielded, and in a moment they would be gone. Thénardier gasped on his wall as the shipwrecked crew of the " Méduse " did on their raft, when they watched the ship which they had sighted fade away on the horizon. He did not dare call to them, for a cry overheard might ruin everything ; but he had an idea, a last idea, an inspiration,

— he took from his pocket the end of Brujon's rope which he had detached from the chimney of the Bâtiment Neuf, and threw it at their feet.

"A cord!" said Babet.

"My cord!" said Brujon.

"The landlord is there," said Montparnasse. They raised their eyes and Thénardier thrust out his head a little.

"Quiet," said Montparnasse. "Have you the other end of the rope, Brujon?"

"Yes."

"Fasten the two ends together. We will throw the rope to him; he will attach it to the wall, and it will be long enough for him to come down."

Thénardier ventured to raise his voice, —

"I am wet through."

"We'll warm you."

"I cannot stir."

"You will slip down, and we will catch you."

"My hands are swollen."

"Only just fasten the rope to the wall."

"I can't."

"One of us must go up," said Montparnasse.

"Three stories!" Brujon ejaculated.

An old plaster conduit pipe, which had served for a stove formerly, lit in the hut, ran along the wall almost to the spot where Thénardier was lying. This pipe, which at that day was full of cracks and holes, has since fallen down, but its traces may be seen. It was very narrow.

"It would be possible to mount by that," said Montparnasse.

"By that pipe?" Babet exclaimed. "A man? Oh no, a boy is required."

"Yes, a boy," Brujon said in affirmative.

"Where can we find one?" Gueulemer said.

"Wait a minute," Montparnasse said; "I have it."

He gently opened the door of the paling, assured himself that there was no passer-by in the street, went out, shut the gate cautiously after him, and ran off in the direction of the Bastille. Seven or eight minutes elapsed, eight thousand centuries for Thénardier; Babet, Brujon, and Gueulemer did not open their lips; the door opened again, and Montparnasse came in, panting and leading Gavroche. The rain continued to make the street completely deserted. Little Gavroche stepped into the enclosure and looked calmly at the faces of the bandits. The rain was dripping from his hair, and Gueulemer said to him, —

"Brat, are you a man?"

Gavroche shrugged his shoulders, and replied, —

"A child like me is a man, and men like you are children."

"What a well-hung tongue the brat has!" Babet exclaimed.

"The boy of Paris is not made of wet paste," Brujon added.

"What do you want of me?" said Gavroche.

Montparnasse answered, —

"Climb up that pipe."

"With this rope," Babet remarked.

"And fasten it," Brujon continued.

" At the top of the wall," Babet added.

" To the cross-bar of the window," Brujon said, finally.

" What next ? " asked Gavroche.

" Here it is," said Gueulemer.

The gamin examined the rope, the chimney, the wall, and the window, and gave that indescribable and disdainful smack of the lips which signifies, " What is it ? "

" There is a man up there whom you will save," Montparnasse continued.

" Are you willing ? " Brujon asked.

" Ass ! " the lad replied, as if the question seemed to him extraordinary, and took off his shoes.

Gueulemer seized Gavroche by one arm, placed him on the roof of the pent-houses, where mouldering planks bent under the boy's weight, and handed him the rope which Brujon had joined again during the absence of Montparnasse. The gamin turned to the chimney, which it was an easy task to enter by a large crevice close to the roof. At the moment when he was going to ascend, Thénardier, who saw safety and life approaching, leaned over the edge of the wall. The first gleam of day whitened his dark forehead, his livid cheek-bones, his sharp savage nose, and his bristling gray beard, and Gavroche recognized him.

" Hilloh ! " he said, " it 's my father. Well, that won't stop me."

And taking the rope between his teeth, he resolutely commenced his ascent. He reached the top of the wall, straddled across it like a horse, and securely fastened the rope to the topmost cross-bar of the window. A moment after, Thénardier was in the street. So soon as he touched the pavement, so soon as he felt himself out of danger, he was no longer wearied, chilled, or trembling. The terrible things he had passed through were dissipated like smoke, and all his strange and ferocious intellect was re-aroused, and found itself erect and free, ready to march onward. The first remark this man made was, —

" Well, whom are we going to eat ? "

It is unnecessary to explain the meaning of this frightfully transparent sentence, which signifies at once killing, assassinating, and robbing. The real meaning of " to eat " is " to devour."

" We must get into hiding," said Brujon. " We will understand each other in three words, and then separate at once. There was an affair that seemed good in the Rue Plumet, — a deserted street ; an isolated house ; old rust-eaten railings looking on a garden, and lone women."

" Well, why not try it ? " Thénardier asked.

" Your daughter Éponine went to look at the thing," Babet answered.

" And has told Magnon it is ' a biscuit,' " Brujon added ; " there's nothing to be done there."

" The girl's no fool," said Thénardier ; " still we must see."

" Yes, yes," Brujon remarked ; " we must see."

Not one of the men seemed to notice Gavroche, who, during this colloquy, was sitting on one of the posts. He waited some minutes, perhaps in the hope that his father would turn to him, and then put on his shoes again, saying, —

"Is it all over? You men don't want me any more, I suppose, as I've got you out of the scrape? I'm off, for I must go and wake my cubs."

And he went off. The five men left the enclosure in turn. When Gavroche had disappeared round the corner of the Rue des Ballets, Babet took Thénardier on one side.

"Do you notice that kid?" he asked him.

"What kid?"

"The one who climbed up the wall and handed you the rope."

"Not particularly."

"Well, I don't know; but I fancy it's your son."

"Bah!" said Thénardier; "do you think so?"

BOOK VII.

SLANG.

CHAPTER I.

THE ORIGIN OF SLANG.

"PIGRITIA" is a terrible word. It engenders a world, *la pègre*, for which read, *robbery ;* and a Hades, *la pégrenne*, for which read, *hunger.* Hence indolence is a mother, and has a son, robbery, and a daughter, hunger. Where are we at this moment? In slang. What is slang? It is at once the nation and the idiom ; it is robbery in its two species, people and language. Four-and-thirty years ago, when the narrator of this grave and sombre history introduced into the middle of a work written with the same object as this one[1] a robber speaking slang, there was amazement and clamor. "Why! what! slang! why, it is frightful ; it is the language of the chain-gang, of hulks and prisons, of everything that is the most abominable in society," etc. We could never understand objections of this nature. Since that period two powerful romance-writers, of whom one was a profound observer of humanity, the other an intrepid

[1] Le dernier Jour d'un Condamné.

friend of the people, — Balzac and Eugène Sue, —
having made bandits talk in their natural tongue, as
the author of "Le dernier Jour d'un Condamné"
did in 1828, the same objections were raised, and
people repeated: "What do writers want with this
repulsive patois? Slang is odious, and produces a
shudder." Who denies it? Of course it does. When
the object is to probe a wound, a gulf, or a society,
when did it become a fault to drive the probe too
deep? We have always thought that it was sometimes an act of courage and at the very least a simple
and useful action, worthy of the sympathetic attention which a duty accepted and carried out deserves.
Why should we not explore and study everything,
and why stop on the way? Stopping is the function
of the probe, and not of the prober.

Certainly it is neither an attractive nor an easy
task to seek in the lowest depths of social order, where
the earth leaves off and mud begins, to grope in these
vague densities, to pursue, seize, and throw quivering
on the pavement that abject idiom which drips with
filth when thus brought to light, that pustulous vo-
cabulary of which each word seems an unclean ring
of a monster of the mud and darkness. Nothing is
more mournful than thus to contemplate, by the light
of thought, the frightful vermin swarm of slang in its
nudity. It seems, in fact, as if you have just drawn
from its sewer a sort of horrible beast made for the
night, and you fancy you see a frightful, living, and
bristling polype, which shivers, moves, is agitated,
demands the shadow again, menaces, and looks.
One word resembles a claw, another a lustreless and

bleeding eye, and some phrases seem to snap like the pincers of a crab. All this lives with the hideous vitality of things which are organized in disorganization. Now, let us ask, when did horror begin to exclude study; or the malady drive away the physician? Can we imagine a naturalist who would refuse to examine a viper, a bat, a scorpion, a scolopendra, or a tarantula, and throw them into the darkness, saying, "Fie, how ugly they are!" The thinker who turned away from slang would resemble a surgeon who turned away from an ulcer or a wart. He would be a philologist hesitating to examine a fact of language, a philosopher hesitating to scrutinize a fact of humanity. For we must tell all those ignorant of the fact, that slang is at once a literary phenomenon and a social result. What is slang, properly so called? It is the language of misery.

Here we may, perhaps, be stopped; the fact may be generalized, which is sometimes a way of palliating it; it may be observed that every trade, every profession, we might also say all the accidents of the social hierarchy, and all the forms of intelligence, have their slang. The merchant who says "Montpellier in demand, Marseille fine quality;" the broker who says, "amount brought forward, premium at end of month;" the gambler who says, "pique, répique, and capot;" the bailiff of the Norman Isles who says, "the holder in fee cannot make any claim on the products of the land during the hereditary seizure of the property of the re-lessor;" the playwright who says, "the piece was goosed;" the actor who says, "I made a hit;" the philosopher who says, "phenomenal triplicity;" the sportsman who says, "a covey of partridges, a leash of woodcocks;" the phrenologist who says, "amativeness, combativeness, secretiveness;" the infantry soldier who says, "my clarionette;" the dragoon who says, "my turkey-cock;" the fencing-master who says, "tierce, carte, disengage;" the printer who says, "hold a chapel;" all — printer, fencing-master, dragoon, infantry man, phrenologist, sportsman, philosopher, actor, playwright, gambler, stock-broker, and merchant — talk slang. The painter who says, "my grinder;" the attorney who says, "my gutter-skipper;" the barber who says, "my clerk;" and the cobbler who says, "my scrub," — all talk slang. Rigorously taken, all the different ways of saying right and left, the sailor's larboard and starboard, the scene-shifter's off-side and prompt-side, and the verger's Epistle-side and Gospel-side, are slang. There is the slang of affected girls as there was the slang of the précieuses, and the Hôtel de Rambouillet bordered to some slight extent the Cour des Miracles. There is the slang of duchesses, as is proved by this sentence, written in a note by a very great lady and very pretty woman of the Restoration : "Vous trouverez dans ces potains-là une foultitude de raisons pour que je me libertise." [1] Diplomatic ciphers are slang, and the Pontifical Chancery, writing 26 for "Rome," *grkztntgzyal* for "Envoy," and *abfxustgrnogrkzu tu* XI. for "the Duke of Modena," talk slang. The mediæval physicians who, in order to refer to carrots, radishes, and

---

[1] "You will find in that tittle-tattle a multitude of reasons why I should take my liberty."

turnips, said, *opoponach, perfroschinum, reptitalinus, dracatholicum, angelorum,* and *postmegorum,* talk slang. The sugar-refiner who says, " clarified syrup, molasses, bastard, common, burned, loaf-sugar," — this honest manufacturer talks slang. A certain school of critics, who twenty years ago said, "one half of Shakespeare is puns and playing on words," spoke slang. The poet and artist who with profound feeling would call M. de Montmorency a bourgeois, if he were not a connoisseur in verses and statues, talk slang. The classic academician who calls flowers Flora, the fruits Pomona, the sea Neptune, love the flames, beauty charms, a horse a charger, the white or tricolor cockade the rose of Bellona, the three-cornered hat the triangle of Mars, — that classic academician talks slang. Algebra, medicine, and botany have their slang. The language employed on shipboard — that admirable sea-language so complete and picturesque, which Jean Bart, Duquesne, Suffren, and Duperré spoke, which is mingled with the straining of the rigging, the sound of the speaking-trumpets, the clang of boarding-axe, the rolling, the wind, the gusts, and the cannon — is an heroic and brilliant slang, which is to the ferocious slang of robbers what the lion is to the jackal.

All this is perfectly true, but whatever people may say, this mode of comprehending the word "slang" is an extension which everybody will not be prepared to admit. For our part, we perceive the precise circumscribed and settled acceptation of the word, and restrict slang to slang. The true slang, the slang *par excellence,* if the two words can be coupled, the immemorial slang which was a kingdom, is nothing else, we repeat, than the ugly, anxious, cunning, treacherous, venomous, cruel, blear-eyed, vile, pro-found, and fatal language of misery. There is at the extremity of all abasements and all misfortunes a last misery, which revolts and resolves to contend with the ensemble of fortunate facts and reigning rights, — a frightful struggle, in which, at one mo-ment crafty, at another violent, at once unhealthy and ferocious, it attacks the social order with pin-pricks by vice, and with heavy blows by crime. For the necessities of this struggle, misery has invented a fighting language, which is called slang. To hold up on the surface and keep from forgetfulness, from the gulf, only a fragment of any language which man has spoken, and which would be lost, — that is to say, one of the elements, good or bad, of which civiliza-tion is composed and complicated, — is to extend the data of social observation and serve civilization itself. Plautus rendered this service, whether voluntarily or involuntarily, by making two Carthaginian soldiers speak Phœnician ; Molière rendered it also by mak-ing so many of his characters talk Levantine and all sorts of patois. Here objections crop out afresh : Phœnician, excellent; Levantine, very good; and even patois may be allowed, for they are languages which have belonged to nations or provinces — but slang ? Of what service is it to preserve slang and help it to float on the surface ?

To this we will only make one remark. Assuredly, if the language which a nation or a province has spoken is worthy of interest, there is a thing still

more worthy of attention and study, and that is the
language which a wretchedness has spoken. It is
the language which has been spoken in France, for
instance, for more than four centuries, not only by a
wretchedness, but by every wretchedness, by every
human wretchedness possible. And then, we insist
upon the fact, to study social deformities and infirmities, and point them out for cure, is not a task in
which choice is permissible. The historian of morals
and ideas has a mission no less austere than the historian of events. The latter has the surface of civilization, the struggles of crowned heads, the births of
princes, the marriages of kings, assemblies, great public men and revolutions, — all the external part ; the
other historian has the interior, — the basis, the people
that labors, suffers, and waits, the crushed woman,
the child dying in agony, the dull warfare of man
with man, obscene ferocities, prejudices, allowed iniquities, the subterranean counter-strokes of the law,
the secret revolutions of minds, the indistinct shivering of multitudes, those who die of hunger, the barefooted, the bare-armed, the disinherited, the orphans,
the unhappy, the infamous, and all the ghosts that
wander about in obscurity. He must go down with
his heart full of charity and severity, at once as a
brother and as a judge, into the impenetrable dungeons in which crawl pell-mell those who bleed and
those who wound, those who weep and those who
cure, those who fast and those who devour, those that
endure evil, and those who commit it. Are the duties
of the historians of hearts and souls inferior to those
of the historians of external facts ? Can we believe

that Alighieri has less to say than Machiavelli? Is the lower part of civilization, because it is deeper and more gloomy, less important than the upper? Do we know the mountain thoroughly if we do not know the caverns?

We will notice, by the way, that from our previous remarks a marked separation, which does not exist in our mind, might be inferred between the two classes of historians. No one is a good historian of the patent, visible, glistening, and public life of a people, unless he is at the same time to a certain extent the historian of their profound and hidden life; and no one is a good historian of the interior unless he can be, whenever it is required, historian of the exterior. The history of morals and ideas penetrates the history of events, and *vice versâ*; they are two orders of different facts which answer to each other, are always linked together, and often engender one another. All the lineaments which Providence traces on the surface of a nation have their gloomy, but distinct, parallels at the base, and all the convulsions of the interior produce up-heavings on the surface. As true history is a medley of everything, the real historian attends to everything. Man is not a circle with only one centre; he is an ellipse with two foci, facts being the one, and ideas the other. Slang is nothing but a vestibule in which language, having some wicked action to commit, disguises itself. It puts on these masks of words and rags of metaphors. In this way it becomes horrible, and can scarce be recognized. Is it really the French language, the great human tongue? It is ready to go on the stage and take up the cue of crime, and suited for all the parts in the repertory of evil. It no longer walks, but shambles ; it limps upon the crutch of the Cour des Miracles, which may be metamorphosed into a club. All the spectres, its dressers, have daubed its face, and it crawls along and stands erect with the double movement of the reptile. It is henceforth ready for any part, for it has been made to squint by the forger, has been verdigrised by the poisoner, blackened by the soot of the incendiary, and the murderer has given it his red.

When you listen at the door of society, on the side of honest men, you catch the dialogue of those outside. You distinguish questions and answers, and notice, without comprehending it, a hideous murmur sounding almost like the human accent, but nearer to a yell than to speech. It is slang ; the words are deformed, wild, imprinted with a species of fantastic bestiality. You fancy that you hear hydras conversing. It is unintelligibility in darkness ; it gnashes its teeth and talks in whispers, supplementing the gloom by enigmas. There is darkness in misfortune, and greater darkness still in crime, and these two darknesses amalgamated compose slang. There is obscurity in the atmosphere, obscurity in the deeds, obscurity in the voices. It is a horrifying, frog-like language, which goes, comes, hops, crawls, slavers, and moves monstrously in that common gray mist composed of crime, night, hunger, vice, falsehood, injustice, nudity, asphyxia, and winter, which is the high noon of the wretched.

Let us take compassion on the chastised, for, alas !

what are we ourselves ? Who am I, who am speaking to you ? Who are you, who are listening to me ? Whence do we come ? And is it quite sure that we did nothing before we were born ? The earth is not without a resemblance to a prison, and who knows whether man is not the ticket-of-leave of Divine justice ? If we look at life closely we find it so made that there is punishment everywhere to be seen. Are you what is called a happy man ? Well, you are sad every day, and each of them has its great grief or small anxiety. Yesterday, you trembled for a health which is dear to you, to-day you are frightened about your own, to-morrow it will be a monetary anxiety, and the day after the diatribe of a calumniator, and the day after that again the misfortune of some friend ; then the weather, then something broken or lost, or a pleasure for which your conscience and your backbone reproach you ; or, another time, the progress of public affairs, and we do not take into account heart-pangs. And so it goes on ; one cloud is dissipated, another forms, and there is hardly one day in one hundred of real joy and bright sunshine. And you are one of that small number who are happy ; as for other men, the stagnation of night is around them. Reflecting minds rarely use the expressions " the happy " and the " unhappy," for in this world, which is evidently the vestibule of another, there are no happy beings. The true human division is into the luminous and the dark. To diminish the number of the dark, and augment that of the luminous, is the object ; and that is why we cry, " Instruction and learning ! " Learning to read is lighting the fire,

and every syllable spelled is a spark.   However, when
we say light, we do not necessarily mean joy; for
men suffer in light, and excess of light burns.   Flame
is the enemy of the wings, and to burn without
ceasing to fly is the prodigy of genius.   When you
know and when you love, you will still suffer, for the
day is born in tears, and the luminous weep, be it
only for the sake of those in darkness.

CHAPTER II.

ROOTS.

SLANG is the language of the dark. Thought is affected in its gloomiest depths, and social philosophy is harassed in its most poignant undulations, in the presence of this enigmatical dialect, which is at once branded and in a state of revolt. There is in this a visible chastisement, and each syllable looks as if it were marked. The words of the common language appear in it, as if branded and hardened by the hangman's red-hot irons, and some of them seem to be still smoking; some phrases produce in you the effect of a robber's fleur-de-lysed shoulder suddenly exposed, and ideas almost refuse to let themselves be represented by these convict substantives. The metaphors are at times so daring that you feel that they have worn fetters. Still, in spite of all this, and in consequence of all this, this strange patois has by right its compartment in that great impartial museum, in which there is room for the oxydized sou as well as the gold medal, and which is called toleration. Slang, whether people allow it or no, has its syntax and poetry. It is a language. If, by the deforming of certain vocables, we perceive that it has been chewed by Mandrin, we feel from

certain metonyms that Villon spoke it. That line
so exquisite and so celebrated, —

> " Mais où sont les neiges d'antan ?
> (But where are the snows of yester-year ?) "

is a line of slang. Antan, *ante annum*, is a slang
word of Thunes, which signified the past year, and,
by extension, formerly. Five-and-thirty years ago,
on the departure of the great chain-gang, in 1827,
there might be read in one of the dungeons of
Bicêtre this maxim, engraved with a nail upon the
wall by a king of Thunes condemned to the galleys,
" Les dabs d'antan trimaient siempre pour la pierre
du Coësre," which means, " The kings of former days
used always to go to be consecrated." In the
thought of that king, the consecration was the
galleys. The word *décarade*, which expresses the
departure of a heavy coach at a gallop, is attributed
to Villon, and is worthy of him. This word, which
strikes fire, contains in a masterly onomatopœia the
whole of Lafontaine's admirable line, —

> " Six forts chevaux tiraient un coche."

From a purely literary point of view, few studies
would be more curious or fertile than that of slang.
It is an entire language within a language, a sort of
sickly grafting which has produced a vegetation, a
parasite which has its roots in the old Gaulish trunk,
and whose sinister foliage crawls up the whole of
one side of the language. This is what might be
called the first or common notion of slang, but to
those who study the language as it should be

studied, that is to say, as geologists study the earth, slang appears like a real alluvium. According as we dig more or less deeply, we find in slang, beneath the old popular French, Provençal, Spanish, Italian, Levantine, that language of the Mediterranean ports, English, and German, Romanic, — in its three varieties of French, Italian, and Roman, — Latin, and finally, Basque and Celtic. It is a deep and strange formation, a subterranean edifice built up in common by all scoundrels. Each accursed race has deposited its stratum, each suffering has let its stone fall, each heart has given its pebble. A multitude of wicked, low, or irritated souls who passed through life, and have faded away in eternity, are found there almost entire, and to some extent still visible, in the shape of a monstrous word.

Do you want Spanish? The old Gothic slang swarms with it. Thus we have *boffette*, a box on the ears, which comes from *bofeton ; vantane*, a window (afterwards vanterne), from *vantana ; gat*, a cat, from *gato ; acite*, oil, from *aceyte*. Do you want Italian? We have *spade*, a sword, which comes from *spada*, and *carvel*, a boat, which comes from *caravella*. From the English we have *bichot*, the *bishop ; raille*, a spy, from *rascal*, *rascalion*, roguish; and *pilche*, a case, from *pilcher*, a scabbard. Of German origin are *caleur*, the waiter, from *kellner; hers*, the master, from *herzog*, or duke. In Latin we find *frangir*, to break, from *frangere; affurer*, to steal, from *fur;* and *cadène*, a chain, from *catena*. There is one word which is found in all continental language with a sort of mysterious power and authority,

and that is the word *magnus :* Scotland makes *mac*
of it, which designates the chief of the clan, Mac
Farlane, Mac Callumore, the great Farlane, the great
Callumore ; slang reduces it to *meck,* afterwards *meg,*
that is to say, the Deity. Do you wish for Basque?
Here is *gahisto,* the devil, which is derived from
gaiztoa, bad, and *sorgabon,* good-night, which comes
from *gabon,* good-evening. In Celtic we find *blavin,*
a handkerchief, derived from *blavet,* running water ;
ménesse, a woman (in a bad sense), from *meinec,*
full of stones ; *barant,* a stream, from *baranton,* a
fountain ; *goffeur,* a locksmith, from *goff,* a blacksmith ; and *guédouze,* death, which comes from
guenn-du, white and black. Lastly, do you wish
for history ? Slang calls crowns " the Maltese," in
memory of the coin which was current aboard the
Maltese galleys.

In addition to the philological origins which we
have indicated, slang has other and more natural
roots, which issue, so to speak, directly from the
human mind. In the first place, there is the direct
creation of words, for it is the mystery of language
to paint with words which have, we know not how
or why, faces. This is the primitive foundation of
every human language, or what might be called the
granite. Slang swarms with words of this nature,
immediate words created all of one piece ; it is impossible to say when, or by whom, without etymolo-
gies, analogies, or derivatives, — solitary, barbarous,
and at times hideous words, which have a singular power of expression, and are alive. The executioner, *le taule* (the anvil's face) ; the forest, *le sabri*

(cudgels); fear or flight, *taf;* the footman, *le larbin;*
the general, prefect, or minister, *pharos* (head man) ;
and the devil, *le rabouin* (the one with the tail).
Nothing can be stranger than these words, which
form transparent masks ; some of them, *le rabouin,*
for instance, are at the same time grotesque and
terrible, and produce the effect of a Cyclopean grim-
ace.   In the second place, there is metaphor, and it
is the peculiarity of a language which wishes to say
everything and conceal everything, to abound in
figures.   Metaphor is an enigma in which the robber
who is scheming a plot, or the prisoner arranging an
escape, takes the refuge.   No idiom is more metaphorical than slang ; *dévisser* (to unscrew) *le coco*
(the cocoa-nut), to twist the neck ; *tortiller* (to wind
up), to eat ; *être gerbé* (sheaved), to be tried ; *un
rat,* a stealer of bread ; *il lansquine,* it rains, — an
old striking figure, which bears to some extent its
date with it, assimilates the long oblique lines of
rain to the serried sloping pikes of the lansquenets,
and contains in one word the popular adage, " It
is raining halberts."   At times, in proportion as
slang passes from the first to the second stage, words
pass from the savage and primitive state to the metaphorical sense.   The devil ceases to be *le rabouin,*
and becomes " the baker," or he who puts in the
oven.   This is wittier but not so grand ; something
like Racine after Corneille, or Euripides after Æschylus.   Some slang phrases which belong to both periods,
and have at once a barbarous and a metaphorical
character, resemble phantasmagorias : *Les sorgueurs
vont sollicer des gails à la lune* (the prowlers are

going to steal horses at night). This passes before the mind like a group of spectres, and we know not what we see. Thirdly, there is expediency : slang lives upon the language, uses it as it pleases, and when the necessity arises limits itself to denaturalizing it summarily and coarsely. At times, with the ordinary words thus deformed and complicated with pure slang, picturesque sentences are composed, in which the admission of the two previous elements, direct creation and metaphor, is visible, — *le cab jaspine, je marronne que la roulotte de Pantin trime dans le sabri,* (the dog barks, I suspect that the Paris diligence is passing through the wood) ; *le dab est sinve, la dabuge est merloussière, la fée est bative,* (the master is stupid, the mistress is cunning, and the daughter pretty). Most frequently, in order to throw out listeners, slang confines itself to adding indistinctly to all the words of the language, a species of ignoble tail, a termination in *aille, orgue, iergue,* or *uche.* Thus : *Vouziergue trouvaille bonorgue ce gigotmuche ?* (Do you find that leg of mutton good?) This was a remark made by Cartouche to a jailer, in order to learn whether the sum offered him for an escape suited him. The termination in *mar* has been very recently added.

Slang, being the idiom of corruption, is itself quickly corrupted. Moreover, as it always tries to hide itself so soon as it feels that it is understood, it transforms itself. Exactly opposed to all other vegetables, every sunbeam kills what it falls on in it. Hence slang is being constantly decomposed and re-composed ; and this is an obscure and rapid labor which never ceases, and it makes more way in ten years than language does in ten centuries. Thus *larton* (head) becomes *lartif; gail* (horse) *gaye; fertanche* (straw) *fertille; momignard* (the child) *momacque; fiques* (clothes) *frusques; chique* (the church) *l'égrugeoir;* and *colabre* (the neck) *colas.* The devil is first *gahisto,* then *le rabouin,* and next " the baker;" a priest is the *ratichon,* and then the *sanglier;* a dagger is the *vingt-deux,* next the *surin,* and lastly the *lingre;* the police are *railles,* then *roussins,* then *marchands de lacet* (handcuff dealers), then *coqueurs,* and lastly *cognes;* the executioner is the *taule,* then *Charlot,* then the *atigeur,* and then the *becquillard.* In the seventeenth century to fight was to " take snuff;" in the nineteenth it is " to break the jaw;" but twenty different names have passed away between these two extremes, and Cartouche would speak Hebrew to Lacenaire. All the words of this language are perpetually in flight, like the men who employ them. Still, from time to time, and owing to this very movement, the old slang reappears and becomes new again. It has its headquarters where it holds its ground. The Temple preserved the slang of the seventeenth century, and Bicêtre, when it was a prison, that of Thunes. There the termination in *anche* of the old Thuners could be heard: *Boyanches-tu?* (do you drink?); *il croyanche* (he believes). But perpetual motion does not the less remain the law. If the philosopher succeeds in momentarily fixing, for the purpose of observation, this language, which is necessarily evaporating, he falls into sorrowful and useful meditations, and no study is more efficacious, or more fertile and instructive. There is not a metaphor or an etymology of slang which does not contain a lesson.

Among these men "fighting" means "pretending:" they "fight" a disease, for cunning is their strength. With them the idea of man is not separated from the idea of a shadow. Night is called *la sorgue* and man *l'orgue:* man is a derivative of night. They have formed the habit of regarding society as an atmosphere which kills them, as a fatal force, and they speak of their liberty as one speaks of his health. A man arrested is a " patient ; " a man sentenced is a " corpse." The most terrible thing for the prisoner within the four stone walls which form his sepulchre is a sort of freezing chastity, and hence he always calls the dungeon the *castus.* In this funereal place external life will appear under its most smiling aspect. The prisoner has irons on his feet, and you may perhaps fancy that he thinks how people walk with their feet: no, he thinks that they dance with them, hence, if he succeed in cutting through his fetters, his first idea is that he can now dance, and he calls the saw a *bastringue.* A name is a *centre*, a profound assimilation. The bandit has two heads, — the one which revolves his deeds and guides him through life, the other which he has on his shoulders on the day of his death ; he calls the head which counsels him in crime, the *sorbonne*, and the one that expiates it the *tronche.* When a man has nothing but rags on his body and vices in his heart, when he has reached that double moral and material degradation which the word *gueux* characterizes in its two significations, he is ripe for crime; he is like a well-sharpened blade; he has two edges, his distress and his villany, and hence slang does not call him a *gueux* but a *réguisé*. What is the bagne? A furnace of damnation, a hell, and the convict calls himself a "fagot." Lastly, what name do malefactors give to the prison? The "college." A whole penitentiary system might issue from this word.

Would you like to know whence came most of the galley songs, — those choruses called in the special vocabularies the *lirlonfa?* Listen to this:

There was at the Châtelet of Paris a large long cellar, which was eight feet below the level of the Seine. It had neither windows nor gratings, and the sole opening was the door; men could enter it, but air not. This cellar had for ceiling a stone arch, and for floor ten inches of mud; it had been paved, but, owing to the leakage of the water, the paving had rotted and fallen to pieces. Eight feet above the ground, a long massive joist ran from one end to the other of this vault; from this joist hung at regular distances chains, three feet long, and at the end of these chains were collars. In this cellar men condemned to the galleys were kept until the day of their departure for Toulon; they were thrust under this beam, where each had his fetters oscillating in the darkness and waiting for him. The chains, like pendant arms, and the collars, like open hands, seized these wretches by the neck; they were riveted and left there. As the chain was too short, they could not lie down; they remained motionless in this cellar,

in this night, under this beam, almost hung, forced
to make extraordinary efforts to reach their loaf or
water-jug, with the vault above their heads and mud
up to their knees, drawn and quartered by fatigue,
giving way at the hips and knees, hanging on by their
hands to the chain to rest themselves, only able to
sleep standing, and awakened every moment by the
choking of the collar — some did not awake. To
eat they were compelled to draw up their bread,
which was thrown into the mud, with the heel all
along the thigh to their hand. How long did they
remain in this state? One month, two months, sometimes six months; one man remained a year. It
was the antechamber of the galleys, and men were
put in it for stealing a hare from the king. In this
hellish sepulchre what did they? They died by inches,
as people can do in a sepulchre, and sang, which they
can do in a hell; for when there is no longer hope,
song remains, — in the Maltese waters, when a galley was approaching, the singing was heard before
the sound of the oars. The poor poacher Survincent,
who passed through the cellar-prison of the Châtelet,
said, "Rhymes sustained me." Poetry is useless;
what is the good of rhymes? In this cellar nearly
all the slang songs were born, and it is from the
dungeon of the Great Châtelet of Paris that comes
the melancholy chorus of Montgomery's galley: *Ti-
maloumisaine, timoulamison.* Most of the songs are
sad, some are gay, and one is tender : —

> "Icicaille est le théâtre
> Du petit dardant." [1]

[1] The archer Cupid.

Do you what you will, you cannot destroy that eternal relic of man's heart, love.

In this world of dark deeds secrets are kept; for secrets are a thing belonging to all, and with these wretches secrecy is the unity which serves as the basis of union. To break secrecy is to tear from each member of this ferocious community something of himself. To denounce is called in the energetic language of slang " to eat the piece," as if the denouncer took a little of the substance of each, and supported himself on a piece of the flesh of each. What is receiving a buffet? The conventional metaphor answers, " It is seeing six-and-thirty candles." Here slang interferes and reads *camoufle* for candle ; life in its ordinary language takes *camouflet* as a synonym for a box on the ears. Hence, by a sort of penetration from bottom to top, and by the aid of metaphor, that incalculable trajectory, slang ascends from the cellar to the academy, and Poulailler saying, " I light my *camoufle*," makes Voltaire write, " Langleviel la Beaumelle deserves a hundred *camouflets*." Searching in slang is a discovery at every step, and the study and investigation of this strange idiom lead to the point of intersection of regular with accursed society. The robber has also his food for powder, or stealable matter in you, in me, in the first passer-by, the *pantre* (*pan*, everybody). Slang is the word converted into a convict. It produces a consternation to reflect that the thinking principle of man can be hurled down so deep that it can be dragged there and bound by the obscure tyranny of fatality, and be fastened to some unknown rivets on this precipice. Alas! will no one come to the help of the human soul in this darkness? Is it its destiny ever to await the mind, the liberator, the immense tamer of Pegasuses and hippogriffs, the dawn-colored combatant, who descends from the azure sky between two wings, the radiant knight of the future? Will it ever call in vain to its help the lance of the light of idealism? Is it condemned always to look down into the gulf of evil and see closer and closer to it beneath the hideous water the demoniac head, this slavering mouth, and this serpentine undulation of claws, swellings, and rings? Must it remain there without a gleam of hope, left to the horror of this formidable and vaguely smelt approach of the monster, shuddering, with dishevelled hair, wringing its arms, forever chained to the rock of night, a sombre Andromeda white and naked in the darkness?

CHAPTER III.

As we see, the whole of slang, the slang of four hundred years ago, as well as that of the present day, is penetrated by that gloomy symbolic spirit which gives to every word at one moment a piteous tone, at another a menacing air. We see in it the old ferocious sorrow of those beggars of the Cour des Miracles, who played at cards with packs of their own, some of which have been preserved for us. The eight of clubs, for instance, represented a large tree bearing eight enormous clover leaves, a sort of fantastic personification of the forest. At the foot of this tree could be seen a lighted fire, at which three hares were roasting a game-keeper on a spit, and behind, over another fire, a steaming caldron from which a dog's head emerged. Nothing can be more lugubrious than these reprisals in painting upon a pack of cards, in the face of the pyres for smugglers, and the caldron for coiners. The various forms which thought assumed in the kingdom of slang, singing, jests, and menaces, all had this impotent and crushed character. All the songs of which a few melodies have come down to us were humble and lamentable enough to draw tears. The *pègre* (thief) calls himself the poor *pègre;* for he is always the hare that hides itself, the mouse that escapes, or the bird that flies away. He hardly protests, but restricts himself to sighing, and one of his groans has reached us: *Je n'entrave que le dail comment meck, le daron des orgues, peut atiger ses mômes et ses momignards, et les locher criblant sans être agité lui même.* (I do not understand how God, the Father of men, can torture His children and His grandchildren, and hear them cry, without being tortured Himself.) The wretch, whenever he has time to think, makes himself little before the law and paltry before society; he lies down on his stomach, supplicates, and implores pity, and we can see that he knows himself to be in the wrong.

Toward the middle of the last century a change took place; the prison songs, and choruses of the robbers assumed, so to speak, an insolent and jovial gesture. The *larifla* was substituted for the plaintive *maluré,* and we find in nearly all the songs of the galleys, the hulks, and the chain-gangs, a diabolical and enigmatical gayety. We hear in them that shrill and leaping chorus which seems illumined by a phosphorescent gleam, and appears cast into the forest by a will-o'-the-wisp playing the fife: —

> " Mirlababi surlababo
> Mirliton ribonribette
> Surlababi mirlababo
> Mirliton ribonribo."

They sang this while cutting a man's throat in a cellar or a thicket. It is a serious symptom that in the eighteenth century the old melancholy of these desponding classes is dissipated, and they begin to laugh ; they mock the great " meg " and the great " dab " (governor), and Louis XV. being given they call the King of France the Marquis de Pantin. The wretches are nearly gay, and a sort of dancing light issues from them, as if their conscience no longer weighed them down. These lamentable tribes of darkness no longer possess the despairing audacity of deeds, but the careless audacity of the mind ; this is a sign that they are losing the feeling of their criminality, and finding some support, of which they are themselves ignorant, among the thinkers and dreamers. It is a sign that robbery and plunder are beginning to be filtered even into doctrines and sophisms, so as to lose a little of their ugliness, and give a good deal of it to the sophisms and the doctrine. Lastly, it is a sign of a prodigious and speedy eruption, unless some diversion arise. Let us halt here for a moment. Whom do we accuse ? Is it the eighteenth century ? Is it her philosophy ? Certainly not. The work of the eighteenth century is healthy and good ; and the Encyclopædists with Diderot at their head, the physicists under Turgot, the philosophers led by Voltaire, and the Utopists commanded by Rousseau, are four sacred legions. The immense advance of humanity toward the light is due to them, and they are the four advance guards of the human races, going toward the four cardinal points of progress, — Diderot toward the beautiful, Turgot toward the useful, Voltaire toward truth, and Rousseau toward justice. But by the side of and below the philosophers were the sophists, — a venomous vegetation mingled with a healthy growth, a hemlock in the virgin forest. While the hangman was burning on the grand staircase of the Palace of Justice the grand liberating books of the age, writers now forgotten were publishing, with the royal privilege, strangely disorganizing books, which were eagerly read by the scoundrels. Some of these publications, patronized, strange to say, by a prince, will be found in the "Bibliothèque secrète." These facts, profound but unknown, were unnoticed on the surface; but at times the very obscurity of a fact constitutes its danger, and it is obscure because it is subterranean. Of all the writers, the one who perhaps dug the most unhealthy gallery at that day in the masses was Restif de la Bretonne.

This work, peculiar to all Europe, produced greater ravages in Germany than anywhere else. In Germany, during a certain period, which was summed up by Schiller in his famous drama of The Robbers, robbery and plunder were raised into a protest against property and labor. They appropriated certain elementary ideas, specious and false, apparently just, and in reality absurd, wrapped themselves up in these ideas, and to some extent disappeared in them, assumed an abstract name, and passed into a theoretical state, and in this way circulated among the laborious, suffering, and honest masses, without even the cognizance of the imprudent chemists who prepared the mixture, and the masses that accepted it. Whenever a fact of this nature is produced it is serious. Suffering engenders passion; and while the prosperous blind themselves, or go to sleep, the hatred of the unfortunate classes kindles its torch at some sullen or ill-constituted mind which is dreaming in a corner, and sets to work examining society. The examination of hatred is a terrible thing. Hence come, if the misfortune of the age desires it, those frightful commotions, formerly called Jacqueries, by the side of which purely political commotions are child's-play, and which are no longer the struggle of the oppressed with the oppressor, but the revolt of want against comfort. Everything is overthrown at such a time. Insurrections are the earthquakes of nations.

The French Revolution, that immense act of probity, cut short this peril, which was perhaps imminent in Europe toward the close of the eighteenth century. The French Revolution, which was nothing but the ideal armed with a sword, rose, and by the same sudden movement closed the door of evil and opened the door of good. It disengaged the question, promulgated the truth, expelled the miasma, ventilated the age, and crowned the people. We may say that it created man a second time by giving him a second soul, — justice. The nineteenth century inherits and profits by its work, and at the present day the social catastrophe which we just now indicated is simply impossible. Blind is he who denounces it, a fool who fears it, for the Revolution is the vaccine of insurrection. Thanks to the Revolution, the social conditions are altered, and the feudal and monarchical diseases are no longer in our blood. There is no middle age left in our constitution, and we are no longer at the time when formidable internal commo-

tions broke out; when the obscure course of a dull
sound could be heard beneath the feet; when the
earth thrown out from the mole-holes appeared on
the surface of civilization; when the soil cracked;
when the roof of caverns opened, and monstrous
heads suddenly emerged from the ground.   The
revolutionary sense is a moral sense, and the feeling
of right being developed, develops the feeling of
duty.   The law of all is liberty, which ends where
the liberty of another begins, according to Robespierre's admirable definition.   Since 1789 the whole
people has been dilated in the sublimated individual.
There is no poor man who, having his right, has not his
radius; the man, dying of hunger, feels within himself
the honesty of France.   The dignity of the citizen
is an internal armor; the man who is free is scrupu-
lous, and the voter reigns.   Hence comes incorrup-
tibility; hence comes the abortiveness of unhealthy
covetousness, and hence eyes heroically lowered before temptation.   The revolutionary healthiness is so
great, that on a day of deliverance, a 14th of July, or
a 10th of August, there is no populace, and the first
cry of the enlightened and progressing crowds is,
"Death to the robbers!"   Progress is an honest
man, and the ideal and the absolute do not steal
pocket-handkerchiefs.   By whom were the carriages
containing the wealth of the Tuileries escorted in
1848?   By the rag-pickers of the Faubourg St.
Antoine.   The rag mounted guard over the treasure.
Virtue rendered these ragged creatures resplendent.
In these carts, in barely closed chests, — some, indeed,
still opened, — there was, amid a hundred dazzling

cases, that old crown of France, all made of diamonds, surmounted by the royal carbuncle and the Regent diamonds, worth thirty millions of francs; barefooted they guarded this crown. Hence Jacquerie is no longer possible, and I feel sorry for the clever men; it is an old fear which has made its last effort, and could no longer be employed in politics. The great spring of the red spectre is now broken. Everybody understands this now. The scarecrow no longer horrifies. The birds treat the manikin familiarly, and deposit their guano upon it, and the bourgeois laugh at it.

CHAPTER IV.

TWO DUTIES : TO WATCH AND TO HOPE.

THIS being the case, is every social danger dissipated ? Certainly not. There is no Jacquerie, and society may be reassured on that side; the blood will not again rush to its head, but it must pay attention to the way in which it breathes. Apoplexy is no longer to be apprehended, but there is consumption, and social consumption is called wretchedness. People die as well when undermined as when struck by lightning. We shall never grow weary of repeating, that to think first of all of the disinherited and sorrowful classes, to relieve, ventilate, enlighten, and love them, to magnificently enlarge their horizon, to lavish upon them education in every shape, to offer them the example of labor, and never that of indolence, to lessen the weight of the individual burden by increasing the notion of the universal object, to limit poverty without limiting wealth, to create vast fields of public and popular activity, to have, like Briareus, a hundred hands to stretch out on all sides to the crushed and the weak, to employ the collective power in opening workshops for every arm, schools for every aptitude, and laboratories for every intellect, to increase wages, diminish the toil, and balance the debit and credit, that is to say, proportion the enjoyment to the effort, and the satisfaction to the wants, — in a word, to evolve from the social machine, on behalf of those who suffer and those who are ignorant, more light and more comfort, — is, and sympathetic souls must not forget it, the first of brotherly obligations, and, let egotistic hearts learn the fact, the first of political necessities. And all this, we are bound to add, is only a beginning, and the true question is this, labor cannot be law, without being a right. But this is not the place to dwell on such a subject.

If nature is called Providence, society ought to call itself foresight. Intellectual and moral growth is no less indispensable than physical improvement; knowledge is a viaticum; thinking is a primary necessity, and truth is nourishment, like wheat. A reason fasting for knowledge and wisdom grows thin, and we must pity minds that do not eat quite as much as stomachs. If there be anything more poignant than a body pining away for want of bread, it is a mind that dies of hunger for enlightenment. The whole of our progress tends toward the solution, and some day people will be stupefied. As the human race ascends, the deepest strata will naturally emerge from the zone of distress, and the effacement of wretchedness will be effected by a simple elevation of the level. We would do wrong to doubt this blessed solution. The past, we grant, is very powerful at the present hour, and is beginning again. This rejuvenescence of a corpse is surprising. It seems victorious; this dead man is a conqueror.

Behold him advancing and arriving ! he arrives with
his legion, superstitions ; with his sword, despotism ;
with his barrier, ignorance ; and during some time
past he has gained ten battles. He advances, he
threatens, he laughs, he is at our gates. But we
have no reason to despair ; let us sell the field on
which Hannibal is encamped. What can we, who
believe, fear ? A recoil of ideas is no more possible
than it is for a river to flow up a hill. But those
who desire no future ought to reflect ; by saying no
to progress they do not condemn the future, but
themselves ; and they give themselves a deadly disease by inoculating themselves with the past. There
is only one way of refusing to-morrow, and that is,
by dying. We wish for no death, — that of the
body as late as possible, and that of the soul never.
Yes, the sphinx will speak, and the problem will be
solved ; the people sketched by the eighteenth century will be finished by the nineteenth. He is an
idiot who doubts it. The future, the speedy burst-
ing into flower of universal welfare, is a divinely
fatal phenomenon. Immense and combined impul-
sions pushing together govern human facts, and lead
them all within a given time to the logical state, that
is to say, to equilibrium, or in other words, to equity.
A force composed of earth and heaven results from
humanity and governs it ; this force is a performer of
miracles, and marvellous denouements are as easy
to it as extraordinary incidents. Aided by science,
which comes from man, and the event, which comes
from another source, it is but little frightened by
those contradictions in the posture of problems which

seem to the vulgar herd impossibilities. It is no less skilful in producing a solution from the approximation of ideas than in producing instruction from the approximation of facts, and we may expect anything and everything from the mysterious power of progress, which, some fine day, confronts the East and the West in a sepulchre, and makes the Imans hold conference with Bonaparte in the interior of the Great Pyramid. In the meanwhile, there is no halt, no hesitation, no check, in the grand forward march of minds. Social philosophy is essentially the science of peace ; it has for its object, and must have as result, the dissolution of passions by the study of antagonisms. It examines, scrutinizes, and analyzes, and then it recomposes ; and it proceeds by the reducing process, by removing hatred from everything.

It has more than once occurred, that a society has been sunk by the wind which is let loose on men. History is full of the shipwrecks of peoples and empires ; one day, that stranger, the hurricane, passes, and carries away manners, laws, and religions. The civilizations of India, Chaldæa, Persia, Assyria, and Egypt have disappeared in turn ; why ? We are ignorant. What are the causes of these disasters ? We do not know. Could those societies have been saved ? Was it any fault of their own ? Did they obstinately adhere to some fatal vice which destroyed them ? What amount of suicide is there in these terrible deaths of a nation and a race ? These are unanswerable questions, for darkness covers the condemned civilizations. They have been under water since they sank, and we have no more to say ; and it is with a species of terror that we see in the background of that sea which is called the past, and behind those gloomy waves, centuries, those immense vessels, — Babylon, Nineveh, Tarsus, Thebes, and Rome, — sunk by the terrific blast which blows from all the mouths of the darkness. But there was darkness then, and we have light; and if we are ignorant of the diseases of ancient civilizations, we know the infirmities of our own, and we contemplate its beauties and lay bare its deformities. Wherever it is wounded we probe it; and at once the suffering is decided, and the study of the cause leads to the discovery of the remedy. Our civilization, the work of twenty centuries, is at once the monster and the prodigy, and is worth saving; it will be saved. To aid it is much, and to enlighten it is also something. All the labors of modern social philosophy ought to converge to this object; and the thinker of the present day has a grand duty to apply the stethoscope to civilization. We repeat it, this auscultation is encouraging; and we intend to finish these few pages, which are an austere interlude in a mournful drama, by laying a stress on this encouragement. Beneath the social mortality the human imperishableness is felt. The globe does not die because of wounds here and there in the shape of craters and eruptions of sulphur, nor of a volcano that bursts forth and scatters purulent matter. The diseases of the people do not kill man.

And yet, whoever follows the social clinics will shake his head at times; and the strongest, the most tender, and the most logical, have their hours

of despondency.   Will the future arrive?   It seems
as if we may almost ask this question on seeing
so much terrible shadow.   There is a sombre, face-
to-face meeting of the egotists and the wretched.
In the egotist we trace prejudices, the cloudiness of
a caste education, appetite growing with intoxication,
and prosperity that stuns, a fear of suffering which
in some goes so far as an aversion to the sufferers,
an implacable satisfaction, and the feeling of self so
swollen that it closes the soul.   In the wretched we
find covetousness, envy, the hatred of seeing others
successful, the great bounds of the human beast
toward gorging, hearts full of mist, sorrow, want,
fatality, and foul and common ignorance.   Must
we still raise our eyes to heaven? Is the luminous
point which we notice there one of those which die
out ?   The ideal is frightful to look on thus lost in
the depths, small, isolated, imperceptible, and brilliant, but surrounded by all those great black menaces monstrously collected around it ; for all that,
though, it is in no more danger than a star in the
yawning throat of the clouds.

BOOK VIII.

ENCHANTMENTS AND DESOLATIONS.

CHAPTER I.

BRIGHT LIGHT.

THE reader has of course understood that Éponine, on recognizing through the railings the inhabitant of the house in the Rue Plumet, to which Magnon sent her, began by keeping the bandits aloof from the house, then led Marius to it; and that after several days of ecstasy before the railings, Marius, impelled by that force which attracts iron to the loadstone, and the lover toward the stones of the house in which she whom he loves resides, had eventually entered Cosette's garden, as Romeo did Juliet's. This had even been an easier task for him than for Romeo; for Romeo was obliged to scale a wall, while Marius had merely to move one of the bars of the decrepit railing loose in its rusty setting, after the fashion of the teeth of old people. As Marius was thin, he easily passed. As there never was anybody in the street, and as Marius never entered the garden save at night, he ran no risk of being seen. From that blessed and holy hour when a kiss affianced these two souls,

Marius went to the garden every night. If, at this moment of her life, Cosette had fallen in love with an unscrupulous libertine, she would have been lost; for there are generous natures that surrender themselves, and Cosette was one of them. One of the magnanimities of a woman is to yield; and love, at that elevation where it is absolute, is complicated by a certain celestial blindness of modesty. But what dangers you incur, ye noble souls! You often give the heart and we take the body; your heart is left you, and you look at it in the darkness with a shudder. Love has no middle term: it either saves or destroys, and this dilemma is the whole of human destiny. No fatality offers this dilemma of ruin or salvation more inexorably than does love, for love is life, if it be not death; it is a cradle, but also a coffin. The same feeling says yes and no in the human heart, and of all the things which God has made, the human heart is the one which evolves the most light, and, alas! the most darkness. God willed it that the love which Cosette encountered was one of those loves which save. So long as the month of May of that year, 1832, lasted, there were every night in this poor untrimmed garden, and under this thicket, which daily became more fragrant and more thick, two beings composed of all the chastities and all the innocences, overflowing with all the felicities of heaven, nearer to the archangels than to man, pure, honest, intoxicated, and radiant, and who shone for each other in the darkness. It seemed to Cosette as if Marius had a crown, and to Marius as if Cosette had a glory.

They touched each other, they looked at each other, they took each other by the hand, they drew close to each other; but there was a distance which they never crossed. Not that they respected it, but they were ignorant of it. Marius felt a barrier in Cosette's purity, and Cosette felt a support in the loyalty of Marius. The first kiss had also been the last; since then Marius had never gone beyond touching Cosette's hand or neck-handkerchief, or a curl with his lips. Cosette was to him a perfume, and not a woman, and he inhaled her. She refused nothing, and he asked for nothing; Cosette was happy and Marius satisfied. They lived in that ravishing state which might be called the dazzling of a soul by a soul; it was the ineffable first em brace of two virginities in the ideal, two swans meeting on the Jungfrau. At this hour of love, the hour when voluptuousness is absolutely silenced by the omnipotence of ecstasy, Marius, the pure and seraphic Marius, would have sooner been able to go home with a street-walker than raise Cosette's gown as high as her ankle. Once in the moonlight Cosette stooped to pick up something on the ground, and her dress opened and displayed her neck. Marius turned his eyes away.

What passed between these two lovers? Nothing; they adored each other. At night, when they were there, this garden seemed a living and sacred spot. All the flowers opened around them and sent them their incense; and they opened their souls and spread them over the flowers. The wanton and vigorous vegetation quivered, full of sap and intoxication, around these two innocents, and they uttered words of love at which the trees shivered. What were these words? Breathings, nothing more ; but they were sufficient to trouble and affect all this nature. It is a magic power which it would be difficult to understand, were we to read in a book this conversation made to be carried away and dissipated like smoke beneath the leaves by the wind. Take away from these whispers of two lovers the melody which issues from the soul, and accompanies them like a lyre, and what is left is only a shadow, and you say, "What! is it only that?" Well, yes, child's-play, repetitions, laughs at nothing, absurdities, foolishness, — all that is the most sublime and profound in the world! the only things which are worth the trouble of being said and being listened to. The man who has never heard, the man who has never uttered these absurdities and poor things is an imbecile and a wicked man. Said Cosette to Marius, —

"Do you know that my name is Euphrasie?"

"Euphrasie? No, it is Cosette."

"Oh, Cosette is an ugly name, which was given me when I was little ; but my real name is Euphrasie. Don't you like that name?"

"Yes ; but Cosette is not ugly."

"Do you like it better than Euphrasie?"

"Well — yes."

"In that case, I like it better too. That is true, Cosette is pretty. Call me Cosette."

Another time she looked at him intently, and exclaimed, —

" You are handsome, sir ; you are good-looking ;
you have wit ; you are not at all stupid ; you are
much more learned than I ; but I challenge you with,
' I love you.' "

And Marius fancied that he heard a strophe sung
by a star. Or else she gave him a little tap when
he coughed, and said, —

" Do not cough, sir ; I do not allow anybody to
cough in my house without permission. It is very
wrong to cough and frighten me. I wish you to
be in good health, because if you were not I should
be very unhappy, and what would you have me
do ? "

And this was simply divine.

Once Marius said to Cosette, —

" Just fancy ; I supposed for a while that your
name was Ursule."

This made them laugh the whole evening. In
the middle of another conversation he happened to
exclaim, —

" Oh ! one day at the Luxembourg I felt disposed
to finish breaking an invalid ! "

But he stopped short, and did not complete the
sentence, for he would have been obliged to allude
to Cosette's garter, and that was impossible. There
was a strange feeling connected with the flesh, before
which this immense innocent love recoiled with a
sort of holy terror. Marius imagined life with Cosette
like this, without anything else, — to come every evening to the Rue Plumet, remove the old complacent
bar of the president's railings, sit down elbow to
elbow on this bench, look through the trees at the

scintillation of the commencing night, bring the fold
in his trouser-knee into cohabitation with Cosette's
ample skirts, to caress her thumb-nail, and to inhale
the same flower in turn forever and indefinitely.
During this time the clouds passed over their heads;
and each time the wind blows it carries off more
of a man's thoughts than of clouds from the sky.
We cannot affirm that this chaste, almost stern love
was absolutely without gallantry. "Paying com-
pliments" to her whom we love is the first way of
giving caresses and an attempted semi-boldness. A
compliment is something like a kiss through a veil,
and pleasure puts its sweet point upon it, while concealing itself. In the presence of the delight the
heart recoils to love more. The cajoleries of Marius,
all saturated with chimera, were, so to speak, of an
azure blue. The birds when they fly in the direction
of the angels must hear words of the same nature,
still, life, humanity, and the whole amount of posi-
tivism of which Marius was capable were mingled
with it. It was what is said in the grotto, as a
prelude to what will be said in the alcove, — a lyrical
effusion, the strophe and the sonnet commingled,
the gentle hyperboles of cooing, all the refinements
of adoration arranged in a posy, and exhaling a subtle
and celestial perfume, an ineffable prattling of heart
to heart.

"Oh!" Marius muttered, "how lovely you are!
I dare not look at you, and that is the reason why
I contemplate you. You are a grace, and I know
not what is the matter with me. The hem of your
dress, where the end of your slipper passes through,

upsets me. And then, what an enchanting light
when your thoughts become visible, for your reason
astonishes me, and you appear to me for instants
to be a dream. Speak, I am listening to you, and
admiring you. Oh, Cosette, how strange and charming it is ; I am really mad. You are adorable, and
I study your feet in the microscope and your soul
with the telescope."

And Cosette made answer, —

" And I love you a little more through all the
time which has passed since this morning."

Questions and answers went on as they could in
this dialogue, which always agreed in the subject
of love, like the elder-pith balls on the nail. Cosette's
entire person was simplicity, ingenuousness, whiteness,
candor, and radiance ; and it might have been said
of her that she was transparent. She produced on
every one who saw her a sensation of April and daybreak, and she had dew in her eyes. Cosette was
a condensation of the light of dawn in a woman's
form. It was quite simple that Marius, as he adored,
should admire. But the truth is, that this little
boarding-school Miss, just freshly turned out of a
convent, talked with exquisite penetration, and made
at times all sorts of true and delicate remarks. Her
chattering was conversation ; and she was never
mistaken about anything, and conversed correctly.
Woman feels and speaks with the infallibility which
is the tender instinct of the heart. No one knows
like a woman how to say things which are at once
gentle and deep. Gentleness and depth, in those
things the whole of woman is contained, and it is

heaven. And in this perfect felicity tears welled in
their eyes at every moment. A lady-bird crushed,
a feather that fell from a nest, a branch of hawthorn
broken, moved their pity, and then ecstasy, gently
drowned by melancholy, seemed to ask for nothing
better than to weep. The most sovereign symptom
of love is a tenderness which becomes at times almost
insupportable. And by the side of all this — for contradictions are the lightning sport of love — they were
fond of laughing with a ravishing liberty, and so
familiarly that, at times, they almost seemed like two
lads. Still, even without these two hearts intoxicated with chastity being conscious of it, unforgettable
nature is ever there, ever there with its brutal and sublime object; and whatever the innocence of souls may
be, they feel in the most chaste *tête-à-tête* the mysterious and adorable distinction which separates a
couple of lovers from a pair of friends.

They idolized each other. The permanent and the
immutable exist, — a couple love, they laugh, they
make little pouts with their lips, they intertwine
their fingers, and that does not prevent eternity.
Two lovers conceal themselves in a garden in the
twilight, in the invisible, with the birds and the
roses; they fascinate each other in the darkness with
their souls which they place in their eyes; they mut-
ter, they whisper, and during this period immense
constellations of planets fill infinity.

CHAPTER II.

THE GIDDINESS OF PERFECT BLISS.

COSETTE and Marius lived vaguely in the intoxication of their madness, and they did not notice the cholera which was decimating Paris in that very month. They had made as many confessions to each other as they could ; but they had not extended very far beyond their names. Marius had told Cosette that he was an orphan, Pontmercy by name, a lawyer by profession, and gaining a livelihood by writing things for publishers ; his father was a colonel, a hero, and he, Marius, had quarrelled with his grandfather, who was very rich. He also incidentally remarked that he was a baron ; but this did not produce much effect on Cosette. Marius a baron ? She did not understand it, and did not know what the word meant, and Marius was Marius to her. For her part, she confided to him that she had been educated at the convent of the Little Picpus ; that her mother was dead, like his ; that her father's name was Fauchelevent, that he was very good and gave a great deal to the poor, but was himself poor, and deprived himself of everything, while depriving her of nothing. Strange to say, in the kind of symphony which Marius had lived in since he found Cosette again, the past, even the most recent, had become so confused and distant to him that what Cosette told him completely satisfied him. He did not even dream of talking to her about the nocturnal adventure in the garret, the Thénardiers, the burning, the strange attitude and singular flight of her father. Marius momentarily forgot all this ; he did not know at night what he had done in the morning, where he had breakfasted, or who had spoken to him ; he had a song in his ears which rendered him deaf to every other thought, and he only existed during the hours when he saw Cosette. As he was in heaven at that time, it was perfectly simple that he should forget the earth. Both of them bore languidly the undefinable weight of immaterial joys ; that is the way in which those somnambulists called lovers live.

Alas ! who is there that has not experienced these things ? Why does an hour arrive when we emerge from this azure, and why does life go on afterwards ?

Love almost takes the place of thought. Love is, indeed, an ardent forgetfulness. It is absurd to ask passion for logic ; for there is no more an absolute logical concatenation in the human heart than there is a perfect geometric figure in the celestial mechanism. For Cosette and Marius nothing more existed than Marius and Cosette ; the whole universe around them had fallen into a gulf, and they lived in a golden moment, with nothing before them, nothing behind them. Marius hardly remembered that Cosette had a father. It was blotted from his brain by his bedazzlement. Of what did these lovers talk ? As we have seen, of flowers, swallows, the setting sun, the rising moon, and all the important things. They had told themselves everything except everything ; for the everything of lovers is nothing. Of what use would it be to talk of her father, the realities, that den, those bandits, that adventure ? And was it quite certain that the nightmare had existed ? They were two, they adored each other, and there was only that, there was nothing else. It is probable that this obliteration of hell behind us is essential to the arrival in Paradise. Have we seen demons ? Are there any ? Have we trembled ? Have we suffered ? We no longer know, and there is a roseate cloud over it all.

Hence these two beings lived in this way, very high up, and with all the unverisimilitude which there is in nature ; neither at the nadir nor at the zenith, but between man and the seraphs, above the mud and below the ether, in the clouds. They were not so much flesh and bone, as soul and ecstasy from head to foot, already too sublimated to walk on earth, and still too loaded with humanity to disappear in ether, and held in suspense like atoms which are waiting to be precipitated ; apparently beyond the pale of destiny, and ignorant of that rut, yesterday, to-day, and to-morrow ; amazed, transported, and floating at moments with a lightness sufficient for a flight in the infinitude, and almost ready for the eternal departure. They slept awake in this sweet lulling ; oh, splendid lethargy of the real overpowered by the ideal ! At times Cosette was so beautiful that Marius closed his eyes before her.

The best way of gazing at the soul is with closed eyes. Marius and Cosette did not ask themselves to what this would lead them, and looked at each other as if they had already arrived. It is a strange claim on the part of men to wish that love should lead them somewhere.

CHAPTER III.

JEAN VALJEAN suspected nothing; for Cosette, not quite such a dreamer as Marius, was gay, and that sufficed to render Jean Valjean happy. Cosette's thoughts, her tender preoccupations, and the image of Marius which filled her soul, removed none of the incomparable purity of her splendid, chaste, and smiling forehead. She was at the age when the virgin wears her love as the angel wears its lily. Jean Valjean was, therefore, happy; and, besides, when two lovers understand each other, things always go well, and any third party who might trouble their love is kept in a perfect state of blindness by a small number of precautions, which are always the same with all lovers. Hence Cosette never made any objections; if he wished to take a walk, "Very good, my little papa," and if he stayed at home, very good, and if he wished to spend the evening with Cosette, she was enchanted. As he always retired at ten o'clock at night, on those occasions Marius did not reach the garden till after that hour, when he heard from the street Cosette opening the door. We need hardly say that Marius was never visible by day, and Jean Valjean did not even remember that Marius existed. One morning, however, he happened to say to Cosette, "Why, the back of your dress is all white!" On the previous evening Marius in a transport had pressed Cosette against the wall. Old Toussaint, who went to bed at an early hour, only thought of sleeping so soon as her work was finished, and was ignorant of everything, like Jean Valjean.

Marius never set foot in the house when he was with Cosette; they concealed themselves in a niche near the steps so as not to be seen or heard from the street, and sat there, often contenting themselves with the sole conversation of pressing hands twenty times a minute, and gazing at the branches of the trees. At such moments, had a thunderbolt fallen within thirty feet of them, they would not have noticed it, so profoundly was the revery of the one absorbed and plunged in the revery of the other. Limpid purities, and spotless hours of almost unbroken similarity! This species of love is a collection of lily leaves and dove's feathers. The whole garden was between them and the street, and each time that Marius came in and out he carefully restored the bar of the railings, so that no disarrangement was visible. He went away generally at midnight, and went back to Courfeyrac's lodgings. Courfeyrac said to Bahorel, —

"Can you believe it? Marius returns home at present at one in the morning."

Bahorel answered, —

"What would you have? There is always a bomb-shell inside a seminarist."

At times Courfeyrac crossed his arms, assumed a stern air, and said to Marius, —

"Young man, you are becoming irregular in your habits."

Courfeyrac, who was a practical man, was not pleased with this reflection of an invisible Paradise cast on Marius ; he was but little accustomed to unpublished passions, hence he grew impatient, and at times summoned Marius to return to reality. One morning he cast this admonition to him, —

"My dear fellow, you produce on me the effect at present of being a denizen of the moon, in the kingdom of dreams, the province of illusion, whose chief city is soap-bubble. Come, don't play the prude, — what is her name ? "

But nothing could make Marius speak, and his nails could have been dragged from him more easily than one of the three sacred syllables of which the ineffable name *Cosette* was composed. True love is luminous as the dawn, and silent as the tomb. Still Courfeyrac found this change in Marius, that he had a beaming taciturnity. During the sweet month of May, Marius and Cosette knew this immense happiness, — to quarrel and become reconciled, to talk for a long time, and with the most minute details, about people who did not interest them the least in the world, — a further proof that in that ravishing opera which is called love, the libretto is nothing. For Marius it was heaven to listen to Cosette talking of dress ; for Cosette to listen to Marius talking politics, to listen, knee against knee, to the vehicles passing along the Rue de Babylone, to look at the same planet in space, or the same worm glistening in the grass, to be silent together, a greater pleasure still than talking, etc.

Still various complications were approaching. One evening Marius was going to the rendezvous along the Boulevard des Invalides; he was walking as usual with his head down, and as he was turning the corner of the Rue Plumet, he heard some one say close to him, —

"Good-evening, Monsieur Marius."

He raised his head and recognized Éponine. This produced a singular effect; he had not once thought of this girl since the day when she led him to the Rue Plumet; he had not seen her again, and she had entirely left his mind. He had only motives to be grateful to her, he owed her his present happiness, and yet it annoyed him to meet her. It is an error to believe that passion, when it is happy and pure, leads a man to a state of perfection; it leads him simply, as we have shown, to a state of forgetfulness. In this situation, man forgets to be wicked, but he also forgets to be good, and gratitude, duty, and essential and material recollections, fade away. At any other time Marius would have been very different to Éponine, but, absorbed by Cosette, he had not very clearly comprehended that this Éponine was Éponine Thénardier, and that she bore a name written in his father's will, — that name to which he would have so ardently devoted himself a few months previously. We show Marius as he was, and his father himself slightly disappeared in his mind beneath the splendor of his love. Hence he replied with some embarrassment, —

" Ah, is it you, Éponine ? "

" Why do you treat me so coldly ?   Have I done you any injury ? "

" No," he answered.

Certainly he had nothing against her ; far from it.   Still he felt that he could not but say " you " to Éponine, now that he said " thou " to Cosette. As he remained silent, she exclaimed, —

" Tell me — "

Then she stopped, and it seemed as if words failed this creature, who was formerly so impudent and bold.   She tried to smile and could not, so continued, —

" Well ? "

Then she was silent again, and looked down on the ground.

" Good-night, Monsieur Marius," she suddenly said, and went away.

CHAPTER IV.

CAB RUNS IN ENGLISH AND BARKS IN SLANG.

THE next day — it was June 3, 1832, a date to which we draw attention owing to the grave events which were at that moment hanging over the horizon of Paris in the state of lightning-charged clouds — Marius at nightfall was following the same road as on the previous evening, with the same ravishing thoughts in his heart, when he saw between the boulevard trees Éponine coming toward him. Two days running, — that was too much; so he sharply turned back, changed his course, and went to the Rue Plumet by the Rue Monsieur. This caused Éponine to follow him as far as the Rue Plumet, a thing she had never done before; hitherto, she had contented herself with watching him as he passed along the boulevard, without attempting to meet him: last evening was the first time that she ventured to address him. Éponine followed him, then, without his suspecting it: she saw him move the railing-bar aside and step into the garden.

"Hilloh!" she said, "he enters the house."

She went up to the railing, felt the bars in turn, and easily distinguished the one which Marius had removed; and she muttered in a low voice, and with a lugubrious accent, — "None of that, Lisette!"

She sat down on the stone-work of the railing, close to the bar, as if she were guarding it. It was exactly at the spot where the railings joined the next wall, and there was there a dark corner, in which Éponine entirely disappeared. She remained thus for more than an hour without stirring or breathing, absorbed in thought. About ten o'clock at night, one of the two or three passers along the Rue Plumet, an old belated citizen, who was hurrying along the deserted and ill-famed street, while passing the railing, heard a dull menacing voice saying, —

"I am not surprised now that he comes every evening."

The passer-by looked around him, saw nobody, did not dare to peer into this dark corner, and felt horribly alarmed. He redoubled his speed, and was quite right in doing so, for in a few minutes six men, who were walking separately, and at some distance from each other, under the walls, and who might have been taken for a drunken patrol, entered the Rue Plumet: the first who reached the railings stopped and waited for the rest, and a second after, all six were together, and began talking in whispered slang.

"It's here," said one of them.

"Is there a cab [dog] in the garden?" another asked.

"I don't know. In any case I have brought a bullet which we will make it eat."

"Have you got some mastic to break a pane?"

"Yes."

"The railings are old," remarked the fifth man, who seemed to have the voice of a ventriloquist.

"All the better," said the second speaker; "it will make no noise when sawn, and won't be so hard to cut through."

The sixth, who had not yet opened his mouth, began examining the railings as Eponine had done an hour ago, and thus reached the bar which Marius had unfastened. Just as he was about to seize this bar, a hand suddenly emerging from the darkness clutched his arm; he felt himself roughly thrust back, and a hoarse voice whispered to him, "There's a cab." At the same time he saw a pale girl standing in front of him. The man had that emotion which is always produced by things unexpected; his hair stood hideously on end. Nothing is more formidable to look at than startled wild beasts. Their affrighted look is hideous. He fell back and stammered, —

"Who is this she-devil?"

"Your daughter."

It was, in truth, Éponine speaking to Thénardier. Upon her apparition, the other five men, that is to say, Claquesous, Gueulemer, Babet, Montparnasse, and Brujon, approached noiselessly, without hurry or saying a word, but with the sinister slowness peculiar to these men of the night. Some hideous tools could be distinguished in their hands, and Gueulemer held a pair of those short pincers which burglars call *fauchons* (small scythes).

"Well, what are you doing here? What do you

want? Are you mad?" Thénardier exclaimed, as far as is possible to exclaim in a whisper. "Have you come to prevent us from working?"

Éponine burst into a laugh and leaped on his neck. "I am here, my little papa, because I am here; are not people allowed to sit down on the stones at present? It is you who ought n't to be here; and what have you come to do, since it is a biscuit? I told Magnon so, and there is nothing to be done here. But embrace me, my good little papa, it is such a time since I saw you. You are out, then?"

Thénardier tried to free himself from Éponine's arms, and growled, —

"There, there, you have embraced me. Yes, I am out, and not in. Now be off."

But Éponine did not loose her hold, and redoubled her caresses.

"My dear papa, how ever did you manage? You must have been very clever to get out of that scrape, so tell me all about it. And where is mamma? Give me some news of her."

Thénardier answered, —

"She's all right. I don't know; leave me and be off, I tell you."

"I do not exactly want to go off," Éponine said with the pout of a spoiled child; "you send me away, though I have n't seen you now for four months, and I have scarce had time to embrace you."

And she caught her father again round the neck.

"Oh, come, this is a bore," said Babet.

"Make haste," said Gueulemer, "the police may pass."

The ventriloquial voice hummed, —

> "Nous n'sommes pas le jour de l'an,
>   A bécoter papa, maman."

Éponine turned to the five bandits : —

"Why, that's Monsieur Brujon. Good-evening, Monsieur Babet; good-evening, Monsieur Claquesous. What, don't you know me, Monsieur Gueulemer? How are you, Montparnasse?"

"Yes, they know you," said Thénardier; "but now good-night, and be off; leave us alone."

"It is the hour of the foxes, and not of the chickens," said Montparnasse.

"Don't you see that we have work here?" Babet added.

Éponine took Montparnasse by the hand. "Mind," he said, "you will cut yourself, for I have an open knife."

"My dear Montparnasse," Éponine replied very gently, "confidence ought to be placed in people, and I am my father's daughter, perhaps. Monsieur Babet, Monsieur Gueulemer, I was ordered to examine into this affair."

It is remarkable that Éponine did not speak slang; ever since she had known Marius that frightful language had become impossible to her. She pressed Gueulemer's great coarse fingers in her little bony hand, which was as weak as that of a skeleton, and continued, — "You know very well that I am no fool, and people generally believe me. I have done

you a service now and then ; well, I have made inquiries, and you would run a needless risk. I swear
to you that there is nothing to be done in this
house."

"There are lone women," said Gueulemer.

"No, they have moved away."

"Well, the candles have n't," Babet remarked; and
he pointed over the trees to a light which was
moving about the garret. It was Toussaint, who was
up so late in order to hang up some linen to dry.
Éponine made a final effort.

"Well," she said, "they are very poor people, and
there is n't a penny piece in the house."

"Go to the devil," cried Thénardier ; "when we
have turned the house topsy-turvy, and placed the
cellar at top and the attics at the bottom, we
will tell you what there is inside, and whether
they are *balles, ronds, or broques* [francs, sous, or
liards]."

And he thrust her away that he might pass.

"My kind M. Montparnasse," Éponine said, "I
ask you, who are a good fellow, not to go in."

"Take care, you 'll cut yourself," Montparnasse
replied.

Thénardier remarked, with that decisive accent of
his, —

"Decamp, fairy, and leave men to do their
business."

Éponine let go Montparnasse's hand, which she
had seized again, and said, —

"So you intend to enter this house ? "

"A little," the ventriloquist said with a grin.

She leaned against the railings, faced these six men armed to the teeth, to whom night gave demoniac faces, and said in a firm, low voice, —

" Well, I will not let you ! "

They stopped in stupefaction, but the ventriloquist completed his laugh. She continued, —

" Friends, listen to me, for it's now my turn to speak. If you enter this garden or touch this railing I will scream, knock at doors, wake people ; I will have you all six seized, and call the police."

" She is capable of doing it," Thénardier whispered to the ventriloquist and Brujon.

She shook her head, and added, —

" Beginning with my father."

Thénardier approached her.

" Not so close, my good man," she said.

He fell back, growling between his teeth, " Why, what is the matter ? " and added, " chienne."

She burst into a terrible laugh.

" As you please, but you shall not enter; but I am not the daughter of a dog, since I am the whelp of a wolf. You are six, but what do I care for that? You are men and I am a woman. You won't frighten me, I can tell you, and you shall not enter this house because it does not please me. If you come nearer I bark ; I told you there was a dog, and I am it. I do not care a farthing for you, so go your way, for you annoy me ! Go where you like, but don't come here, for I oppose it. Come on, then, you with your stabs and I with my feet."

She advanced a step toward the bandits and said, with the same frightful laugh, —

"Confound it! I'm not frightened. This summer I shall be hungry, and this winter I shall be cold. What asses these men must be to think they can frighten a girl! Afraid of what? You have got dolls of mistresses who crawl under the bed when you talk big, but I am afraid of nothing!"

She fixed her eye on Thénardier, and said, — "Not even of you, father."

Then she continued, as she turned her spectral, bloodshot eyeballs on each of the bandits in turn, —

"What do I care whether I am picked up to-morrow on the pavement of the Rue Plumet stabbed by my father, or am found within a year in the nets of St. Cloud, or on Swan's Island, among old rotting corks and drowned dogs?"

She was compelled to break off, for she was attacked by a dry cough, and her breath came from her weak, narrow chest like the death-rattle.

She continued, —

"I have only to cry out and people will come, patatras. You are six, but I am the whole world."

Thénardier moved a step toward her.

"Don't come near me," she cried.

He stopped, and said gently, —

"Well, no; I will not approach you; but do not talk so loud. Do you wish to prevent us from working, my daughter? And yet we must earn a livelihood. Do you no longer feel any affection for your father?"

"You bore me," said Éponine.

"Still we must live; we must eat — "

"Burst!"

This said, she sat down on the coping of the railings and sang, —

> " Mon bras si dodu,
>   Ma jambe bien faite,
>   Et le temps perdu."

She had her elbow on her knee, and her chin in her hand, and balanced her foot with a careless air. Her ragged gown displayed her thin shoulder-blades, and the neighboring lamp lit up her profile and attitude. Nothing more resolute or more surprising could well be imagined. The six burglars, amazed and savage at being held in check by a girl, went under the shadow of the lamp and held council, with humiliated and furious shrugs of their shoulders. She, however, looked at them with a peaceful and stern air.

" There's something the matter with her," said Babet ; " some reason for it. Is she fond of the cab ? It's a pity to miss the affair. There are two women who live alone, an old cove who lives in a yard, and very decent curtains up to the windows. The old swell must be a sheney, and I consider the affair a good one."

" Well, do you fellows go in," Montparnasse exclaimed, " and do the trick. I will remain here with the girl, and if she stirs — "

He let the knife which he held in his hand glisten in the lamp-light. Thénardier did not say a word, and seemed ready for anything they pleased. Brujon, who was a bit of an oracle, and who, as we know, " put up the job," had not yet spoken, and seemed thoughtful. He was supposed to recoil at nothing, and it was notorious that he had plundered a police office through sheer bravado. Moreover, he wrote verses and songs, which gave him a great authority. Babet questioned him.

"Have you nothing to say, Brujon?"

Brujon remained silent for a moment, then tossed his head in several different ways, and at length decided on speaking, —

"Look here. I saw this morning two sparrows fighting, and to-night I stumble over a quarrelsome woman : all that is bad, so let us be off."

They went away, and while doing so Montparnasse muttered, —

"No matter ; if you had been agreeable I would have cut her throat."

Babet replied, —

"I wouldn't ; for I never strike a lady."

At the corner of the street they stopped, and exchanged in a low voice this enigmatical dialogue.

"Where shall we go and sleep to-night?"

"Under Pantin [Paris]."

"Have you your key about you, Thénardier?"

"Of course."

Éponine, who did not take her eyes off them, saw them return by the road along which they had come. She rose and crawled after them, along the walls and the houses. She followed them thus along the boulevard ; there they separated, and she saw the six men bury themselves in the darkness, where they seemed to fade away.

CHAPTER V.

AFTER the departure of the bandits the Rue Plumet resumed its calm, nocturnal aspect. What had just taken place in this street would not have astonished a forest, for the thickets, the coppices, the heather, the interlaced branches, and the tall grass, exist in a sombre way; the savage crowd catches glimpses there of the sudden apparitions of the invisible world; what there is below man distinguishes there through the mist what is beyond man, and things unknown to us living beings confront each other there in the night. Bristling and savage nature is startled by certain approaches, in which it seems to feel the supernatural; the forces of the shadow know each other and maintain a mysterious equilibrium between themselves. Teeth and claws fear that which is unseizable, and blood-drinking bestiality, voracious, starving appetites in search of prey, the instincts armed with nails and jaws, which have for their source and object the stomach, look at and sniff anxiously the impassive spectral lineaments prowling about in a winding-sheet or standing erect in this vaguely-rustling robe, and which seems to them to live a dead and terrible life. These brutalities, which are only physical, have a confused fear of dealing with an immense obscurity condensed in an unknown being. A black figure barring the passage stops the wild beast short; what comes from the cemetery intimidates and disconcerts what comes from the den; ferocious things are afraid of sinister things, and wolves recoil on coming across a ghoul.

CHAPTER VI.

MARIUS ACTUALLY GIVES COSETTE HIS ADDRESS.

WHILE this sort of human-faced dog was mounting guard against the railing, and six bandits fled before a girl, Marius was by Cosette's side. The sky had never been more star-spangled and more charming, the trees more rustling, or the smell of the grass more penetrating; never had the birds fallen asleep beneath the foliage with a softer noise; never had all the harmonies of universal serenity responded better to the internal music of love; never had Marius been more enamoured, happier, or in greater ecstasy. But he had found Cosette sad, she had been crying, and her eyes were red. It was the first cloud in this admirable dream. Marius's first remark was, —

"What is the matter with you?"

And she replied, —

"I will tell you."

Then she sat down on the bench near the house, and while he took his seat, all trembling, by her side, she continued, —

"My father told me this morning to hold myself in readiness, for he had business to attend to, and we were probably going away."

Marius shuddered from head to foot. When we

reach the end of life, death signifies a departure, but at the beginning, departure means death. For six weeks past Marius had slowly and gradually taken possession of Cosette; it was a perfectly ideal but profound possession. As we have explained, in first love men take the soul long before the body; at a later date they take the body before the soul, and at times they do not take the soul at all, — the Faublas and Prudhommes add, because there is none to take; but the sarcasm is fortunately a blasphemy. Marius, then, possessed Cosette in the way that minds possess; but he enveloped her with his entire soul, and jealously seized her with an incredible conviction. He possessed her touch, her breath, her perfume, the deep flash of her blue eyes, the softness of her skin when he touched her hand, the charming mark which she had on her neck, and all her thoughts. They had agreed never to sleep without dreaming of each other, and had kept their word. He, therefore, possessed all Cosette's dreams. He looked at her incessantly, and sometimes breathed on the short hairs which she had on the back of her neck, and said to himself that there was not one of those hairs which did not belong to him. He contemplated and adored the things she wore, her bows, — her cuffs, her gloves, and slippers, — like sacred objects of which he was the master. He thought that he was the lord of the small tortoise-shell combs which she had in her hair; and he said to himself, in the confused stammering of delight that came on, that there was not a seam of her dress, not a mesh of her stockings, not a wrinkle in her bodice, which was not his. By the side of

Cosette he felt close to his property, close to his creature, close to his despot and his slave. It seemed that they had so blended their souls that if they had wished to take them back it would have been impossible for them to recognize them. This is mine — no, it is mine — I assure you that you are mistaken. This is really I — what you take for yourself is myself; Marius was something which formed part of Cosette, and Cosette was something that formed part of Marius. Mairus felt Cosette live in him ; to have Cosette, to possess Cosette, was to him not very different from breathing. It was in the midst of this faith, this intoxication, this virgin, extraordinary, and absolute possession, and this sovereignty, that the words " We are going away " suddenly fell on him, and the stern voice of reality shouted to him, " Cosette is not thine." Marius awoke. For six weeks, as we said, he had been living out of life, and the word "depart" made him roughly re-enter it. He could not find a word to say, and Cosette merely noticed that his hand was very cold. She said to him in her turn, — " What is the matter with you ? "

He answered, in so low a voice that Cosette could scarce hear him, —

" I do not understand what you said."

She continued, —

" This morning my father told me to prepare my clothes and hold myself ready ; that he would give me his linen to put in a portmanteau ; that he was obliged to make a journey ; that we were going away ; that we must have a large trunk for myself and a small one for him ; to get all this ready within a week, and that we should probably go to England."

" Why, it is monstrous ! " Marius exclaimed.

It is certain that at this moment, in Marius's mind, no abuse of power, no violence, no abomination of the most prodigious tyrants, no deed of Busiris, Tiberius, or Henry VIII., equalled in ferocity this one, — M. Fauchelevent taking his daughter to England because he had business to attend to. He asked, in a faint voice, —

" And when will you start ? "

" He did not say when."

" And when will you return ? "

" He did not tell me."

And Marius rose and said coldly, —

" Will you go, Cosette ? "

Cosette turned to him, her beautiful eyes full of agony, and answered, with a species of wildness, —

" Where ? "

" To England ; will you go ? "

" What can I do ? " she said, clasping her hands.

" Then you will go ? "

" If my father goes."

" So you are determined to go ? "

Cosette seized Marius's hand and pressed it as sole reply.

" Very well," said Marius ; " in that case I shall go elsewhere."

Cosette felt the meaning of this remark even more than she comprehended it ; she turned so pale that her face became white in the darkness, and stammered, —

"What do you mean?"

Marius looked at her, then slowly raised his eyes to heaven, and replied, —

"Nothing."

When he looked down again he saw Cosette smiling at him; the smile of the woman whom we love has a brilliancy which is visible at night.

"How foolish we are! Marius, I have an idea."

"What is it?"

"Follow us if we go away! I will tell you whither, and you can join me where I am."

Marius was now a thoroughly wide-awake man, and had fallen back into reality; hence he cried to Cosette, —

"Go with you! Are you mad? Why, it would require money, and I have none! Go to England! Why, I already owe more than ten louis to Courfeyrac, one of my friends, whom you do not know! I have an old hat, which is not worth three francs, a coat with buttons missing in front, my shirt is all torn, my boots let in water, I am out at elbows, but I have not thought of it for six weeks, and did not tell you. Cosette, I am a wretch; you only see me at night and give me your love : were you to see me by day you would give me a sou. Go to England! Why, I have not enough to pay for the passport!"

He threw himself against a tree, with his arms over his head and his forehead pressed to the bark, neither feeling the wood that grazed his skin nor the fever which spotted his temples, motionless and ready to fall, like the statue of despair. He remained for a long time in this state — people would remain for an eternity in such abysses.   At length he turned and heard behind a little stifled, soft, and sad sound ; it was Cosette sobbing ; she had been crying for more than two hours by the side of Marius, who was reflecting.   He went up to her, fell on his knees, seized her foot, which peeped out from under her skirt, and kissed it.   She let him do so in silence, for there are moments when a woman accepts, like a sombre and resigned duty, the worship of love.

"Do not weep," he said.

She continued, —

"But I am perhaps going away, and you are not able to come with me."

He said, "Do you love me ? "

She replied by sobbing that Paradisaic word, which is never more charming than through tears, "I adore you."

He pursued, with an accent which was an inexpressible caress, —

"Do not weep.   Will you do so much for me as to check your tears ? "

"Do you love me ? " she said.

He took her hand.

"Cosette, I have never pledged my word of honor to any one, because it frightens me, and I feel that my father is by the side of it.   Well, I pledge you my most sacred word of honor that if you go away I shall die."

There was in the accent with which he uttered these words such a solemn and calm melancholy that

Cosette trembled, and she felt that chill which is produced by the passing of a sombre and true thing. In her terror she ceased to weep.

"Now listen to me," he said; "do not expect me to-morrow."

"Why not?"

"Do not expect me till the day after."

"Oh, why?"

"You will see."

"A day without your coming!—oh, it is impossible!"

"Let us sacrifice a day, to have, perhaps, one whole life."

And Marius added in a low voice and aside,— "He is a man who makes no change in his habits, and he never received anybody before the evening."

"What man are you talking about?" Cosette asked.

"I? I did not say anything."

"What do you hope for, then?"

"Wait till the day after to-morrow."

"Do you desire it?"

"Yes, Cosette."

He took her head between his two hands, as she stood on tiptoe to reach him and tried to see his hopes in his eyes. Marius added,—

"By the bye, you must know my address, for something might happen; I live with my friend Courfeyrac, at No. 16, Rue de la Verrerie."

He felt in his pockets, took out a knife, and scratched the address on the plaster of the wall.

In the mean while Cosette had begun looking in his eyes again.

"Tell me your thought, Marius, for you have one. Tell it to me. Oh, tell it to me, so that I may pass a good night!"

"My thought is this: it is impossible that God can wish to separate us. Expect me the day after to-morrow."

"What shall I do till then?" Cosette said. "You are in the world, and come and go; how happy men are! but I shall remain all alone. Oh, I shall be so sad! What will you do to-morrow night, tell me?"

"I shall try something."

"In that case I shall pray to Heaven, and think of you, so that you may succeed. I will not question you any more, as you do not wish it, and you are my master. I will spend my evening in singing the song from 'Euryanthe,' of which you are so fond, and which you heard one night under my shutters. But you will come early the next evening, and I shall expect you at nine o'clock exactly. I warn you. Oh, good Heaven! how sad it is that the days are so long! You hear; I shall be in the garden as it is striking nine."

"And I too."

And without saying a word, moved by the same thought, carried away by those electric currents which place two lovers in continual communication, both intoxicated with voluptuousness, even in their grief, fell into each other's arms without noticing that their lips were joined together, while their up-raised eyes, overflowing with ecstasy and full of tears, contemplated the stars. When Marius left, the street was deserted, for it was the moment when Éponine followed the bandits into the boulevard. While Marius dreamed with his head leaning against a tree an idea had crossed his mind, — an idea, alas! which himself considered mad and impossible. He had formed a violent resolution.

CHAPTER VII.

AN OLD HEART AND A YOUNG HEART FACE TO FACE.

FATHER GILLENORMAND at this period had just passed his ninety-first birthday, and still lived with his daughter at No. 6, Rue des Filles-de-Calvaire, in the old house which was his own property. He was, it will be remembered, one of those antique old men whose age falls on without bending them, and whom even sorrow cannot bow. Still, for some time past his daughter had said, "My father is breaking." He no longer slapped the servants, or rapped so violently with his cane the staircase railing where Basque kept him waiting. The Revolution of July had not exasperated him for more than six months, and he had seen almost with tranquillity in the *Moniteur* this association of words, M. Humblot-Conté, Peer of France. The truth is, that the old man was filled with grief; he did not bend, he did not surrender, for that was not possible either with his moral or physical nature; but he felt himself failing inwardly. For four years he had been awaiting Marius with a firm foot, — that is really the expression, — with the conviction that the wicked young scapegrace would ring his bell some day; and now he had begun to say to himself, when depressed, that Marius might remain away a little too long. It was not death that was insupportable to him, but the idea that perhaps he might not see Marius again. This idea had never occurred to him till one day, and at present it rose before him constantly, and chilled him to death. Absence, as ever happens in natural and true feelings, had only heightened the grandfather's love for the ungrateful boy who had gone away like that. It is on December nights, when the thermometer is almost down at zero, that people think most of the sun. M. Gillenormand was, or fancied himself, utterly incapable of taking a step toward his grandson; "I would rot first," he said to himself. He did not think himself at all in the wrong, but he only thought of Marius with profound tenderness, and the dumb despair of an old man who is going down into the valley of the shadows. He was beginning to lose his teeth, which added to his sorrow. M. Gillenormand, without confessing it to himself, however, for he would have been furious and ashamed of it, had never loved a mistress as he loved Marius. He had hung up in his room, as the first thing he might see on awaking, an old portrait of his other daughter, the one who was dead, Madame de Pontmercy, taken when she was eighteen. He incessantly regarded this portrait, and happened to say one day, while gazing at it, —

"I can notice a likeness."

"To my sister?" Mlle. Gillenormand remarked; "oh, certainly."

The old man added, "And to him too."

When he was once sitting, with his knees against

each other, and his eyes almost closed in a melancholy posture, his daughter ventured to say to him, —

"Father, are you still so furious against — " She stopped, not daring to go further.

"Against whom ? " he asked.

"That poor Marius."

He raised his old head, laid his thin wrinkled fist on the table, and cried, in his loudest and most irritated accent, —

"Poor Marius, you say ! That gentleman is a scoundrel, a scamp, a little vain ingrate, without heart or soul, a proud and wicked man ! "

And he turned away, so that his daughter might not see a tear which he had in his eyes. Three days later he interrupted a silence which had lasted four hours to say to his daughter gruffly, —

"I had had the honor of begging Mademoiselle Gillenormand never to mention his name to me."

Aunt Gillenormand gave up all attempts, and formed this profound diagnostic : " My father was never very fond of my sister after her folly. It is clear that he detests Marius." "After her folly " meant, " since she married the Colonel." Still, as may be conjectured, Mademoiselle Gillenormand failed in her attempt to substitute her favorite, the officer of lancers, in Marius's place. Théodule had met with no success, and M. Gillenormand refused to accept the *qui pro quo ;* for the vacuum in the heart cannot be stopped by a bung. Théodule, on his side, while sniffing the inheritance, felt a repugnance to the labor of pleasing, and the old gentleman annoyed the lancer, while the lancer offended the old gentleman. Lieutenant Théodule was certainly gay but gossiping, frivolous but vulgar, a good liver but bad company ; he had mistresses, it is true, and he talked a good deal about them, it is also true, but then he talked badly. All his qualities had a defect, and M. Gillenormand was worn out with listening to the account of the few amours he had had round his barracks in the Rue de Babylone. And then Lieutenant Théodule called sometimes in uniform with the tricolor cockade, which rendered him simply impossible. M. Gillenormand eventually said to his daughter, " I have had enough of Théodule, for I care but little for a warrior in peace times. You can receive him if you like, but for my part I do not know whether I do not prefer the sabrers to the trailing of sabres, and the clash of blades in a battle is less wretched, after all, than the noise of scabbards on the pavement. And then, to throw up one's head like a king of clubs, and to lace one's self like a woman, to wear stays under a cuirass, is doubly ridiculous. When a man is a real man he keeps himself at an equal distance from braggadocio and foppishness. So keep your Théodule for yourself." Though his daughter said to him, " After all, he is your grand-nephew," it happened that M. Gillenormand, who was grandfather to the end of his nails, was not a grand-uncle at all ; the fact is, that as he was a man of sense and comparison, Théodule only served to make him regret Marius the more.

One evening, it was the 4th of June, which did not

prevent Father Gillenormand from having an excellent fire in his chimney, he had dismissed his daughter, who was sewing in the adjoining room. He was alone in his apartment with the pastoral hangings, with his feet on the andirons, half enveloped in his nine-leaved Coromandel screen, sitting at a table on which two candles burned under a green shade, swallowed up in his needle-worked easy-chair, and holding a book in his hand, which he was not reading. He was dressed, according to his mode, as an "Incroyable," and resembled an old portrait of Garat. This would have caused him to be followed in the streets ; but whenever he went out, his daughter wrapped him up in a sort of episcopal wadded coat, which hid his clothing. At home he never wore a dressing-gown, save when he got up and went to bed. "It gives an old look," he was wont to say. Father Gillenormand was thinking of Marius bitterly and lovingly, and, as usual, bitterness gained the upper hand. His savage tenderness always ended by boiling over and turning into indignation, and he was at the stage when a man seeks to make up his mind and accept that which lacerates. He was explaining to himself that there was no longer any reason for Marius's return, that if he had meant to come home he would have done so long before, and all idea of it must be given up. He tried to form the idea that it was all over, and that he should die without seeing that "gentleman" again. But his whole nature revolted, and his old paternity could not consent. "What," he said, and it was his mournful burden, "he will not come back ! " and his old bald head fell on his chest, and he vaguely fixed a lamentable and irritated glance upon the ashes on his hearth. In the depth of this reverie his old servant Basque came in and asked, —

" Can you receive M. Marius, sir ? "

The old man sat up, livid, and like a corpse which is roused by a galvanic shock. All his blood flowed to his heart, and he stammered, —

" M. Marius ! Who ? "

" I do not know," Basque replied, intimidated and disconcerted by his master's air, " for I did not see him. It was Nicolette who said to me just now, ' There is a young man here ; say it is M. Marius.' "

Father Gillenormand stammered in a low voice, " Show him in."

And he remained in the same attitude, with hanging head and eye fixed on the door. It opened, and a young man appeared ; it was Marius, who stopped in the doorway as if waiting to be asked in. His almost wretched clothes could not be seen in the obscurity produced by the shade, and only his calm, grave, but strangely sorrowful face could be distinguished. Father Gillenormand, as if stunned by stupor and joy, remained for a few minutes seeing nothing but a brilliancy, as when an apparition rises before us. He was ready to faint, and perceived Marius through a mist. It was really he, it was really Marius ! At length, after four years ! He took him in entirely, so to speak, at a glance, and found him handsome, noble, distinguished, grown, a thorough man, with a proper attitude and a charming air. He felt inclined to open his arms and call the boy to him, his bowels were swelled with ravishment, affectionate words welled up and overflowed his bosom. At length all this tenderness burst forth and reached his lips, and through the contrast which formed the basis of his character a harshness issued from it. He said roughly, —

"What do you want here?"

Marius replied with an embarrassed air, —

"Sir —"

Monsieur Gillenormand would have liked for Marius to throw himself into his arms, and he was dissatisfied both with Marius and himself. He felt that he was rough and Marius cold, and it was an insupportable and irritating anxiety to the old gentleman to feel himself so tender and imploring within, and unable to be otherwise than harsh externally. His bitterness returned, and he abruptly interrupted Marius.

"In that case, why do you come?"

The "in that case" meant "if you have not come to embrace me." Marius gazed at his ancestor's marble face.

"Sir —"

The old gentleman resumed in a stern voice, —

"Have you come to ask my pardon? Have you recognized your error?"

He believed that he was putting Marius on the right track, and that "the boy" was going to give way. Marius trembled, for it was a disavowal of his father that was asked of him, and he lowered his eyes and replied, "No, sir."

"Well, in that case," the old man exclaimed impetuously, and with a sharp sorrow full of anger, "what is it you want of me?"

Marius clasped his hands, advanced a step, and said, in a weak, trembling voice, —

"Take pity on me, sir."

This word moved M. Gillenormand; had it come sooner it would have softened him, but it came too late. The old gentleman rose, and rested both hands on his cane; his lips were white, his forehead shook, but his lofty stature towered over the stooping Marius.

"Pity on you, sir! The young man asks pity of an old man of ninety-one! You are entering life, and I am leaving it; you go to the play, to balls, to the coffee-house, the billiard-table; you are witty, you please women, you are a pretty fellow, while I spit on my logs in the middle of summer; you are rich with the only wealth there is, while I have all the poverty of old age, infirmity, and isolation. You have your two-and-thirty teeth, a good stomach, a quick eye, strength, appetite, health, gayety, a forest of black hair, while I have not even my white hair left. I have lost my teeth, I am losing my legs, I am losing my memory, for there are three names of streets which I incessantly confound, — the Rue Charlot, the Rue du Chaume, and the Rue St. Claude. Such is my state; you have a whole future before you, full of sunshine, while I am beginning to see nothing, as I have advanced so far into night. You are in love, that is a matter of course, while I am not beloved by a soul in the world, and yet you ask me for pity! By Jove! Molière forgot that. If that is the way in which you lawyers jest at the palais, I compliment you most sincerely upon it, for you are droll fellows."

And the octogenarian added, in a serious and wrathful voice, —

"Well; what is it you want of me?"

"I am aware, sir," said Marius, "that my presence here displeases you; but I have only come to ask one thing of you, and then I shall go away at once."

"You are a fool!" the old man said. "Who told you to go away?"

This was the translation of the tender words which he had at the bottom of his heart. "Ask my pardon, why don't you? and throw your arms round my neck." M. Gillenormand felt that Marius was going to leave him in a few moments, that his bad reception offended him, and that his harshness expelled him; he said all this to himself, and his grief was augmented by it, and as his grief immediately turned into passion his harshness grew the greater. He had wished that Marius should understand, and Marius did not understand, which rendered the old gentleman furious. He continued, —

"What! you insulted me, your grandfather; you left my house to go the Lord knows whither; you broke your aunt's heart; you went away to lead a bachelor's life, — of course that's more convenient, — to play the fop, come home at all hours, and amuse yourself; you have given me no sign of life; you have incurred debts without even asking me to pay them; you have been a breaker of windows and a brawler; and at the end of four years you return to my house and have nothing more to say to me than that ! "

This violent way of forcing the grandson into tenderness only produced silence on the part of Marius. M. Gillenormand folded his arms, — a gesture which with him was peculiarly imperious, — and bitterly addressed Marius, —

" Let us come to an end. You have come to ask something of me, you say. Well, what is it ? Speak ! "

" Sir," said Marius, with the look of a man who feels that he is going to fall over a precipice, " I have come to ask your permission to marry."

M. Gillenormand rang the bell, and Basque poked his head into the door.

" Send my daughter here."

A second later the door opened again, and Mlle. Gillenormand did not enter, but showed herself. Marius was standing silently, with drooping arms and the face of a criminal, while M. Gillenormand walked up and down the room. He turned to his daughter and said to her, —

" It is nothing. This is M. Marius ; wish him good-evening. This gentleman desires to marry. That will do. Be off ! "

The sound of the old man's sharp, hoarse voice announced a mighty fury raging within him. The aunt looked at Marius in terror, seemed scarce to recognize him, did not utter a syllable, and disappeared before her father's breath like a straw before a hurricane. In the mean while M. Gillenormand had turned back, and was now leaning against the mantel-piece.

"You marry! at the age of one-and-twenty! You have settled all that, and have only a permission to ask, a mere formality! Sit down, sir. Well, you have had a revolution since I had the honor of seeing you last; the Jacobins had the best of it, and you are of course pleased. Are you not a republican since you became a baron? Those two things go famously together, and the republic is a sauce for the barony. Are you one of the decorated of July? Did you give your small aid to take the Louvre, sir? Close by, in the Rue St. Antoine, opposite the Rue des Nonaindières, there is a cannon-ball imbedded in the wall of a house three stories up, with the inscription, 'July 28, 1830.' Go and look at it, for it produces a famous effect. Ah! your friends do very pretty things! By the way, are they not erecting a fountain on the site of the Duc de Berry's monument? So you wish to marry? May I ask, without any indiscretion, who the lady is?"

He stopped, and before Marius had time to answer, he added violently, —

"Ah! have you a profession, a fortune? How much do you earn by your trade as a lawyer?"

"Nothing," said Marius, with a sort of fierceness and almost stern resolution.

"Nothing? Then you have only the twelve hundred livres which I allow you to live on?"

Marius made no reply, and M. Gillenormand continued, —

"In that case, I presume that the young lady is wealthy?"

"Like myself."

" What ! no dowry ? "

" No."

" Any expectations ? "

" I do not think so."

" Quite naked ! And what is the father ? "

" I do not know."

" And what is her name ? "

" Mademoiselle Fauchelevent."

" Mademoiselle Fauchewhat ? "

" Fauchelevent."

" Ptt ! " said the old gentleman.

" Monsieur ! " Marius exclaimed.

M. Gillenormand interrupted him, with the air of a man who is talking to himself, —

" That is it, one-and-twenty, no profession, twelve hundred livres a year, and the Baroness Pontmercy will go and buy two sous' worth of parsley at the green-grocer's ! "

" Sir," Marius replied in the wildness of the last vanishing hope, " I implore you, I conjure you in Heaven's name, with clasped hands I throw myself at your feet, — sir, permit me to marry her ! "

The old man burst into a sharp, melancholy laugh, through which he coughed and spoke, —

" Ah, ah, ah ! you said to yourself, ' I 'll go and see that old periwig, that absurd ass ! What a pity that I am not five-and-twenty yet ! how I would send him a respectful summons ! Old fool, you are too glad to see me ; I feel inclined to marry Mamselle Lord-knows-who, the daughter of Monsieur Lord-knows-what. She has no shoes and I have no shirt ; that matches. I am inclined to throw into the river my career, my youth, my future, my life, and take a plunge into wretchedness with a wife round my neck — that is my idea, and you must consent : ' and the old fossil will consent. Go in, my lad, fasten your paving-stone round your neck, marry your Pousselevent, your Coupelevent, — never, sir, never ! "

" Father — "

" Never ! "

Marius lost all hope through the accent with which this " never " was pronounced. He crossed the room slowly, with hanging head, tottering, and more like a man that is dying than one who is going away. M. Gillenormand looked after him, and at the moment when the door opened and Marius was about to leave the room he took four strides with the senile vivacity of an impetuous and spoiled old man, seized Marius by the collar, pulled him back energetically into the room, threw him into an easy-chair, and said, —

" Tell me all about it."

The word *father* which had escaped from Marius's lips produced this revolution. Marius looked at M. Gillenormand haggardly, but his inflexible face expressed nought now but a rough and ineffable goodness. The ancestor had made way for the grandfather.

" Well, speak ; tell me of your love episodes, tell me all. Sapristi ! how stupid young men are ! "

" My father ! " Marius resumed.

The old gentleman's entire face was lit up with an indescribable radiance.

" Yes, that is it, call me father, and you 'll see."

There was now something so gentle, so good, so open, and so paternal in this sharpness, that Marius, in this sudden passage from discouragement to hope, was, as it were, stunned and intoxicated. As he was seated near the table the light of the candles fell on his seedy attire, which Father Gillenormand studied with amazement.

"Well, father," said Marius.

"What!" M. Gillenormand interrupted him, "have you really no money? You are dressed like a thief."

He felt in a drawer and pulled out a purse, which he laid on the table.

"Here are one hundred louis to buy a hat with."

"My father," Marius continued, "my kind father. If you only knew how I love her! You cannot imagine it. The first time I saw her was at the Luxembourg, where she came to walk. At the beginning I paid no great attention to her, and then I know not how it happened, but I fell in love with her. Oh, how wretched it made me! I see her now every day at her own house, and her father knows nothing about it. Just fancy, they are going away; we see each other at night in the garden; her father means to take her to England; and then I said to myself, 'I will go and see my grandfather and tell him about it.' I should go mad first, I should die, I should have a brain fever, I should throw myself into the water. I must marry her, or else I shall go mad. That is the whole truth, and I do not believe that I have forgotten anything. She lives in a garden with a railing to it, in the Rue Plumet: it is on the side of the Invalides."

Father Gillenormand was sitting radiantly by Marius's side : while listening and enjoying the sound of his voice he enjoyed at the same time a lengthened pinch of snuff. At the words "Rue Plumet" he broke off inhaling, and allowed the rest of the snuff to fall on his knees.

"Rue Plumet! Did you say Rue Plumet? Only think! Is there not a barrack down there? Oh yes, of course there is : your cousin Théodule, the officer, the lancer, told me about it — a little girl, my dear fellow, a little girl! By Jove! yes, Rue Plumet, which used formerly to be called Rue Blomet. I remember it all now, and I have heard about the petite behind the railings in the Rue Plumet. In a garden, a Pamela. Your taste is not bad. I am told she is very tidy. Between ourselves, I believe that ass of a lancer has courted her a little ; I do not exactly know how far matters have gone, but, after all, that is of no consequence. Besides, there is no believing him ; he boasts. Marius, I think it very proper that a young man like you should be in love, for it becomes your age, and I would sooner have you in love than a Jacobin. I would rather know you caught by a petticoat, ay, by twenty petticoats, than by Monsieur de Robespierre. For my part, I do myself the justice of saying that, as regards sans-culottes, I never loved any but women. Pretty girls are pretty girls, hang it all! and there is no harm in that. And so she receives you behind her father's back, does she? That's all right, and I had affairs of the same sort, more than one. Do you know what a man does in such cases? He does not regard the matter ferociously, he does not hurl himself into matrimony, or conclude with marriage and M. le Maire in his scarf. No, he is, although foolish, a youth of spirits and of good sense. Glide, mortals, but do not marry. Such a young man goes to his grandfather, who is well inclined after all, and who has always a few rolls of louis in an old drawer, and he says to him, 'Grandpapa, that's how matters stand;' and grandpapa says, 'It is very simple; youth must make and old age break. I have been young and you will be old. All right, my lad, you will re-quite it to your grandson. Here are two hundred pistoles; go and amuse yourself, confound you!' That is the way in which the matter should be arranged; a man does not marry, but that is no obstacle: do you understand?"

Marius, petrified and incapable of uttering a word, shook his head in the negative. The old gentleman burst into a laugh, winked his agèd eyelid, tapped him on the knee, looked at him in both eyes with a mysterious and radiant air, and said with the tender-est shrug of the shoulders possible, —

"You goose! make her your mistress!"

Marius turned pale; he had understood nothing of what his grandfather had been saying, and this maundering about the Rue Blomet, Pamela, the bar-racks, the lancer, had passed before Marius like a phantasmagoria. Nothing of all this could affect Cosette, who was a lily, and the old gentleman was wandering. But this divagation had resulted in a sentence which Marius understood, and which was a mortal insult to Cosette, and the words, *Make her your mistress,* passed through the pure young man's heart like a sword-blade. He rose, picked up his hat which was on the ground, and walked to the door with a firm, assured step. Then he turned, gave his grandfather a low bow, drew himself up again, and said, —

"Five years ago you outraged my father; to-day you outrage my wife. I have nothing more to ask of you, sir; farewell!"

Father Gillenormand, who was stupefied, opened his mouth, stretched out his arms, strove to rise, and ere he was able to utter a word, the door had closed again, and Marius had disappeared. The old gentleman remained for a few minutes motionless, and as if thunderstruck, unable to speak or breathe, as though a garroter's hand were compressing his throat. At length he tore himself out of his easy-chair, ran to the door as fast as a man can run at ninety-one, opened it, and cried, —

"Help! help!"

His daughter appeared, and then his servants; he went on with a lamentable rattle in his throat, —

"Run after him! catch him up! How did I offend him? He is mad and going away! Oh Lord, oh Lord! this time he will not return."

He went to the window which looked on the street, opened it with his old trembling hands, bent half his body out of it, while Basque and Nicolette held his skirts, and cried, —

"Marius! Marius! Marius! Marius!"

But Marius could not hear him, for at this very moment he was turning the corner of the Rue St.

Louis. The nonagenarian raised his hands twice or thrice to his temples with an expression of agony, tottered back, and sank into an easy-chair, pulseless, voiceless, and tearless, shaking his head and moving his lips with a stupid air, and having nothing left in his eyes or heart but a profound and gloomy rigidity which resembled night.

BOOK IX.

WHERE ARE THEY GOING?

CHAPTER I.

JEAN VALJEAN.

THAT same day, about four in the afternoon, Jean Valjean was seated on one of the most solitary slopes of the Champ de Mars. Either through prudence, a desire to reflect, or simply in consequence of one of those insensible changes of habits which gradually introduce themselves into all existences, he now went out very rarely with Cosette. He had on his workman's jacket and gray canvas trousers, and his long peaked cap concealed his face. He was at present calm and happy by Cosette's side; what had startled and troubled him for a while was dissipated; but during the last week or fortnight anxieties of a fresh nature had sprung up. One day, while walking along the boulevard, he noticed Thénardier; thanks to his disguise, Thénardier did not recognize him, but after that Jean Valjean saw him several times again, and now felt a certainty that Thénardier was prowling about the quarter. This was sufficient to make him form a grand resolution, for Thénardier

present was every peril at once; moreover, Paris
was not quiet, and political troubles offered this inconvenience to any man who had something in his
life to hide, — that the police had become very restless
and suspicious, and when trying to find a man like
Pepin or Morey, might very easily discover a man
like Jean Valjean. He therefore resolved to leave
Paris, even France, and go to England; he had
warned Cosette, and hoped to be off within a week.
He was sitting on the slope, revolving in his mind all
sorts of thoughts, — Thénardier, the police, the journey, and the difficulty of obtaining a passport. From
all these points of view he was anxious; and lastly,
an inexplicable fact, which had just struck him, and
from which he was still hot, added to his alarm.
On the morning of that very day he, the only person
up in the house, and walking in the garden before
Cosette's shutters were opened, suddenly perceived
this line on the wall, probably scratched with a
nail, 16 *Rue de la Verrerie.*

It was quite recent; the lines were white on the
old black mortar, and a bed of nettles at the foot of
the wall was powdered with fine fresh plaster. This
had probably been inscribed during the night. What
was it, — an address, a signal for others, or a warning for himself? In any case, it was evident that the
secrecy of the garden was violated, and that strangers entered it. He remembered the strange incidents
which had already alarmed the house, and his mind
was at work on this subject; but he was careful not
to say a word to Cosette about the line written on
the wall, for fear of alarming her. In the midst of

his troubled thoughts he perceived, from a shadow which the sun threw, that some one was standing on the crest of the slope immediately behind him. He was just going to turn, when a folded paper fell on his knees, as if a hand had thrown it over his head ; he opened the paper and read these words, written in large characters, and in pencil : LEAVE YOUR HOUSE.

Jean Valjean rose smartly, but there was no longer any one on the slope ; he looked round him, and perceived a person, taller than a child and shorter than a man, dressed in a gray blouse and dust-colored cotton-velvet trousers, bestriding the parapet, and slipping down into the moat of the Champ de Mars. Jean Valjean at once went home very thoughtfully.

CHAPTER II.

MARIUS.

Marius had left M. Gillenormand's house in a wretched state; he had gone in with very small hopes, and came out with an immense despair. However, — those who have watched the beginnings of the human heart will comprehend it, — the lancer, the officer, the fop, cousin Théodule, had left no shadow on his mind, not the slightest. The dramatic poet might apparently hope for some complications to be produced by this revelation, so coarsely made to the grandson by the grandfather; but what the drama would gain by it truth would lose. Marius was at that age when a man believes nothing that is wrong; later comes the age when he believes everything. Suspicions are only wrinkles, and early youth has none; what o'erthrows Othello glides over Candide. Suspect Cosette? Marius could have committed a multitude of crimes more easily. He began walking about the streets, the resource of those who suffer, and he thought of nothing which he might have remembered. At two in the morning he went to Courfeyrac's lodging and threw himself on his mattress full dressed; it was bright sunshine when he fell asleep, with that frightful oppressive sleep

which allows ideas to come and go in the brain.
When he awoke he saw Courfeyrac, Enjolras, Feuilly,
and Combeferre, all ready to go out, and extremely
busy. Courfeyrac said to him, —

"Are you coming to General Lamarque's funeral?"
It seemed to him as if Courfeyrac were talking
Chinese. He went out shortly after them, and put
in his pockets the pistols which Javert had intrusted
to him at the affair of February 3, and which still
remained in his possession. They were still loaded,
and it would be difficult to say what obscure notion
he had in his brain when he took them up. The
whole day he wandered about, without knowing
where; it rained at times, but he did not perceive
it; he bought for his dinner a halfpenny roll, put it
in his pocket, and forgot it. It appears that he took
a bath in the Seine without being conscious of it,
for there are moments when a man has a furnace
under his skull, and Marius had reached one of those
moments. He hoped for nothing, feared nothing
now, and had taken this step since the previous day.
He awaited the evening with a feverish impatience,
for he had but one clear idea left, that at nine o'clock
he should see Cosette. This last happiness was now
his sole future; after that came the shadow. At
times, while walking along the most deserted boulevards, he imagined that he could hear strange noises
in Paris; then he thrust his head out of his reverie,
and said, — "Can they be fighting?" At nightfall,
at nine o'clock precisely, he was at the Rue Plumet,
as he had promised Cosette. He had not seen her
for eight-and-forty hours; he was about to see her

again. Every other thought was effaced, and he only felt an extraordinary and profound joy. Those minutes in which men live ages have this sovereign and admirable thing about them, that at the moment when they pass they entirely occupy the heart.

Marius removed the railing and rushed into the garden. Cosette was not at the place where she usually waited for him, and he crossed the garden and went to the niche near the terrace. "She is waiting for me there," he said; but Cosette was not there. He raised his eyes and saw that the shutters of the house were closed; he walked round the garden, and the garden was deserted. Then he returned to the garden, and, mad with love, terrified, exasperated with grief and anxiety, he rapped at the shutters, like a master who returns home at a late hour. He rapped, he rapped again, at the risk of seeing the window open and the father's frowning face appear and ask him, — "What do you want?" This was nothing to what he caught a glimpse of. When he had rapped, he raised his voice, and called Cosette. "Cosette!" he cried: "Cosette!" he repeated imperiously. There was no answer. It was all over; there was no one in the garden, no one in the house. Marius fixed his desperate eyes on this mournful house, which was as black, as silent, and more empty, than a tomb. He gazed at the stone bench on which he had spent so many adorable hours by Cosette's side; then he sat down on the garden steps, with his heart full of gentleness and resolution; he blessed his love in his heart, and said to himself that since Cosette was gone all left him was to die. All at once he heard a voice which seemed to come from the street, crying through the trees, —

" Monsieur Marius ! "

He drew himself up.

" Hilloh ! " he said.

" Monsieur Marius, are you there ? "

" Yes."

" Monsieur Marius," the voice resumed, " your friends are waiting for you at the barricade in the Rue de la Chanvrerie."

This voice was not entirely strange to him, and resembled Éponine's rough, hoarse accents. Marius ran to the railings, pulled aside the shifting bar, passed his head through, and saw some one, who seemed to be a young man, running away in the gloaming.

CHAPTER III.

JEAN VALJEAN's purse was useless to M. Mabœuf, who in his venerable childish austerity had not accepted the gift of the stars; he had not allowed that a star could coin itself into louis d'or, and he had not guessed that what fell from heaven came from Gavroche. Hence he carried the purse to the police commissary of the district, as a lost object, placed by the finder at the disposal of the claimants. The purse was really lost; we need hardly say that no one claimed it, and it did not help M. Mabœuf. In other respects M. Mabœuf had continued to descend: and the indigo experiments had succeeded no better at the Jardin des Plantes than in his garden of Austerlitz. The previous year he owed his housekeeper her wages; and now, as we have seen, he owed his landlord his rent. The Government pawnbrokers' office sold the copper-plates of his *Flora*, at the expiration of thirteen months, and a coppersmith had made stewpans of them. When his plates had disappeared, as he could no longer complete the unbound copies of his *Flora*, which he still possessed, he sold off plates and text to a secondhand bookseller as defective. Nothing was then left him of the labor of his whole life, and he began eating the money produced by these copies. When he saw that this poor resource was growing exhausted he gave up his garden, and did not attend to it ; before, and long before, he had given up the two eggs and the slice of beef which he ate from time to time, and now dined on bread and potatoes. He had sold his last articles of furniture, then everything he had in duplicate, in linen, clothes, and coverlids, and then his herbals and plates ; but he still had his most precious books, among them being several of great rarity, such as the " Les Quadrins Historiques de la Bible," the edition of 1560 ; " La Concordance des Bibles," of Pierre de Besse ; " Les Marguerites de la Marguerite," of Jean de la Haye, with a dedication to the Queen of Navarre ; the work on the " Duties and Dignity of an Ambassador," by the Sieur de Villiers Hotman ; a " Florilegium Rabbinicum," of 1644 ; a Tibullus, of 1567, with the splendid imprint " Venetiis, in ædibus Manutianis ; " and lastly a Diogenes Laertius, printed at Lyons in 1644, in which were the famous various readings of the Vatican manuscript 411, of the thirteenth century, and those of the two Venetian *codices* 393 and 394, so usefully consulted by Henri Estienne, and all the passages in the Doric dialect, only to be found in the celebrated twelfth century manuscript of the Naples library. M. Mabœuf never lit a fire in his room, and went to bed with the sun, in order not to burn a candle ; it seemed as if he no longer had neighbors, for they shunned him when he went out, and he noticed it. The wretchedness of a child interests a mother, the wretchedness of a youth interests an old man, but the wretchedness of an old man interests nobody, and it is the coldest of all distresses. Still M. Mabœuf had not entirely lost his childlike serenity; his eye acquired some vivacity when it settled on his books, and he smiled when he regarded the Diogenes Laertius, which was a unique copy. His glass case was the only furniture which he had retained beyond what was indispensable. One day Mother Plutarch said to him, —

" I have no money to buy dinner with."

What she called dinner consisted of a loaf and four or five potatoes.

" Can't you get it on credit ? " said M. Mabœuf.

" You know very well that it is refused me."

M. Mabœuf opened his bookcase, looked for a long time at all his books in turn, as a father, obliged to decimate his children, would look at them before selecting, then took one up quickly, put it under his arm, and went out. He returned two hours after with nothing under his arm, laid thirty sous on the table, and said, —

" You will get some dinner."

From this moment Mother Plutarch saw a dark veil, which was not raised again, settle upon the old gentleman's candid face. The next day, the next after that, and every day, M. Mabœuf had to begin again ; he went out with a book and returned with a piece of silver. As the second-hand booksellers saw that he was compelled to sell, they bought for twenty sous books for which he had paid twenty francs, and frequently to the same dealers. Volume by volume his whole library passed away, and he said at times, "And yet I am eighty years of age," as if he had some lurking hope that he should reach the end of his days ere he reached the end of his books. His sorrow grew, but once he had a joy : he went out with a Robert Estienne, which he sold for thirty-five sous on the Quai Malaquais, and came home with an Aldus which he had bought for forty sous in the Rue de Grès. "I owe five sous," he said quite radiantly to Mother Plutarch, but that day he did not dine. He belonged to the Horticultural Society, and his poverty was known. The President of the Society called on him, promised to speak about him to the Minister of Commerce and Agriculture, and did so. "What do you say ?" the minister exclaimed. "I should think so ! an old savant ! a botanist ! an inoffensive man ! we must do something for him." The next day M. Mabœuf received an invitation to dine with the minister, and, trembling with joy, showed the letter to Mother Plutarch. "We are saved !" he said. On the appointed day he went to the minister's, and noticed that his ragged cravat, his long, square-cut coat, and shoes varnished with white of egg, astounded the footman. No one spoke to him, not even the minister, and at about ten in the evening, while still waiting for a word, he heard the minister's wife, a handsome lady in a low-necked dress, whom he had not dared to approach, ask, "Who can that old gentleman be ?" He went home afoot at midnight through the pouring rain ; he had sold an Elzevir to pay his hackney coach in going.

Every evening, before going to bed, he had fallen

into the habit of reading a few pages of his Diogenes Laertius ; for he knew enough of Greek to enjoy the peculiarities of the text which he possessed, and had no other joy now left him. A few weeks passed away, and all at once Mother Plutarch fell ill. There is one thing even more sad than having no money to buy bread at a baker's, and that is, not to have money to buy medicine at the chemist's. One night the doctor had ordered a most expensive potion, and then the disease grew worse, and a nurse was necessary. M. Mabœuf opened his bookcase, but there was nothing left in it ; the last volume had departed, and the only thing left him was the Diogenes Laertius. He placed the unique copy under his arm and went out, — it was June 4, 1832 ; he proceeded to Royol's successor at the Porte St. Jacques, and returned with one hundred francs. He placed the pile of five-franc pieces on the old servant's table, and entered his bedroom without uttering a syllable. At dawn of the next day he seated himself on the overturned post in his garden, and over the hedge he might have been seen the whole morning, motionless, with drooping head, and eyes vaguely fixed on the faded flower-beds. It rained every now and then, but the old man did not seem to notice it ; but in the afternoon extraordinary noises broke out in Paris, resembling musket-shots, and the clamor of a multitude. Father Mabœuf raised his head, noticed a gardener passing, and said, —

"What is the matter ? "

The gardener replied, with the spade on his back, and with the most peaceful accent, —

" It 's the riots."

" What !   Riots ? "

" Yes ; they are fighting."

" Why are they fighting ? "

" The Lord alone knows," said the gardener.

" In what direction ? "

" Over by the arsenal."

Father Mabœuf went into his house, took his hat, mechanically sought for a book to place under his arm, found none, said, " Ah, it is true ! " and went out with a wandering look.

BOOK X.

THE FIFTH OF JUNE, 1832.

CHAPTER I.

THE SURFACE OF THE QUESTION.

OF what is a revolt composed? Of nothing and of everything, of an electricity released by degrees, of a flame which suddenly breaks out, of a wandering strength and a passing breath. This breath meets with heads that talk, brains that dream, souls that suffer, passions that burn, and miseries which yell, and carries them off with it. Whither? It is chance work; through the State, through the laws, through prosperity and the insolence of others. Irritated convictions, embittered enthusiasms, aroused indignations, martial instincts suppressed, youthful courage exalted, and generous blindnesses; curiosity, a taste for a change, thirst for something unexpected, the feeling which causes us to find pleasure in reading the announcement of a new piece, or on hearing the machinist's whistle; vague hatreds, rancors, disappointments, every vanity which believes that destiny has been a bankrupt to it; straitened circumstances, empty dreams, ambitions surrounded with escarpments, every man who hopes for an issue from an overthrow, and, lastly, at the very bottom, the mob, that mud which takes fire, — such are the elements of riot. The greatest and the most infamous, beings who prowl about beyond the pale of everything while awaiting an opportunity, gypsies, nameless men, highway vagabonds, the men who sleep o' nights in a desert of houses with no other roof but the cold clouds of heaven, those who daily ask their bread of chance and not of toil ; the unknown men of wretchedness and nothingness, bare arms and bare feet, belong to the riot. Every man who has in his soul a secret revolt against any act of the State, of life, or of destiny, borders on riot ; and so soon as it appears he begins to quiver and to feel himself lifted by the whirlwind.

Riot is a species of social atmospheric waterspout, which is suddenly formed in certain conditions of temperature, and which in its revolutions mounts, runs, thunders, tears up, razes, crushes, demolishes, and uproots, bearing with it grand and paltry natures, the strong man and the weak mind, the trunk of a tree and the wisp of straw. Woe to the man whom it carries as well as to the one it dashes at, for it breaks one against the other. It communicates to those whom it seizes a strange and extraordinary power ; it fills the first comer with the force of events and converts everything into projectiles ; it makes a cannon-ball of a stone, and a general of a porter. If we may believe certain oracles of the crafty policy, a little amount of riot is desirable from the governing point of view. The system is, that riot strengthens

those governments which it does not overthrow; it
tries the army; it concentrates the bourgeoisie,
strengthens the muscles of the police, and displays
the force of the social framework. It is a lesson
in gymnastics, and almost hygiene; and power feels
better after a riot, as a man does after a rubbing
down. Riot, thirty years ago, was also regarded
from other stand-points. There is for everything a
theory which proclaims itself as "common sense,"
a mediation offered between the true and the false:
explanation, admonition, and a somewhat haughty
extenuation which, because it is composed of blame
and apology, believes itself wisdom, and is often
nothing but pedantry. An entire political school,
called the "Juste milieu," emanated from this, and
between cold water and hot water there is the luke-
warm-water party. This school, with its false depth
entirely superficial, which dissects effects without
going back to causes, scolds, from the elevation of
semi-science, the agitations of the public streets.

If we listen to this school we hear: "The riots
which complicated the deed of 1830 deprived that
grand event of a portion of its purity. The revolution of July was a fine blast of the popular wind,
suddenly followed by a blue sky, and the riot caused
a cloudy sky to reappear, and compelled the revolution, originally so remarkable through unanimity, to
degenerate into a quarrel. In the revolution of July,
as in every progress produced by a shock, there were
secret fractures; the riot rendered them perceptible.
After the revolution of July only the deliverance was
felt, but after the riots the catastrophe was felt.

Every riot closes shops, depresses the funds, conster-
nates the Stock Exchange, suspends trade, checks
business, and entails bankruptcies; there is no money,
trade is disconcerted, capital is withdrawn, labor is
at a discount, there is fear everywhere, and counter-
strokes take place in every city, whence come gulfs.
It is calculated that the first day of riot costs France
twenty millions of francs, the second forty, and the
third sixty. Hence a riot of three days costs one hundred and twenty millions; that is to say, if we only
regard the financial result, is equivalent to a disaster,
shipwreck, or lost action, which might annihilate a
fleet of sixty vessels of the line. Indubitably, riots,
historically regarded, had their beauty; the war of
the paving-stones is no less grand or pathetic than
the war of thickets; in the one there is the soul of
forests, in the other the heart of cities; one has Jean
Chouan, the other has Jeanne. Riots lit up luridly
but splendidly all the most original features of the
Parisian character, — generosity, devotion, stormy
gayety, students proving that bravery forms a part
of intellect, the National Guard unswerving, bivouacs
formed by shop-keepers, fortresses held by gamins,
and contempt of death in the passers-by. Schools
and legions came into collision, but, after all, there
was only the difference of age between the combatants, and they are the same race; the same stoical
men who die at the age of twenty for their ideas,
and at forty for their families; the army, ever sad in
civil wars, opposed prudence to audacity; and the
riots, while manifesting the popular intrepidity, were
the education of the bourgeois courage. That is all

very well, but is all this worth the blood shed? And
then add to the bloodshed the future darkened, progress compromised, anxiety among the better classes,
honest liberals despairing, foreign absolutism delighted at these wounds dealt to revolution by itself,
and the conquered of 1830 triumphing and shouting,
'Did we not say so?' Add Paris possibly aggran-
dized, France assuredly diminished. Add — for we
must tell the whole truth — the massacres which too
often dishonored the victory of order, which became
ferocious, over liberty which went mad, and we must
arrive at the conclusion that riots have been fatal."

Thus speaks that wisdom, almost, with which the
bourgeoisie, that people, almost, are so readily contented. For our part, we regret the word riots as
being too wide, and consequently too convenient,
and make a distinction between one popular movement and another; we do not ask ourselves whether
a riot costs as much as a battle. In the first place,
why a battle? Here the question of war arises. Is
war less a scourge than riot is a calamity? And then,
are all riots calamities? And even supposing that
July 14 cost one hundred and twenty millions, the
establishment of Philip V. in Spain cost France two
billions, and even were the price equal we should
prefer the 14th July. Besides, we reject these figures, which seem reasons and are only words, and a
riot being given, we examine it in itself. In all that
the doctrinaire objection we have just reproduced
says, the only question is the effect, and we seek for
the cause.

CHAPTER II.

THERE is riot, and there is insurrection; they are two passions, one of which is just, the other unjust. In democratic States, the only ones based on justice, it sometimes happens that the fraction usurps power; in that case the whole people rises, and the necessary demand for its rights may go so far as taking up arms. In all the questions which result from collective sovereignty, the war of all against the fraction is insurrection, and the attack of the fraction on the masses is a riot; according as the Tuileries contain the king or the convention, they are justly or unjustly attacked. The same guns pointed at the mob are in the wrong on August 14, and in the right on the 14th Vendémiaire. Their appearance is alike, but the base is different; the Swiss defend what is false, and Bonaparte what is true. What universal suffrage has done in its liberty and its sovereignty cannot be undone by the street. It is the same in matters of pure civilization, and the instinct of the masses, clear-sighted yesterday, may be perturbed to-morrow. The same fury is legitimate against Terray and absurd against Turgot. Smashing engines, pillaging store-houses, tearing up rails, the demolition of docks, the wrong ways of multitudes, the denial of popular justice to progress, Ramus assassinated by the scholars, and Rousseau expelled from Switzerland by stones, — all this is riot. Israel rising against Moses, Athens against Phocion, Rome against Scipio, are riots, while Paris attacking the Bastille is insurrection. The soldiers opposing Alexander, the sailors mutinying against Christopher Columbus, are the same revolt, — an impious revolt; why? Because Alexander does for Asia with the sword what Columbus does for America with the compass; Alexander, like Columbus, finds a world. These gifts of a world to civilization are such increments of light, that any resistance in such a case is culpable. At times the people breaks its fidelity to itself, and the mob behaves treacherously to the people. Can anything, for instance, be stranger than the long and sanguinary protest of the salt smugglers, a legitimate chronic revolt which at the decisive moment, on the day of salvation, and in the hour of the popular victory, espouses the throne, turns royalist, and instead of an insurrection against the government becomes a riot for it? These are gloomy masterpieces of ignorance. The salt smuggler escapes from the royal gallows, and with the noose still round his neck mounts the white cockade. "Death to the salt taxes" brings into the world, "Long live the king." The killers of St. Bartholomew, the murderers of September, the massacrers of Avignon, the assassins of Coligny, of Madame de Lamballe, the assassins of Brune, the Miquelets, the Verdets, and the Cadenettes, the Companions of Jehu, and the Chevaliers du

Brassard, — all this is riot. The Vendée is a grand Catholic riot. The sound of right in motion can be recognized, and it does not always come from the trembling of the overthrown masses ; there are mad furies and cracked bells, and all the tocsins do not give the sound of bronze. The commotion of passions and ignorances differs from the shock of progress. Rise, if you like, but only to grow, and show me in what direction you are going, for insurrection is only possible with a forward movement. Any other uprising is bad, every violent step backwards is riot, and recoiling is an assault upon the human race. Insurrection is the outburst of the fury of truth ; the paving-stones which insurrection tears up emit the spark of right, and they only leave to riot their mud. Danton rising against Louis XVI. is insurrection ; Hébert against Danton is riot.

Hence it comes that if insurrection in given cases may be, as Lafayette said, the most holy of duties, riot may be the most fatal of attacks. There is also some difference in the intensity of caloric ; insurrection is often a volcano, a riot often a straw fire. Revolt, as we have said, is sometimes found in the power. Polignac is a rioter, and Camille Desmoulins is a government. At times insurrection is a resurrection. The solution of everything by universal suffrage being an absolutely modern fact, and all history anterior to that fact being for four thousand years filled with violated right and the suffering of the peoples, each epoch of history brings with it the protest which is possible to it. Under the Cæsars there was no insurrection, but there was Juvenal. The *facit indig-*

natio takes the place of the Gracchi.   Under the Cæsars there is the Exile of Syene, and there is also the man of the " Annals." We will not refer to the immense Exile of Patmos, who also crushes the real world with a protest in the name of the ideal world, converts a vision into an enormous satire, and casts on Rome-Nineveh, Rome-Babylon, and Rome-Sodom the flashing reflection of the Apocalypse.   John on his rock is the sphinx on its pedestal.   We cannot understand him, for he is a Jew, and writes in Hebrew ; but the man who writes the " Annals" is a Latin, or, to speak more correctly, a Roman.   As the Neros reign in the black manner, they must be painted in the same.   Work produced by the graver alone would be pale, and so a concentrated biting prose must be poured into the lines.   Despots are of some service to thinkers, for chained language is terrible language, and the writer doubles and triples his style when silence is imposed by a master on the people.   There issues from this silence a certain mysterious fulness which filters and fixes itself in bronze in the thought.   Compression in history produces conciseness in the historian, and the granitic solidity of certain celebrated prose is nothing but a pressure put on by the tyrant. Tyranny forces the writer into contraction of the diameter, which is increase of strength.   The Ciceronian period, scarce sufficient for Verres, would be blunted upon a Caligula.   The less spread in the phrase, the more weight in the blow.   The thoughts of Tacitus come straight from the shoulder.   The honesty of a great heart condensed in justice and truth is annihilating.

We must observe, by the way, that Tacitus is not historically superimposed on Cæsar, and the Tiberii are reserved for him. Cæsar and Tacitus are two successive phenomena, whose meeting seems to be mysteriously prevented by Him who regulates the entrances and exits on the stage of centuries. Cæsar is great, Tacitus is great, and God spares these two grandeurs by not bringing them into collision. The judge, in striking Cæsar, might strike too hard and be unjust, and God does not wish that. The great wars of Africa and Spain, the Cilician pirates destroyed, civilization introduced into Gaul, Britain, and Germany, — all this glory covers the Rubicon. There is in this a species of delicacy on the part of divine justice, hesitating to let loose on the illustrious usurper the formidable historian, saving Cæsar from the sentence of a Tacitus, and granting extenuating circumstances to genius. Assuredly despotism remains despotism, even under the despot of genius. There is corruption under illustrious tyrants, but the moral plague is more hideous still under infamous tyrants. In such reigns nothing veils the shame; and the producers of examples, Tacitus like Juvenal, buffet more usefully in the presence of this human race this ignominy, which has no reply to make. Rome smells worse under Vitellius than under Sylla; under Claudius and Domitian there is a deformity of baseness corresponding with the ugliness of the tyrant. The foulness of the slaves is the direct product of the despots; a miasma is extracted from these crouching consciences in which the master is reflected; the public power is unclean, heads are small, consciences flat, and souls vermin; this is the case under Caracalla, Commodus, and Heliogabalus, while from the Roman senate under Cæsar there only issues the smell of dung peculiar to eagles' nests. Hence the apparently tardy arrival of Juvenal and Tacitus, for the demonstrator steps in at the hour for the experiment to be performed.

But Juvenal or Tacitus, like Isaiah in biblical times and Dante in the Middle Ages, is the man; riot and insurrection are the multitude, which is sometimes wrong, sometimes right. In the most general cases riot issues from a material fact, but insurrection is always a moral phenomenon. Riot is Masaniello; insurrection is Spartacus. Insurrection is related to the mind, riot to the stomach; Gaster is irritated, but Gaster is certainly not always in the wrong. In questions of famine, riot, the Buzançais one, for instance, has a true, pathetic, and just starting point, and yet it remains a riot. Why? Because, though right in the abstract, it is wrong in form. Ferocious though legitimate, violent though strong, it has struck at random. It marches like a blind elephant, crushing things in its passage; it has left behind it the corpses of old men, women, and children, and has shed, without knowing why, the blood of the unoffending and the innocent. To nourish the people is a good motive, but to slaughter it is a bad means.

All armed protests, even the most legitimate, even August 10 and July 14, set out with the same trouble, and before right is disengaged there are tumult and foam. At the outset an insurrection is a riot, in the same way as the river is a torrent, and generally pours itself into that ocean, Revolution. Sometimes, however, insurrection, which has come from those lofty mountains which command the moral horizon, justice, wisdom, reason, and right, and is composed of the purest snow of the ideal, after a long fall from rock to rock, after reflecting the sky in its transparency, and being swollen by a hundred confluents in its majestic course, suddenly loses itself in some bourgeois bog, as the Rhine does in the marshes. All this belongs to the past, and the future will be different; for universal suffrage has this admirable thing about it, that it dissolves riot in its origin, and, by giving insurrection a vote, deprives it of the weapon. The disappearance of war, street wars as well as frontier wars, — such is the inevitable progress. Whatever To-day may be, peace is To-morrow. However, the bourgeois, properly so called, makes but a slight distinction between insurrection and riot. To him everything is sedition, pure and simple rebellion, the revolt of the dog against the master, an attempt to bite, which must be punished with the chain and the kennel, a barking, until the day when the dog's head, suddenly enlarged, stands out vaguely in the shadow with a lion's face. Then the bourgeois shouts, " Long live the people ! "

This explanation given, how does the movement of 1832 stand to history? Is it a riot or an insurrection? It is an insurrection. It may happen that in the course of our narrative of a formidable event we may use the word " riot," but only to qualify surface facts, and while still maintaining the distinction between the form riot and the basis insurrection. The movement of 1832 had in its rapid explosion and mournful extinction so much grandeur that even those who only see a riot in it speak of it respectfully. To them it is like a remnant of 1830 ; for, as they say, excited imaginations cannot be calmed in a day, and a revolution does not stop short with a precipice, but has necessarily a few undulations before it returns to a state of peace, like a mountain in redescending to the plain. There are no Alps without Jura, nor Pyrenees without Asturia. This pathetic crisis of contemporary history, which the memory of the Parisians calls the " time of the riots," is assuredly a characteristic hour among the stormy hours of this age. One last word before we return to our story.

The facts which we are going to record belong to that dramatic and living reality which the historian sometimes neglects through want of time and space, but they contain — we insist upon it — life, heartbeats, and human thrills. Small details, as we think we have said, are, so to speak, the foliage of great events, and are lost in the distance of history. The period called the riots abounds in details of this nature, and the judicial inquiries, through other than historic reasons, have not revealed everything, or perhaps studied it. We are, therefore, going to bring into light among the peculiarities known and published, things which are not known and facts over which the forgetfulness of some and the death of others have passed. Most of the actors in these gigantic scenes have disappeared. On the next day they held their tongues, but we may say that we saw what we are about to narrate. We will change a few names, for history recounts and does not denounce, but we will depict true things. The nature of our book will only allow us to display one side and one episode, assuredly the least known, of the days of June 5 and 6, 1832; but we will do so in such a way that the reader will be enabled to catch a glimpse of the real face of this frightful public adventure behind the dark veil which we are about to lift.

CHAPTER III.

A BURIAL GIVES OPPORTUNITY FOR A REVIVAL.

IN the spring of 1832, although for three months cholera had chilled minds and cast over their agitation a species of dull calm, Paris had been for a long time ready for a commotion. As we have said, the great city resembles a piece of artillery when it is loaded, — a spark need only fall and the gun goes off. In June, 1832, the spark was the death of General Lamarque. Lamarque was a man of renown and of action, and had displayed in succession, under the Empire and the Restoration, the two braveries necessary for the two epochs, — the bravery of the battle-field and the bravery of the oratorical tribune. He was eloquent as he had been valiant, and a sword was felt in his words; like Foy, his predecessor, after holding the command erect, he held liberty erect; he sat between the Left and the extreme Left, beloved by the people because he accepted the chances of the future, and beloved by the mob because he had served the Emperor well. He was with Gérard and Drouet one of the Napoleon's marshals *in petto*, and the treaties of 1815 affected him like a personal insult. He hated Wellington with a direct hatred, which pleased the multitude, and for the last seventeen years, scarcely paying attention to intermediate events, he had majestically nursed his grief for Waterloo. In his dying hour he pressed to his heart a sword which the officers of the Hundred Days had given him; and while Napoleon died uttering the word *army*, Lamarque died pronouncing the word *country*. His death, which was expected, was feared by the people as a loss, and by the Government as an opportunity. This death was a mourning, and like everything which is bitter, mourning may turn into revolt. This really happened. On the previous evening, and on the morning of June 5th, the day fixed for the interment of Lamarque, the Faubourg St. Antoine, close to which the procession would pass, assumed a formidable aspect. This tumultuous network of streets was filled with rumors, and people armed themselves as they could. Carpenters carried off the bolts of their shop "to break in doors with;" one of them made a dagger of a stocking-weaver's hook, by breaking off the hook and sharpening the stump. Another in his fever "to attack" slept for three nights in his clothes. A carpenter of the name of Lombier met a mate, who asked him, "Where are you going?" "Why, I have no weapon, and so I am going to my shop to fetch my compasses." "What to do?" "I don't know," Lombier said. A porter of the name of Jacqueline arrested any workman who happened to pass, and said, "Come with me." He paid for a pint of wine, and asked, "Have you work?" "No." "Go to Filspierre's, between the Montreuil and Charonne barrières, and you will find work." At Filspierre's cartridges and arms were distributed.

Some well-known chiefs went the rounds, that is to say, ran from one to the other to collect their followers. At Barthélemy's, near the Barrière du Trône, and at Capel's, the Petit Chapeau, the drinkers accosted each other with a serious air, and could be heard saying, " Where is your pistol ? " " Under my blouse ; and yours ? " " Under my shirt." In the Rue Traversière, in front of Roland's workshop, and in the yard of the Maison Brulée, before the workshop of Bernier the tool-maker, groups stood whispering. The most ardent among them was a certain Mavot, who never stopped longer than a week at a shop, for his masters sent him away, " as they were obliged to quarrel with him every day." Mavot was killed the next day on the barricade of the Rue Menilmontant. Pretot, who was also destined to die in the struggle, seconded Mavot, and replied to the question " What is your object ? " " Insurrection." Workmen assembled at the corner of the Rue de Bercy, awaiting a man of the name of Lemarin, revolutionary agent for the Faubourg St. Marceau, and passwords were exchanged almost publicly.

On June 5, then, a day of sunshine and shower, the funeral procession of General Lamarque passed through Paris with the official military pomp, somewhat increased by precautions. Two battalions with covered drums and reversed muskets, ten thousand of the National Guard with their sabres at their side, and the batteries of the artillery of the National Guard escorted the coffin, and the hearse was drawn by young men. The officers of the Invalides followed immediately after, bearing laurel branches, and

then came a countless, agitated, and strange multitude, the sectionists of the friends of the people, the
school of law, the school of medicine, refugees of all
nations, Spanish, Italian, German, Polish flags, horizontal tricolor flags, every banner possible, children
waving green branches, stone-cutters and carpenters
out of work at this very time, and printers easy to
recognize by their paper caps, marching two and
two, three and three, uttering cries, nearly all shaking sticks, and some sabres, without order, but with
one soul, at one moment a mob, at another a column.
Squads selected their chiefs, and a man armed with
a brace of pistols, which were perfectly visible, seemed
to pass others in review, whose files made way for
him.   On the sidewalks of the boulevards, on the
branches of the trees, in the balconies, at the windows and on the roofs, there was a dense throng of
men, women, and children, whose eyes were full
of anxiety.   An armed crowd passed, and a startled
crowd looked at it; on its side Government was observing, with its hand on the sword-hilt.   There might
be seen, — all ready to march, cartridge-boxes full,
guns and carbines loaded, — on the Place Louis XV.,
four squadrons of carbineers in the middle, with
trumpeters in front; in the Pays Latin, and at the
Jardin des Plantes, the municipal guard échelonned
from street to street; at the Halle-aux-Vins a squadron of dragoons, at the Grève one half of the 12th
Light Infantry, the other half at the Bastille ; the
6th Dragoons at the Celestins, and the court of the
Louvre full of artillery.   The rest of the troops were
confined to barracks, without counting the regiments

in the environs of Paris. The alarmed authorities held suspended over the threatening multitude twenty-four thousand soldiers in the city and thirty thousand in the suburbs.

Various rumors circulated in the procession, legitimist intrigues were talked about, and they spoke about the Duke of Reichstadt, whom God was marking for death at the very moment when the crowd designated him for Emperor. A person who was never discovered announced that at appointed hours two overseers, gained over, would open to the people the gates of a small arm-factory. An enthusiasm blended with despondency was visible in the uncovered heads of most of the persons present, and here and there too in this multitude, suffering from so many violent but noble emotions, might be seen criminal faces and ignoble lips, that muttered, " Let us plunder." There are some agitations which stir up the bottom of the marsh and bring clouds of mud to the surface of the water; this is a phenomenon familiar to a well-constituted police force. The procession proceeded with feverish slowness from the house of death along the boulevards to the Bastille. It rained at intervals, but the rain produced no effect on this crowd. Several incidents, such as the coffin carried thrice round the Vendôme column, stones thrown at the Duc de Fitzjames, who was noticed in a balcony with his hat on his head, the Gallic cock torn from a popular flag and dragged in the mud, a policeman wounded by a sword-thrust at the Porte St. Martin, an officer of the 12th Light Infantry saying aloud, "I am a Republican," the Polytechnic school coming up, after forcing the gates, and the cries of " Long live the Polytechnic School ! " " Long live the Republic ! " marked the passage of the procession. At the Bastille long formidable files of spectators, coming down from the Faubourg St. Antoine, effected their junction with the procession, and a certain terrible ebullition began to agitate the crowd. A man was heard saying to another, " You see that fellow with the red beard ; he will say when it is time to fire." It seems that this red beard reappeared with the same functions in a later riot, the Quenisset affair.

The hearse passed the Bastille, followed the canal, crossed the small bridge, and reached the esplanade of the bridge of Austerlitz, where it halted. At this moment a bird's-eye view of the crowd would have offered the appearance of a comet, whose head was on the esplanade, and whose tail was prolonged upon the boulevard as far as the Porte St. Martin. A circle was formed round the hearse, and the vast crowd was hushed. Lafayette spoke, and bade farewell to Lamarque : it was a touching and august moment, — all heads were uncovered, and all hearts beat. All at once a man on horseback, dressed in black, appeared in the middle of the group with a red flag, though others say with a pike surmounted by a red cap. Lafayette turned his head away, and Excelmans left the procession. This red flag aroused a storm and disappeared in it : from the Boulevard Bourdon to the bridge of Austerlitz one of those clamors which resemble billows stirred up the multitude, and two prodigious cries were raised, "Lamarque to the Panthéon!" — " Lafayette to the Hôtel de Ville!" Young men, amid the acclamations of the crowd, began dragging Lamarque in the hearse over the bridge of Austerlitz, and Lafayette in a hackney coach along the Quai Morland. In the crowd that surrounded and applauded Lafayette people noticed and pointed out to each other a German of the name of Ludwig Snyder, who has since died a centenarian, who also went through the campaign of 1776, and had fought at Trenton under Washington, and under Lafayette at Brandywine.

The municipal cavalry galloped along the left bank to stop the passage of the bridge, while on the right the dragoons came out of the Célestins and deployed along the Quai Morland. The people who were drawing Lafayette suddenly perceived them at a turning of the quay, and cried, " The Dragoons!" The troops advanced at a walk, silently, with their pistols in the holsters, sabres undrawn, and musquetoons slung with an air of gloomy expectation. Two hundred yards from the little bridge they halted, the coach in which was Lafayette went up to them, they opened their ranks to let it pass, and then closed up again. At this moment the dragoons and the crowd came in contact, and women fled in terror. What took place in this fatal minute? No one could say, for it is the dark moment when two clouds clash together. Some state that a bugle-call sounding the charge was heard on the side of the Arsenal, others that a dragoon was stabbed with a knife by a lad. The truth is, that three shots were suddenly fired, one killing Major Cholet, the second an old deaf woman who was closing her window in the Rue Contrescarpe, while the third grazed an officer's shoulder. A woman cried, "They have begun too soon!" and all at once on the side opposite the Quai Morland, a squadron of dragoons, which had been left in barracks, was seen galloping up the Rue Bassompierre and the Boulevard Bourdon, with naked swords, and sweeping everything before it.

Now all is said, the tempest is unchained, stones shower, the fusillade bursts forth : many rush to the water's edge and cross the small arm of the Seine, which is now filled up : the timber-yards on Isle Louviers, that ready-made citadel, bristle with combatants, stakes are pulled up, pistols are fired, a barricade is commenced, the young men, driven back, pass over the bridge of Austerlitz with the hearse at the double, and charge the municipal guard : the carabineers gallop up, the dragoons sabre, the crowd disperses in all directions, a rumor of war flies to the four corners of Paris : men cry "To arms!" and run, overthrow, fly, and resist. Passion spreads the riot as the wind does fire.

CHAPTER IV.

THE EBULLITIONS OF OTHER DAYS.

NOTHING is more extraordinary than the commencement of a riot, for everything breaks out everywhere at once. Was it foreseen? Yes. Was it prepared? No. Where does it issue from? From the pavement. Where does it fall from? The clouds. At one spot the insurrection has the character of a plot, at another of an improvisation. The first-comer grasps a current of the mob and leads it whither he pleases. It is a beginning full of horror, with which a sort of formidable gayety is mingled. First there is a clamor; shops are closed, and the goods disappear from the tradesmen's windows; then dropping shots are heard; people fly; gateways are assailed with the butts of muskets, and servant-maids may be heard laughing in the yards of the houses and saying, "There's going to be a row."

A quarter of an hour had not elapsed: this is what was going on simultaneously at twenty different points of Paris. In the Rue St. Croix de la Bretonnerie, twenty young men, with beards and long hair, entered a wine-shop and came out a moment after carrying a horizontal tricolor flag covered with crape, and having at their head three men armed, one with a sabre, the second with a gun, and the third with a pike. In the Rue des Nonaindières, a well-dressed bourgeois, who had a large stomach, a sonorous voice, bald head, lofty forehead, black beard, and one of those rough moustaches which cannot be kept from bristling, publicly offered cartridges to passers-by. In the Rue St. Pierre Montmartre bare-armed men carried about a black flag, on which were read these words, in white letters : "Republic or death." In the Rue des Jeûneurs, Rue du Cadran, Rue Montorgueil, and Rue Mandar, groups appeared waving flags, on which could be distinguished in gold letters the word "Section," with a number. One of these flags was red and blue, with an imperceptible parting line of white. A weapon factory in the Boulevard St. Martin and three gunsmiths' shops — the first in the Rue Beaubourg ; the second, Rue Michel le Comte ; and the third, Rue du Temple — were pillaged. In a few minutes the thousand hands of the mob seized and carried off two hundred and thirty guns nearly all double-barrelled, sixty-four sabres, and eighty-three pistols. In order to arm as many persons as possible, one took the musket, the other the bayonet. Opposite the Quai de la Grève young men armed with muskets stationed themselves in the rooms of some ladies in order to fire ; one of them had a wheel-lock gun. They rang, went in and began making cartridges, and one of the ladies said afterwards, "I did not know what cartridges were till my husband told me." A crowd broke into a curiosity-shop on the Rue des Vieilles-Haudriettes, and took from it yataghans and Turkish weapons. The corpse of a mason killed by a bullet lay in the Rue de la Perle. And then, on the right bank and the left bank, on the quays, on the boulevards, in the Quartier Latin, and on the Quartier of the Halles, panting men, workmen, students, and sectionists read proclamations, shouted " To arms ! " broke the lanterns, unharnessed vehicles, tore up the pavement, broke in the doors of houses, uprooted trees, searched cellars, rolled up barrels, heaped up paving-stones, furniture, and planks, and formed barricades.

Citizens were forced to lend a hand; the rioters went to the wives, compelled them to surrender the sabre and musket of their absent husbands, and then wrote on the door in chalk, " The arms are given up." Some signed with their own names receipts for musket and sabre, and said, " Send for them to-morrow at the Mayoralty." Isolated sentries and National Guards proceeding to their gathering-place were disarmed in the streets. Epaulettes were torn from the officers, and in the Rue du Cimetière St. Nicolas an officer of the National Guard, pursued by a party armed with sticks and foils, found refuge with great difficulty in a house, where he was compelled to remain till night, and then went away in disguise. In the Quartier St. Jacques the students came out of their lodging-houses in swarms, and went up the Rue Sainte Hyacinthe to the Café du Progrès, or down to the Café des Sept Billards in the Rue des Mathurins ; there the young men stood on benches and distributed arms ; and the timber-yard in the Rue Transnonain was pillaged to make

barricades.   Only at one spot did the inhabitants offer
resistance, — at the corner of the Rue Sainte Avoye
and Simon le Franc, where they themselves destroyed
the barricade.   Only at one point too did the insurgents give way ; they abandoned a barricade begun
in the Rue du Temple, after firing at a detachment
of the National Guard, and fled along the Rue de
la Corderie.   The detachment picked up on the barricade a red flag, a packet of cartridges, and three
hundred pistol bullets ; the National Guards tore up
the flag, and carried off the strips on the point of
their bayonets.   All this which we are describing
here slowly and successively was going on simultaneously at all parts of the city, in the midst of
a vast tumult, like a number of lightning flashes in
a single peal of thunder.

In less than an hour twenty-seven barricades issued
from the ground in the single quarter of the Halles ;
in the centre was that famous house No. 50, which
was the fortress of Jeanne and her hundred-and-six
companions, and which, flanked on one side by a
barricade at St. Merry, and on the other by a barricade in the Rue Maubuée, commanded the three
streets, Des Arcis, St. Martin, and Aubry le Boucher,
the last of which it faced.   Two square barricades
retreated, the one from the Rue Montorgueil into la
Grande Truanderie, the other from the Rue Geoffroy
Langevin into the Rue Sainte Avoye.   This is without counting innumerable barricades in twenty other
districts of Paris, as the Marais and the Montagne
Sainte Geneviève ; one in the Rue Ménilmontant,
in which a gate could be seen torn off its hinges ;

and another near the little bridge of the Hôtel Dieu, made of an overthrown vehicle. Three hundred yards from the Préfecture of Police, at the barricade in the Rue des Ménétriers, a well-dressed man distributed money to the artisans ; at the barricade in the Rue Grenetat a horseman rode up and handed to the man who seemed to be the chief of the barricade a roll, which looked like money. " Here," he said, " is something to pay the expenses, — the wine, etc." A light-haired young man, without a cravat, went from one barricade to another, carrying the passwords ; and another, with drawn sabre and a blue forage-cap on his head, stationed sentries. In the interior, within the barricades, the wine-shops and cabarets were converted into guard-rooms, and the riot was managed in accordance with the most skilful military tactics. The narrow, uneven, winding streets, full of corners and turnings, were admirably selected, — the vicinity of the Halles more especially, a network of streets more tangled than a forest. The society of the Friends of the People had, it was said, taken the direction of the insurrection in the Sainte Avoye district, and a plan of Paris was found on the body of a man killed in the Rue du Ponceau.

What had really assumed the direction of the insurrection was a sort of unknown impetuosity that was in the atmosphere. The insurrection had suddenly built barricades with one hand, and with the other seized nearly all the garrison posts. In less than three hours the insurgents, like a powder-train fired, had seized and occupied on the right bank the Arsenal, the Mayoralty of the Place Royale, all the

Marais, the Popincourt arms-factory, the Galiote, the Château d'Eau, and all the streets near the Halles ; on the left bank the Veterans' barracks, Sainte Pélagie, the Place Maubert, the powder manufactory of the Deux Moulins, and all the barrières. At five in the evening they were masters of the Bastille, the Lingerie, and the Blancs-Manteaux ; while their scouts were close to the Place des Victoires and menaced the Bank, the barracks of the Petits-Pères and the Post-office. One third of Paris was in the hands of the revolt. On all points the struggle had begun on a gigantic scale, and the result of the disarmaments, the domiciliary visits, and the attack on the gunsmiths' shops, was that the fight which had begun with stone-throwing was continued with musket-shots.

About six in the evening the Passage du Saumon became the battle-field ; the rioters were at one end and the troops at the other, and they fired from one gate at the other. An observer, a dreamer, the author of this book, who had gone to have a near look at the volcano, found himself caught between two fires in the passage, and had nothing to protect him from the bullets but the projecting semi-columns which used to separate the shops ; he was nearly half an hour in this delicate position. In the mean while the tattoo was beaten, the National Guards hurriedly dressed and armed themselves, the legions issued from the Mayoralty, and the regiments from the barracks. Opposite the Passage de l'Ancre a drummer was stabbed ; another was attacked in the Rue du Cygne by thirty young men, who ripped up

his drum and took his sabre, while a third was killed
in the Rue Grenier St. Lazare. In the Rue Michel
le Comte three officers fell dead one after the other,
and several municipal guards, wounded in the Rue
des Lombards, recoiled. In front of the Cour Ba-
tave, a detachment of National Guards found a red
flag, bearing this inscription, " Republican Revolution, No. 127." Was it really a revolution? The
insurrection had made of the heart of Paris a sort
of inextricable, tortuous, and colossal citadel; there
was the nucleus, there the question would be solved;
all the rest was merely skirmishing. The proof that
all would be decided there lay in the fact that fighting had not yet begun there.

In some regiments the troops were uncertain,
which added to the startling obscurity of the crisis;
and they remembered the popular ovation which, in
July, 1830, greeted the neutrality of the 53d line.
Two intrepid men, tried by the great wars, Marshal
de Lobau and General Bugeaud, commanded, —
Bugeaud under Lobau. Enormous patrols, composed of battalions of the line enclosed in entire
companies of the National Guard, and preceded by
the Police Commissary in his scarf, went to recon-
noitre the insurgent streets. On their side, the insurgents posted vedettes at the corner of the streets,
and audaciously sent patrols beyond the barricades.
Both sides were observing each other; the Government, with an army in its hand, hesitated, night was
setting in, and the tocsin of St. Mary was beginning
to be heard. Marshal Soult, the Minister of War at
that day, who had seen Austerlitz, looked at all this

with a gloomy air. These old sailors, habituated to correct manœuvres, and having no other resource and guide but tactics, the compass of battles, are completely thrown out when in the presence of that immense foam which is called the public anger. The wind of revolutions is not favorable for sailing. The National Guards of the suburbs ran up hastily and disorderly; a battalion of the 12th Light Infantry came at the double from St. Denis; the 14th line arrived from Courbevoie, the batteries of the military school had taken up position at the Carrousel, and guns were brought in from Vincennes.

Solitude set in at the Tuileries. Louis Philippe was full of serenity.

CHAPTER V.

ORIGINALITY OF PARIS.

DURING the two past years Paris, as we said, had seen more than one insurrection. With the exception of the insurgent districts, as a rule, nothing is more strangely calm than the physiognomy of Paris during a riot. Paris very soon grows accustomed to everything — it is only a riot; and Paris has so much to do that it does not put itself out of the way for such a trifle. These colossal cities alone can offer such spectacles. These immense enclosures alone can contain simultaneously civil war and a strange tranquillity. Usually, when the insurrection begins, when the drum, the tattoo, and the assembly are heard, the shopkeeper confines himself to saying:

"Ah, there seems to be a row in the Rue St. Martin."

Or, —

"The Faubourg St. Antoine."

And he often adds, negligently, —

"Somewhere over that way."

At a later date, when the heart-rending and mournful sound of musketry and platoon fire can be distinguished, the shopkeeper says, —

"Bless me, it is growing hot!"

A moment later, if the riot approaches and spreads, he precipitately closes his shop and puts on his uniform; that is to say, places his wares in safety, and risks his person. Men shoot themselves on a square, in a passage, or a blind alley; barricades are taken, lost, and retaken, blood flows, the grape-shot pock-mark the fronts of the houses, bullets kill people in their beds, and corpses encumber the pavement. A few yards off you hear the click of the billiard-balls in the coffee-houses. The theatres open their doors and play farces; and gossips talk and laugh two yards from these streets full of war. Hackney coaches roll along, and their fares are going to dine out, sometimes in the very district where the fighting is. In 1831 a fusillade was interrupted in order to let a wedding pass. During the insurrection of May 12, 1839, in the Rue St. Martin, a little old infirm man, dragging a hand-truck surmounted by a tricolor rag, and carrying bottles full of some fluid, came and went from the barricade to the troops, and from the troops to the barricade, impartially offering glasses of cocoa, first to the Government and then to anarchy. Nothing can be stranger; and this is the peculiar character of Parisian riots, which is not found in any other capital, as two things are required for it, — the grandeur of Paris and its gayety, the city of Voltaire and of Napoleon. This time, however, in the insurrection of June 5, 1832, the great city felt something which was perhaps stronger than itself, and was frightened. Everywhere, in the most remote and disinterested districts, doors, windows, and shutters were closed in broad daylight. The courageous armed, the cowardly hid themselves, and the careless and busy passengers disappeared. Many streets were as empty as at four in the morning. Alarming details were hawked about, and fatal news spread, — that *they* were masters of the Bank; that at the cloisters of St. Merry alone they were six hundred, intrenched with loopholes in a church; that the line was not sure; that Armand Carrel had been to see Marshal Clausel, and the latter said to him, "Have a regiment first;" that Lafayette, though ill, had said to them, "I am with you, and will follow you wherever there is room for a chair;" that people must be on their guard, for at night burglars would plunder isolated houses in the deserted corners of Paris (in this could be recognized the imagination of the police, that Anne Radcliffe blended with government); that a battery had been established in the Rue Aubry-le-Boucher; that Lobau and Bugeaud were agreed, and that at midnight, or at daybreak at the latest, four columns would march together on the centre of the revolt, the first coming from the Bastille, the second from the Porte St. Martin, the third from the Grève, and the fourth from the Halles; that perhaps, too, the troops would evacuate Paris, and retire on the Champ de Mars; that no one knew what would happen, but this time it was certainly very serious. People were alarmed too by the hesitation of Marshal Soult; why did he not attack at once? It is certain that he was greatly absorbed, and the old lion seemed to scent an unknown monster in the darkness.

Night came, and the theatres were not opened, the patrols went their rounds with an air of irritation, passers-by were searched, and suspected persons arrested. At nine o'clock there were more than eight hundred persons taken up, and the Préfecture of Police, the Conciergerie, and La Force were crowded. At the Conciergerie, especially, the long vault called the Rue de Paris was strewn with trusses of straw, on which lay a pile of prisoners, whom Lagrange, the man of Lyons, valiantly harangued. All this straw, moved by all these men, produced the sound of a shower. Elsewhere the prisoners slept in the open air on lawns; there was anxiety everywhere, and a certain trembling, not at all usual to Paris. People barricaded themselves in the houses; wives and mothers were alarmed, and nothing else but this was heard, "Oh heavens! he has not come in!" Only the rolling of a few vehicles could be heard in the distance, and people listened in the doorways to the noises, cries, tumults, and dull, indistinct sounds, of which they said, "That is the cavalry," or, "It is the galloping of tumbrils;" to the bugles, the drums, the firing, and before all to the lamentable tocsin of St. Merry. They waited for the first artillery round, and men rose at the corner of the streets and disappeared, after shouting, "Go in." And they hastened to bolt their doors, saying, "How will it all end?" From moment to moment, as the night became darker, Paris seemed to be more lugubriously colored by the formidable flashes of the revolt.

BOOK XI.

THE ATOM FRATERNIZES WITH THE HURRICANE.

CHAPTER I.

THE ORIGIN OF THE POETRY OF GAVROCHE AND THE INFLUENCE OF AN ACADEMICIAN UPON IT.

AT the moment when the insurrection, breaking out through the collision between the people and the troops in front of the Arsenal, produced a retrograde movement in the multitude that followed the hearse, and which pressed with the whole length of the boulevards upon the head of the procession, there was a frightful reflux. The ranks were broken, and all ran or escaped, some with cries of attack, others with the pallor of flight. The great stream which covered the boulevards divided in a second, overflowed on the right and left, and spread in torrents over two hundred streets at once, as if a dyke had burst. At this moment a ragged lad who was coming down the Rue Ménilmontant, holding in his hand a branch of flowering laburnum which he had picked on the heights of Belleville, noticed in the shop of a dealer in bric-à-brac an old hostler pistol. He threw his branch on the pavement, and cried, —

"Mother What's-your-name, I'll borrow your machine."

And he ran off with the pistol. Two minutes after, a crowd of frightened cits, flying through the Rue Amelot and the Rue Basse, met the lad, who was brandishing his pistol and singing, —

> "La nuit on ne voit rien,
>   Le jour on voit très bien,
>   D'un écrit apocryphe
>   Le bourgeois s'ébouriffe,
>   Pratiquez la vertu,
>   Tutu, chapeau pointu!"

It was little Gavroche going to the wars; on the boulevard he noticed that his pistol had no hammer. Who was the composer of this couplet which served to punctuate his march, and all the other songs which he was fond of singing when he had a chance? Who knows? Himself, perhaps. Besides, Gavroche was acquainted with all the popular tunes in circulation, and mingled with them his own chirping, and, as a young vagabond, he made a *pot-pourri* of the voices of nature and the voices of Paris. He combined the repertoire of the birds with that of the studios, and he was acquainted with artists' students, a tribe contiguous to his own. He had been for three months, it appears, apprenticed to a painter, and had one day delivered a message for M. Baour Lormian, one of the Forty; Gavroche was a gamin of letters.

Gavroche did not suspect, by the way, that on that wretched rainy night, when he offered the hospitality of his elephant to the two boys, he was performing the offices of Providence to his two brothers. His brothers in the evening, his father in the morning, — such had been his night. On leaving the Rue des Ballets at dawn, he hurried back to the elephant, artistically extracted the two boys, shared with them the sort of breakfast which he had invented, and then went away, confiding them to that good mother, the street, who had almost brought himself up. On leaving them he appointed to meet them on the same spot at night, and left them this speech as farewell, — "I am going to cut my stick, otherwise to say, I intend to bolt, or as they say at court, I shall make myself scarce. My brats, if you do not find papa and mamma, come here again to-night. I will give you your supper and put you to bed." The two lads, picked up by some policeman and placed at the station, or stolen by some mountebank, or simply lost in that Chinese puzzle, Paris, did not return. The substrata of the existing social world are full of such lost traces. Gavroche had not seen them again, and ten or twelve weeks had elapsed since that night. More than once he had scratched his head and asked himself, "Where the deuce are my two children?"

He reached the Rue du Pont aux Choux, and noticed that there was only one shop still open in that street, and it was worthy of reflection that it was a confectioner's. It was a providential opportunity to eat one more apple-puff before entering the unknown. Gavroche stopped, felt in his pockets, turned them inside out, found nothing, not even a sou, and began shouting, "Help!" It is hard to go without the last cake, but for all that Gavroche went on his way. Two minutes after he was in the Rue St. Louis, and on crossing the Rue du Parc Royal he felt the necessity of compensating himself for the impossible apple-puff, and gave himself the immense treat of tearing down in open daylight the play-bills. A little farther on, seeing a party of stout gentry who appeared to him to be retired from business, he shrugged his shoulders and spat out this mouthful of philosophic bile, —

"How fat annuitants are! they wallow in good dinners. Ask them what they do with their money, and they don't know. They eat it, eat their belly-ful."

CHAPTER II.

GAVROCHE ON THE MARCH.

HOLDING a pistol without a cock in the streets is such a public function, that Gavroche felt his humor increase at every step. He cried between the scraps of the Marseillaise which he sang, —

"All goes well. I suffer considerably in my left paw. I have broken my rheumatism, but I am happy, citizens. The bourgeois have only to hold firm, and I am going to sing them some subversive couplets. What are the police? Dogs. Holy Moses! we must not lack respect for the dogs. Besides, I should be quite willing to have one [1] for my pistol. I have just come from the boulevard, my friends, where it's getting warm, and the soup is simmering; it is time to skim the pot. Forward, my men, and let an impure blood inundate the furrows! I give my days for my country. I shall not see my concubine again; it's all over. Well, no matter! Long live joy! Let us fight, crebleu! I have had enough of despotism!"

At this moment the horse of a lancer in the National Guard, who was passing, fell. Gavroche laid his pistol on the pavement, helped the man up,

---

[1] The hammer of a pistol is called a dog in France.

and then helped to raise the horse, after which he picked up his pistol and went his way again. In the Rue de Thorigny all was peace and silence; and this apathy, peculiar to the Marais, contrasted with the vast surrounding turmoil. Four gossips were conversing on the step of a door; Scotland has trios of witches, but Paris has quartettes of gossips, and the "Thou shalt be king" would be as lugubriously cast at Bonaparte at the Baudoyer crossway, as to Macbeth on the Highland heath, — it would be much the same croak. The gossips in the Rue Thorigny only troubled themselves about their own affairs; they were three portresses, and a rag-picker with her dorser and her hook. They seemed to be standing all four at the four corners of old age, which are decay, decrepitude, ruin, and sorrow. The rag-picker was humble, for in this open-air world the rag-picker bows, and the portress protects. The things thrown into the street are fat and lean, according to the fancy of the person who makes the pile, and there may be kindness in the broom. This rag-picker was grateful, and she smiled, — what a smile! — at the three portresses. They were making remarks like the following, —

"So your cat is as ill-tempered as ever?"

"Well, good gracious! you know that cats are naturally the enemy of dogs. It's the dogs that complain."

"And people too."

"And yet cats' fleas do not run after people."

"Dogs are really dangerous. I remember one year when there were so many dogs that they were obliged to put it in the papers. It was at that time when there were large sheep at the Tuileries to drag the little carriage of the King of Rome. Do you remember the King of Rome?"

"I preferred the Duc de Bordeaux."

"Well, I know Louis XVII., and I prefer him."

"How dear meat is, Mame Patagon!"

"Oh, don't talk about it! Butcher's meat is a horror, — a horrible horror. It is only possible to buy bones now."

Here the rag-picker interposed, —

"Ladies, trade does not go on well at all, and the rubbish is abominable. People do not throw away anything now, but eat it all."

"There are poorer folk than you, Vargoulême."

"Ah, that 's true," the rag-picker replied deferentially, "for I have a profession."

There was a pause, and the rag-picker, yielding to that need of display which is at the bottom of the human heart, added, —

"When I go home in the morning I empty out my basket and sort the articles; that makes piles in my room. I put the rags in a box, the cabbage-stalks in a tub, the pieces of linen in my cupboard, the woollen rags in my chest of drawers, old papers on the corner of the window, things good to eat in my porringer, pieces of glass in the fire-place, old shoes behind the door, and bones under my bed."

Gavroche had stopped, and was listening.

"Aged dames," he said, "what right have you to talk politics?"

A broadside, composed of a quadruple yell, assailed him.

"There's another of the villains."

"What's that he has in his hand, — a pistol?"

"Just think, that rogue of a boy!"

"They are never quiet unless when they are over-throwing the authorities."

Gavroche disdainfully limited his reprisals to lift-ing the tip of his nose with his thumb, and open-ing his hand to the full extent. The rag-picker exclaimed, —

"The barefooted scamp!"

The one who answered to the name of Mame Patagon struck her hands together with scandal.

"There are going to be misfortunes, that's sure. The young fellow with the beard round the corner, I used to see him pass every morning with a girl in a pink bonnet on his arm; but this morning I saw him pass, and he was giving his arm to a gun. Mame Bacheux says there was a revolution last week at, at, at, at, — where do the calves come from? — at Pontoise. And then, just look at this atrocious young villain's pistol. It seems that the Célestins are full of cannon. What would you have the Govern-ment do with these vagabonds who can only invent ways to upset the world, after we were beginning to get over all the misfortunes which fell — good gracious! — on that poor Queen whom I saw pass in a cart! And all this will raise the price of snuff. It is infamous, and I will certainly go and see you guillotined, malefactor."

"You snuffle, my aged friend," said Gavroche; "blow your promontory."

And he passed on. When he was in the Rue

Pavée his thoughts reverted to the rag-picker, and he had this soliloquy, —

"You are wrong to insult the revolutionists, Mother Cornerpost. This pistol is on your behalf, and it is for you to have in your baskets more things good to eat."

All at once he heard a noise behind ; it was the portress Patagon, who had followed him, and now shook her fist at him, crying, —

"You are nothing but a bastard."

"At that I scoff with all my heart," said Gavroche.

A little later he passed the Hôtel Lamoignon, where he burst into this appeal, —

"Go on to the battle."

And he was attacked by a fit of melancholy ; he regarded his pistol reproachfully, and said to it, —

"I am going off, but you will not go off."

One dog may distract another ; [1] a very thin whelp passed, and Gavroche felt pity for it.

"My poor little creature," he said to it, "you must have swallowed a barrel, as you show all the hoops."

Then he proceeded toward the Orme St. Gervais.

[1] Another allusion to the hammer (chien) of the pistol.

CHAPTER III.

JUST INDIGNATION OF A BARBER.

THE worthy barber who had turned out the two children for whom Gavroche had opened the elephant's paternal intestines, was at this moment in his shop, engaged in shaving an old legionary who had served under the Empire. The barber had naturally spoken to the veteran about the riot, then about General Lamarque, and from Lamarque they had come to the Emperor. Hence arose a conversation between the barber and the soldier which Prudhomme, had he been present, would have enriched with arabesques, and entitled, " A dialogue between a razor and a sabre."

" How did the Emperor ride, sir ? " the barber asked.

" Badly. He did not know how to fall off, and so he never fell off."

" Had he fine horses ? He must have had fine horses ! "

" On the day when he gave me the cross I noticed his beast. It was a white mare. It had its ears very far apart, a deep saddle, a fine head marked with a black star, a very long neck, prominent knees, projecting flanks, oblique shoulders, and a strong crupper. It was a little above fifteen hands high."

" A fine horse," said the barber.

" It was His Majesty's beast."

The barber felt that after this remark a little silence was befitting ; then he went on, —

" The Emperor was wounded only once, I believe, sir ? "

The old soldier replied, with the calm and sovereign accent of the man who has felt wounds, —

" In the heel, at Ratisbon. I never saw him so well dressed as on that day. He was as clean as a halfpenny."

" And you, sir, I suppose, have received sword-wounds ? "

" I," said the soldier ; " oh, a mere flea-bite. I received two sabre-cuts on my neck at Marengo ; I got a bullet in my right arm at Jena, another in the left hip at Jena ; at Friedland a bayonet-thrust, — there ; at the Muskowa seven or eight lance-prods, never mind where ; at Lützen, a piece of shell carried off a finger, and — oh, yes ! at Waterloo a bullet from a case-shot in my thigh. That's all."

" How glorious it is," the barber exclaimed, with a Pindaric accent, " to die on the battle-field ! On my word of honor, sooner than die on a bed of disease, slowly, a bit every day, with drugs, cataplasms, clysters, and medicine, I would sooner have a cannon-ball in my stomach ! "

" And you 're right," said the soldier. He had scarce ended ere a frightful noise shook the shop ; a great pane of glass was suddenly smashed, and the barber turned livid.

" Good Lord ! " he cried, " it is one."

" What ? "

" A cannon-ball."

" Here it is."

And he picked up something which was rolling on the ground ; it was a pebble. The barber ran to his broken pane, and saw Gavroche flying at full speed towards the Marché St. Jean. On passing the barber's shop Gavroche, who had the two lads at his heart, could not resist the desire of wishing him good-evening, and threw a stone through his window.

" Just look," the barber yelled, who had become blue instead of livid, " he does harm for harm's sake. What had I done to that villain ? "

CHAPTER IV.

THE CHILD ASTONISHES THE OLD MAN.

On reaching St. Jean market, the post at which had been disarmed already, Gavroche proceeded "to effect his junction" with a band led by Enjolras, Courfeyrac, Combeferre, and Feuilly. They were all more or less armed, and Bahorel and Prouvaire had joined them, and swelled the group. Enjolras had a double-barrelled fowling-piece, Combeferre a National Guard's musket bearing the number of a legion, and in his waist-belt two pistols, which his unbuttoned coat allowed to be seen; Jean Prouvaire an old cavalry carbine, and Bahorel a rifle; Courfeyrac brandished a sword drawn from a cane, while Feuilly with a naked sabre in his hand walked along shouting, "Long live Poland!" They reached the Quai Morland without neck-cloths or hats, panting for breath, drenched with rain, but with lightning in their eyes. Gavroche calmly approached them, —

"Where are we going?"

"Come," said Courfeyrac.

Behind Feuilly marched or rather bounded Bahorel, a fish in the water of revolt. He had a crimson waistcoat, and uttered words which smash everything. His waistcoat upset a passer-by, who cried wildly, "Here are the reds!"

"The reds, the reds!" Bahorel answered; "that's a funny fear, citizen. For my part, I do not tremble at a poppy, and the little red cap does not inspire me with any terror. Citizen, believe me, we had better leave a fear of the red to horned cattle."

He noticed a corner wall, on which was placarded the most peaceful piece of paper in the world, a permission to eat eggs, a Lent mandamus addressed by the Archbishop of Paris to his "flock." Bahorel exclaimed, —

"A flock! a polite way of saying geese." And he tore the paper down. This conquered Gavroche, and from this moment he began studying Bahorel.

"Bahorel," Enjolras observed, "you are wrong; you should have left that order alone, for we have nothing to do with it, and you uselessly expended your anger. Keep your stock by you; a man does not fire out of the ranks any more with his mind than with his gun."

"Every man has his own way, Enjolras," Bahorel replied; "the bishop's prose offends me, and I insist on eating eggs without receiving permission to do so. Yours is the cold burning style, while I amuse myself; moreover, I am not expending myself, but getting the steam up, and if I tore that order down, Hercle! it is to give me an appetite."

This word *hercle* struck Gavroche, for he sought every opportunity of instructing himself, and this tearing down of posters possessed his esteem. Hence he asked, —

"What's the meaning of *hercle?*"

Bahorel answered, —

"It means cursed name of a dog in Latin."

Here Bahorel noticed at a window a pale young man, with a black beard, who was watching them pass, probably a Friend of the A. B. C. He shouted to him, —

"Quick with the cartridges, *para bellum !*"

"A handsome man [bel homme], that's true," said Gavroche, who now comprehended Latin.

A tumultuous crowd accompanied them, — students, artists, young men affiliated to the Cougourde of Aix, artisans, and lightermen, armed with sticks and bayonets, and some, like Combeferre, with pistols passed through their trouser-belt. An old man, who appeared very aged, marched in this band; he had no weapon, and hurried on, that he might not be left behind, though he looked thoughtful. Gavroche perceived him.

"Keksekça?" said he to Courfeyrac.

"That is an antique."

It was M. Mabœuf.

CHAPTER V.

THE OLD MAN.

WE will tell what had occurred. Enjolras and
his friends were on the Bourdon Boulevard near the
granaries at the moment when the dragoons charged,
and Enjolras, Courfeyrac, and Combeferre were among
those who turned into the Rue Bassompierre shouting, "To the barricades!" In the Rue Lesdiguières
they met an old man walking along, and what attracted their attention was, that he was moving very
irregularly, as if intoxicated. Moreover, he had his
hat in his hand, although it had rained the whole
morning, and was raining rather hard at that very
moment. Courfeyrac recognized Father Mabœuf,
whom he knew through having accompanied Marius
sometimes as far as his door. Knowing the peaceful
and more than timid habits of the churchwarden and
bibliomaniac, and stupefied at seeing him in the midst
of the tumult, within two yards of cavalry charges,
almost in the midst of the musketry fire, bareheaded
in the rain, and walking about among bullets, he
accosted him, and the rebel of five-and-twenty and
the octogenarian exchanged this dialogue : —

"Monsieur Mabœuf, you had better go home."

"Why so?"

"There is going to be a row."

"Very good."

"Sabre-cuts and shots, Monsieur Mabœuf."

"Very good."

"Cannon-shots."

"Very good.   Where are you gentlemen going?"

"To upset the Government."

"Very good."

And he began following them, but since that moment had not said a word.   His step had become suddenly firm, and when workmen offered him an arm, he declined it with a shake of the head.   He walked almost at the head of the column, having at once the command of a man who is marching and the face of a man who is asleep.

"What a determined old fellow!" the students muttered; and the rumor ran along the party that he was an ex-conventionalist, an old regicide.   The band turn into the Rue de la Verrerie, and little Gavroche marched at the head, singing at the top of his voice, which made him resemble a bugler.   He sang:—

> "Voici la lune qui paraît,
>   Quand irons-nous dans la forêt?
> Demandait Charlot à Charlotte.

> "Tou tou tou
>   Pour Chatou.
> Je n'ai qu'un Dieu, qu'un roi, qu'un liard et qu'une botte.

> "Pour avoir bu de grand matin
>   La rosée à même le thym,
>   Deux moineaux étaient en ribotte.

> "Zi zi zi
>   Pour Passy.
> Je n'ai qu'un Dieu, qu'un roi, qu'un liard et qu'une botte.

" Et ces deux pauvres petits loups,
Comme deux grives étaient soûls ;
Un tigre en riait dans sa grotte.

" Don don don
Pour Meudon.
Je n'ai qu'un Dieu, qu'un roi, qu'un liard et qu'une botte.

" L'un jurait et l'autre sacrait,
Quand irons-nous dans la forêt ?
Demandait Charlot à Charlotte.

" Tin tin tin
Pour Pantin.
Je n'ai qu'un Dieu, qu'un roi, qu'un liard et qu'une botte."

They proceeded towards St. Merry.

CHAPTER VI.

RECRUITS.

THE band swelled every moment, and near the Rue des Billettes, a tall, grayish-haired man, whose rough bold face Courfeyrac, Enjolras, and Combeferre noticed, though not one of them knew him, joined them. Gavroche, busy singing, whistling, and shouting, and rapping the window-shutters with his pistol-butt, paid no attention to this man. As they went through the Rue de la Verrerie they happened to pass Courfeyrac's door.

"That's lucky," said Courfeyrac, "for I have forgotten my purse and lost my hat."

He left the band and bounded up-stairs, where he put on an old hat and put his purse in his pocket. He also took up a large square box of the size of a portmanteau, which was concealed among his dirty linen. As he was running down-stairs again his portress hailed him.

"Monsieur de Courfeyrac!"

"Portress, what is your name?" Courfeyrac retorted.

She stood in stupefaction.

"Why, you know very well, sir, that my name is Mother Veuvain."

"Well, then, if ever you call me M. de Courfeyrac again I shall call you Mother de Veuvain. Now speak; what is it?"

"Some one wishes to speak to you."

"Who is it?"

"I don't know."

"Where is he?"

"In my lodge."

"Oh, the devil!" said Courfeyrac.

"Why! he has been waiting for more than an hour for you to come in."

At the same time a species of young workman, thin, livid, small, marked with freckles, dressed in an old blouse and a pair of patched cotton-velvet trousers, who looked more like a girl attired as a boy than a man, stepped out of the lodge and said to Courfeyrac in a voice which was not the least in the world a feminine voice, —

"Monsieur Marius, if you please?"

"He is not here."

"Will he come in to-night?"

"I do not know."

And Courfeyrac added, "I shall not be in to-night."

The young man looked at him intently and asked, —

"Why not?"

"Because I shall not."

"Where are you going?"

"How does that concern you?"

"Shall I carry your chest for you?"

"I am going to the barricades."

" May I go with you ? "

" If you like," Courfeyrac replied; " the street is free, and the pavement belongs to everybody."

And he ran off to join his friends again; when he had done so, he gave one of them the box to carry, and it was not till a quarter of an hour after that he noticed that the young man was really following them. A mob does not go exactly where it wishes, and we have explained that a puff of wind directs it. They passed St. Merry, and found themselves, without knowing exactly why, in the Rue St. Denis.

BOOK XII.

CORINTH.

CHAPTER I.

HISTORY OF CORINTH FROM ITS FOUNDATION.

THE Parisians, who at the present day on entering the Rue Rambuteau from the side of the Halles notice on their right, opposite the Rue Mondétour, a basket-maker's shop having for sign a basket in the shape of Napoleon the Great, with this inscription :

NAPOLÉON EST FAIT
TOUT EN OSIER,

do not suspect the terrible scenes which this very site saw hardly thirty years ago. Here were the Rue de la Chanvrerie, which old title-deeds write Chanverrerie, and the celebrated wine-shop called Corinth. Our readers well remember all that has been said about the barricade erected at this spot, and eclipsed by the way by the St. Merry barricade. It is on this famous barricade of the Rue de la Chanvrerie, which has now fallen into deep night, that we are going to throw a little light.

For the clearness of our narrative, we may be permitted to have recourse to the simple mode which we employed for Waterloo. Those persons who wish to represent to themselves in a tolerably exact manner the mass of houses which at that day stood near Sainte Eustache at the northeast corner of the Halles de Paris, at the spot where the opening of the Rue Rambuteau now is, need only imagine an N whose two vertical strokes are the Rue de la Grande Truanderie and the Rue de la Chanvrerie, and of which the Rue de la Petite Truanderie would be the crossstroke. The old Rue Mondétour intersected the three strokes with the most tortuous angles, so that the Dædalian entanglement of these four streets was sufficient to make, upon a space of one hundred square yards, between the Halles and the Rue St. Denis on one side, between the Rue du Cygne and the Rue des Prêcheurs, on the other side, seven islets of houses, strangely cut, of different heights, standing sideways, and as if accidentally, and scarce separated by narrow cracks, like the blocks of stone in a dock. We say narrow cracks, and cannot give a fairer idea of these obscure, narrow, angular lanes, bordered by tenements eight stories in height. These houses were so decrepit that in the Rues de la Chanvrerie and La Petite Truanderie, the frontages were supported by beams running across from one house to the other. The street was narrow and the gutter wide; the passer-by walked on a constantly damp pavement, passing shops like cellars, heavy posts shod with iron, enormous piles of filth, and gates armed with extraordinarily old palings. The Rue Rambuteau has devastated all this. The name of Mondétour exactly describes the windings of all this lay-stall. A little farther on it was found even better expressed by the Rue Pirouette, which threw itself into the Rue Mondétour. The wayfarer who turned out of the Rue St. Denis into the Rue de la Chanvrerie saw it gradually contract before him, as if he had entered an elongated funnel. At the end of the street, which was very short, he found the passage barred on the side of the Halles by a tall row of houses, and he might have fancied himself in a blind alley had he not perceived on his right and left two black cuts through which he could escape. It was the Rue Mondétour, which joined on one side the Rue des Prêcheurs, on the other the Rue du Cygne. At the end of this sort of blind alley, at the corner of the right-hand cutting, a house lower than the rest, forming a species of cape in the street, might be noticed. It is in this house, only two stories high, that an illustrious cabaret had been installed for more than three hundred years. This inn produced a joyous noise at the very spot which old Théophile indicated in the two lines :

> " Là branle le squelette horrible
> D'un pauvre amant qui se pendit."

The spot was good, and the landlords succeeded each other from father to son. In the time of Mathurin Régnier, this cabaret was called the *Pot-aux-Roses*, and as rebuses were fashionable, it had for a sign a poteau (post) painted in rose-color. In the last century, worthy Natoire, one of the fantastic masters disdained at the present day by the stiff school, having got tipsy several times in this inn at the same

table where Régnier had got drunk, painted, out of
gratitude, a bunch of currants on the pink post. The
landlord, in his delight, changed his sign, and had
the words gilded under the bunch, *Au raisin de
Corinthe*, — hence the name of Corinth. Nothing
is more natural to drunkards than ellipses, for they
are the zigzags of language. Corinth had gradually
dethroned the rose-pot, and the last landlord of the
dynasty, Father Hucheloup, not being acquainted
with the tradition, had the post painted blue.

A ground-floor room in which was the bar, a first-
floor room in which was a billiard-table, a spiral
wooden staircase piercing the ceiling, wine on the
tables, smoke on the walls, and candles by daylight, —
such was the inn. A staircase with a trap in the
ground-floor room led to the cellar, and the apartments of the Hucheloups, on the second floor, were
reached by a staircase more like a ladder, and
through a door hidden in the wall of the large first-
floor room. Under the roof were two garrets, the
nests of the maid-servants, and the kitchen shared
the ground-floor with the bar. Father Hucheloup
might have been born a chemist, but was really a
cook, and customers not only drank but ate in his
wine-shop. Hucheloup had invented an excellent
dish, which could be eaten only at his establishment;
it was stuffed carp, which he called *carpes au gras*.
This was eaten by the light of a tallow candle, or a
lamp of the Louis XVI. style, on tables on which
oil-cloth was nailed in lieu of a table-cloth. People
came from a long distance; and Hucheloup one fine
morning had thought it advisable to inform passers-

by of his "speciality:" he dipped a brush in a pot
of blacking, and as he had an orthography of his
own, he improvised on his wall the following remarkable inscription: —

CARPES HO GRAS.

One winter the showers and the hail amused themselves with effacing the "s" which terminated the
first word, and the "G" which began the last, and
the following was left: —

CARPE HO RAS.

By the aid of time and rain a humble gastronomic
notice had become a profound counsel. In this way
it happened that Hucheloup, not knowing French,
had known Latin, had brought philosophy out of the
kitchen, and while simply wishing to eclipse Carême,
equalled Horace. And the striking thing was that
this also meant "enter my inn." Nothing of all this
exists at the present day; the Mondétour labyrinth
was gutted and widened in 1847, and probably is
no longer to be found. The Rue de la Chanvrerie
and Corinth have disappeared under the pavement
of the Rue Rambuteau. As we have said, Corinth
was a meeting-place, if not a gathering-place, of
Courfeyrac and his friends, and it was Grantaire
who discovered it. He went in for the sake of the
carpe ho ras, and returned for the sake of the
carp *au gras.* People drank there, ate there, and
made a row there: they paid little, paid badly, or
paid not at all, but were always welcome. Father

Hucheloup was a worthy fellow.   Hucheloup, whom we have just called a worthy fellow, was an eating-house keeper with a moustache, — an amusing variety. He always looked ill-tempered, appeared wishful to intimidate his customers, growled at persons who came in, and seemed more disposed to quarrel with them than serve them.   And yet we maintain people were always welcome.   This peculiarity filled his bar, and brought to him young men who said, " Let us go and have a look at Father Hucheloup."   He had been a fencing-master, and would suddenly break out into a laugh ; he had a rough voice, but was a merry fellow.   He had a comical background with a tragical appearance ; he asked for nothing better than to frighten you, something like the snuff-boxes which had the shape of a pistol, — the detonation produces a sneeze.   He had for wife a Mother Huche-loup, a bearded and very ugly being.   About 1830 Father Hucheloup died, and with him disappeared the secret of the carp *au gras*.   His widow, who was almost inconsolable, carried on the business, but the cooking degenerated and became execrable, and the wine, which had always been bad, was frightful.   Courfeyrac and his friends, however, continued to go to Corinth, — through pity, said Bossuet.

Widow Hucheloup was short of breath and shape-less, and had rustic recollections, which she deprived of their insipidity by her pronunciation.   She had a way of her own of saying things which seasoned her reminiscences of her village and the spring : it had formerly been her delight, she declared, to hear " the red-beasts singing in the awe-thorns." [1] The first-floor room, where the restaurant was, was a large, long apartment, crowded with stools, chairs, benches, and tables, and an old rickety billiard-table. It was reached by the spiral staircase which led to a square hole in the corner of the room, like a ship's hatchway. This apartment, lighted by only one narrow window and a constantly-burning lamp, had a garret-look about it, and all the four-legged articles of furniture behaved as if they had only three. The white-washed wall had for sole ornament the following quatrain in honor of Mame Hucheloup : —

" Elle étonne à dix pas, elle épouvante à deux,
    Une verrue habite en son nez hasardeux ;
    On tremble à chaque instant qu'elle ne vous la mouche,
    Et qu'un beau jour son nez ne tombe dans sa bouche."

This was written in charcoal on the wall. Mame Hucheloup, very like her description, walked past this quatrain from morning till night with the most perfect tranquillity. Two servant-girls, called Matelote and Gibelotte, and who were never known by other names, helped Mame Hucheloup in placing on the tables bottles of blue wine, and the various messes served to the hungry guests in earthenware bowls. Matelote, stout, round, red-haired, and noisy, an ex-favorite sultana of the defunct Hucheloup, was uglier than the ugliest mythological monster ; and yet, as it is always proper that the servant should

---

[1] The original malapropism, " les loups-de-gorge chanter dans les ogrépines," is utterly untranslatable. The above is only an attempt to convey some approximative idea.

be a little behind the mistress, she was not so ugly
as Mame Hucheloup.   Gibelotte, tall, delicate, white
with a lymphatic whiteness, with blue circles round
her eyes, and drooping lids, ever exhausted and
oppressed, and suffering from what may be called
chronic lassitude, the first to rise, the last to go
to bed, waited on everybody, even the other servant,
silently and gently, and smiling a sort of vague,
sleepy smile through her weariness.   Before entering
the restaurant the following line written by Courfeyrac
in chalk was legible : " Régale si tu peux et mange
si tu l'oses."

CHAPTER II.

LAIGLE of Meaux, as we know, liked better to live with Joly than any one else, and he had a lodging much as the bird has a branch. The two friends lived together, ate together, slept together, and had everything in common, even a little Musichetta. They were what they call *bini* in the house of the Assistant Brothers. On the morning of June 5 they went to breakfast at Corinth. Joly had a cold in his head, and Laigle's coat was threadbare, while Joly was well dressed. It was about nine in the morning when they pushed open the door of Corinth, and went up to the first-floor room, where they were received by Matelote and Gibelotte.

"Oysters, cheese, and ham," said Laigle.

They sat down at a table ; the room was empty; there was no one in it but themselves. Gibelotte, recognizing Joly and Laigle, placed a bottle of wine on the table, and they attacked the first dozen of oysters. A head appeared in the hatchway and a voice said, —

"As I was passing I smelt a delicious perfume of Brie cheese, so I stepped in."

It was Grantaire ; he took a stool and sat down

at the table. Gibelotte, on seeing Grantaire, placed two bottles of wine on the table, which made three.

"Are you going to drink these two bottles?" Laigle asked Grantaire, who replied, —

"All men are ingenious, but you alone are ingenuous. Two bottles never yet astonished a man."

The others began with eating, but Grantaire began with drinking; a pint was soon swallowed.

"Why, you must have a hole in your stomach," said Laigle.

"Well, you have one in your elbow," Grantaire retorted, and after emptying his glass, he added, —

"Oh yes, Laigle of the funeral orations, your coat is old."

"I should hope so," Laigle replied, "for my coat and I live comfortably together. It has assumed all my wrinkles, does not hurt me anywhere, has moulded itself on my deformities, and is complacent to all my movements, and I only feel its presence because it keeps me warm. Old coats and old friends are the same thing."

"Grantaire," Joly asked, "have you come from the boulevard?"

"No."

"Laigle and I have just seen the head of the procession pass. It is a marvellous sight."

"How quiet this street is!" Laigle exclaimed. "Who could suspect that Paris is turned topsy-turvy? How easy it is to see that formerly there were monasteries all round here! Du Breuil and Sauval give a list of them, and so does the Abbé

Lebeuf. There was all around where we are now sitting a busy swarm of monks, shod and barefooted, tonsured and bearded, gray, black, white, Franciscans, Minims, Capuchins, Carmelites, little Augustines, great Augustines, old Augustines — "

"Don't talk about monks," Grantaire interrupted, "for it makes me want to scratch myself." Then he exclaimed, —

"Bouh! I have just swallowed a bad oyster, and that has brought back my hypochondria. Oysters are spoiled, servant-girls are ugly, and I hate the human race. I passed just now before the great public library in the Rue Richelieu, and that pile of oyster-shells, which is called a library, disgusts me with thinking. What paper! What ink! What pot-hooks and hangers! All that has been written! What ass was that said man was a featherless biped? And then, too, I met a pretty girl I know, lovely as spring, and worthy to be called Floréal, who was ravished, transported, happy in Paradise, the wretch, because yesterday a hideous banker spotted with small-pox deigned to throw his handkerchief to her! Alas! woman looks out for a keeper quite as much as a lover; cats catch mice as well as birds. This girl not two months ago was living respectably in a garret, and fitted little copper circles into the eyelet-holes of stays, — what do you call it? She sewed, she had a flockbed, she lived by the side of a pot of flowers, and was happy. Now she is a bankeress, and the transformation took place last night. I met the victim this morning perfectly happy, and the hideous thing was that the wretched creature was quite as pretty this morning as she was yesterday, and there was no sign of the financier on her face. Roses have this more or less than women, that the traces which the caterpillars leave on them are visible. Ah! there is no morality left in the world, and I call as witnesses the myrtle, symbol of love, the laurel, symbol of war, the olive, that absurd symbol of peace, the apple-tree, which nearly choked Adam with its pips, and the fig-tree, the grandfather of petticoats. As for justice, do you know what justice is? The Gauls covet Clusium, Rome protects Clusium and asks what wrong Clusium has done them. Brennus answers, 'The wrong which Alba did to you, the wrong that Fidène did to you, the wrong that the Equi, Volscians, and Sabines did to you. They were your neighbors, and the Clusians are ours. We understand neighborhood in the same way as you do. You stole Alba, and we take Clusium.' Rome says, ' You shall not take Clusium.' and Brennus took Rome, and then cried ' Væ victis ! ' That is what justice is ! Oh, what beasts of prey there are in the world ! What eagles, what eagles! the thought makes my flesh creep."

He held out his glass to Joly, who filled it, then drank, and continued almost without having been interrupted by the glass of wine, which no one noticed, not even himself : —

"Brennus who takes Rome is an eagle; the banker who takes the grisette is an eagle ; and there is no more shame in one than the other. So let us believe nothing; there is only one reality, drinking. Of whatever opinion you may be, whether you back the lean cock, like the canton of Uri, or the fat cock, like the canton of Glaris, it is of no consequence; drink. You talk to me about the boulevard, the procession, etc. ; what, are we going to have another revolution ? This poverty of resources astonishes me on the part of le bon Dieu ; and He must at every moment set to work greasing the groove of events. Things stick and won't move, — look sharp then with a revolution ; le bon Dieu has always got his hands black with that filthy cart-wheel grease. In his place I should act more simply, I should not wind up my machinery at every moment, but lead the human race evenly ; I should knit facts mesh by mesh without breaking the thread ; I should have no temporary substitutes, and no extraordinary repertory. What you fellows call progress has two motive-powers, men and events, but it is a sad thing that something exceptional is required every now and then. For events as for men the ordinary stock company is not sufficient ; among men there must be geniuses, and among events revolutions. Great accidents are the law, and the order of things cannot do without them ; and, judging from the apparition of comets, we might be tempted to believe that Heaven itself feels a want of leading actors. At the moment when it is least expected, God bills the wall of the firmament with a meteor, and some strange star follows, underlined by an enormous tail ; and that causes the death of Cæsar. Brutus gives him a dagger-thrust, and God deals him a blow with a comet. Crac ! here is an aurora borealis, here is a revolution, here is a great man :

'93 in big letters, Napoleon in a line by itself, and the comet of 1811 at the head of the bill. Ah! what a fine blue poster, spangled all over with unexpected flashes! Boum! boum! an extraordinary sight. Raise your eyes, idlers. Everything is in disorder, the star as well as the drama. Oh Lord! It is too much and not enough; and these resources, drawn from exceptional circumstances, seem magnificence and are only poverty. My friends, Providence has fallen into the stage of expedients. What does a revolution prove? That God is running short : He produces a *coup d'état*, because there is a solution of continuity between the present and the future, and He is unable to join the ends. In fact, this confirms me in my conjectures as to the state of Jehovah's fortune ; and on seeing so much discomfort above and below, so much paltriness and pinching and saving and distress both in heaven and on earth, from the bird which has not a seed of grain, to myself who have not one hundred thousand francs a year, — on seeing human destiny which is very much worn, and even royal destiny which is threadbare, as witness the Prince de Condé hanged, — on seeing winter, which is only a rent in the zenith through which the wind blows, — on seeing so many rags, even in the bran-new morning purple on the tops of the hills, — on seeing drops of dew, those false pearls, and hoar-frost, that paste jewelry, — on seeing humanity unripped and events patched, and so many spots on the sun, so many holes in the moon, and so much wretchedness everywhere, — I suspect that God is not rich. There is an appearance, it is true, but I see the pressure, and He gives a revolution just as a merchant whose cash-box is empty gives a ball. We must not judge the gods by appearances, and under the gilding of heaven I catch a glimpse of a poor universe. There is a bankruptcy in creation, and that is why I am dissatisfied. Just see, this is June 5, and it is almost night; I have been waiting since morning for day to come, and it has not come, and I will wager that it does not come at all. It is the irregularity of a badly-paid clerk. Yes, everything is badly arranged, nothing fits into anything, this old world is thrown out of gear, and I place myself in the ranks of the opposition. Everything goes crooked, and the universe is close-fisted; it is like the children, — those who ask get nothing, and those who don't ask get something. And then, again, it afflicts me to look at that bald-headed Laigle of Meaux, and I am humiliated by the thought that I am of the same age as that knee. However, I criticise but do not insult; the universe is what it is, and I speak without any evil meaning, and solely to do my duty by my conscience. Ah! by all the saints of Olympus, and by all the gods of Paradise, I was not made to be a Parisian, that is to say, to be constantly thrown like a shuttle-cock between two battledores, from a group of idlers to a group of noisy fellows. No! I was meant to be a Turk, looking all day at Egyptian damsels performing those exquisite dances, wanton like the dreams of a chaste man, or a Beauceron peasant, or a Venetian gentleman surrounded by fair ladies, or a little German prince, supplying one half a soldier to the Germanic

Confederation, and employing his leisure hours in drying his stockings on his hedge, that is to say, his frontier! Such were the destinies for which I was born. Yes, I said Turk, and I will not recall it. I do not understand why the Turks are usually looked upon askance, for Mahom has some good points. Let us respect the inventor of harems of houris, and Paradises of Odalisques, and we ought not to insult Mahometism, the only religion adorned with a hen-coop! After this, I insist on drinking, for the earth is a great piece of stupidity. And it appears that all those asses are going to fight, to break each other's heads and massacre one another in the heart of summer, in the month of June, when they might go off with a creature on their arm to inhale in the fields the perfume of that immense cup of tea of cut hay. Really, too many follies are committed. An old broken lantern, which I saw just now at a bric-à-brac dealer's, suggests a reflection to me, 'it is high time to enlighten the human race.' Yes, I am sad again, and it has come from swallowing an oyster and a revolution the wrong way. I am growing lugubrious again. Oh, frightful old world! On your surface people strive, are destitute, prostitute themselves, kill themselves, and grow accustomed to it!"

And after this burst of eloquence Grantaire had a burst of coughing, which was well deserved.

"Talking of a revolution," said Joly, "it seebs that Barius is certaidly in love."

"Do you know with whom?" Laigle asked.

"Do."

"No?"

"Do, I tell you."

"The loves of Marius!" Grantaire exclaimed, "I can see them from here. Marius is a fog and will have found a vapor. Marius is of the poetic race. Who says poet says madman. *Tymbræus Apollo.* Marius and his Marie, or his Maria, or his Mariette, or his Marion, must be a funny brace of lovers. I can fancy what it is : ecstasies in which kissing is forgotten. Chaste on earth but connected in the infinitude. They are souls that have feelings, and they sleep together in the stars."

Grantaire was attacking his second bottle, and perhaps his second harangue, when a new head emerged from the staircase hatchway. It was a boy under ten years of age, ragged, very short and yellow, with a bull-dog face, a quick eye, and an enormous head of hair; he was dripping with wet, but seemed happy. The lad choosing without hesitating among the three, though he knew none of them, addressed Laigle of Meaux.

"Are you Monsieur Bossuet?" he asked.

"I am called so," Laigle replied; "what do you want?"

"A big blonde on the boulevard said to me, 'Do you know Mother Hucheloup's?' I said, 'Yes, Rue Chanvrerie, the widow of the old buffer.' He says to me, 'Go there; you will find Monsieur Bossuet there, and say to him from me, A — B — C.' I suppose it's a trick played you, eh? He gave me ten sous."

"Joly, lend me ten sous," said Laigle; and turning to Grantaire, "Grantaire, lend me ten sous."

This made twenty sous, which Laigle gave the lad. "Thank you, sir," he said.

"What is your name?" Laigle asked.

"Navet, Gavroche's friend."

"Stay with us," Laigle said.

"Breakfast with us," Grantaire added.

The lad replied, "I can't, for I belong to the procession, and have to cry, 'Down with Polignac!'"

And, drawing his foot slowly after him, which is the most respectful of bows possible, he went away. When he was gone, Grantaire remarked, —

"That is the pure gamin, and there are many varieties in the gamin genus. The notary-gamin is called 'skip-the-gutter;' the cook-gamin is called 'scullion;' the baker-gamin is called 'paper-cap;' the footman-gamin is called 'tiger;' the sailor-gamin is called 'cabin-boy;' the soldier-gamin is called 'drummer-boy;' the painter-gamin is called 'dauber;' the tradesman-gamin is called 'errand-boy;' the courtier-gamin is called 'favorite;' the royal-gamin is called 'dauphin;' and the divine-gamin is called 'Bambino.'"

In the mean while Laigle meditated, and said in a low voice, —

"A — B — C, that is to say, funeral of General Lamarque."

"The tall, fair man," Grantaire observed, "is Enjolras, who has sent to warn you."

"Shall we go?" asked Bossuet.

"It's raining," said Joly; "I have sworn to go

through fire but dot through water, and I do dot wish to bake by cold worse."

"I shall stay here," Grantaire remarked; "I prefer a breakfast to a hearse."

"Conclusion, we remain," Laigle continued; "in that case let us drink. Besides, we may miss the funeral without missing the row."

"Ah, the row!" cried Joly, "I 'b id that."

Laigle rubbed his hands.

"So the revolution of 1830 is going to begin over again. Indeed, it disturbs people by brushing against them."

"I do not care a rap for your revolution," Grantaire remarked, "and I do not execrate the present Government, for it is the crown tempered by the cotton nightcap, a sceptre terminating in an umbrella. In such weather as this Louis Philippe might use his royalty for two objects, — stretch out the sceptre-end against the people, and open the umbrella-end against the sky."

The room was dark, and heavy clouds completely veiled the daylight. There was no one in the wine-shop or in the streets, for everybody had gone "to see the events."

"Is it midday or midnight?" Bossuet asked; "I can see nothing; bring a candle, Gibelotte."

Grantaire was drinking sorrowfully.

"Enjolras disdains me," he muttered. "Enjolras said to himself, 'Joly is ill and Grantaire is drunk,' and so he sent Navet to Bossuet. And yet, if he had fetched me, I would have followed him. All the worse for Enjolras! I will not go to his funeral."

This resolution formed, Bossuet, Grantaire, and Joly did not stir from the wine-shop, and at about 2 P.M. the table at which they sat was covered with empty bottles. Two candles burned on it, one in a perfectly green copper candlestick, the other in the neck of a cracked water-bottle. Grantaire had led Joly and Bossuet to wine, and Bossuet and Joly had brought Grantaire back to joy. As for Grantaire, he gave up wine at midday, as a poor inspirer of illusions. Wine is not particularly valued by serious sots, for in ebriety there is black magic and white magic, and wine is only the white magic. Grantaire was an adventurous drinker of dreams. The blackness of a formidable intoxication yawning before him, far from arresting, attracted him, and he had given up bottles and taken to the dram-glass, which is an abyss. Not having at hand either opium or hashish, and wishing to fill his brain with darkness, he turned to that frightful mixture of brandy, stout, and absinthe, which produces such terrible lethargies. Of these three vapors, beer, brandy, and absinthe, the lead of the soul is made : they are three darknesses in which the celestial butterfly is drowned ; and there are formed in a membraneous smoke, vaguely condensed into a bat's wing, three dumb furies, Nightmare, Night, and Death, which hover over the sleeping Psyche. Grantaire had not yet reached that phase ; far from it : he was prodigiously gay, and Bossuet and Joly kept even with him. Grantaire added to the eccentric accentuation of words and ideas the vagary of gestures ; he laid his left hand on his knee with a dignified air, and with his neckcloth unloosed, straddling his stool, and with his full glass in his right hand, he threw these solemn words at the stout servant-girl Matelote : —

"Open the gates of the Palace! Let every man belong to the Académie Française, and have the right of embracing Madame Hucheloup! Let us drink."

And turning to the landlady, he added, —

"Antique female, consecrated by custom, approach, that I may contemplate thee."

And Joly exclaimed, —

"Batelote and Gibelotte, don't give Grantaire ady-bore drink. He is spending a frightful sum, and odly since this borning has devoured in shabeful prodigality two francs, ninety-five centibes."

And Grantaire went on, —

"Who has unhooked the stars without my leave, in order to place them on the table in lieu of candles ? "

Bossuet, who was very drunk, had retained his calmness, and was sitting on the sill of the open window, letting the rain drench his back, while he gazed at his two friends. All at once he heard behind him a tumult, hurried footsteps, and shouts of "To arms!" He turned, and noticed in the Rue St. Denis, at the end of the Rue Chanvrerie, Enjolras passing, carbine in hand, Gavroche with his pistol, Feuilly with his sabre, Courfeyrace with his sword, Jean Prouvaire with his musquetoon, Combeferre with his gun, Bahorel with his, and the whole armed and stormy band that followed them. The Rue de la Chanvrerie was not a pistol-shot in length, so

Bossuet improvised a speaking-trumpet with his two
hands round his mouth, and shouted, —

"Courfeyrac ! Courfeyrac ! hilloh ! "

Courfeyrac heard the summons, perceived Bossuet,
and walked a few steps down the Rue de la Chanvrerie, exclaiming, " What do you want?" which was
crossed by a " Where are you going ? "

" To make a barricade," Courfeyrac answered.

" Well, why not make it here ? the spot is good."

" That is true, Eagle," Courfeyrac remarked.

And at a sign from Courfeyrac the mob rushed
into the Rue de la Chanvrerie.

CHAPTER III.

THE ground was, in fact, admirably suited; the entrance of the street was wide, the end narrowed, and, like a blind alley, Corinth formed a contraction in it, the Rue de Mondétour could be easily barred right and left, and no attack was possible save by the Rue St. Denis; that is to say, from the front and in the open. Bossuet drunk had had the inspiration of Hannibal sober. At the sound of the band rushing on, terror seized on the whole street, and not a passer-by but disappeared. More quickly than a flash of lightning, shops, stalls, gates, doors, Venetian blinds, and shutters of every size were shut from the ground-floor to the roofs, at the end, on the right, and on the left. An old terrified woman fixed up a mattress before her window with clothes-props, in order to deaden the musketry, and the public-house alone remained open, — and for an excellent reason, because the insurgents had rushed into it.

"Oh Lord! oh Lord!" Mame Hucheloup sighed.

Bossuet ran down to meet Courfeyrac, and Joly, who had gone to the window, shouted, —

"Courfeyrac, you ought to have brought an umbrella. You will catch cold."

In a few minutes twenty iron bars were pulled down from the railings in front of the inn, and ten yards of pavement dug up. Gavroche and Bahorel seized, as it passed, the truck of a lime-dealer of the name of Anceau, and found in it three barrels of lime, which they placed under the piles of paving-stones; Enjolras had raised the cellar-flap, and all Mame Hucheloup's empty casks went to join the barrels of lime; Feuilly, with his fingers accustomed to illumine the delicate sticks of fans, reinforced the barrels and the trucks with two massive piles of stones, — rough stones, improvised like the rest, and taken from no one knew where. The supporting shores were pulled away from the frontage of an adjoining house, and laid on the casks. When Courfeyrac and Bossuet turned round, one half the street was already barred by a rampart taller than a man, for there is nothing like the hand of the people to build up anything that is built by demolishing. Matelote and Gibelotte were mixed up with the workmen, and the latter went backwards and forwards, loaded with rubbish, and her lassitude helped at the barricade. She served paving-stones, as she would have served wine, with a sleepy look. An omnibus drawn by two white horses passed the end of the street; Bossuet jumped over the stones, ran up, stopped the driver, ordered the passengers to get out, offered his hand to "the ladies," dismissed the conductor, and returned, pulling the horses on by the bridles.

"Omnibuses," he said, "must not pass before Corinth. *Non licet omnibus adire Corinthum.*"

A moment after, the unharnessed horses were straggling down the Rue Mondétour, and the omnibus lying on its side completed the barricade. Mame Hucheloup, quite upset, had sought refuge on the first-floor; her eyes were wandering and looked without seeing, and her cries of alarm dared not issue from her throat.

"It is the end of the world," she muttered.

Joly deposited a kiss on Mame Hucheloup's fat, red, wrinkled neck, and said to Grantaire, "My dear fellow, I have always considered a woman's neck an infinitely delicate thing." But Grantaire had reached the highest regions of dithyramb. When Matelote came up to the first-floor, he seized her round the waist and burst into loud peals of laughter at the window.

"Matelote is ugly," he cried; "Matelote is the ideal of ugliness; she is a chimera. Here is the secret of her birth, — a Gothic Pygmalion, who was carving cathedral gargoyles, fell in love on a fine morning with the most horrible of them. He implored love to animate it, and this produced Matelote. Look at her, citizens! She has chromate-of-lead-colored hair, like Titian's mistress, and is a good girl; I will answer that she fights well, for every good girl contains a hero. As for Mother Hucheloup, she is an old brave. Look at her mustachios; she inherited them from her husband. She will fight too, and the couple will terrify the whole of the suburbs. Comrades, we will overthrow the Government so truly as there are fifteen intermediate acids between margaric acid and formic acid; however, it is a matter of perfect indifference to me.   My father always detested me because I could not understand mathematics; I only understand love and liberty. I am Grantaire, the good fellow; never having had any money, I have not grown accustomed to it, and for that reason have never wanted it; but, had I been rich, there would be no poor left! You would have seen! Oh, if good hearts had large purses, how much better things would be! I can imagine the Saviour with Rothschild's fortune! What good he would do! Matelote, embrace me! You are voluptuous and timid; you have cheeks that claim the kiss of a sister, and lips that claim the kiss of a lover!"

"Hold your tongue, barrel!" Courfeyrac said.

Grantaire replied, —

"I am the Capitoul and master of the Floral games!"

Enjolras, who was standing on the top of the barricade, gun in hand, raised his handsome, stern face. Enjolras, as we know, blended the Spartan with the Puritan; he would have died at Thermopylæ with Leonidas, and burned Drogheda with Cromwell.

"Grantaire," he cried, "go and sleep off your wine elsewhere; this is the place for intoxication, and not for drunkenness.   Do not dishonor the barricade."

These stinging words produced on Grantaire a singular effect, and it seemed as if he had received a glass of cold water in his face.   He appeared suddenly sobered, sat down near the window, gazed at Enjolras with inexpressible tenderness, and said to him, —

" Let me sleep here."

" Go and sleep elsewhere," Enjolras cried.

But Grantaire, still fixing on him his tender and misty eyes, answered, —

" Let me sleep here till I die here."

Enjolras looked at him disdainfully.

" Grantaire, you are incapable of believing, thinking, wishing, living, and dying."

Grantaire replied in a grave voice, —

" You will see."

He stammered a few more unintelligible words, then his head fell noisily on the table, and — as is the usual effect of the second period of ebriety into which Enjolras had roughly and suddenly thrust him — a moment later he was asleep.

CHAPTER IV.

AN ENDEAVOR TO CONSOLE THE WIDOW HUCHELOUP.

BAHOREL, delighted with the barricade, exclaimed, "How well the street looks décolleté ! "

Courfeyrac, while gradually demolishing the public-house, tried to console the widowed landlady.

"Mother Hucheloup, were you not complaining the other day that you had been summoned by the police, because Gibelotte shook a counterpane out of the window ? "

"Yes, my good Monsieur Courfeyrac. Ah ! good gracious ! are you going to put that table too in your horror ? Yes, and the Government also condemned me to a fine of one hundred francs on account of a flower-pot that fell out of the garret into the street. Is that not abominable ? "

"Well, Mother Hucheloup, we are going to avenge you."

Mother Hucheloup did not exactly see the advantage accruing to her from the reparation made her. She was satisfied after the fashion of the Arab woman who, having received a box on the ears from her husband, went to complain to her father, crying vengeance, and saying, "Father, you owe my husband affront for affront." The father asked, "On which cheek did you receive the blow?" "On the left cheek." The father boxed her right cheek, and said, "Now you must be satisfied. Go and tell your husband that he buffeted my daughter, but I have buffeted his wife." The rain had ceased, and recruits began to arrive. Artisans brought under their blouses a barrel of gunpowder, a hamper containing carboys of vitriol, two or three carnival torches, and a basket full of lamps, "remaining from the king's birthday," which was quite recent, as it was celebrated on May 1. It was said that this ammunition was sent by a grocer in the Faubourg St. Antoine named Pépin. The only lantern in the Rue de la Chanvrerie, and all those in the surrounding streets, were broken. Enjolras, Combeferre, and Courfeyrac directed everything, and now two barricades were erected simultaneously, both of which were supported by Corinth and formed a square; the larger one closed the Rue de la Chanvrerie, and the smaller the Rue Mondétour on the side of the Rue du Cygne. This latter barricade, which was very narrow, was merely made of barrels and paving-stones. There were about fifty workmen there, of whom three were armed with guns, for on the road they had borrowed a gunsmith's entire stock.

Nothing could be stranger or more motley than this group: one had a sleeved waistcoat, a cavalry sabre, and a pair of holster pistols; another was in shirt-sleeves, with a round hat, and a powder-flask hung at his side; while a third was cuirassed with nine sheets of gray paper, and was armed with a saddler's awl. There was one who shouted, "Let us exterminate to the last, and die on the point of our bayonet !" This man had no bayonet. Another displayed over his coat the belts and pouch of a National Guard, with these words sewn in red worsted on the cover, "Public order." There were many muskets, bearing the numbers of legions, few hats, no neckties, a great many bare arms, and a few pikes ; add to this all ages, all faces, short pale youths, and bronzed laborers at the docks. All were in a hurry, and while assisting each other, talked about the possible chances, — that they were sure of one regiment, and Paris would rise. There were terrible remarks, with which a sort of cordial joviality was mingled ; they might have been taken for brothers, though they did not know one another's names. Great dangers have this beauty about them, that they throw light on the fraternity of strangers.

A fire was lighted in the kitchen, and men were melting in a bullet-mould, bowls, spoons, forks, and all the pewter articles of the public-house. They drank while doing this, and caps and slugs lay pell-mell on the table with glasses of wine. In the billiard-room Mame Hucheloup, Matelote, and Gibelotte, variously affected by terror, — as one was brutalized by it, another had her breath stopped, while the third was awakened, — were tearing up old sheets and making lint ; three insurgents helped them, — three hairy, bearded, and moustached fellows, who pulled the linen asunder with the fingers of a sempstress and made them tremble. The tall man, whom Courfeyrac, Combeferre, and Enjolras had noticed as he joined the band at the corner of the

Rue des Billettes, was working at the small barricade and making himself useful; Gavroche was working at the large one; and as for the young man who had waited for Courfeyrac at his lodgings and asked after M. Marius, he disappeared just about the time when the omnibus was overthrown.

Gavroche, who was perfectly radiant, had taken the arrangements on himself; he came, went, ascended, descended, went up again, rustled and sparkled. He seemed to be there for the encouragement of all. Had he a spur? Certainly, in his misery. Had he wings? Certainly, in his joy. Gavroche was a whirlwind; he was seen incessantly, and constantly heard, and he filled the air, being everywhere at once. He was a sort of almost irritating ubiquity, and it was impossible to stop with him. The enormous barricade felt him on its crupper; he annoyed the idlers, excited the slothful, reanimated the fatigued, vexed the thoughtful, rendered some gay and gave others time to breathe, set some in a passion and all in motion; he piqued a student and stung a workman; he halted, then started again, flew over the turmoil and the efforts, leaped from one to the other, murmured, buzzed, and harassed the whole team; he was the fly of the immense revolutionary coach. Perpetual movement was in his little arms, and perpetual clamor in his little lungs.

"Push ahead; more paving-stones, more barrels, more vehicles! Where are there any? We want a hodload of plaster to stop up this hole. Your barricade is very small, and must mount. Put everything into it; smash up the house; a barricade is Mother Gibou's tea. Hilloh! there's a glass door."

This made the workmen exclaim, —

"A glass door! What would you have us do with that, tubercule?"

"Hercules yourselves," Gavroche retorted; "a glass door in a barricade is excellent, for though it does not prevent the attack, it makes it awkward to take it. Have you never boned apples over a wall on which there was broken glass? A glass door cuts the corns of the National Guards when they try to climb up the barricade. By Job! glass is treacherous. Well, you fellows have no very bright imagination."

He was furious with his useless pistol, and went from one to the other, saying, "A gun! I want a gun! Why don't you give me a gun?"

"A gun for you?" said Combeferre.

"Well, why not?" Gavroche answered; "I had one in 1830, when we quarrelled with Charles X."

Enjolras shrugged his shoulders.

"When all the men have guns we will give them to boys."

Gavroche turned firmly, and answered him, —

"If you are killed before me I will take yours."

"Gamin!" said Enjolras.

"Puppy!" said Gavroche.

A dandy lounging past the end of the street created a diversion; Gavroche shouted to him, —

"Come to us, young man! What, will you do nothing for your old country?"

The dandy fled.

CHAPTER V.

PREPARATIONS.

THE journals of the day which stated that the barricade in the Rue de la Chanvrerie, that "almost impregnable fortress," as they called it, reached the level of a first-floor, are mistaken, for the truth is that it did not exceed an average height of six or seven feet. It was so built that the combatants could at will either disappear behind it or ascend to its crest by means of a quadruple row of paving-stones arranged like steps inside. Externally the front of the barricade, composed of piles of paving-stones and barrels, held together by joists and planks passed through the wheels of the truck and the omnibus, had a bristling and inextricable appearance. A gap, sufficiently wide for one man to pass, was left between the house-wall and the end of the barricade farthest from the wine-shop, so that a sortie was possible. The pole of the omnibus was held upright by ropes, and a red flag fixed to this pole floated over the barricade. The small Mondétour barricade, concealed behind the wine-shop, could not be seen, but the two barricades combined formed a real redoubt. Enjolras and Courfeyrac had not thought it advisable to barricade the other portion of the Rue

Mondétour, which opens on to the Halles, as they doubtless wished to maintain a possible communication with the outside, and had but little fear of being attacked by the difficult and dangerous Rue des Prêcheurs. With the exception of this issue left free, which constituted what Folard would have called in a strategic style a *boyau*, and of the narrow passage in the Rue de la Chanvrerie, the interior of the barricade, in which the wine-shop formed a salient angle, presented an irregular quadrilateral enclosed on all sides. There was a space of twenty yards between the great barricade and the tall houses which formed the end of the street, so that it might be said that the barricade leaned against these houses, which were all inhabited, but closed from top to bottom.

All this labor was completed without any obstacle, in less than an hour, during which this handful of men had not seen a single bearskin-cap or bayonet. The few citizens who still ventured at this moment of riot into the Rue St. Denis took a glance into the Rue de la Chanvrerie, perceived the barricade, and doubled their pace. When the two barricades were completed and the flag was hoisted, a table was pulled from the wine-shop into the street, and Courfeyrac got upon it. Enjolras brought up the square chest, which Courfeyrac opened, and it proved to be full of cartridges. When they saw these cartridges the bravest trembled, and there was a moment's silence. Courfeyrac distributed the cartridges smilingly, and each received thirty: many had powder, and began making others with the bullets which had been cast; as for the powder barrel, it was on a separate table, near the door, and was held in reserve. The drum-beat call to arms, which was traversing the whole of Paris, did not cease, but in the end it had become a monotonous sound, to which they no longer paid any attention. This noise at one moment retired, at another came nearer, with lugubrious undulations. The guns and carbines were loaded all together, without precipitation and with a solemn gravity. Enjolras then stationed three sentries outside the barricades, one in the Rue de la Chanvrerie, the second in the Rue des Prêcheurs, the third at the corner of the Petite Truanderie. Then, when the barricades were built, the posts assigned, the guns loaded, the sentries set, the insurgents alone in these formidable streets, through which no one now passed, surrounded by dumb and, as it were, dead houses, in which no human movement palpitated, enveloped in the menacing darkness, in the midst of that silence and obscurity in which they felt something advancing, and which had something tragical and terrifying about it, isolated, armed, determined, and tranquil — waited.

CHAPTER VI.

DURING the hours of waiting, what did they do?
We are bound to tell it, because this is historical.

While the men were making cartridges and the
women lint, while a large stewpan full of melted
tin and lead, intended for the bullet-mould, was
smoking on a red-hot chafing-dish, while the vedettes
were watching with shouldered guns on the barricade, while Enjolras, whom it was impossible to distract, watched the vedettes, Combeferre, Courfeyrac,
Jean Prouvaire, Feuilly, Bossuet, Joly, Bahorel, and
a few others, assembled, as in the most peaceful days
of their student conversations, and in one corner of
the wine-shop converted into a casemate, two paces
from the barricade which they had raised, and with
their loaded and primed muskets leaning against the
back of their chairs, — these fine young men, so near
their last hour, wrote love verses.

What verses? Here they are: —

Do you remember those days gone by,
    Our youth's high spring-tide? The sweet glad spell
Held us a season, when you and I
    Lived but to love and to look well?

Then all your years together with mine
    Would not make two-score when all was said;
Our nest it was so cosy and fine,
    Spring hid within till Winter had fled.

What days!   Manuel, how lofty, how chaste!
    Paris, turned godly, would be improved.
And how Foy thundered — and in your waist
    Was a pin, that pricked when my fingers roved!

All eyes looked your way.   At Prado's where
    Your briefless barrister dined with you,
You were so pretty, the roses there
    Turned and eyed you, in envy too.

I seemed to hear them whisper, "How fair!
    What wealth of ringlets, what rich perfume!
They are wings she hides 'neath her mantle there;
    Her bonnet's a blossom all a-bloom!"

Arm linked in arm, together we strayed;
    Passers thought, as we went our way,
Light-hearted Cupid a match had made
    'Twixt tender April and gallant May.

We lived so merrily hidden away,
    Feeding on Love's dear forbidden fruit.
Swifter than aught that my lips could say
    Your heart replied, when your lips were mute.

In the Sorbonne 't was, that idyllic spot,
    I dreamed of you through the long night-hours.
'T is thus a youthful lover self-taught
    In the Latin Quarter sights Love-land's towers.

O Place Maubert! O Place Dauphine!
  Dear sky-built palace-attic where
You drew your stocking on, unseen —
  I gazed at a star in the ceiling there!

Lamennais, Malebranche, forgotten they,
  And Plato too, mastered so carefully;
But I fathomed God's Infinite Love one day
  In a flower, — the flower you gave to me.

I was your slave.   You my subject were.
  O golden attic! to watch you pass
Back and forth, dressing, at daybreak there,
  Your girl's face smiling from that old glass!

O golden dawn! O golden days!
  Who can outlive them, forget them wholly?
The ribbons too, flowers and gauze and lace,
  Wherein Love stammered its first sweet folly.

Our garden, — a tulip-pot held the whole!
  Your petticoat curtained the window-pane;
I kept for myself the earthen-ware bowl,
  And gave you the cup of porcelain.

And such mishaps too, for mirth and woe!
  Your muff had caught fire, your tippet was gone;
And that portrait of Shakespeare we valued so
  Sold for a song — to be supped upon.

I'd beg and you would your alms bestow,
  A kiss from your fair round arm I'd steal.
Our board was that Dante in folio,
  And a hundred chestnuts our humble meal.

And that one moment, and all its joy
  When your lips met mine and the first kiss given,
You fled, dishevelled and rosy and coy ;
  I grew quite pale and believed in Heaven !

Do you remember our countless joys ?
  Those neckerchiefs rumpled ? ah, well-a-day !
And now from heavier hearts what sighs
  To skies all darkened are borne away !

The hour, the spot, the recollections of youth recalled, a few stars which were beginning to glisten in the sky, the funereal repose of these deserted streets, the imminence of the inexorable adventure which was preparing, gave a pathetic charm to these verses murmured in a low voice in the twilight by Jean Prouvaire, who, as we said, was a gentle poet.

In the mean while a lamp had been lit on the small barricade, and on the large one, one of those wax torches such as may be seen on Shrove Tuesday in front of the vehicles crowded with masks that are proceeding to the Courtille. These torches, we know, came from the Faubourg St. Antoine. The torch was placed in a species of lantern of paving-stones closed on three sides to protect it from the wind, and arranged so that the entire light should fall on the flag. The street and the barricade remained plunged in darkness, and nothing was visible save the red flag formidably illumined, as if by an enormous dark-lantern. This light added a strange and terrible purple to the scarlet of the flag.

CHAPTER VII.

THE RECRUIT OF THE RUE DES BILLETTES.

NIGHT had quite set in, and nothing occurred, only confused rumors and fusillades now and then could be heard, but they were rare, badly maintained, and distant. This respite, which was prolonged, was a sign that the Government was taking its time and collecting its strength. These fifty men were waiting for the coming of sixty thousand. Enjolras was attacked by that impatience which seizes on powerful minds when they stand on the threshold of formidable events. He looked up Gavroche, who was busy manufacturing cartridges in the ground-floor room by the dubious light of two candles placed on the bar for precaution, on account of the gunpowder sprinkled over the tables. These two candles threw no rays outside, and the insurgents allowed no light in the upper floors. Gavroche was at this moment greatly occupied, though not precisely with his cartridge.

The recruit from the Rue des Billettes had come into the room and seated himself at the least-lighted table. A Brown Bess of the large model had fallen to his share, and he held it between his legs. Gavroche up to this moment, distracted by a hundred " amusing " things, had not even seen this man.

When he entered, Gavroche looked after him, mechanically admiring his musket, but when the man was seated the gamin suddenly rose. Those who might have watched this man would have noticed him observe everything in the barricade, and the band of insurgents with singular attention; but when he entered the room he fell into a state of contemplation, and seemed to see nothing of what was going on. The gamin approached this pensive man, and began walking round him on tiptoe, in the same way as people move round a man whom they are afraid of awaking. At the same time all the grimaces of an old man passed over his childish face, at once so impudent and so serious, so giddy and so profound, so gay and so affecting, and these grimaces signified, "Oh, stuff! it is not possible, I must see double — I am dreaming — can it be? — no, it is not — yes, it is — no, it is not." Gavroche balanced himself on his heels, clenched his fists in his pockets, moved his neck like a bird, and expended on an enormously outstretched lip all the sagacity of a lower lip. He was stupefied, uncertain, convinced, and dazzled. He had the look of the chief of the eunuchs at the slave-market discovering a Venus among the girls, and the air of an amateur recognizing a Raphael in a pile of daubs. All about him was at work the instinct that scents and the intellect that combines; it was plain that an event was happening to Gavroche. It was when he was deepest in thought that Enjolras accosted him.

"You are little," he said, "and will not be seen. Go out of the barricades, slip along the houses, pass through as many streets as you can, and come back to tell me what is going on."

Gavroche drew himself up.

"So little ones are good for something! That's lucky! I'm off. In the mean while, trust to the little and distrust the big;" and Gavroche, raising his head and dropping his voice, added, as he pointed to the man of the Rue des Billettes, —

"You see that tall fellow?"

"Well?"

"He's a spy."

"Are you sure?"

"Not a fortnight back he pulled me down by the ear from the cornice of the Pont Royal where I was taking the air."

Enjolras hurriedly left the gamin and whispered a few words to a laborer from the wine-docks who was present. The laborer went out and returned almost immediately, followed by three others. The four men, four broad-shouldered porters, stationed themselves silently behind the table at which the man of the Rue des Billettes was seated, in evident readiness to fall upon him, and then Enjolras walked up to the man and asked him, —

"Who are you?"

At this sudden question the man started; he looked into the depths of Enjolras's candid eyeballs, and seemed to read his thoughts. He gave a smile, which was at once the most disdainful, energetic, and resolute possible, and answered, with a haughty gravity, —

"I see what you mean, — well, yes!"

" Are you a spy ? "

" I am an agent of the authority ! "

" And your name is — "

" Javert."

Enjolras gave the four men a sign, and in a twinkling, before Javert had time to turn round, he was
collared, thrown down, bound, and searched. They
found on him a small round card fixed between two
pieces of glass, and bearing on one side the arms of
France, with the motto, " Surveillance and vigilance,"
and on the other this notice, " JAVERT, Police Inspector, fifty-two years of age," and the signature of the
Prefect of Police of that day, M. Gisquet. He had
also a watch, and a purse containing some pieces of
gold, and both were left him. Behind his watch at
the bottom of his fob a paper was found, which
Enjolras unfolded, and on which he read these lines,
written by the Prefect of Police himself : —

" So soon as his political mission is concluded,
Javert will assure himself by a special watch whether it is true that criminals assemble on the slope
of the right bank of the Seine, near the bridge of
Jena."

When the search was ended, Javert was raised
from the ground, his arms were tied behind his back,
and he was fastened in the middle of the room to
the celebrated post which in olden times gave its
name to the wine-shop. Gavroche, who had watched
the whole scene and approved of everything with a
silent shake of the head, went up to Javert, and
said, —

" The mouse has trapped the cat."

All this took place so quickly that it was completed before those outside the wine-shop were aware of it. Javert had not uttered a cry, but on seeing him fastened to the post, Courfeyrac, Bossuet, Combeferre, Joly, and the men scattered over the two barricades, flocked in. Javert, who was surrounded with cords so that he could not stir, raised his head with the intrepid serenity of a man who has never told a falsehood.

"It is a spy," said Enjolras; and turning to Javert, " You will be shot two minutes before the barricade is taken."

Javert replied, with his most imperious accent, —

" Why not at once ? "

" We are saving of powder."

" Then settle the affair with a knife."

" Spy," said the beautiful Enjolras, " we are judges, and not assassins."

Then he called Gavroche.

" You be off now and do what I told you."

" I am off," Gavroche cried, but stopped just as he reached the door.

" By the way, you will give me his gun. I leave you the musician, but I want his clarinet."

The gamin gave a military salute, and gayly slipped round the large barricade.

CHAPTER VIII.

WAS HIS NAME LE CABUC?

THE tragical picture we have undertaken would not be complete, the reader would not see in their exact and real relief those great moments of social lying-in and revolutionary giving birth, in which there are throes blended with effort, if we were to omit in our sketch an incident full of an epic and stern horror, which occurred almost immediately after Gavroche's departure.

Bands of rioters, it is well known, resemble a snowball, and, as they roll along, agglomerate many tumultuous men, who do not ask one another whence they come. Among the passers-by who joined the band led by Enjolras, Combeferre, and Courfeyrac, there was a man wearing a porter's jacket, much worn at the shoulders, who gesticulated and vociferated, and had the appearance of a drunken savage. This man, whose name or nickname was Le Cabuc, and who was entirely unknown to those who pretended to know him, was seated, in a state of real or feigned intoxication, with four others, round a table which they had dragged out of the wine-shop. This Cabuc, while making the others drink, seemed to be gazing thoughtfully at the large house behind the

barricade, whose five stories commanded the whole
street and faced the Rue St. Denis. All at once he
exclaimed, —

"Do you know what, comrades? We must fire
from that house. When we are at the windows,
hang me if any one can come up the street."

"Yes, but the house is closed," said one of the
drinkers.

"We 'll knock."

"They won't open."

"Then we 'll break in the door."

Le Cabuc ran up to the door, which had a very
massive knocker, and rapped ; as the door was not
opened he rapped again, and no one answering, he
gave a third rap, but the silence continued.

"Is there any one in here? " Le Cabuc shouted.
But nothing stirred, and so he seized a musket and
began hammering the door with the butt end. It was
an old, low, narrow, solid door, made of oak, lined
with sheet iron inside and a heavy bar, and a thorough
postern gate. The blows made the whole house
tremble, but did not shake the door. The inmates,
however, were probably alarmed, for a little square
trap window was at length lit up and opened on
the third story, and a candle and the gray-haired
head of a terrified old man, who was the porter,
appeared in the orifice. The man who was knocking
left off.

"What do you want, gentlemen? " the porter
asked.

"Open the door ! " said Le Cabuc.

"I cannot, gentlemen."

" Open, I tell you ! "

" It is impossible, gentlemen."

Le Cabuc raised his musket and took aim at the porter, but as he was below and it was very dark the porter did not notice the fact.

" Will you open? Yes or no."

" No, gentlemen."

" You really mean it ? "

" I say no, my kind — "

The porter did not finish the sentence, for the musket was fired ; the bullet entered under his chin and came out of his neck, after passing through the jugular vein. The old man fell in a heap, without heaving a sigh, the candle went out, and nothing was visible save a motionless head lying on the sill of the window, and a small wreath of smoke ascending to the roof.

" There," said Le Cabuc, as he let the butt of the musket fall on the pavement again.

He had scarce uttered the word ere he felt a hand laid on his shoulder with the tenacity of an eagle's talon, and he heard a voice saying to him, —

" On your knees ! "

The murderer turned, and saw before him Enjolras's white, cold face. Enjolras held a pistol in his hand, and had hurried up on hearing the shot fired, and clutched with his left hand Le Cabuc's blouse, shirt, and braces.

" On your knees ! " he repeated.

And with a sovereign movement the frail young man of twenty bent like a reed the muscular and thick-set porter, and forced him to kneel in the mud.

Le Cabuc tried to resist, but he seemed to have been seized by a superhuman hand. Enjolras, pale, bare-neck, with his dishevelled hair and feminine face, had at this moment I know not what of the ancient Themis. His dilated nostrils, his downcast eyes, gave to his implacable Greek profile that expression of wrath and that expression of chastity which, in the opinion of the old world, are becoming to justice. All the insurgents had hurried up, and then ranged themselves in a circle at a distance, feeling that it was impossible for them to utter a word in the presence of what they were going to see. Le Cabuc, con-quered, no longer attempted to struggle, and trembled all over : Enjolras loosed his grasp, and took out his watch.

"Pray or think!" he said ; "you have one minute to do so."

"Mercy!" the murderer stammered, then hung his head and muttered a few inarticulate execrations.

Enjolras did not take his eyes off the watch; he let the minute pass, and then put the watch again in his fob. This done, he seized Le Cabuc by the hair, who clung to his knees with a yell, and placed the muzzle of the pistol to his ear. Many of these intrepid men, who had so tranquilly entered upon the most frightful of adventures, turned away their heads. The explosion was heard, the assassin fell on his head on the pavement, and Enjolras drew himself up and looked round him with a stern air of conviction. Then he kicked the corpse and said, —

"Throw this outside."

Three men raised the body of the wretch, which was still writhing in the last mechanical convulsions of expiring life, and threw it over the small barricade into the Mondétour lane. Enjolras stood pensive; some grand darkness was slowly spreading over his formidable serenity. Presently he raised his voice, and all were silent.

"Citizens," said Enjolras, "what that man did is frightful, and what I have done is horrible; he killed, and that is why I killed, and I was obliged to do so, as insurrection must have its discipline. Assassination is even more of a crime here than elsewhere, for we stand under the eye of the Revolution, we are the priests of the Republic, we are the sacred victims to duty, and we must not do aught that would calumniate our combat. I, therefore, tried and condemned this man to death; for my part, constrained to do what I have done, but abhorring it, I have also tried myself, and you will shortly see what sentence I have passed."

All who listened trembled.

"We will share your fate," Combeferre exclaimed.

"Be it so!" Enjolras continued. "One word more. In executing that man I obeyed Necessity; but Necessity is a monster of the old world, and its true name is Fatality. Now, it is the law of progress that monsters should disappear before angels, and Fatality vanish before Fraternity. It is a bad moment to utter the word love; but no matter, I utter it, and I glorify it. Love, thou hast a future; Death, I make use of thee, but I abhor thee. Citizens, in the future there will be no darkness, no thunderclaps; neither ferocious ignorance nor bloodthirsty retaliation; and as there will be no Satan left, there will be no Saint Michael. In the future no man will kill another man; the earth will be radiant, and the human race will love. The day will come, citizens, when all will be concord, harmony, light, joy, and life, and we are going to die in order that it may come."

Enjolras was silent, his virgin lips closed, and he stood for some time at the spot where he had shed blood, in the motionlessness of a marble statue. His fixed eyes caused people to talk in whispers around him. Jean Prouvaire and Combeferre shook their heads silently, and leaning against each other in an angle of the barricade, gazed, with an admiration in which there was compassion, at this grave young man, who was an executioner and priest, and had, at the same time, the light and the hardness of crystal. Let us say at once, that after the action, when the corpses were conveyed to the Morgue and searched, a police-agent's card was found on Le Cabuc; the author of this work had in his hands, in 1848, the special report on this subject made to the Prefect of Police in 1832. Let us add that, if we may believe a strange but probably well-founded police tradition, Le Cabuc was Claquesous. It is certainly true that after the death of Cabuc, Claquesous was never heard of again, and left no trace of his disappearance. He seemed to have become amalgamated with the invisible; his life had been gloom, and his end was night.

The whole insurgent band were still suffering from

the emotion of this tragical trial, so quickly begun and so quickly ended, when Courfeyrac saw again at the barricade the short young man who had come to his lodgings to ask for Marius; this lad, who had a bold and reckless look, had come at night to rejoin the insurgents.

BOOK XIII.

MARIUS ENTERS THE SHADOW.

CHAPTER I.

FROM THE RUE PLUMET TO THE QUARTIER ST. DENIS.

The voice which summoned Marius through the twilight to the barricade in the Rue de la Chanvrerie had produced on him the effect of the voice of destiny. He wished to die, and the opportunity offered; he rapped at the door of the tomb, and a hand held out the key to him from the shadows. Such gloomy openings in the darkness just in front of despair are tempting; Marius removed the bar which had so often allowed him to pass, left the garden, and said, "I will go." Mad with grief, feeling nothing fixed and solid in his brain, incapable of accepting anything henceforth of destiny, after the two months spent in the intoxication of youth and love, and crushed by all the reveries of despair at once, he had only one wish left, — to finish with it all at once. He began walking rapidly, and he happened to be armed, as he had Javert's pistols in his pocket. The young man whom he fancied that he had seen had got out of his sight in the streets.

Marius, who left the Rue Plumet by the boulevard, crossed the esplanade and bridge of the Invalides, the Champs Élysées, the square of Louis XV.,
and reached the Rue de Rivoli. The shops were
open there, the gas blazed under the arcades, ladies
were making purchases, and people were eating ices
at the Café Laiter and cakes at the English pastry-
cook's. A few post-chaises, however, were leaving
at a gallop the Hôtel des Princes and Meurice's.
Marius entered the Rue St. Honoré by the passage
Delorme. The shops were closed there, the tradesmen were conversing before their open doors, people
walked along, the lamps were lighted, and from the
first-floor upwards the houses were illumined as
usual. Cavalry were stationed on the square of the
Palais Royal. Marius followed the Rue St. Honoré,
and the farther he got from the Palais Royal the
fewer windows were lit up; the shops were entirely
closed, nobody was conversing on the thresholds, the
street grew darker, and at the same time the crowd
denser, for the passers-by had now become a crowd.
No one could be heard speaking in the crowd, and
yet a hollow, deep buzzing issued from it. Near the
Fountain of Arbre Sec there were motionless mobs,
and sombre groups standing among the comers and
goers like stones in the middle of a running stream.
At the entrance of the Rue des Prouvaires, the crowd
no longer moved; it was a resisting, solid, compact,
almost impenetrable mob of persons packed together
and conversing in a low voice. There were hardly
any black coats or round hats present, only fustian
jackets, blouses, caps, and bristling beards. This

multitude undulated confusedly in the night mist, and its whispering had the hoarse accent of a rustling; and though no one moved, a tramping in the mud could be heard. Beyond this dense crowd there was not a window lit up in the surrounding streets, and the solitary and decreasing rows of lanterns could only be seen in them. The street-lanterns of that day resembled large red stars suspended from ropes, and cast on to the pavement a shadow which had the shape of a large spider. These streets, however, were not deserted, and piled muskets, moving bayonets, and troops bivouacking could be distinguished in them. No curious person went beyond this limit, and circulation ceased there; there the mob ended and the army began.

Marius wished with the will of a man who no longer hopes; he had been summoned and was bound to go. He found means to traverse the crowd and bivouacking troops; he hid himself from the patrols and avoided the sentries. He made a circuit, came to the Rue de Béthisy, and proceeded in the direction of the markets; at the corner of the Rue des Bourdonnais the lanterns ceased. After crossing the zone of the mob he passed the border of troops, and now found himself in something frightful. There was not a wayfarer, nor a soldier, nor a light, nothing but solitude, silence, and night, and a strangely-piercing cold; entering a street was like entering a cellar. Still he continued to advance: Some one ran close past him: was it a man? — a woman? Were there more than one? He could not have said, for it had passed and vanished.

By constant circuits he reached a lane, which he judged to be the Rue de la Poterie, and toward the middle of that lane came across an obstacle. He stretched out his hands and found that it was an overturned cart, and his feet recognized pools of water, holes, scattered and piled-up paving-stones; it was a barricade which had been begun and then abandoned. He clambered over the stones and soon found himself on the other side of the obstacle; he walked very close to the posts, and felt his way along the house walls. A little beyond the barricade he fancied that he could see something white before him, and on drawing nearer it assumed a form. It was a pair of white horses, the omnibus horses unharnessed by Bossuet in the morning, which had wandered, haphazard, from street to street all day, and at last stopped here, with the stolid patience of animals which no more comprehend the actions of man than man comprehends the actions of Providence. Marius left the horses behind him, and as he entered a street which seemed to be the Rue du Contrat Social, a musket-shot, which came no one could say whence, and traversed the darkness at hazard, whizzed close past him, and pierced above his head a copper shaving-dish, hanging from a hairdresser's shop. In 1846 this dish with the hole in it was still visible at the corner of the pillars of the markets. This shot was still life, but from this moment nothing further occurred; the whole itinerary resembled a descent down black steps, but for all that Marius did not the less advance.

CHAPTER II.

AN OWL'S-EYE VIEW OF PARIS.

ANY being hovering over Paris at this moment, with the wings of a bat or an owl, would have had a gloomy spectacle under his eyes. The entire old district of the markets, which is like a city within a city, which is traversed by the Rues St. Denis and St. Martin, and by a thousand lanes which the insurgents had converted into their redoubt and arsenal, would have appeared like an enormous black hole dug in the centre of Paris. Here the eye settled on an abyss, and, owing to the broken lamps and the closed shutters, all brilliancy, life, noise, and movement had ceased in it. The invisible police of the revolt were watching everywhere and maintaining order, that is to say, night. To hide the small number in a vast obscurity, and to multiply each combatant by the possibilities which this obscurity contains, this is the necessary tactics of insurrection, and at nightfall every window in which a candle gleamed received a bullet; the light was extinguished, and sometimes the occupant killed. Hence, nothing stirred; there was nought but terror, mourning, and stupor in the houses, and in the streets a sort of sacred horror. Not even the long rows of windows and floors, the network of chimneys and roofs, and the vague reflections which glisten on the muddy and damp pavement, could be perceived. The eye which had looked down from above on this mass of shadow might perhaps have noticed here and there indistinct gleams, which made the broken and strange lines, and the profile of singular buildings, stand out, something like flashes flitting through ruins ; at such spots were the barricades. The rest was a lake of darkness and mystery, oppressive and funereal, above which motionless and mournful outlines rose, — the Tower of St. Jacques, St. Merry church, and two or three other of those grand edifices of which man makes giants and night phantoms. All around this deserted and alarming labyrinth, in those districts where the circulation of Paris was not stopped, and where a few lamps glistened, the aerial observer would have distinguished the metallic scintillation of bayonets, the dull rolling of artillery, and the buzz of silent battalions which was augmented every moment ; it was a formidable belt, slowly contracting and closing in on the revolt.

The invested district was now but a species of monstrous cavern ; everything seemed there asleep or motionless, and, as we have seen, each of the streets by which it could be approached only offered darkness. It was a stern darkness, full of snares, full of unknown and formidable collisions, into which it was terrifying to penetrate and horrible to remain, where those who entered shuddered before those who awaited them, and those who awaited shuddered before those who were about to come. Invisible com-

batants were intrenched at the corner of every street,
like sepulchral traps hidden in the thickness of the
night. It was all over; no other light could be
hoped for there henceforth save the flash of musketry,
no other meeting than the sudden and rapid apparition of death. Where, how, when, they did not
know, but it was certain and inevitable: there, in
the spot marked out for the contest, the Government
and the insurrection, the National Guards and the
popular society, the bourgeoisie and the rioters, were
about to grope their way toward one another. There
was the same necessity for both sides, and the only
issue henceforth possible was to be killed or conquer.
It was such an extreme situation, such a powerful
obscurity, that the most timid felt resolute and the
most daring terrified. On both sides, however, there
was equal fury, obstinacy, and determination; on one
side advancing was death, and no one dreamed of
recoiling; on the other, remaining was death, and
no one thought of flying. It was necessary that all
should be over by the morrow, that the victory
should be with one side or the other, and the insurrection either become a revolution or a riot.
The Government understood this as well as the
partisans, and the smallest tradesman felt it. Hence
came an agonizing thought with the impenetrable
gloom of this district, where all was about to be
decided; hence came a redoubled anxiety around
this silence, whence a catastrophe was going to issue.
Only one sound could be heard, — a sound as heart-
rending as a death-rattle and as menacing as a male-
diction, the tocsin of St. Merry. Nothing could be

so chilling as the clamor of this distracted and despairing bell as it lamented in the darkness.

As often happens, nature seemed to have come to an understanding with what men were going to do, and nothing deranged the mournful harmonies of the whole scene. The stars had disappeared, and heavy clouds filled the entire horizon with their melancholy masses. There was a black sky over these dead streets, as if an intense pall were cast over the immense tomb. While a thoroughly political battle was preparing on the same site which had already witnessed so many revolutionary events, — while the youth, the secret associations, and the schools in the name of principles, and the middle classes in the name of interests, were coming together to try a final fall, — while everybody was hurrying up and appealing to the last and decisive hour of the crisis, in the distance and beyond that fatal district, at the lowest depths of the unfathomable cavities of that old wretched Paris which is disappearing under the splendor of happy and opulent Paris, the gloomy voice of the people could be heard hoarsely growling. It is a startling and sacred voice, composed of the yell of the brute and the word of God, which terrifies the weak and warns the wise, and which at once comes from below like the voice of the lion, and from above like the voice of thunder.

CHAPTER III.

THE EXTREME BRINK.

MARIUS had reached the markets; there all was calmer, darker, and even more motionless than in the neighboring streets. It seemed as if the frozen peace of the tomb had issued from the ground and spread over the sky. A ruddy tinge, however, brought out from the black background the tall roofs of the houses which barred the Rue de la Chanvrerie on the side of St. Eustache. It was the reflection of the torch burning on the Corinth barricade, and Marius walked toward that ruddy hue; it led him to the Marché aux Poirées, and he caught a glimpse of the Rue des Prêcheurs, into which he turned. The sentry of the insurgents watching at the other end did not notice him; he felt himself quite close to what he was seeking, and he walked on tiptoe. He thus reached the corner of that short piece of the Mondétour lane which was, as will be remembered, the sole communication which Enjolras had maintained with the outer world. At the corner of the last house on his left he stopped and peeped into the lane. A little beyond the dark corner formed by the lane and the Rue de la Chanvrerie, which formed a large patch of shadow in which he was himself buried, he noticed a little light on the pavement, a portion of a wine-shop, a lamp flickering in a sort of shapeless niche, and men crouching down with guns on their knees, — all this was scarce ten yards from him, and was the interior of the barricade. The houses that lined the right-hand side of the lane hid from him the rest of the wine-shop, the large barricade, and the flag. Marius had but one step to take, and then the unhappy young man sat down on a post, folded his arms, and thought of his father.

He thought of that heroic Colonel Pontmercy, who had been such a proud soldier, who had defended under the Republic the frontier of France, and touched under the Empire the frontier of Asia ; who had seen Genoa, Alexandria, Milan, Turin, Madrid, Vienna, Dresden, Berlin, and Moscow ; who had left on all the victorious battle-fields of Europe drops of the same blood which Marius had in his veins ; who had grown gray before age in discipline and command ; who had lived with his waist-belt buckled, his epaulettes falling on his chest, his cockade blackened by smoke, his brow wrinkled by his helmet, in barracks, in camp, in bivouacs, and in hospitals, and who, at the expiration of twenty years, had returned from the great wars with his scarred cheek and smiling face, simple, tranquil, admirable, pure as an infant, having done everything for France and nothing against her. He said to himself that his own day had now arrived, that his hour had at length struck, that after his father he too was going to be brave, intrepid, and bold, to rush to meet bullets, offer his chest to the bayonets, shed his blood, seek the enemy, seek death ; that he in his turn was about to wage war and go into the battle-field, and that the battle he would enter was the street, and the war he was about to wage civil war ! He saw civil war opening like a gulf before him, and that he was going to fall into it ; then he shuddered.

He thought of his father's sword, which his grandfather had sold to the old-clothes dealer, and which he had so painfully regretted. He said to himself that this valiant and chaste sword had done well to escape from him, and disappear angrily in the darkness ; that it fled away thus because it was intelligent, and foresaw the future, — the riots, the war of gutters, the war of paving-stones, fusillades from cellar-traps, and blows dealt and received from behind ; that, coming from Marengo and Austerlitz, it was unwilling to go to the Rue de la Chanvrerie, and after what it had done with the father refused to do that with the son ! He said to himself that if that sword had been here, if, after receiving it at his dead father's bedside, he had dared to take it, and carry it into this nocturnal combat between Frenchmen in the streets, it would assuredly have burned his hands, and have flashed before him like the glaive of the archangel ! He said to himself that it was fortunate it was not there, but had disappeared, — that this was well, this was just, that his grandfather had been the true guardian of his father's glory, and that it was better for the Colonel's sword to have been put up to auction, sold to the second-hand dealer, or broken up as old

iron, than come to-day to make the flank of the
country bleed. And then he began weeping bitterly.
It was horrible, but what was he to do? He could
not live without Cosette, and since she had departed
all left him was to die. Had he not pledged her
his word of honor that he would die? She had
gone away knowing this, and it was plain that she
was pleased with Marius's dying; and then it was
clear that she no longer loved him, since she had
gone away thus without warning him, without a
word, without a letter, and yet she knew his address!
Of what use was it to live; and why should he live
now? And then, to have come so far and then
recoil! to have approached the danger and run away!
to have come to look at the barricade and then slip
off! to slip off, trembling and saying, "After all, I
have had enough of that. I have seen it, that is
sufficient; it is civil war, and I will be off!" To
abandon his friends who expected him, who perhaps
had need of him, who were a handful against an
army! To be false to everything at once, — to love,
to friendship, to his word! to give his poltroonery
the pretext of patriotism! Oh, that was impossible,
and if his father's phantom were there in the shadows,
and saw him recoil, it would lash him with the flat
of its sabre, and cry to him, "Forward, coward!"

A prey to this oscillation of his thoughts, he hung
his head, but suddenly raised it again, for a species
of splendid rectification had just taken place in his
mind. There is a dilation of thought peculiar to
the vicinity of the tomb; and to be near death makes
a man see correctly. The vision of the action upon

which he saw himself perhaps on the point of entering, no longer appeared to him lamentable, but superb;
the street was become transfigured by some internal
labor of the soul before his mental eye.   All the tumultuous notes of interrogation of reverie crowded
back upon him, but without troubling him, and he
did not leave a single one unanswered.   Why would
his father be indignant ? Are there not cases in which
insurrection attains to the dignity of duty ?   What
was there degrading for the son of Colonel Pontmercy in the combat which was about to begin ?
It is no longer Montmirail or Champaubert, it is
something else ; it is no longer a question of a sacred
territory, but of a holy idea.   The country complains;
be it so, but humanity applauds.   Is it true, besides,
that the country complains ? France bleeds, but liberty smiles, and on seeing the smile of liberty France
forgets her wound.   And then, regarding things from
a higher point still, what did people mean by talking
of a civil war ?

What is the meaning of civil war ? Is there such
a thing as a foreign war ? Is not every war between
men a war between brothers ? War can only be quali-
fied by its object, and there is neither foreign war
nor civil war, there is only just or unjust war.   Up
to the day when the great human concordat is concluded, war, at least that which is the effort of the
hurrying future against the laggard past, may be necessary.   What reproach can be urged against such a
war ? War does not become a disgrace, or the sword
a dagger, until it assassinates right, progress, reason,
civilization, and truth.   In such a case, whether civil

war or foreign war, it is iniquitous, and is called crime. Beyond that holy thing justice, what right would one form of war have to despise another? By what right would the sword of Washington ignore the pike of Camille Desmoulins? Which is the greater, Leonidas contending against the foreigner, or Timoleon against the tyrant? One is the defender, the other is the liberator. Must we brand, without investigating the object, every taking up of arms in the interior of a city? If so, mark with contumely Brutus, Marcel, Arnould of Blankenheim, and Coligny. A war of thickets — a street war? Why not? Such was the war of Ambiorix, of Artevelde, of Marnix, and Pelagius. But Ambiorix struggled against Rome, Artevelde against France, Marnix against Spain, and Pelagius against the Moors, — all against the foreigner. Well, monarchy is the foreigner, oppression is the foreigner, divine right is the foreigner, and despotism violates the moral frontier as invasion does the geographical frontier. Expelling the tyrant or expelling the English is, in either case, a reconquest of territory. An hour arrives when a protest is insufficient; after philosophy, action is needed; living strength completes what the idea has sketched out: Prometheus vinctus begins, Aristogiton ends, the Encyclopædia enlightens minds, and August 10 electrifies them. After Æschylus, Thrasybulus; after Diderot, Danton. Multitudes have a tendency to accept the master, and their mass deposits apathy. A crowd is easily led into habits of obedience. These must be stirred up, impelled, and roughly treated by the very blessing of their deliverance, their eyes be hurt by the truth, and light hurled at them in terrible handfuls. They must themselves be to some extent thunderstruck by their own salvation, for such a dazzling awakes them. Hence comes the necessity of tocsins and wars : it is necessary that great combatants should rise, illumine nations by audacity, and shake up that sorry humanity over which divine right, Cæsarian glory, strength, fanaticism, irresponsible power, and absolute majesties cast a shadow, — a mob stupidly occupied in contemplating these gloomy triumphs of the night in their crepuscular splendor. But what ? Whom are you talking of ? Do you call Louis Philippe the tyrant ? No ; no more than Louis XVI. These are both what history is accustomed to call good kings ; but principles cannot be broken up, the logic of truth is rectilinear, and its peculiarity is that it lacks pliability. No concession therefore ; every encroachment on man must be repressed : there is the right divine in Louis XVI., there is the " because a Bourbon" in Louis Philippe ; both represent to a certain extent the confiscation of right, and they must be combated in order to sweep away universal usurpation ; it must be so, for France is always the one who begins, and when the master falls in France he falls everywhere. In a word, what cause is more just, and consequently what war is greater, than to re-establish social truth, give back its throne to liberty, restore the people to the people and the sovereignty to man, to replace the crown on the head of France, to restore reason and equity in their plenitude, to suppress every germ of antagonism by giving back individuality, to annihilate the obstacle which the royalty offers to the immense human concord, and to place the human race once again on a level with right? Such wars construct peace. An enormous fortalice of prejudice, privileges, superstitions, false-hoods, exactions, abuses, violences, iniquities, and darknesses, is still standing on the earth with its towers of hatred, and it must be thrown down, and the monstrous mass crumble away. To conquer at Austerlitz is great, but to take the Bastille is immense.

No one but will have noticed in himself that the mind — and this is the marvel of its unity compli-cated with ubiquity — has the strange aptitude of reasoning almost coldly in the most violent extremi-ties, and it often happens that weird passions and deep despair, in the very agony of their blackest soliloquies, handle subjects and discuss theses. Logic is mingled with the convulsion, and the thread of syllogism floats, without breaking, through the storm of the thoughts: such was Marius's state of mind. While thinking thus, crushed but resolute, and yet hesitating and shuddering at what he was going to do, his eyes wandered about the interior of the barri-cade. The insurgents were conversing in whispers, without moving, and that almost silence which marks the last phase of expectation was perceptible. Above them, at a third-floor window, Marius distinguished a species of spectator or of witness who seemed sin-gularly attentive; it was the porter killed by Le Cabuc. From below, this head could be vaguely perceived in the reflection of the torch burning on the barricade, and nothing was stranger in this dense and vacillating light than this motionless, livid, and amazed face, with its bristling hair, open and fixed eyes, and gaping mouth, bending over the street in an attitude of curiosity. It might be said that this dead man was contemplating those who were going to die. A long stream of blood, which had flowed from his head, descended from the window to the first-floor, where it stopped.

BOOK XIV.

THE GRANDEUR OF DESPAIR.

CHAPTER I.

THE FLAG: ACT FIRST.

NOTHING came yet: it had struck ten by St. Merry's, and Enjolras and Combeferre were sitting musket in hand near the sally-port of the great barricade. They did not speak, but were listening, trying to catch the dullest and most remote sound of marching. Suddenly, in the midst of this lugubrious calm, a clear, young, gay voice, which seemed to come from the Rue St. Denis, burst forth, and began singing distinctly, to the old popular tune of "Au clair de la lune," these lines, terminating with a cry that resembled a cock-crow: —

> "Mon nez est en larmes,
>   Mon ami Bugeaud,
>   Prêt'-moi tes gendarmes
>   Pour leur dire un mot.
>   En capote bleue,
>   La poule au shako,
>   Voici la banlieue !
>   Co-cocorico ! "

They shook hands.

" 'T is Gavroche," said Enjolras.

" He is warning us," said Combeferre.

Hurried footsteps troubled the deserted streets, and a being more active than a clown was seen climbing over the omnibus, and Gavroche leaped into the square, out of breath, and saying, —

" My gun !   Here they are ! "

An electric shudder ran along the whole barricade, and the movement of hands seeking guns was heard.

" Will you have my carbine ? "   Enjolras asked the gamin.

" I want the big gun," Gavroche answered, and took Javert's musket.

Two sentries had fallen back and come in almost simultaneously with Gavroche ; they were those from the end of the street and the Petite Truanderie. The vedette in the Lane des Prêcheurs remained at his post, which indicated that nothing was coming from the direction of the bridges and the markets. The Rue de la Chanvrerie, in which a few paving-stones were scarce visible in the reflection of the light cast on the flag, offered to the insurgents the aspect of a large black gate vaguely opened in a cloud of smoke.   Every man proceeded to his post : forty-three insurgents, among whom were Enjolras, Combeferre, Courfeyrac, Bossuet, Joly, Bahorel, and Gavroche, knelt behind the great barricade, with the muzzles of their guns and carbines thrust out between the paving-stones as through loop-holes, attentive, silent, and ready to fire.   Six, commanded by

Feuilly, installed themselves at the upper windows of Corinth. Some minutes more elapsed, and then a measured, heavy tramp of many feet was distinctly heard from the direction of St. Leu; this noise, at first faint, then precise, and then heavy and re-echoing, approached slowly, without halt or interruption, and with a tranquil and terrible continuity. Nothing was audible but this; it was at once the silence and noise of the statue of the Commander; but the stony footfall had something enormous and multiple about it, which aroused the idea of a multitude at the same time as that of a spectre; you might have fancied that you heard the fearful statue Legion on the march. The tramp came nearer, nearer still, and then ceased; and the breathing of many men seemed to be audible at the end of the street. Nothing, however, was visible, though quite at the end in the thick gloom could be distinguished a multitude of metallic threads, fine as needles and almost imperceptible, which moved about like that indescribable phosphoric network which we perceive under our closed eyelids just at the moment when we are falling asleep. These were bayonets and musket-barrels on which the reflection of the torch confusedly fell. There was another pause, as if both sides were waiting. All at once a voice which was the more sinister because no one could be seen, and it seemed as if the darkness itself was speaking, shouted, " Who goes there? "

At the same time the click of muskets being cocked could be heard. Enjolras replied with a sonorous and haughty accent, —

" French Revolution ! "

" Fire ! " the voice commanded.

A flash lit up all the frontages in the street, as if the door of a furnace had been suddenly opened and shut, and a frightful shower of bullets hurled against the barricade, and the flag fell. The discharge had been so violent and dense that it cut the staff asunder, that is to say, the extreme point of the omnibus pole. Bullets ricochetting from the cornices of the houses penetrated the barricade and wounded several men. The impression produced by this first discharge was chilling ; the attack was rude, and of a nature to make the boldest think. It was plain that they had to do with a whole regiment at the least.

" Comrades," Courfeyrac cried, " let us not waste our powder, but wait till they have entered the street before returning their fire."

" And before all," Enjolras said, " let us hoist the flag again ! "

He picked up the flag, which had fallen at his feet : outside, the ring of ramrods in barrels could be heard ; the troops were reloading. Enjolras continued, —

" Who has a brave heart among us ? Who will plant the flag on the barricade again ? "

Not one replied ; for to mount the barricade at this moment, when all the guns were doubtless again aimed at it, was simply death, and the bravest man hesitates to condemn himself. Enjolras even shuddered as he repeated, —

" Will no one offer ? "

CHAPTER II.

SINCE the arrival at Corinth and the barricade had been begun no one paid any further attention to Father Mabœuf. M. Mabœuf, however, had not quitted the insurgents : he had gone into the ground-floor room of the wine-shop and seated himself behind the bar, where he was, so to speak, annihilated in himself. He seemed no longer to see or think. Courfeyrac and others had twice or thrice accosted him, warning him of the peril and begging him to withdraw, but he had not appeared to hear them. When no one was speaking to him his lips moved as if he were answering some one, and so soon as people addressed him his lips left off moving, and his eyes no longer seemed alive. A few hours before the barricade was attacked he had assumed a posture which he had not quitted since, with his two hands on his knees, and his head bent forward, as if he were looking into a precipice. Nothing could have drawn him out of this attitude, and it did not appear as if his mind were in the barricade. When every one else went to his post the only persons left in the room were Javert tied to the post, an insurgent with drawn sabre watching over Javert, and Mabœuf. At the moment of the attack, at the detonation, the physical shock affected and as it were awoke him; he suddenly rose, crossed the room, and at the moment when Enjolras repeated his appeal, " Does no one offer ?" the old man was seen on the threshold of the wine-shop. His presence produced a species of commotion in the groups, and the cry was raised, —

" It is the voter, the conventionalist, the representative of the people ! "

He probably did not hear it : he walked straight up to Enjolras, the insurgents making way for him with a religious fear, tore the flag from Enjolras, who recoiled with petrifaction, and then, no one daring to arrest or help him, this old man of eighty, with shaking head but firm step, slowly began ascending the staircase of paving-stones formed inside the barricade. This was so gloomy and so grand that all around him cried, " Off with your hats ! " With each step he ascended the scene became more frightful ; his white hair, his decrepit face, his high, bald, and wrinkled forehead, his hollow eyes, his amazed and open mouth, and his old arm raising the red banner, stood out from the darkness and were magnified in the sanguinary brightness of the torch, and the spectators fancied they saw the spectre of '93 issuing from the ground, holding the flag of terror in its hand. When he was on the last step, when this trembling and terrible phantom, standing on the pile of ruins, in the presence of twelve hundred invisible gun-barrels, stood facing death, and as if stronger than it, the whole barricade assumed a supernatural and colossal aspect in the darkness. There was one of those silences which occur only at the sight of prodigies, and in the midst of this silence the old man brandished the red flag and cried, —

"Long live the revolution! Long live the republic! Fraternity, equality, and death!"

A low and quick talking, like the murmur of a hurried priest galloping through a mass, was heard; it was probably the police commissary making the legal summons at the other end of the street; then the same loud voice which had shouted "Who goes there?" cried, —

"Withdraw!"

M. Mabœuf, livid, haggard, with his eyeballs illumined by the mournful flames of mania, raised the flag about his head and repeated, —

"Long live the republic!"

"Fire!" the voice commanded.

A second discharge, resembling a round of grape-shot, burst against the barricade; the old man sank on his knees, then rose again, let the flag slip from his hand, and fell back on the pavement like a log, with his arms stretched out like a cross. Streams of blood flowed under him, and his old, pale, melancholy face seemed to be gazing at heaven. One of those emotions stronger than man, which makes him forget self-defence, seized on the insurgents, and they approached the corpse with respectful horror.

"What men these regicides are!" said Enjolras.

Courfeyrac whispered in Enjolras's ear, —

"This is only between ourselves, as I do not wish to diminish the enthusiasm; but this man was anything rather than a regicide. I knew him, and his name was Mabœuf. I do not know what was the matter with him to-day, but he was a brave idiot. Look at his head."

"The head of an idiot and the heart of Brutus!" Enjolras replied; then he raised his voice: —

"Citizens! such is the example which the old give to the young. We hesitated and he came; we recoiled and he advanced. This is what those who tremble with old age teach those who tremble with fear! This aged man is august before his country; he has had a long life and a magnificent death! Now let us place his corpse under cover; let each of us defend this dead old man as he would defend his living father; and let his presence in the midst of us render the barricade impregnable!"

A murmur of gloomy and energetic adhesion followed these words. Enjolras bent down, raised the old man's head and sternly kissed him on the forehead; then, stretching out his arms and handling the dead man with tender caution, as if afraid of hurting him, he took off his coat, pointed to the blood-stained holes, and said, —

"This is now our flag!"

CHAPTER III.

GAVROCHE HAD BETTER HAVE ACCEPTED THE CARBINE OF ENJOLRAS.

A LONG black shawl of Widow Hucheloup's was thrown over Father Mabœuf : six men made a litter of their muskets, the corpse was laid on them, and they carried it with bare heads and solemn slowness to a large table in the ground-floor room. These men, entirely engaged with the grave and sacred thing they were doing, did not think of the perilous situation in which they were, and when the corpse was carried past the stoical Javert, Enjolras said to the spy, —

"Your turn will come soon."

During this period little Gavroche, who alone had not left his post, and had remained on the watch, fancied he could see men creeping up to the barricade : all at once he cried, "Look out!" Courfeyrac, Enjolras, Jean Prouvaire, Combeferre, Joly, Bahorel, and Bossuet all hurried tumultuously out of the wine-shop ; but it was almost too late, for they saw a flashing line of bayonets undulating on the crest of the barricade. Municipal Guards of tall stature penetrated, some by striding over the omnibus, others through the sally-port, driving before them the gamin, who fell back, but did not fly. The moment was critical; it was that first formidable minute of inundation when the river rises to the level of the dam and the water begins to filter through the fissures of the dyke. One second more and the barricade was captured. Bahorel dashed at the first Municipal Guard who entered, and killed him with a shot from his carbine; the second killed Bahorel with a bayonet-thrust. Another had already levelled Courfeyrac, who was shouting "Help!" while the tallest of all of them, a species of Colossus, was marching upon Gavroche, with his bayonet at the charge. The gamin raised in his little arms Javert's enormous musket, resolutely aimed at the giant, and pulled the trigger. But the gun did not go off, as Javert had not loaded it: the Municipal Guard burst into a laugh, and advanced upon the lad. Before the bayonet had reached Gavroche, however, the musket fell from the soldier's hands, for a bullet struck him in the middle of the forehead, and he fell on his back. A second bullet struck the other guard, who had attacked Courfeyrac, in the middle of the chest, and laid him low.

The shots were fired by Marius, who had just entered the barricade.

CHAPTER IV.

THE BARREL OF GUNPOWDER.

Marius, still concealed at the corner of the Rue
Mondétour, had watched the first phase of the combat with shuddering irresolution. Still he was unable
to resist for any length of time that mysterious and
sovereign dizziness which might be called the appeal
from the abyss ; and at the sight of the imminence
of the peril, of M. Mabœuf's death, that mournful
enigma, Bahorel killed, Courfeyrac shouting for help,
this child menaced, and his friends to succor or revenge, all hesitation vanished, and he rushed into
the medley, pistols in hand. With the first shot
he saved Gavroche, and with the second delivered
Courfeyrac. On hearing the shots, and the cries of
the guards, the assailants swarmed up the intrench-
ment, over the crest of which could now be seen
more than half the bodies of Municipal Guards,
troops of the line, and National Guards from the
suburbs, musket in hand. They already covered
more than two thirds of the barricade, but no longer
leaped down into the enclosure, and hesitated, as if
they feared some snare. They looked down into the
gloomy space as they would have peered into a
lion's den ; and the light of the torch only illumined

bayonets, bearskin shakos, and anxious and irritated faces.

Marius had no longer a weapon, as he had thrown away his discharged pistols ; but he had noticed the barrel of gunpowder near the door of the ground-floor room. As he half turned to look in that direction a soldier levelled his musket at him, and at the moment when the soldier was taking steady aim at Marius, a hand was laid on the muzzle of his musket and stopped it up ; the young workman in the velvet trousers had rushed forward. The shot was fired, the bullet passed through the hand, and probably through the workman, for he fell, but it did not hit Marius. Marius, who was entering the wine-shop, hardly noticed this ; still he had confusedly seen the gun pointed at him, and the hand laid on the muzzle, and had heard the explosion. But in minutes like this things that men see vacillate, and they do not dwell on anything, for they feel them-selves obscurely impelled toward deeper shadows still, and all is mist. The insurgents, surprised but not terrified, had rallied, and Enjolras cried, " Wait ; do not throw away your shots !" and, in truth, in the first moment of confusion they might wound each other. The majority had gone up to the first-floor and attic windows, whence they commanded the assailants ; but the more determined, with Enjolras, Courfeyrac, Jean Prouvaire, and Combeferre, were haughtily standing against the houses at the end, unprotected, and facing the lines of soldiers and guards who crowned the barricade. All this was done without precipitation, and with that strange and menacing gravity which precedes a combat ; on both sides men were aiming at each other within point-blank range, and they were so near that they could converse. When they were at the point where the spark was about to shoot forth, an officer wearing a gorget and heavy epaulettes stretched out his sword and said, —

" Throw down your arms ! "

" Fire ! " Enjolras commanded.

The two detonations took place at the same moment, and everything disappeared in smoke, — a sharp and stifling smoke, — in which the dying and the wounded writhed, with faint and hollow groans. When the smoke dispersed, the two lines of combatants could be seen thinned, but at the same spot, and silently reloading their guns. All at once a thundering voice was heard shouting, —

" Begone, or I will blow up the barricade ! "

All turned to the quarter whence the voice came.

Marius had entered the wine-shop, fetched the barrel of gunpowder, and then, taking advantage of the smoke and obscure mist which filled the intrenched space, glided along the barricade up to the cage of paving-stones in which the torch was fixed. To tear out the torch, place in its stead the barrel of powder, throw down the pile of paving-stones on the barrel, which was at once unheaded with a sort of terrible obedience, had only occupied so much time as stooping and rising again ; and now all, National Guards and Municipal Guards, officers and privates, collected at the other end of the barricade, gazed at him in stupor, as he stood with one foot on the paving-stones, the torch in his hand, his haughty face illumined by a fatal resolution, approaching the flame of the torch to the formidable heap, in which the broken powder-barrel could be distinguished, and uttering the terrifying cry, —

" Begone, or I will blow up the barricade ! "

Marius, on this barricade after the octogenarian, was the vision of the young revolution after the apparition of the old one.

" Blow up the barricade ! " a sergeant said, " and yourself too ! "

Marius answered, " And myself too ! "

And he lowered the torch toward the barrel of gunpowder ; but there was no one left on the barricade. The assailants, leaving their dead and their wounded, fell back pell-mell and in disorder to the end of the street, and disappeared again in the night. It was a *sauve qui peut*.

The barricade was saved.

CHAPTER V.

END OF THE VERSES OF JEAN PROUVAIRE.

ALL surrounded Marius, and Courfeyrac fell on his neck.

"Here you are!"

"What happiness!" said Combeferre.

"You arrived just in time," said Bossuet.

"Were it not for you I should be dead!" Courfeyrac remarked.

"Without you I should have been gobbled!" Gavroche added.

Marius asked, —

"Who is the leader?"

"Yourself," Enjolras replied.

Marius the whole day through had had a furnace in his brain, but now it was a whirlwind; and this whirlwind which was in him produced on him the effect of being outside him and carrying him away. It seemed to him as if he were already an immense distance from life, and his two luminous months of joy and love suddenly terminated at this frightful precipice. Cosette lost to him, this barricade, M. Mabœuf letting himself be killed for the Republic, himself chief of the insurgents, — all these things seemed to him a monstrous nightmare, and he was obliged to make a mental effort in order to remind himself that all which surrounded him was real. Marius had not lived long enough yet to know that nothing is so imminent as the impossible, and that what must be always foreseen is the unforeseen. He witnessed the performance of his own drama as if it were a piece of which he understood nothing. In his mental fog he did not recognize Javert, who, fastened to his post, had not made a movement of his head during the attack on the barricade, and saw the revolt buzzing round him with the resignation of a martyr and the majesty of a judge. Marius did not even notice him. In the mean while the assailants no longer stirred; they could be heard marching and moving at the end of the street, but did not venture into it, either because they were waiting for orders, or else required reinforcements, before rushing again upon this impregnable redoubt. The insurgents had posted sentries, and some who were medical students had begun dressing wounds. All the tables had been dragged out of the wine-shop, with the exception of the two reserved for the lint and the cartridges, and the one on which Father Mabœuf lay; they had been added to the barricade, and the mattresses off the beds of Widow Hucheloup and the girls had been put in their place. On these mattresses the wounded were laid; as for the three poor creatures who inhabited Corinth, no one knew what had become of them, but they were at length found hidden in the cellar.

A poignant emotion darkened the joy of the liberated barricade; the roll-call was made, and one of the insurgents was missing. Who was he? One of the dearest and most valiant, Jean Prouvaire. He was sought for among the dead, but was not there; he was sought for among the wounded, and was not there; he was evidently a prisoner. Combeferre said to Enjolras, —

"They have our friend, but we have their agent; do you insist on the death of this spy?"

"Yes," Enjolras replied, "but less than the life of Jean Prouvaire."

This was said in the bar-room close to Javert's post.

"Well," Combeferre continued, "I will fasten a handkerchief to my cane, and go as a flag of truce to offer to give them their man for our man."

"Listen," said Enjolras, as he laid his hand on Combeferre's arm.

There was a meaning click of guns at the end of the street, and a manly voice could be heard crying, —

"Long live France! Long live the future!"

They recognized Prouvaire's voice; a flash passed and a detonation burst forth; then the silence returned.

"They have killed him," Combeferre exclaimed.

Enjolras looked at Javert and said to him, —

"Your friends have just shot you."

CHAPTER VI.

DEATH'S AGONY AFTER LIFE'S AGONY.

It is a singularity of this sort of war, that the attack on barricades is almost always made in the front, and that the assailants generally refrain from turning positions, either because they suspect ambuscades, or are afraid to enter winding streets. The whole attention of the insurgents was, consequently, directed to the great barricade, which was evidently the constantly threatened point, and the contest would infallibly recommence there. Marius, however, thought of the little barricade, and went to it; it was deserted, and only guarded by the lamp which flickered among the paving-stones. However, the Mondétour lane and the branches of the Little Truanderie were perfectly calm. As Marius, after making his inspection, was going back, he heard his name faintly uttered in the darkness, —

"Monsieur Marius!"

He started, for he recognized the voice which had summoned him two hours back through the garden railings in the Rue Plumet, but this voice now only seemed to be a gasp; he looked around him and saw nobody. Marius fancied that he was mistaken, and that it was an illusion added by his mind to the

extraordinary realities which were pressing round
him. He took a step to leave the remote angle in
which the barricade stood.

"Monsieur Marius!" the voice repeated; this time
he could not doubt, for he had heard distinctly; he
looked around but saw nothing.

"At your feet," the voice said.

He stooped down, and saw in the shadow a form
crawling toward him on the pavement. It was the
speaker. The lamp enabled him to distinguish a
blouse, torn cotton-velvet trousers, bare feet, and
something that resembled a pool of blood; Marius
also caught a glimpse of a pale face raised to him,
and saying, —

"Do you not recognize me?"

"No."

"Éponine."

Marius eagerly stooped down; it was really that
hapless girl, dressed in male clothes.

"What brought you here? What are you doing?"

"Dying," she said to him.

There are words and incidents that wake up
crushed beings; Marius cried with a start, —

"You are wounded! Wait, I will carry you into
the wine-shop! Your wound will be dressed! Is it
serious? How shall I catch hold of you so as not
to hurt you? Where is it you suffer? Help, good
God! But what did you come to do here?"

And he tried to pass his hand under her to lift
her, and as he did so he touched her hand; she
uttered a faint cry.

"Have I hurt you?" Marius asked.

" A little."

" But I only touched your hand."

She raised her hand to Marius's eyes, and he could see a hole right through it.

" What is the matter with your hand ? " he said.

" It is pierced."

" Pierced ? "

" Yes."

" What with ? "

" A bullet."

" How ? "

" Did you see a musket aimed at you ? "

" Yes, and a hand laid on the muzzle."

" It was mine."

Marius shuddered.

" What madness ! poor child ! But all the better ; if that is your wound, it is nothing, so let me carry you to a bed. Your wound will be dressed, and people do not die of a bullet through the hand."

She murmured, —

" The bullet passed through my hand but came out of my back, so it is useless to move me from here. I will tell you how you can do me more good than a surgeon ; sit down by my side on that stone."

He obeyed ; she laid her head on his knees, and without looking at him, said, —

" Oh, how good that is, how comforting ! See, I no longer suffer ! "

She remained silent for a moment, then turned her head with an effort and gazed at Marius.

" Do you know this, Monsieur Marius ? It annoyed me that you entered that garden, though it was very foolish of me, as I showed you the house; and then, too, I ought to have remembered that a young gentleman like you — "

She broke off, and leaping over the gloomy transitions which her mind doubtless contained, she added with a heart-rending smile, —

" You thought me ugly, did you not ? "

Then she continued, —

" You are lost, and no one will leave the barricade now. I brought you here, you know, and you are going to die, I feel sure of it. And yet, when I saw the soldier aiming at you, I laid my hand on the muzzle of his gun. How droll that is ! But the reason was that I wished to die with you. When I received that bullet I dragged myself here, and as no one saw me I was not picked up. I waited for you and said, ' Will he not come ? ' Oh, if you only knew how I bit my blouse, for I was suffering so terribly ! But now I feel all right. Do you remember the day when I came into your room and looked at myself in your glass, and the day when I met you on the boulevard near the washerwomen ? How the birds sang ! and it is not so very long ago. You gave me five francs, and I said to you, ' I do not want your money.' I hope you picked up your coin, for you are not rich, and I did not think of telling you to pick it up. The sun was shining and it was not at all cold. Do you remember, Monsieur Marius ? Oh, I am so happy, for everybody is going to die ! "

She had a wild, grave, and heart-rending look, and her ragged blouse displayed her naked throat. While speaking, she laid her wounded hand on her chest, in which there was another hole, and whence every moment a stream of blood spirted like a jet of wine from an open bung. Marius gazed at this unfortunate creature with profound compassion.

"Oh," she suddenly continued, "it is coming back! I suffocate!"

She raised her blouse and bit it, and her limbs stiffened on the pavement. At this moment Gavroche's crowing voice could be heard from the barricade: the lad had got on to a table to load his musket, and was gayly singing the song so popular at that day, —

> "En voyant Lafayette,
> Le gendarme répète:
> Sauvons-nous! sauvons-nous! sauvons-nous!"

Éponine raised herself and listened; then she muttered, —

"It is he."

And, turning to Marius, added, —

"My brother is here, but he must not see me, or he would scold me."

"Your brother?" Marius asked, as he thought most bitterly and sadly of the duties toward the Thénardiers which his father had left him; "which is your brother?"

"That little fellow."

"The one who is singing?"

"Yes."

Marius made a move.

"Oh, do not go away!" she said; "it will not be long just now."

She was almost sitting up, but her voice was very low, and every now and then interrupted by the death-rattle. She put her face as close as she could to that of Marius, and added with a strange expression, —

"Come, I will not play you a trick : I have had a letter addressed to you in my pocket since yesterday ; I was told to put it in the post, but kept it, as I did not wish it to reach you. But perhaps you will not be angry with me when we meet again ere long, for we shall meet again, shall we not ? Take your letter."

She convulsively seized Marius's hand with her wounded hand, but seemed no longer to feel the suffering. She placed Marius's hand in her blouse pocket, and he really felt a paper.

"Take it," she said.

Marius took the letter, and she gave a nod of satisfaction and consolation.

"Now, for my trouble, promise me — "

And she stopped.

"What ? " Marius asked.

"Promise me ! "

"I do promise ! "

"Promise to kiss me on the forehead when I am dead ; I shall feel it."

She let her head fall again on Marius's knees and her eyes closed ; he fancied the poor soul departed. Éponine remained motionless ; but all at once, at the moment when Marius believed her eternally asleep, she slowly opened her eyes, on which the gloomy profundity of death was visible, and said to

him with an accent whose gentleness seemed already
to come from another world, —

"And then, look you, Monsieur Marius, I think
that I was a little in love with you."

She tried to smile once more, and expired.

CHAPTER VII.

GAVROCHE CALCULATES DISTANCES.

MARIUS kept his promise; he deposited a kiss on this livid forehead, upon which an icy perspiration beaded. It was not an infidelity to Cosette, but a pensive and sweet farewell to an unhappy soul. He had not taken without a quiver the letter which Éponine gave him; for he at once suspected an event in it, and was impatient to read it. The heart of man is so constituted, — and the unfortunate child had scarce closed her eyes ere Marius thought of unfolding the paper. He gently laid her on the ground and went off, for something told him that he could not read this letter in the presence of a corpse. He walked up to a candle on the ground-floor room; it was a little note folded and sealed with the elegant care peculiar to women. The address was in a feminine handwriting, and ran, —

"To Monsieur Marius Pontmercy, at M. Courfeyrac's, No. 16, Rue de la Verrerie."

He broke the seal and read: —

"MY WELL-BELOVED, — Alas! my father insists on our going away at once. We shall be this evening at No. 7, Rue de l'Homme Armé. In a week we shall be in England.   COSETTE."

"June 4."

Such was the innocence of their love, that Marius did not even know Cosette's handwriting.

What had happened may be told in a few words. Éponine had done it all. After the night of June 3 she had had a double thought, — to foil the plans of her father and the bandits upon the house in the Rue Plumet, and separate Marius and Cosette. She had changed rags with the first scamp she met, who thought it amusing to dress up as a woman, while Éponine disguised herself as a man. It was she who gave Jean Valjean the expressive warning, " Remove ! " and he had gone straight home and said to Cosette, " We shall start this evening and go to the Rue de l'Homme Armé with Toussaint. Next week we shall be in London." Cosette, startled by this unexpected blow, had hastily written two lines to Marius, but how was she to put the letter in the post ? She never went out alone, and Toussaint, surprised by such an errand, would certainly show the letter to M. Fauchelevent. In this state of anxiety, Cosette noticed through the railings Éponine in male clothes, who now incessantly prowled round the garden. Cosette had summoned " this young workman," and given him the letter and a five-franc piece, saying, " Carry this letter at once to its address," and Éponine put the letter in her pocket. The next day she went to Courfeyrac's and asked for Marius, not to hand him the letter, but " to see," — a thing which every jealous, loving soul will understand. There she waited for Marius, or at any rate Courfeyrac — always to see. When Courfeyrac said to her, " We are going to the barricades," an idea crossed her mind, — to throw herself into this death as she would have done into any other, and thrust Marius into it. She followed Courfeyrac, assured herself of the spot where the barricade was being built, and feeling certain, since Marius had not received the letter, that he would go at nightfall to the usual meeting-place, she went to the Rue Plumet, waited for Marius there, and gave him that summons in the name of his friends, which, as she thought, must lead him to the barricade. She reckoned on Marius's despair when he did not find Cosette, and she was not mistaken, and then she returned to the Rue de la Chanvrerie. We have just seen what she did there ; she died with the tragic joy of jealous hearts, which drag the beloved being down to death with them and say, " No one shall have him ! "

Marius covered Cosette's letter with kisses ; she loved him, then, and for a moment he had an idea that he ought not to die ; but then he said to himself, " Her father is taking her to England, and my grandfather will not give his consent to the marriage ; no change has taken place in fatality." Dreamers like Marius undergo such supreme despondencies, and desperate resolves issue from them ; the fatigue of living is insupportable, and death is sooner over. Then he thought that two duties were left him to accomplish, — inform Cosette of his death and send her his last farewell, and save from the imminent catastrophe which was preparing, that poor boy, Éponine's brother and Thénardier's son. He had a pocket-book about him, the same which had contained the paper on which he had written so many love-thoughts for Cosette; he tore out a leaf, and wrote in pencil these few lines, —

"Our marriage was impossible; I asked my grandfather's consent, and he refused to give it; I have no fortune, nor have you. I ran to your house, and did not find you there; you remember the pledge I made to you, and I have kept it. I die. I love you; and when you read this my soul will be near you and smile upon you."

Having nothing with which to seal this letter, he merely folded it, and wrote on it the address : —

"To Mademoiselle Cosette Fauchelevent, at M. Fauchelevent's, No. 7, Rue de l'Homme Armé."

The letter folded, he stood for a moment in thought, then opened his pocket-book again, and wrote with the same pencil these lines on the first page.

"My name is Marius Pontmercy. Carry my body to my grandfather, M. Gillenormand, No. 6, Rue des Filles du Calvaire, in the Marais."

He returned the book to his coat pocket, and then summoned Gavroche. The lad, on hearing Marius's voice, ran up with his joyous and devoted face.

"Will you do something for me ? "

"Everything," said Gavroche. "God of Gods ! my goose would have been cooked without you."

"You see this letter ? "

"Yes."

"Take it. Leave the barricade at once," — Gavroche began scratching his ear anxiously, — "and to-morrow morning you will deliver it at its address, No. 7, Rue de l'Homme Armé."

The heroic lad replied, —

" Well, but during that time the barricade will be attacked, and I shall not be here."

" The barricade will not be attacked again till daybreak, according to all appearances, and will not be taken till to-morrow afternoon."

The new respite which the assailants granted to the barricade was really prolonged ; it was one of those intermissions frequent in night-fights, which are always followed by redoubled obstinacy.

" Well," said Gavroche, " suppose I were to deliver your letter to-morrow morning ? "

" It will be too late, for the barricade will probably be blockaded, all the issues guarded, and you will be unable to get out.   Be off at once."

Gavroche could not find any reply, so he stood there undecided, and scratching his head sorrowfully. All at once he seized the letter with one of those bird-like movements of his.

" All right," he said.

And he ran off toward the Mondétour lane. Gavroche had an idea which decided him, but which he did not mention ; it was the following : —

" It is scarce midnight ; the Rue de l'Homme Armé is no great distance off.   I will deliver the letter at once, and be back in time."

BOOK XV.

THE RUE DE L'HOMME ARMÉ.

CHAPTER I.

BLOTTING, BLABBING.

WHAT are the convulsions of a city compared with the convulsions of a soul? Man is even a greater profundity than the people. Jean Valjean at this very moment was suffering from a frightful internal earthquake, and all the gulfs were reopened within him. He too was quivering, like Paris, on the threshold of a formidable and obscure revolution. A few hours had sufficed to cover his destiny and his conscience with shadows, and of him, as of Paris, it might be said, " The two principles are face to face." The white angel and the black angel are about to wrestle with each other on the brink of the abyss; which will hurl the other down?

On the evening of that same day, Jean Valjean, accompanied by Cosette and Toussaint, proceeded to the Rue de l'Homme Armé, where a tremendous incident was fated to take place. Cosette had not left the Rue Plumet without an attempt at resistance, and for the first time since they had lived

together, the will of Cosette and the will of Jean
Valjean had shown themselves distinct, and had con-
tradicted each other, though they did not come into
collision. There was objection on one side and in-
flexibility on the other : for the abrupt counsel,
"Remove!" thrown to Jean Valjean by a stranger, had
alarmed him to such a point as to render him absolute. He fancied himself tracked and pursued, and
Cosette was compelled to yield. The pair reached
the Rue de l'Homme Armé without exchanging a
syllable, for each was so deep in personal thought,
while Jean Valjean was so anxious that he did not
notice Cosette's sadness, and Cosette was so sad that
she did not notice Jean Valjean's anxiety. Jean
Valjean had brought Toussaint with him, which he
had never done in his previous absences, but he foresaw that he might possibly never return to the Rue
Plumet, and he could neither leave Toussaint behind
him nor tell her his secret. Moreover, he felt her to
be devoted and sure ; the treachery of a servant to
a master begins with curiosity, and Toussaint, as if
predestined to be Jean Valjean's servant, was not
curious. She was wont to say through her stammering in her patois of a Barneville peasant, "I am so,
I do my work, and the rest does not concern me."
In his departure from the Rue Plumet, which was
almost a flight, Jean Valjean took away with him
nothing but the fragrant little portmanteau, christened by Cosette the "inseparable." Packed trunks
would have required porters, and porters are witnesses ; a hackney-coach had been called to the gate
in the Rue de Babylone and they went away in it.

It was with great difficulty that Toussaint obtained permission to pack up a little stock of linen and clothes, and a few toilet articles; Cosette herself only took her desk and blotting-book. Jean Valjean, in order to heighten the solitude and mystery of this disappearance, had so arranged as to leave the Rue Plumet at nightfall, which had given Cosette the time to write her note to Marius. They reached the Rue de l'Homme Armé when it was quite dark, and went to bed in perfect silence.

The apartments in this street were situated on a second floor in a back-yard, and consisted of two bed-rooms, a dining-room, and a kitchen adjoining, with a closet in which was a flock-bed, that fell to the lot of Toussaint. The dining-room was at the same time ante-room and separated the two bed-rooms, and the apartments were provided with the necessary articles of furniture. Human nature is so constituted that men become reassured almost as absurdly as they are alarmed; hence Jean Valjean had scarce reached the Rue de l'Homme Armé ere his anxiety cleared away and was gradually dissipated. There are calming places which act to some extent mechanically on the mind, and when a street is obscure the inhabitants are peaceful. Jean Valjean felt a contagious tranquillity in this lane of old Paris, which is so narrow that it is barred against vehicles by a cross-beam, which is dumb and deaf amid the noisy town, full of twilight in broad daylight, and, so to speak, incapable of feeling emotions between its two rows of tall centenary houses, which are silent like old folks are. There is in this street a stagnant oblivion,

and Jean Valjean breathed again in it, for how was
it possible that he could be found there ?   His first
care was to place the " inseparable " by his side ; he
slept soundly, and night counsels, we might add,
night appeases.   The next morning he woke up
almost gay.   He considered the dining-room charming, though it was hideous, for it was furnished with
an old round table, a low side-board surmounted by
a mirror, a rickety easy-chair, and a few chairs
encumbered with Toussaint's parcels.   In one of
these parcels Jean Valjean's National Guard uniform
could be seen through an opening.

As for Cosette, she ordered Toussaint to bring a
basin of broth to her bed-room, and did not make
her appearance till evening.   At about five o'clock,
Toussaint, who went about very busy with getting
things to rights, placed a cold fowl on the dinner-
table, which Cosette consented to look at, through
deference for her father.   This done, Cosette pro-
testing a persistent headache, said good-night to
Jean Valjean, and shut herself up in her bed-room.
Jean Valjean ate a wing of the fowl with appetite,
and with his elbows on the table, and gradually
growing reassured, regained possession of his serenity.   While he was eating this modest dinner, he
vaguely heard twice or thrice stammering Toussaint
say to him, "There is a disturbance, sir, and people
are fighting in Paris."   But, absorbed in a multitude
of internal combinations, he had paid no attention to
her ; truth to tell, he had not heard her.   He rose
and began walking from the door to the window,
and from the window to the door with calmness.

Cosette, his sole preoccupation, reverted to his mind, not that he was alarmed by this headache, a slight nervous attack, a girl's pouting, a momentary cloud, which would disappear in a day or two, but he thought of the future, and, as usual, thought of it gently.   After all, he saw no obstacle to his happy life resuming its course : at certain hours everything seems impossible, at others everything appears easy, and Jean Valjean was in one of those good hours. They usually arrive after bad hours, as day does after night, through that law of succession and contrast which is the basis of our nature, and which superficial minds call antithesis.   In this peaceful street where he had sought shelter, Jean Valjean freed himself from all that had troubled him for some time past, and from the very fact that he had seen so much darkness he was beginning to perceive a little azure.   To have left the Rue Plumet without any complication or incident was a good step gained, and perhaps it would be wise to leave the country, were it only for a few months, and go to London. Well, they would go ; what did he care whether he were in England or France, provided that he had Cosette by his side?   Cosette was his nation, Cosette sufficed for his happiness, and the idea that he perhaps did not suffice for Cosette's happiness, that idea which had formerly been his fever and sleeplessness, did not even present itself to his mind.   All his past sorrows had collapsed, and he was in the centre of optimism.   Cosette, being by his side, seemed to be his, and this is an optical effect which everybody has experienced.   He arranged in his mind, and with all possible facility, the departure for England with Cosette, and he saw his felicity reconstructed, no matter where, in the perspectives of his reverie.

While slowly walking up and down, his eye suddenly fell on something strange. He noticed, facing him in the inclined mirror over the side-board, and read distinctly : —

" MY WELL-BELOVED, — Alas ! my father insists on our going away at once. We shall be this evening at No. 7, Rue de l'Homme Armé. In a week we shall be in England. COSETTE."
" June 4."

Jean Valjean stopped with haggard gaze. Cosette, on arriving, had laid her blotting-book on the side-board facing the mirror, and, immersed in her painful thoughts, had forgotten it, without even noticing that she had left it open at the very page on which she had dried the few lines she had written and intrusted to the young workman passing along the Rue Plumet. The writing was imprinted on the blotting-paper and the mirror reflected the writing. The result was what is called in geometry a symmetric image, so that the writing reversed on the blotting-paper was placed straight in the mirror, and offered its natural direction, and Jean Valjean had before his eyes the letter written on the previous evening by Cosette to Marius. It was simple and crushing. Jean Valjean walked up to the mirror and read the lines again, but did not believe in them. They produced on him the effect of appearing in a flash of lightning : it was an hallucination ; it was impossible; it was not. Gradually his perception became more precise, he looked at Cosette's blotting-book, and the feeling of the real fact returned to him. He took up the blotting-book, saying, "It comes from that." He feverishly examined the lines imprinted on the blotting-paper, but as they ran backward he could see no meaning in the strange scrawl. Then he said to himself, "Why, it means nothing; there is nothing written there." And he drew a long breath with inexpressible relief. Who has not felt such wild delight in horrible moments? The soul does not surrender to despair till it has exhausted every illusion.

He held the book in his hand and gazed at it, stupidly happy, almost ready to laugh at the hallucination of which he had been the dupe. All at once his eyes fell again on the mirror, and he saw the vision again; the lines stood on it with inexorable clearness. This time it was no mirage, it was palpable, it was the writing turned straight in the mirror, and he comprehended the fact. Jean Valjean tottered, let the blotting-book slip from his grasp, and fell into the old easy-chair by the side of the sideboard with hanging head and glassy, wandering eye. He said to himself that it was evident that the light of this world was eclipsed, and that Cosette had written that to somebody. Then he heard his soul, which had become terrible again, utter a hoarse roar in the darkness. Just attempt to take from the lion the dog he has in his cage! Strange, and sad to say, at that moment Marius had not yet received Cosette's letter, and accident had treacherously carried it to

Jean Valjean before delivering it to Marius. Jean Valjean up to that day had never been conquered by a trial; he had been subjected to frightful assaults, not a blow of evil fortune had been spared him, and the ferocity of fate, armed with all social revenge and contempt, had taken him for its victim and furiously attacked him. He had accepted, when it was necessary, every extremity; he had surrendered his reacquired inviolability as man, given up his liberty, risked his head, lost everything and suffered everything, and he had remained disinterested and stoical to such an extent that at times he seemed to be oblivious of self, like a martyr. His conscience, hardened to all possible assaults of adversity, might seem quite impregnable; but any one who had now gazed into his heart would have been compelled to allow that it was growing weak. In truth, of all the tortures he had undergone in this long trial to which fate subjected him, this was the most formidable, and never had such a vise held him before. He felt the mysterious agitation of all his latent sensibilities, he felt the twitching of an unknown fibre. Alas! the supreme trial, we may say the sole trial, is the loss of the being whom we love.

Poor old Jean Valjean did not assuredly love Cosette otherwise than as a father; but, as we have already remarked, the very widowhood of his life had introduced all the forms of love into this paternity: he loved Cosette as his daughter, loved her as his mother, and loved her as his sister, and, as he had never had a mistress or a wife, that feeling too, the most clinging of all, was mingled with the others, vague, ignorant, pure with the purity of blindness, unconscious, heavenly, angelic, and divine, less as a feeling than an instinct, less as an instinct than an attraction, imperceptible, invisible, but real; and love, properly so called, was in his enormous tenderness for Cosette as the vein of gold is in the mountain, dark and virginal. Our readers must study for a moment this state of the heart; no marriage was possible between them, not even that of souls, and yet it is certain that their destinies were wedded. Excepting Cosette, that is to say, excepting a childhood, Jean Valjean, during the whole of his life, had known nothing about things that may be loved. Those passions and loves which succeed each other had not produced in him those successive stages of green, light green, or dark green, which may be noticed on leaves that survive the winter, and in men who pass their fiftieth year. In fine, as we have more than once urged, all this internal fusion, all this ensemble, whose resultant was a lofty virtue, ended by making Jean Valjean a father to Cosette, — a strange father, forged out of the grandsire, the son, the brother, and the husband, which were in Jean Valjean; a father in whom there was even a mother; a father who loved Cosette and adored her, and who had this child for his light, his abode, his family, his country, and his paradise. Hence, when he saw that it was decidedly ended, that she was escaping from him, slipping through his fingers, concealing herself, that she was a cloud, that she was water; when he had before his eyes this crushing evidence : " Another is the object of her heart, another is the wish of

her life, she has a lover, I am only the father, I
no longer exist;" when he could no longer doubt,
when he said to himself, "She is leaving me," the
sorrow he experienced went beyond the limits of
the possible. To have done all that he had done to
attain this, and to be nothing! Then, as we have
just stated, he had a quivering of revolt from head
to foot; he felt even in the roots of his hair the immense reawaking of selfishness, and the "I" yelled
in the depths of this man's soul.

There are such things as internal earthquakes; the
penetration of a desperate certainty into a man is not
effected without removing and breaking certain profound elements which are at times the man himself.
Grief, when it attains that pitch, is a frantic flight of all
the forces of the conscience, and such crises are fatal.
Few among us emerge from them equal to ourselves
and firm in our duty; for when the limit of suffering
is exceeded, the most imperturbable virtue is disconcerted. Jean Valjean took up the blotting-book and
convinced himself afresh; he bent down as if petrified, and with fixed eye, over the undeniable lines,
and such a cloud collected within him that it might
be believed that the whole interior of his soul was in
a state of collapse. He examined this revelation
through the exaggerations of reverie with an apparent
and startling calmness, for it is a formidable thing
when a man's calmness attains the coldness of a
statue. He measured the frightful step which his
destiny had taken without any suspicion on his part,
he recalled his fears of the past summer, so madly
dissipated, he recognized the precipice; it was still

the same, but Jean Valjean was no longer at the top but at the bottom. It was an extraordinary and crushing fact that he had fallen without perceiving it, the whole light of his life had fled while he still fancied he could see the sun. His instinct did not hesitate; he brought together certain circumstances, certain dates, certain blushes, and certain palenesses of Cosette, and said to himself, "It is he!" The divination of despair is a species of mysterious bow which never misses its mark, and with its first shaft it hit Marius. He did not know the name, but at once found the man; he perceived distinctly at the bottom of the implacable evocation of memory the unknown prowler of the Luxembourg, that villanous seeker of amourettes, that romantic idler, that imbecile, that coward,—for it is cowardice to exchange loving glances with girls who have by their side a father who loves them. After feeling quite certain that this young man was at the bottom of the situation, and that all this came from him, Jean Valjean, the regenerated man, the man who had toiled. so heavily in his soul, the man who had made so many efforts to resolve his whole life, his whole misery, and his whole misfortune into love, looked into himself and saw there a spectre — hatred.

Great griefs contain exhaustion, and discourage us with life; the man into whom they enter feels something retire from him. In youth their visit is mournful, at a later date it is sinister. Alas! when the blood is hot, when the hair is black, when the head is upright on the body like the flame on the candle, when the heart, full of a yearning love, still has palpitations which may be given to it in return, when a man has time to recover from the wound, when all women are there, and all the smiles, and all the future, and the whole horizon, when the strength of life is complete,— if despair be a frightful thing under such circumstances, what is it then in old age, when years are growing more and more livid, at that twilight hour when the stars of the tomb are beginning to become visible ? While Jean Valjean was thinking, Toussaint came in ; he rose and asked her, —

"Do you know whereabout it is ? "

Toussaint, in her stupefaction, could only answer,—

"I beg your pardon, sir."

Jean Valjean continued, —

"Did you not say just now that they were fighting ? "

"Oh yes, sir," Toussaint replied; "over at St. Merry."

There are some mechanical movements which come to us, without our cognizance, from our deepest thoughts. It was doubtless under the impulse of a movement of this nature, of which he was scarce conscious, that Jean Valjean found himself five minutes later in the street. He was bareheaded, and sat down on the bench before his house, seemingly listening.

Night had set in.

CHAPTER II.

THE GAMIN THE ENEMY OF LAMPS.

How long did he remain there? What was the ebb and flow of this tragical meditation? Did he draw himself up? Did he remain bowed down? Had he been bent till he was broken? Could he recover himself and stand again upon something solid in his conscience? Probably he could not have said himself. The street was deserted, and a few anxious citizens who hurriedly returned home scarce noticed him, for each for himself is the rule in times of peril. The lamplighter came as usual to light the lamp which was exactly opposite the door of No. 7, and went away. Jean Valjean would not have appeared to be a living man to any one who might have examined him in this gloom, and he sat on his bench motionless, like a statue of ice. His despair had got beyond congelation. The tocsin and vague stormy rumors could be heard, and in the midst of all these convulsions of the bell blended with the riot, the clock of St. Paul struck the eleventh hour, solemnly and without hurrying; for the tocsin is man, the hour is God. The passing of the hour produced no effect on Jean Valjean, and he did not stir. Almost immediately after, however, a sudden detonation

broke out in the direction of the markets, followed by
a second even more violent; it was probably that
attack on the barricade of the Rue de la Chanvrerie
which we have just seen repulsed by Marius. At
this double discharge, whose fury seemed increased
by the stupor of the night, Jean Valjean started;
he turned in the direction whence the sound came,
but then fell back on his bench, crossed his arms,
and his head slowly bent down again on his chest.
He resumed his dark dialogue with himself.

All at once he raised his eyes, for there was some
one in the street; he heard footsteps close to him,
and by the light of the lamp he perceived a livid,
young, and radiant face, in the direction of the street
which runs past the Archives. It was Gavroche,
who had just arrived from the Rue de la Chanvrerie;
Gavroche was looking up in the air, and appeared
to be seeking. He saw Jean Valjean distinctly, but
paid no attention to him. Gavroche, after looking
up in the air, looked down on the ground; he stood
on tiptoe, and felt the doors and ground-floor windows; they were all shut, bolted, and barred.
After examining the fronts of several houses barricaded in this way, the gamin shrugged his shoulders,
and then resumed his self-colloquy with himself, thus,
"By Jove!" Then he looked up in the air again.
Jean Valjean, who a moment previously in his
present state of mind would neither have spoken
to nor answered any one, felt an irresistible impulse
to address this lad.

"My little boy," he said, "what is the matter
with you?"

"Why, I'm hungry," Gavroche answered bluntly. And he added, "Little yourself!"

Jean Valjean felt in his pocket and pulled out a five-franc piece. But Gavroche, who was a species of wagtail, and rapidly passed from one gesture to another, had just picked up a stone. He had noticed the lamp.

"Hilloh!" he said, "you have still got lights here. You are not acting rightly, my friends; that is disorderly conduct. Break it for me."

And he threw the stone at the lamp, whose glass fell with such a noise that the citizens concealed behind their curtains in the opposite house cried, "There is '93!" The lamp oscillated violently and went out; the street suddenly became dark.

"That's it, old street," said Gavroche, "put on your nightcap." Then, turning to Jean Valjean, he said, —

"What do you call that gigantic monument which you have there at the end of the street? It's the Archives, isn't it? Let's pull down some of those great brutes of columns and make a tidy barricade."

Jean Valjean walked up to Gavroche.

"Poor creature!" he said in a low voice, and as if speaking to himself, "he is hungry."

And he placed the five-franc piece in his hand. Gavroche raised his nose, amazed at the size of this double sou; he looked at it in the darkness, and the whiteness of the double sou dazzled him. He was acquainted with five-franc pieces by hearsay, and their reputation was agreeable to him; he was delighted to see one so closely, and said, "Let us contemplate the tiger." He looked at it for some moments in ecstasy; then, turning to Jean Valjean, he held out the coin to him, and said majestically, —

"Citizen, I prefer breaking the lamps. Take back your ferocious animal, for I am not to be corrupted. It has five claws, but can't scratch me."

"Have you a mother?" Jean Valjean asked.

Gavroche replied, —

"Perhaps more than you."

"Well," Jean Valjean continued, "keep that money for your mother."

Gavroche was affected. Moreover, he had noticed that the man who was addressing him had no hat on, and this inspired him with confidence.

"Really, then," he said, "it is not to prevent me breaking the lamps?"

"Break as many as you like."

"You are a worthy man," said Gavroche.

And he put the five-franc piece in one of his pockets. Then, with increasing confidence, he added, —

"Do you belong to this street?"

"Yes; why?"

"Can you point me out No. 7?"

"What do you want at No. 7?"

Here the lad stopped, for he feared lest he had said too much. He energetically plunged his nails into his hair, and confined himself to answering, —

"Ah, there it is."

An idea flashed across Jean Valjean's mind, for agony has lucidities of that nature. He said to the boy, —

" Have you brought me the letter which I am expecting ? "

" You," said Gavroche, " you ain't a woman."

" The letter is for Mademoiselle Cosette, is it not ? "

" Cosette ? " Gavroche grumbled ; " yes, I think it is that absurd name."

" Well," Jean Valjean continued, " you have to deliver the letter to me ; so give it here."

" In that case, you must be aware that I am sent from the barricade ? "

" Of course," said Jean Valjean.

Gavroche thrust his hand into another of his pockets, and produced a square folded letter ; then he gave the military salute.

" Respect for the despatch," he said ; " it comes from the Provisional Government."

" Give it to me," said Jean Valjean.

Gavroche held the paper above his head.

" You must not imagine that it is a love-letter, though it is for a woman ; it is for the people ; we are fighting, and we respect the sex ; we are not like people in the world of fashion, where there are lions that send poulets to camels."

" Give it to me."

" After all," Gavroche continued, " you look like an honest man."

" Make haste."

" Here it is."

And he handed the paper to Jean Valjean.

" And make haste, Monsieur Chose, since Mamselle Chosette is waiting."

Gavroche felt pleased at having made this pun. Jean Valjean added, —

"Must the answer be taken to St. Merry?"

"You would make in that way," Gavroche exclaimed, "one of those pastries vulgarly called *brioches* [blunders]. That letter comes from the barricade in the Rue de la Chanvrerie, and I am going back to it. Good-night, citizen."

This said, Gavroche went away, or, to speak more correctly, resumed his birdlike flight to the spot whence he had escaped. He plunged again into the darkness, as if there were a hole there, with the rigid rapidity of a projectile: the lane of l'Homme Armé became once again silent and solitary. In a twinkling, this strange lad, who had shadows and dreams within him, buried himself in the gloom of these rows of black houses, and was lost in it like smoke in darkness, and it might have been fancied that he was dispersed, had vanished, had not, a few minutes after his disappearance, a noisy breakage of glass, and the splendid echo of a lamp falling on the pavement, suddenly reawakened the indignant citizens. It was Gavroche passing along the Rue de Chaume.

CHAPTER III.

WHILE COSETTE AND TOUSSAINT SLEEP.

JEAN VALJEAN re-entered with Marius's letter: he groped his way up-stairs, pleased with the darkness like an owl that holds its prey, gently opened and closed the door, listened whether he could hear any sound, convinced himself that Cosette and Toussaint were, according to all appearances, asleep, and plunged into the Fumade lighting-bottle three or four matches before he could procure a spark, for his hand trembled so, as what he had just done was a robbery. At last his candle was lit, he sat down at the table, opened the letter, and read. In such violent emotions men do not read, they hurl down, so to speak, the paper they hold, clutch it like a victim, crumple it, bury in it the nails of their fury or delight, they run to the end, they dash at the beginning: the attention is feverish, it understands the essential facts, it seizes on one point, and all the rest disappears. In the note from Marius to Cosette Jean Valjean only saw these words, —

"I die: when you read this my soul will be near you."

In the presence of this line he felt a horrible bedazzlement ; he remained for a moment as if crushed
by the change of emotion which took place in him.
He gazed at Marius's letter with a species of drunken
amazement, he had before his eyes this splendor, —
the death of the hated being. He uttered a frightful
cry of internal joy. So all was over, and the dénouement arrived more quickly than he could have dared
to hope. The being that encumbered his destiny
was disappearing ; he went away of his own accord,
freely and willingly, without his doing anything in
the matter, without any fault on the part of him, Jean
Valjean ; " that man " was going to die, perhaps was
already dead. Here his fever made its calculations ;
" No, he is not yet dead. The letter was evidently
written to be read by Cosette on the next morning :
since the two volleys he had heard between eleven
o'clock and midnight nothing had occurred : the barricade would not be seriously attacked till daybreak ;
but no matter, from the moment when 'that man' is
mixed up in this war, he is lost, he is caught in the
cog-wheels." Jean Valjean felt himself delivered ;
he was going to find himself once more alone with
Cosette ; the rivalry ceased and the future began
again. He need only keep the note in his pocket,
and Cosette would never know what had become of
" that man ; " " I have only to let things take their
course. That man cannot escape, and if he is not
dead yet, it is certain that he is going to die. What
happiness ! " All this said internally, he became
gloomy : he went down and aroused the porter.
About an hour later Jean Valjean left the house in

the uniform of a National Guard and armed. The porter had easily obtained for him in the neighborhood the articles to complete his equipment: he had a loaded musket and a full cartouche-box. He proceeded in the direction of the markets.

CHAPTER IV.

GAVROCHE'S EXCESS OF ZEAL.

IN the mean while an adventure had happened to Gavroche; after conscientiously stoning the lamp in the Rue du Chaume, he approached the Rue des Vieilles Haudriettes, and not seeing "a cat" there, found the opportunity excellent for striking up a song at the full pitch of his lungs. His march, far from being checked by the singing, became accelerated, and he sowed along the sleeping or terrified houses the following incendiary verses : —

> "L'oiseau médit dans les charmilles,
> Et prétend qu' hier Atala
> Avec un Russe s'en alla.
> Où vont les belles filles,
> Lon la.

> "Mon ami Pierrot, tu babilles,
> Parce que l'autre jour Mila
> Cogna sa vitre, et m'appela.
> Où vont les belles filles,
> Lon la.

> "Les drôlesses sont fort gentilles,
> Leur poison qui m'ensorcela
> Griserait Monsieur Orfila.
> Où vont les belles filles,
> Lon la.

" J'aime l'amour et ses bisbilles,
   J'aime Agnès, j'aime Paméla,
   Lise en m'allumant se brûla.
     Où vont les belles filles,
       Lon la.

" Jadis, quand je vis les mantilles
   De Suzette et de Zéila,
   Mon âme à leurs plis se mêla.
     Où vont les belles filles,
       Lon la.

" Amour, quand, dans l'ombre où tu brilles,
   Tu coiffes de roses Lola,
   Je me damnerais pour cela.
     Où vont les belles filles,
       Lon la.

" Jeanne, à ton miroir tu t'habilles !
   Mon cœur un beau jour s'envola ;
   Je crois que c'est Jeanne qui l'a.
     Où vont les belles filles,
       Lon la.

" Le soir, en sortant des quadrilles,
   Je montre aux étoiles Stella,
   Et je leur dis : ' Regardez-la.'
     Où vont les belles filles,
       Lon la."

Gavroche, while singing, was lavish of his panto-
mime, for gesture is the mainstay of a chorus. His
face, an inexhaustible repertory of masks, made grimaces more convulsive and more fantastic than the
mouths of a torn sheet in a stiff breeze. Unluckily,
as he was alone and in the dark, this was neither

seen nor visible. Much wealth is lost in this way. Suddenly he stopped short.

"We must interrupt the romance," he said.

His catlike eye had just distinguished inside a gateway what is called in painting an ensemble, that is to say, a being and a thing; the thing was a hand-cart, the being an Auvergnat sleeping inside it. The shafts of the cart were upon the pavement, and the Auvergnat's head leaned on the backboard of the truck. His body lay along this inclined plane, and his feet touched the ground. Gavroche, with his experience of the things of this world, recognized a drunkard : it was some street-corner porter who had drunk too much and was sleeping too much.

"Such is the use," Gavroche thought, "to which summer nights may be turned. The Auvergnat sleeps in his truck. I take the truck for the republic, and leave the Auvergnat for the monarchy."

His mind had just been illumined by this flash.

"That truck would be famous on our barricade!"

The Auvergnat was snoring. Gavroche gently pulled the truck behind and the Auvergnat in front, that is to say, by the feet, and in a second the porter was lying imperturbably flat on the pavement. The truck was liberated. Gavroche, accustomed constantly to face unexpected events, had always everything about him. He felt in one of his pockets and pulled out a scrap of paper and a piece of red pencil stolen from some carpenter. He wrote

République Française

Received this truck.

And he signed, GAVROCHE.

This done, he placed the paper in the snoring porter's velvet waistcoat pocket, seized the hand-cart, and started in the direction of the markets, thrusting the truck before him at a gallop with a glorious triumphal row. This was dangerous, for there was a post at the Royal Printing Office, and Gavroche did not think of that. This post was held by suburban National Guards ; a certain amount of alarm was beginning to arouse the squad, and heads were raised in the guard-beds. Two lamps broken so shortly after each other, and this singing at the pitch of the lungs, were a good deal for these cowardly streets, which like to go to bed at sunset, and put the extinguisher on their candle at so early an hour. For an hour past the gamin had been making in this peaceful district the noise of a fly in a bottle. The suburban sergeant listened and waited, for he was a prudent man. The wild rolling of the truck filled up the measure of possible awaiting, and determined the sergeant to attempt a reconnoisance.

" There must be a whole band of them," he said, " so we will advance gently."

It was clear that the hydra of anarchy had emerged from its box, and was playing the deuce in the quarter, so the sergeant ventured out of the guard-house on tiptoe. All at once, Gavroche, pushing his truck, found himself, just as he was turning out of the Rue des Vieilles Haudriettes, face to face with a uniform, a shako, a pompon, and a musket. For the second time he stopped short.

"Hilloh!" he said, "it's he.   Good-day, public order."

Gavroche's surprises were short and rapidly thawed.

"Where are you going, scamp?" the sergeant cried.

"Citizen," said Gavroche, "I have not yet called you bourgeois, so why do you insult me?"

"Where are you going, scoundrel?"

"Sir," Gavroche continued, "it is possible that you were a man of sense yesterday, but you must have sent in your resignation this morning."

"I ask you where you are going, villain?"

Gavroche answered, —

"You speak politely.   Really, no one would fancy you that age.   You ought to sell your hair at one hundred francs apiece, and that would bring you in five hundred francs."

"Where are you going, where are you going, where are you going, bandit?"

Gavroche retorted, —

"Those are ugly words.   The first time they give you the breast they ought to wash your mouth out better."

The sergeant levelled his bayonet.

"Will you tell me where you are going or not, wretch?"

"My general," said Gavroche, "I am going to fetch the doctor for my wife, who is taken in labor."

"To arms!" the sergeant shouted.

It is the masterpiece of powerful minds to save themselves by what has ruined them; and Gavroche measured the whole situation at a glance. It was the truck that had compromised him, and so the truck must now protect him. At the moment when the sergeant was going to rush on Gavroche, the truck, converted into a projectile and launched at full speed, rolled upon him furiously, and the sergeant, struck in the stomach, fell back into the gutter, while his musket was discharged in the air. On hearing their sergeant's cry, the guard hurried forth pell-mell ; the shot produced a general firing at random, after which the guns were reloaded, and they began again. This blindman's-buff firing lasted a good quarter of an hour, and killed sundry panes of glass. In the mean while, Gavroche, who had turned back, stopped five or six streets off, and sat down panting on the bench at the corner of the Enfants Rouges, and listened. After breathing for a few minutes, he turned in the direction where the musketry was raging, raised his left hand to the level of his nose, and thrust it out thrice, while striking the back of his head with his right hand, — a sovereign gesture, in which the Parisian gamins have condensed French irony, and which is evidently effective, as it has already lasted more than half a century. This gayety was troubled by a bitter reflection.

"Yes," he said, "I am delighted, I overflow with joy, I crack my sides, but I am losing my way, and shall be obliged to steer a roundabout course. I only hope I shall reach the barricade betimes."

After saying this he ran off again, and while running asked himself, "Where was I ? " and he began